In Praise of Younger Men

"The Demon's Mistress" by *New York Times* **bestselling author Jo Beverley**
A wealthy widow's proposition to a young officer could prove to be his redemption or his downfall. . . .

"A Man Who Can Dance" by *New York Times* **bestselling author Cathy Maxwell**
A governess offers lessons in the art of wooing to a studious bachelor—only to fall in love herself with his newfound charm. . . .

"Written in the Stars" by Jaclyn Reding
In order to fulfill an ancient family prophecy, a young woman is destined to marry a younger man—or else court disaster. . . .

"Forevermore" by Lauren Royal
A sensible woman throws caution to the wind when her fantasy man becomes a flesh-and-blood reality with an offer she can't refuse. . . .

In Praise of Younger Men

Jo Beverley

Cathy Maxwell

Jaclyn Reding

Lauren Royal

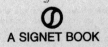

A SIGNET BOOK

SIGNET
Published by New American Library, a division of
Penguin Putnam Inc., 375 Hudson Street,
New York, New York 10014, U.S.A.
Penguin Books Ltd, 27 Wrights Lane,
London W8 5TZ, England
Penguin Books Australia Ltd, Ringwood,
Victoria, Australia
Penguin Books Canada Ltd, 10 Alcorn Avenue,
Toronto, Ontario, Canada M4V 3B2
Penguin Books (N.Z.) Ltd, 182–190 Wairau Road,
Auckland 10, New Zealand

Penguin Books Ltd, Registered Offices:
Harmondsworth, Middlesex, England

First published by Signet, an imprint of New American Library,
a division of Penguin Putnam Inc.

First Printing, March 2001
10 9 8 7 6 5 4 3 2 1

Contents

A Man Who Can Dance
A SCOTTISH TALE

—◆◆◆—

Cathy Maxwell

For June Stephenson, Book Guru

Chapter One

On a fine day in May when the sun was shining and spring had at last arrived, Graham McNab received the news he'd worked hard to earn: Edinburgh's finest doctor, Mr. Fielder, was releasing him from his studies.

"There's nothing more I can teach you, lad. You've a gift, a power to heal. Go and use it." Mr. Fielder gave Graham a letter of recommendation written in his own hand and a gift of a set of razor-sharp surgical knives.

Graham had dreamed of this day since he was a child. He'd always been a healer. The other children in the small village where he'd grown up had brought their pets to him. Dogs, rabbits, horses, cattle, birds, and a chipmunk—all had been his patients.

But it wasn't until his parents had died of the dreaded smallpox and there'd been nothing he could do to save them had he decided he must go to Edinburgh to learn the art of medicine. He'd been fourteen at the time and had walked to the city from his home, the village of Kirriemuir, begging room and board from his uncle, Sir Edward Brock, in exchange for work in his shipping business.

Graham's goal had not been an easy one for a poor highland boy. Edinburgh University had turned up its

academic nose at a student who had none of Latin and
Greek. And Uncle Edward had been a harsh taskmaster,
never missing an opportunity to discourage Graham's
dreams of being a doctor.

Mr. Fielder's patronage had been a godsend. Graham
had toiled nights over shipping ledgers and overseeing
his uncle's accounts and his days apprenticed to the wise
physician. He'd tutored himself in the language of medicine, sometimes going days without sleep.

Now, nothing could stop him. He'd reached the stars. His
destiny lay before him.

Shifting his leather bag over to his other shoulder,
Graham smiled at the added weight of the new surgical
knives. He could not wait to share his news with Sarah, the
governess to his uncle's twin daughters, and Graham's closest friend in the household. She would be as delighted as
he was.

The house came into view. The yellow brick offices
and living quarters of Sir Edward Brock were a well
known Edinburgh landmark. On the other side of the
road were the warehouses and beyond them, the ships
that transported goods between Scotland and the world.

The road was teeming with activity on such a lovely
day. The quayside walk was a popular one among locals.
While they strolled and visited, merchants plied their
wares and his uncle's ostlers loaded bags of grain onto
a wagon or rolled kegs into the warehouse. Brock Shipping appeared, and was, a prosperous concern.

Graham paused and took pride in his role building
the company's success . . . but the time had come to
leave the world of commerce. He stood on the threshold
of great things.

And then, from the down the road, he noticed a snow-
white horse prancing toward him. The animal was so
magnificent, people stepped to the side and watched it
pass.

Or so Graham thought until he saw men take off their
hats and bow and women frown. 'Twas then he noticed
the rider—and could not take his eyes off of her.

She was the most beautiful woman Graham had ever seen.

The green velvet of her riding habit faithfully followed ripe, buxom curves. Her cheeks were rosy and her Dresden blue eyes bright with laughter. Silver blond ringlets, the color of the sun's rays, peeked out from beneath a dashing cavalier's hat with a jaunty plume.

So intent had he been on his work and studies, he'd not had time to consider the opposite sex—until this moment. He was smitten.

But he was not her only admirer. A literal cavalry of gentlemen rode with her. Some were wigged soldiers in scarlet uniforms with mountains of gold braid dripping from their chests. Others wore jackets cut of the finest stuff and hand sewn to fit their wearers' shoulders. Their boots shone from champagne blacking and jewels flashed in the lace falls of their cravats.

She laughingly commented on something one of the gentlemen had said . . . and as she did, she looked straight at Graham.

Their gazes met.

His heart beat double-time. His ears rang with the sound of a thousand bells. He couldn't breathe. He couldn't think. The busy street, the ostlers' calls, the sun, the stars, the very heavens faded from his mind and there was only her. Beautiful her.

Her lips parted slightly and he knew she felt the same pull of attraction, the same aura of wonderment. She even turned in her saddle so she could maintain eye contact as she rode past until one of her many suitors placed himself between her and Graham.

He took a step, unwilling to let her go—

His feet tripped over something in his path. He stumbled. Reaching out, he caught himself before he hit the ground, but it was too late. She was gone from view.

"What were you ogling, you clumsy bumpkin?" a bored, snide voice questioned.

Graham turned to come face-to-face with his cousin, Blair.

The two of them were of the same age, six and twenty,

and had similar russet-colored hair, but there, all similarities ended. Graham was tall and strong, his body strengthened by years of physical labor in his uncle's warehouse, his hair unfashionably long, albeit tied back in a neat queue.

Blair didn't even have his father's height and disdained work in any form. He considered himself a gentleman and a gentleman never lifted a finger in labor. Instead, he paraded around Edinburgh dressed in the latest trends from garish striped vests to collar points starched so high, he had trouble moving his head. He wore his hair short *á la Brutus*. Drinking, gambling, and wenching comprised his chief pursuits. Ah, yes, and dueling. Blair was a renowned swordsman. He was one of a party of elegantly attired, idle young men who could terrorize a neighborhood if they'd a mind to.

While Graham studied to save life, Blair was willing to dispatch it over a whim or imagined insult.

The cousins did not like each other.

Blair twirled the walking stick he'd used to trip Graham and smiled. "You should watch where you are going."

"You should keep your walking stick out of my path," Graham answered. He turned, praying for one more glimpse of the woman of his dreams.

"Look at him drooling over the Garrison Commander's daughter," Blair said to Cullen, his almost constant companion and another one of the Bully Boys, the name Blair's companions labeled themselves.

"Have you looked in your glass lately, McNab?" Blair said. "Women like Lucinda Whitlow aren't attracted to giants—"

Lucinda Whitlow. Her name! Graham rolled the syllables over in his mind, loving the sound of them.

"—And she is going to marry me," Blair concluded.

Now he had Graham's complete, undivided attention. "She's marrying you?" The idea was preposterous. His cousin was a faithless rogue when it came to women. "You're joking."

"No, I'm not," Blair answered with his usual air of

superiority. He pulled from his coat an invitation engraved on heavy vellum.

In bold letters at the top was printed: A MAN WHO CAN DANCE CAN DO ALL THINGS WELL. Graham knew the saying. 'Twas a Scottish wives' tale of a lass who found true marital happiness in the arms of a dancing man.

Curious, Graham easily snagged the card out of Blair's hand before his cousin could blink. Below the heading was a request for the gentlemen of Sir Edward Brock's family to be the Garrison Commander's guests at a ball to be held four days hence. The ball was being given in the honor of Miss Lucinda Whitlow for the express purpose of introducing her to all eligible bachelors in Edinburgh.

Blair leaned close. "The Garrison Commander wishes to see his daughter married. The rumor is he is anxious to seek his fortune in India, but he doesn't wish to subject his very lovely daughter to the fevers and dangers of the tropics. He wants her married posthaste and the man she chooses at the ball will receive a most excellent dowry for his pains." He pulled the invitation out of Graham's hands. "I will be that man. No one in Edinburgh is a finer dancer."

Graham stared into his cousin's smirking face. 'Twas true. Blair was a dancer. Still . . .

"It isn't addressed to you alone," Graham said. "*All* the eligible gentleman in Uncle Edward's house are invited."

"And you believe that includes you?" Blair hooted his opinion, a sound Cullen echoed, and pointed out, "By *gentle*men, the Garrison Commander isn't referring to quacks and sawbones." He whacked the side of Graham's instrument bag with the walking stick. "Are your drills and saws in there, coz? Have you cut open any bodies yet this morning and played with the innards?"

In the past, Graham had always ignored Blair's barbs. But not today.

Today, something inside Graham snapped. After years of being the butt of jokes, he wanted to put Blair firmly in his place.

Nor did his sense of chivalry want to see Miss Whitlow go to such a mean-spirited, lazy man as Blair. She deserved better.

Graham looked his cousin in the eye. "I'm going to the ball." He turned to walk toward the house but Blair quickly moved into his path, his narrow eyes glittering.

"Don't make a fool of yourself, coz."

"I won't," Graham replied tightly.

Blair snorted his opinion. "You'll embarrass the family. You've never been to a ball. What would you wear? The homespun you have on now?" He laughed. "I daresay you can't even dance."

"I'll learn." Graham stepped around Blair and continued his way to the house.

"You'll make a fool of yourself," Blair promised. The blunt words reverberated on the suddenly silent street.

Graham stopped and turned. Their argument had an audience. The ostlers, all of them men he knew and who respected him, were watching as were the neighbors, their eyes round at the unexpected boon of juicy gossip.

Even Uncle Edward was there. He'd come out of the warehouse, his brown periwig slightly askew on his head.

Pride exerted itself. For years he'd lived as his uncle's hireling, but he was a man now, a man with a profession. Graham straightened to his full height. "Miss Whitlow will be my bride."

Blair grinned and placed his hands on his hips. "Would you care to make a wager of it?" he asked softly.

"A wager?"

Blair swaggered forward. "I'll bet ten gold coins I will win the hand of Miss Whitlow."

"You?" Graham put all the contempt he felt for his cousin in that one word.

"Yes, myself." He opened his arms, a magician revealing he had no tricks. "What of you, coz? Are you *gentleman* enough to accept the wager? Or do you doubt your abilities with the ladies?"

At any other time, Graham could have walked off from such nonsense—but not today. Aware of their audience, he asked, "What do you expect of me in return? You know I have no gold."

"I will stake you," Uncle Edward said. All eyes turned to him, many people surprised a father would hazard against his only son. After all, everyone knew Sir Edward doted on Blair.

Too late, Graham had a sense of foreboding. "And your terms, sir?"

Uncle Edward smiled benevolently. " 'Tis for the good of my own soul," he said.

"But if I don't win . . . ?" Graham prodded.

"Ah, well." Uncle Edward considered the matter a few moments and then offered, "If you don't win, you can work the wager off in my business as you have been."

Graham reeled from the thought. 'Twould take him years to pay off such a debt. And yet . . . he remembered the moment of connection between himself and Miss Whitlow. The air had vibrated with its power. She had been as attracted to him as he had to her. He knew it all the way to his soul.

He looked to his uncle. "I shall need the clothes of a gentleman."

"My personal tailor shall attend you," Uncle Edward replied. "If you win the wager, the new coat will be my wedding gift to you."

If he lost, Graham had no doubt the price would be added to his debt.

An instant's hesitation, then, "I'll accept the wager." He heard himself say those words almost as if in a dream. Fate played a hand in this moment. Not even the weight of his doctor's bag and instruments could deter him.

The ostlers gave a cheer. The neighbors challenged them to friendly wagers and the whole street returned to life.

"What if neither of them win the girl's hand?" Old Nate, one of the ostlers called out. Everyone listened up.

Uncle Edward answered, "She'd be a foolish lass to

ignore two such handsome men . . . but if she does, the wager will be a draw."

Everyone agreed his was a good solution. They went back to their betting.

Blair smiled. "I hope you can dance, coz."

"I'll know how to dance well enough," Graham promised.

"You'd best," Blair answered and strutted back to join his cronies.

Graham glanced at Uncle Edward who was laughing at something one of the neighbors said. He seemed very pleased with himself—and Graham wondered what he had done out of pride.

And love. He had no doubt he was in love. A man couldn't feel such an irresistible attraction and not be in love, could he?

Graham reminded himself the time had come for him to marry. With a lovely bride at his side like Miss Whitlow, his medical practice would flourish.

Everything was right except one small item—he didn't know how to dance.

Without another word, he set off toward the house in search of his friend Sarah. She would help him. He knew she would.

Blair came to his father's side. "Was everything as you wished?"

"You did better than expected, my son." He smiled grimly. "It will take years for Graham to work off ten pieces of gold. Just make sure you win the wager. I don't care how you do it. Brock Shipping can't survive without Graham." His words were true. Sir Edward had no head for business. Before Graham, he'd been about to go bankrupt. Graham had made him rich.

Over the years, Sir Edward had done everything in his power to keep Graham from becoming a doctor, including bribery. Unfortunately, the city's most noted doctor, Mr. Fielder, had thwarted him by accepting Graham as an apprentice and willingly let the lad work around the long hours he'd been forced to spend in Sir Edward's business.

One of these days, he'd see Mr. Fielder pay for his interference.

Sir Edward placed his hand on his beloved son's shoulder. "Make sure you win the Garrison Commander's daughter."

Blair pulled his sword from its walking stick scabbard, the blade gleaming sharp in the sunlight. "I will do all in my power, Father. Even if I must run through the other suitors."

Chapter Two

The door to the schoolroom flew open. "Sarah, you must teach me to dance," Graham demanded, his handsome face tight with anxiety.

Sarah Ambrose looked up from her lesson on map reading, her glasses perched on the end of her nose. He never barged in on her lessons. Or had ever expressed the curious urge to dance.

"*Mister* McNab," she said pointedly, a gentle reminder they had a wide-eyed audience, Sir Edward's ten-year-old twin daughters, "I am in the middle of lessons." She tapped the map book with the drawing pencil she used as a pointer to reclaim the girls' attention but it was already too late.

Jean and Janet called out his name, happy for the interruption. They adored their cousin who, unlike their brother, usually had a moment for a kind word.

But not today.

Graham shocked Sarah by striding across the room, grabbing her firmly by the elbow and steering her out of her seat and toward the connecting door that led to her private quarters. He was a big man and when he made up his mind to move, no one could gainsay him. Certainly not Sarah who at five foot four only came up to his chest. "Excuse me, Jean, Janet," he threw over his shoulder. "Your teacher will return in a moment."

"Mister McNab—Graham! Wait, what do you think you are doing?" She pushed her glasses up her nose before they fell off.

He closed the connecting door firmly behind them. She shoved the drawing pencil into the careless topknot of her soft brown hair and reached to open it. "Have you lost your reason?"

He blocked her attempt with the flat of his palm on the door, his long, hard body pinning her in place. "No, I'm in love."

Now, he had Sarah's undivided attention.

She leaned her back against the door, uncertain if she'd heard him correctly. At two and thirty, she was six years older but considered him a compatriot. They were both neither servants in the true sense of the words— well, perhaps herself more than him—and yet, outsiders to Sir Edward's class. Graham's friendship was the bright spot in her otherwise humdrum life. He was one of the few men she trusted. She thought she knew everything about him.

Obviously not.

"Love?" she tested the word—and backed away from it, cautious. "Were you in 'love' this morning when I saw you at breakfast?"

"No. But I am now and, Sarah, you are my only hope." He took both her hands. "You must teach me to dance."

She couldn't follow his train of thought. "Why?"

"Because I don't know how," he replied earnestly.

"Yes," she agreed. "That's usually the way it is with people who need dancing lessons." She shook her head. None of what he said made sense, nor did she want to consider the implications to herself. If he was in love . . .

She reached for the door handle behind her. "We'll discuss this later. I must return to the twins." And maybe, in the meantime, she prayed he would come to his senses.

Graham covered her hand on the door handle with his and opened the door, squashing Sarah between his body and the door frame in a way that brought a hot rush of color to her face, and said, "Jean, Janet, place your slates on Miss Ambrose's desk and run see Nurse. I think she has treacle tea for you."

He didn't have to make the suggestion twice. The girls

jumped to obey, their slates clattering as they were thrown on the desk.

Sarah made an exasperated sound and slipped through the door to chase them back but it was too late. Janet was the latter one through the schoolroom door, slamming it shut behind her.

She whirled on Graham. "Why did you do that? They are never good students in the best circumstances and, now, I won't get anything out of them for the rest of the day."

"Good," he replied happily. "You have time to start teaching me how to dance."

She stared into the light green eyes that she'd thought she'd known as well as her own gray ones and realized he'd become a stranger. The thought was unsettling, as was her almost stomach-churning reaction to his claiming to be . . . in . . . *love*.

"This is sudden. Too sudden," she avowed. He'd always been too involved in work and his studies to care about frivolities. "I mean, last night you were anticipating this day because Mister Fielder was to release you from your apprenticeship."

"Oh, yes, he did," Graham answered offhandedly and Sarah was more bewildered. Becoming a doctor had been Graham's sole goal in life.

She sat in her "teacher" chair behind her desk. "Perhaps you should start from the beginning."

"I'd rather start with the dancing lessons." He leaned on her desk. "Please, Sarah, help me."

She crossed her arms. "Talk first, lessons second."

The set of his mouth flattened stubbornly. Sarah thought Graham had the most amazing mouth. It conveyed all his emotions. Now it told her he didn't want to be questioned. Too bad. "Talk, Graham."

He frowned but then the corners of his mouth twisted into rueful resignation. With a sigh, he hitched one leg up on the edge of her desk and launched into the most astounding story she'd ever heard about seeing a Miss Whitlow, the Garrison Commander's daughter, who apparently had all the virtues of womanhood without opening her mouth and how her father was hosting a ball to find her a husband.

She listened, her eyebrows climbing higher and higher. "So you wish to learn to dance to impress this young woman whose father is blatantly auctioning her off?"

He frowned, then corrected, "He's holding a search."

"And you want to dance in such a way as to convince him and her you would be a good lover."

Her blunt words startled him. She made an impatient sound. "Graham, I have been about in the world. I know the implications of the Scottish proverb on the invitation."

"Yes . . . and no," he admitted. "I mean, there should be some decency involved."

"Exactly," she murmured, withholding further opinion.

"There's more," he said, and told her about the wager, his focus dropping to the slates on her desk as he spoke, his expression taking on a new intensity.

"You didn't accept the challenge, did you?" she asked, fearing the answer.

Graham's gaze met hers. "I did."

Sarah released a soft groan, but she was not surprised. Everyone knew Blair was jealous of his tall, intelligent cousin. She'd witnessed the petty insults and small cruelties he'd inflicted on Graham over the years. She'd considered it a sign of Graham's strength that he had not struck back. However, a day of reckoning was bound to have come.

What disturbed her were the whispers she'd overheard among the household staff about how Sir Edward did not want Graham to leave the shipping firm. Blair's timing was too fortuitous.

She looked up at him. "They mean for you to lose."

Graham straightened. "I won't." He paused and added, "*If* you teach me to dance."

"Me? If I?" she repeated blindly. She rose from her chair and started stacking and restacking the girls' slates with more force than necessary, her mind jumbled with objections and fears and—

"It's an insane wager." She shoved the slates away

and faced him. "Graham, go tell your uncle you've changed your mind. Back out while you have time. They don't mean for you to win," she said, rapping her knuckles on the desk to emphasize each word. "They will take every advantage of you without any regret."

He stepped back, his features hardened with the resolute sense of purpose that was so much a part of him. "I will win, Sarah. Miss Whitlow is in love with me."

"Love?" The word sounded alien to her ears. "Because she looked at you? Did either of your speak? Did you introduce yourselves?" The challenges flew out of her mouth before she'd had a chance to consider their wisdom.

"Sometimes words are not necessary."

"Not even a simple 'hello, how are you'?"

" 'Twas love at first sight," he replied stonily.

" 'Twas *lust* at first sight!" Sarah snapped back. She wanted to shake him she was so angry. Unreasonably angry.

He took another step toward the door, his sparkling eyes growing colder, more distant. "I thought you would understand."

Oh, she understood. There had been a time when she, too, had been willing to forsake all for love. When she'd believed in shining stars, happily ever afters, and, oh, yes, love at first sight. Her "love" had left her at the altar, his promises empty, meaningless.

Nothing seared the soul like love. It had almost destroyed her.

She'd needed a full year, crammed with the most painful moments of her life to recover. Even now, the feelings of shame and humiliation from his rejection hovered near her. Graham was the first man she'd opened herself to in years. Perhaps, because he was several years younger, she had not feared for her heart with him.

However, because of their close friendship, she had to make him see reason. She chose her words carefully. "This wager . . . it could destroy your life." She paused, needing to make him understand and, yet, unwilling to confess her own miserable experience. "As a governess,

I have lived in different households. My experiences have allowed me to observe human nature." She gripped the edge of the table, her knuckles turning white. "Once the first bloom of love fades—and it fades quickly, Graham, mark my words—what is left in its place is not to be desired."

The tension eased in him slightly. "There is a connection between Miss Whitlow and myself. Something special."

"Graham, what if you win and are forced to marry this young woman—"

"I *want* to marry her."

Sarah released her hold on the desk, pushing it back to accent her words. "Or do you just not want Blair to have her?"

Graham jerked his head to one side as if she had struck him. Sarah closed her eyes. 'Twas not like her to lash out.

"You don't have to help me, Sarah."

His words pierced her heart. She opened her eyes. He was moving toward the door. He reached for the door handle. "And yes, I'm bloody tired of playing the lackey. If dancing to claim a woman's hand is how I can make my uncle and cousin respect me, then I will." He opened the door.

"Graham—"

He stopped, waiting.

Sarah balled her hands into fists. She didn't know what to say. But before her mind could form words to heal the rift between them, Betty, the cheeky upstairs maid hailed Graham.

"Mister McNab, I've been looking for you. What is this I hear about a wager and a dance?" Betty appeared in the doorway, a big, happy smile stretched across her face, her hips twitching saucily. Her cinch belt was laced so tight her breasts appeared to be popping forward like two beehives on a table.

Graham was forced to take a step back into the classroom lest he be run over.

"They say the Garrison Commander's daughter practi-

cally fell off her horse when she first laid eyes on you,"
Betty crooned. " 'Course, I don't blame her. You would
turn my head any day." Her breasts quivered with her
words.

Sarah spoke up to let the forward puss know Graham
was not alone. "Don't you have cleaning to do, Betty?"

The maid didn't even bother a glance in Sarah's direction. "I've got all my chores done and a wee bit of time
on my hands. They say you might be needing a dancing
lesson or two, Mister McNab. I'm a good dancer." She
bumped Graham with her beehive breasts.

Inexplicably, jealousy stabbed through Sarah with
blinding force. "Mister McNab doesn't need your help."

Betty slipped from Sarah's grasp and moved into the
schoolroom. "Then who will teach him to dance?"

"I will," Sarah replied.

"You?" Betty asked doubtfully.

"You?" Graham said happily.

"Yes, *me*," Sarah answered.

"But I thought—" Graham started.

She cut him off, not wanting to examine her motives
too closely. " 'Tis the least I can do for a friend,
Graham."

He gave a sudden, happy whoop, scooped her up in
his arms, and twirled her around. "I knew I could count
on you, Sarah. I knew it."

"Yes," she agreed numbly, her cheek against his hard
chest. His movements made her a little dizzy and she
was startled by tears stinging her eyes. What had she
gotten herself into?

He set Sarah on her feet. "Can we start now?" he
asked, his eyes alive with anticipation.

"No," Sarah said quickly. "The twins will be back . . .
we should meet later. Say, nine o'clock in the downstairs
ballroom. Sir Edward is going out this evening."

"That will be perfect," Graham said.

"I beg your pardon," Betty demanded rudely, obviously irritated at being ignored. "But do you know how
to dance, Miss Ambrose?"

"Yes, I do."

"Then why haven't I seen you dance?" Betty asked.

Sarah matched her cat smile with a bright one of her own. "We don't travel in the same circles or frequent the same places, Betty."

The maid's eyes narrowed at the implied insult. "So where do you dance?"

"Here." Sarah walked over to her desk, her symbol of authority. "In the schoolroom. Teaching dance is one of my responsibilities."

"And she's a good dancer," Graham said loyally although Sarah doubted he'd ever seen her dance.

"*I'm* a good dancer," Betty corrected. "And he is a man not a child, Miss Ambrose. He needs a *woman* to teach him to dance."

"I am a woman, Betty," Sarah said, a hint of warning in her voice.

"No, you are a *teacher*." Betty shuddered and then started for the door, her hips swaying with the wanton sensuality. "You stay up here in your little tower and look down on the rest of us."

"You'd best remember your place, Betty," Sarah said evenly.

Betty turned. "I want him to win, Miss Ambrose. Can you say the same?"

The maid's challenge caught Sarah off guard. For a second, class distinction evaporated between them and Sarah sensed Betty knew and saw more than Sarah would want her to. More than Sarah would admit to.

Graham came to her rescue.

"Betty, Sarah is graceful and elegant, intelligent and kind. In short, everything a woman should be. Perhaps you'd best go back to your work."

The expression on Betty's face made it clear she didn't agree with him and had a thing or two she wanted to add, but then thought differently. With an almost insolent curtsy, she excused herself. "I'd best be doing my duties. Perhaps I'll mosey by the ballroom this evening to see how your lessons are going."

" 'Tis not necessary, Betty," Graham said.

"I wouldn't do it because it was necessary, Mister

McNab. I'd do it for you." The maid disappeared down the hall—leaving Sarah behind slightly rattled.

Graham sensed her thoughts. "Don't mind her, Sarah. She's a haughty puss and too full of herself." He gave her shoulders a reassuring squeeze. "But we'll show her. We'll show all of them, including Blair. You'll teach me to be the finest dancer in Edinburgh."

"And you will claim Miss Whitlow's hand." The words sounded hollow in her ears.

"Yes," he agreed with a smile. "I'll see you this evening. And thank you."

"For what? We haven't started the lessons."

"For the friendship, Sarah. For the friendship." He left the room.

Sarah stood quiet for a moment listening to his footsteps go down the hall. His parting words disturbed her as had most of what he'd said this afternoon. In less than an hour, her life seemed to have been tossed upside down.

She then turned a full circle taking in her surroundings as if seeing them for the first time . . . no longer certain of her own mind. "A teacher."

No one had ever suggested she was lacking before. They'd all assumed she was happy with her life and *she thought* she had been until Graham asked her to teach him to dance.

Her gaze fell upon a slim red-leather book beneath the slates. Her present for Graham. She had forgotten to give it to him. 'Twas a copy of Nicolò Machiavelli's *The Prince*.

The book had belonged to her father. Graham had borrowed it when she'd first arrived at Sir Edward's. Their lively argument over the moral implications of Machiavelli's theories had been the start of their friendship.

Now, friendship didn't seem enough.

Chapter Three

The upcoming dancing lesson lurked on the edge of Sarah's mind for the rest of the afternoon, making it hard for her to concentrate on Jean's cross stitching and Janet's music lesson. She sent the twins back to Nurse for their supper with a touch of relief.

Walking into her private quarters, she headed straight toward the looking glass hanging over her washstand and studied her reflection. Carefully, she removed her glasses.

Betty was wrong. Sarah might love books, she might have chosen a chaste, academic life to Betty's earthy pursuits, but she was still a woman.

And yet, she had the sudden sense she'd been living her life in a cocoon.

At one time, she'd loved to dance. At one time, she'd been courted and worn bright pretty colors instead of dove gray or lavender. At one time, other women considered her a worthy rival. The likes of Betty would never have laughed at her.

Sarah tugged on the black velvet ribbon holding her topknot in place. Her heavy hair fell down past her shoulders and she saw in the looking glass a hint of the girl she had once been.

Where was that girl now?

She lifted her hair with her fingers and turned her head this way and that with a critical eye. Perhaps, it was time for a new style. Maybe she had gotten into a rut.

Sarah reached for her comb. A half hour later, she wore a style very much like her topknot although tidied up a bit with tendrils curling down around her ears and neck.

A new hairstyle demanded a change of dress. Thoughtfully, she inspected her meager wardrobe. The dress she thought best for dancing was the robin's-egg blue one she saved for Sundays, a dress bosomy Betty would turn up her nose at.

Boldly, Sarah pulled off the demure lace ruching decorating the edge of the bodice. Now the dress looked a touch more daring . . . and Sarah was surprised by how anxious she was to try it on. She even preened a bit in front of the mirror, an indulgence she would have chastised the twins over.

Of course, she couldn't avoid noticing her bosom needed a bit of uplift and she knew exactly what to do. She stuffed the lace ruching in her bodice and was quite pleased with the results.

She pinched her cheeks and her lips to bring out the color and she remembered an old trick. Picking up a tallow candle, she attempted to use the wick black to darken her lashes. Her movements were awkward. Years ago, she'd been more adept at this process—

"What are you doing with that candle, Miss Ambrose?"

Sarah gave a start at the sound of Jean's voice and almost poked her eye out with the candle. She turned, surprised to discover the twins in the doorway connecting her quarters to the schoolroom.

"Um, yes, what can I do for you?" she said, hiding the candle behind her back. Her lashes on one eye felt heavy. She blinked several times.

"We came to say good night," Janet said. She entered the room. "You look so pretty, Miss Ambrose."

"Do I?" Sarah said. She ran a hand over Janet's shiny carrot-bright hair. "Thank you."

"Are you going to teach Graham to dance?" Jean asked, following her sister. "Nurse says you must."

"I'm going to try," Sarah answered. She dropped the candle on the washstand and held out her arms to give the girls a hug good night, a ritual they observed every evening.

However, this time as she kissed their downy cheeks, she found herself wishing they were hers. For years, when people had asked, she'd insisted she was happy enough taking care of others' children.

Now, Graham's unexpected romance had given rise to all sorts of feelings she'd refused to recognize. Feelings she'd denied.

"Come along, Jean, Janet," Nurse said. She always hovered on the other side of the door while the twins wished their governess a good night. But tonight, she'd opened the door wide. "And you, Miss Ambrose, you teach Mister McNab how to cut a fine figure on the dance floor. I put a bit of money on him myself. 'Twould be a fine thing to see him married to the Garrison Commander's daughter."

"Yes, it would," Sarah agreed with less enthusiasm.

"He deserves the best. He's a fine man." Nurse held out her hands to lead the twins to their beds for the night and Sarah realized the appointed hour to meet Graham was close at hand.

Sarah turned to her reflection in the mirror. She put on her eyeglasses, then took them off again, then put them on. She really didn't need them except for close reading, but they made her feel mature, dignified. "You're in danger of becoming a fool," she warned herself. She'd just stuffed her bodice and yet worried over eyeglasses.

With those words, she left her room, eyeglasses on her nose. A second later, she returned, set them on the washstand, and dashed out.

Downstairs, all was quiet. Bailey, the butler, usually lingered somewhere close to the front door when Sir Edward was out but not even he was to be seen. Curious how deserted the rooms were but it was not Sarah's problem.

She hurried to the ballroom in the back of the house overlooking the garden, pushed open the door, and froze, dumbfounded by the scene in front of her.

The high-ceilinged room was ablaze with light and full of people. All the servants were here—Cook, Bailey, the downstairs and dairy maids, the scullery girl, and the ostlers, too.

Graham stood at the forefront. He'd loosened his neck cloth and taken off his brown wool coat. Betty nudged his shoulder with her beehive breasts as she moved closer to tell him something. She'd changed her hairstyle, too, so that it hung freely down to her waist in a shining curtain.

Fortunately, when Sarah entered the room, Graham sidled away from Betty's pushy breasts and called a greeting, "We have quite a crowd here. They've come to watch me learn to dance."

"Watch?" Sarah frowned. As governess, she rarely mingled with the other servants. It just wasn't done. "Well, they can't," she decided firmly. She addressed Bailey. "You must leave immediately. After all, what will Sir Edward say when he sees every candle in the house lit?"

"We're burning candle stubs," Cook said with her broad Northern accent. "Been saving them. Besides, the master will be gone for hours. We can do what we wish till then." She paused. "I say, Miss Ambrose, have you changed something about yourself?" Her eagle gaze honed in on Sarah's bosom.

"I'm not wearing my eyeglasses," Sarah replied primly, turning slightly to avoid "bosom discovery." Perhaps she had overdone it a bit.

"Your hair," Graham said warmly. "You've changed it. I like the new style, Miss Ambrose." He addressed her formally in front of the others. "But I miss the eyeglasses," he added quietly.

His response touched her. She wondered what else he might say if they were alone.

The moment was spoiled by Betty's brassy, "I think she's changed a bit more than her spectacles."

The other maids giggled. They'd noticed the bosom, but suddenly Sarah didn't care. "How did you all know we were holding a dance lesson in here?"

Betty answered, "You told Mister McNab in front of me. I told Cook, Cook told Mister Bailey, Mister Bailey told the others."

"I see," Sarah said. "Well, I don't think Mister McNab needs an audience for the dance lessons. Bailey, would you please see everyone out?"

Bailey was a white-haired gent who had been trained in London. His opinion carried a great deal of weight in the household. "Miss Ambrose, with all due respect, what harm can come of it? We want to help Mister McNab."

"Don't tell me. You've wagered money," Sarah said.

"Aye, some have. But not myself. I'd support anything Mister McNab does," the butler said proudly. "He saved me niece who was dying of a fever. I want to see him win his lady love."

"Your niece was young. She would have recovered," Graham said modestly.

" 'Twas not another doctor in all Edinburgh who would come to see her without coin up front," Bailey replied. He looked to Sarah. "Me brother's family is poor and I know the girl was very sick. Mister McNab has a gift. A healing gift. We are all proud of him."

"Aye," Cook agreed. "He saved my sister's eye. She would not leave the house. Now, she is the merriest of souls. He didn't ask a penny for it either."

"I couldn't," Graham stated. "I didn't do that much."

"You cared. Sometimes that is enough," Cook countered.

And there were stories from the ostlers and other servants, too, all tales of Graham's generosity while he stood in the center appearing embarrassed by such glowing testimonials.

Their tales humbled Sarah. In the three years she'd known Graham, they'd rarely talked about his medicine. She knew he'd worked with Mr. Fielder late into the night but she hadn't really grasped the physical reality of what he did, what it meant to others. Now, surrounded by lives he'd touched, her selfish denunciation of Miss Whitlow seemed petty.

Betty's claim that Sarah lived in a tower away from everyone and everything took on a ring of truth.

The time had come to make amends. Sobered of her vanity, Sarah wished she had her eyeglasses.

"Sarah, what do I do?" Graham leaned toward her, his face pale.

"What do you mean?"

"Look at them. They expect me to win the wager."

Because you are a hero in their eyes, she wanted to tell him, but the words would only embarrass him further.

"You'd best learn to dance," she replied in her brisk "governess" voice. She gave his arm a reassuring squeeze and took charge. "And we must make him the greatest dancer in Edinburgh," she said to the others.

"In Scotland," one of the ostlers corrected and everyone cheered.

Sarah rubbed her hands together in anticipation, feeling a bit like a hero herself. "Let's get started. Form two lines." They moved to her direction.

One of the ostlers had brought a fiddle. She motioned for him to stand in the corner, saying, "Excellent. With music, the lesson will go quickly. Now, Mister McNab, We're going to teach you the quadrille since the ball will probably open with one. You stand beside me and watch the first time. Does everyone know the quadrille?"

Heads nodded.

"The first step," she said to Graham, "is the *chaine anglaise.*"

"The what?" 'Twas Nate, one of the ostlers, who spoke.

"Chaine anglaise," Sarah repeated. She demonstrated.

"Ach," Nate said with recognition. "You mean, the Cat's Chasing the Ladies."

"What?" Now it was Sarah's turn to be confused.

Nate performed a perfect *chaine anglaise.* "Yes, that's it," Sarah said. "Follow it with a two *chassés,* one right, one left, while you lift the right hand of the opposite partner."

Again Nate spoke up, addressing the others, "I think what Miss Ambrose means with her fancy Frog words is that she wants a 'Fiddle Your Feet' right, 'Fiddle Your

Feet' left while the lasses do the same in the other direction." Immediately people attempted the step and he was right.

"Why thank you, Mister Nate," Sarah said. "I appreciate your help."

"I'm happy to oblige, governess," the ostler responded with complete seriousness and Sarah felt her lips twitch. Beside her, Graham covered his own smile.

She didn't even mind the ostler's impertinent use of her title governess. He made her feel one of them . . . and she'd never been included before.

Funny how good it was to be a part of this small community.

"Let's try the dance, if you already know the steps," Sarah said. "Mister McNab can watch and pick up the dance as we go along."

Everyone agreed to the idea. Sarah tapped a beat and, on the count of three, the fiddler started playing a sprightly reel.

Feet began moving, hands clapping, and the first couple—Bailey and Cook—stepped to the center. Sarah was delighted at how well everyone danced. With their help, teaching Graham would be easy.

He was clapping, too . . . but she noticed he didn't keep good time to the music. His hands were a beat off and he couldn't seem to move them and tap his toe at the same time. She watched, fascinated. Graham was so perfect in every other way, this small flaw made him human.

Her thoughts focused on his hands themselves. She'd seen his fingers stained with ink from accounting books and observed him hefting bags of grain or spices from the Orient or kegs of molasses, but she'd not seen him heal.

She leaned closer so he could hear her over the merrymaking. "Why didn't you mention whenever you doctored to the servants?"

"I'm a doctor. 'Tis what I do." He shrugged. "Besides, I didn't think you were interested."

The response surprised her. "Why not?"

He shot her an amused glance. "Sarah, you have the twins to worry over. You would not want to hear me fretting about a child with a fever."

Details fell into place, times when he'd seemed preoccupied. "I would have listened," she said. "I'm your friend."

He lifted an eyebrow, but she didn't elaborate. Somehow, her words hadn't come out exactly the way she'd meant them.

Fortunately, she was saved from examining her motives too closely by the last measure of music. The dance ended. The time had arrived to throw Graham into the fray.

She took his hand and started for the line. Betty stepped forward. "I'd be happy to dance with Mister McNab while you call the steps, Miss Ambrose."

"*I'll* dance with him," Sarah asserted. " 'Tis best I lead him through the first time."

Betty's mouth pursed into a pout. For a second, Sarah feared the maid would accuse her of wanting to keep Graham to herself—and she would be right. Sarah didn't want to share. Not with a woman sporting Betty's bosom and easy morals.

Betty's too-knowing gaze narrowed. Sarah braced herself, but then Graham rescued the situation. "Miss Ambrose is my teacher, Betty," he said and the maid had no choice but to flounce back to her place opposite Nate.

Sarah tried to hide a flicker of triumph, without much success. After all, Graham had chosen her. "We'll start again. Bailey and Cook first, again."

"Be careful," Cook whispered to her. "You may bounce out of your bodice without all that stuffing in there."

Sarah's lips parted in shock and then, such was her good mood, she started laughing. Cook laughed with her. "You are a rum one, Miss Ambrose. I had not thought it."

"And you are a bit of a rogue," Sarah countered. The two of them had rarely spoken before. Graham and Bailey questioned what was so funny but Cook and Sarah were cohorts now and wouldn't tell.

The dancing started. Sarah and Graham would be the last ones. She called out the steps for Graham as the others took their turns hoping he'd find the beat. He couldn't. She'd never seen the like. His eyes were alive with his delight in the music. His head nodded to the tempo but the rest of him was going in different directions—and then their turn came to step to the center.

Graham grabbed her hands with a bruising grip, lifted his feet, and proceeded with the worst approximation of a *chaine anglaise* or even a "chase the ladies" she had ever witnessed. He'd shown more grace when he'd twirled her in the schoolroom. Now, he bounced and bobbed, his feet moving but not in any discernible order and she was hard pressed to avoid being trampled.

They stomped left and stomped right. The other dancers scrambled out of Graham's way, and eventually even the fiddler quit playing to gape at Graham's dancing feet.

Worse, Graham was so involved in these steps of his own creation, it took him a moment to realize the silence. He came to a standstill. "What? Is something the matter? Why aren't you all dancing? Sarah?"

With a raised hand, Sarah warded off his questions, needing a moment to catch her breath. Whatever Graham had been doing, he'd been doing vigorously.

"You were fine," she lied. " 'Tis a good first effort."

"But—?" he prompted.

Betty snickered and Sarah decided to make a clean break of it. "Pay better attention to where you place your feet. All beginners have this problem," she added quickly. "We'll resolve it. Bailey, you stand on one side of Mister McNab. Nate, you take the other. We'll go over the steps slowly. Men only."

"Should I play, Miss Ambrose?" the fiddler asked.

"The first time, we'll count the beats. When he has the rhythm, then we'll add the music." Sarah was certain Graham's problem could be corrected easily.

She started counting, "Right foot up, and down and one . . . two . . . three." They repeated the steps several times and all seemed fine but adding the music and tempo was a different story. Graham tromped on Bailey's foot.

The butler doubled over with a groan.

"I'm sorry." The words burst out of Graham. He backed away and accidentally punched his elbow into Nate's stomach. The air left the ostler in a whoosh.

Bailey hobbled over to sit in a chair. " 'Tis all right, Mister McNab. I don't think anything is broken."

"I'm . . . not . . . feeling . . . so good," Nate wheezed out.

"Let me see," Graham said, but Sarah grabbed him in the crook of the arm and swung him back around in place.

"You can examine them both later," she said and, indeed, Nate was getting his wind back and Bailey could move his foot. "We don't have time to waste. The hour is growing late. Sir Edward could come home at any time. Now, let's try it again—"

"It's already too late," Sir Edward's deep voice said from the doorway. "I'm home, Miss Ambrose."

Chapter Four

Sarah whirled around to face Sir Edward. Graham came to stand beside her . . . but everyone else took a step back. The scullery girl even ran to cower behind the chair Bailey sat in.

Sir Edward walked into the room with slow measured steps. Blair trailed behind swinging his walking stick, his hat at a cocky angle. His father stopped in front of Sarah and Graham.

Under Sir Edward's scrutiny, Sarah reminded herself she had no need to feel guilty and, yet, she felt like a child caught with her hands in the honey pot.

Graham came forward protectively. "They are teaching me to dance."

"Ummmhmmmm." Sir Edward's gaze moved past Graham to where Bailey sat and then to Cook and the others. He took his time, studying each servant carefully and moving on to the next only when he received a proper squirm. He saved Sarah for the last.

She refused to cower. She was a governess, not a menial.

"Miss Ambrose, do you value being in my employ?"

"Uncle—" Graham started but Sarah cut him off.

"Yes, Sir Edward, I do." She clasped her hands so he wouldn't notice they were shaking.

"Then you will cease organizing the servants in such silly endeavors like dancing or I shall have a meeting with you in my library."

Sarah's heart leaped to her throat. The only time Sir Edward ordered an employee to the library was to deliver the sack.

"Uncle, this is my doing," Graham said sternly. "Don't blame Sarah."

Sir Edward considered his nephew a moment. 'Twas always a war of wills and there was no telling who would be the winner. This time, Sir Edward deferred first, "Very well," he murmured, "then I will advise *you* to stop inciting the servants or I will be forced to ask Miss Ambrose to leave my employ."

The muscle in Graham's jaw hardened. "You can't hold her responsible for my actions."

"I can and will," Sir Edward answered. "You are free to go, Miss Ambrose."

Graham opened his mouth to protest, but Sarah lightly touched his arm in warning. Nothing good would come out of continued confrontation. Head dutifully bowed, she slipped by the men and walked toward the door. As she passed, Blair leered at her pumped-up bosom. She curled her lip in distaste but he didn't notice since he hadn't raised his gaze. Men!

However, once outside the door in the dark hallway, Sarah rebelled. She wouldn't go to her room like a chastened child. Instead, she slipped into an alcove and hid in the deep shadows, determined to wait for Graham. Then she would rail in private to him about her employer's high-handedness.

In the ballroom, Sir Edward addressed his butler. "Bailey, we obviously do not give the servants enough responsibilities if they have time to dance while in my employ. Or perhaps I should cut back wages, hmmmm?"

"Uncle," Graham said, a quiet warning.

His uncle studied him for a moment under hooded eyes. Graham was his conscience and always had been. His uncle nodded to the butler. "We'll discuss the matter in the morning, Bailey."

"Yes, sir," Bailey answered, visibly relieved because he knew like the others Graham had swayed his uncle to common sense once again.

His uncle didn't wait but turned and started for the

door. "Come along, Blair. The hour is late." He didn't wait for his son's response but walked out of the room.

Blair lingered behind.

He strutted in front of the line of servants, obviously enjoying the fact he made them ill at ease. He stopped in front of Graham. His lips twisted into a smirk.

"Nice dancing, coz. I believe my money is safe."

" 'Tis not the dancing we are wagering over but Miss Whitlow," Graham answered. "And there are other suitors," he added pointedly. "I am not your only competition."

"There *were*," Blair corrected. He unsheathed his walking stick to reveal the sword inside. Graham smelled the blood before he saw its stain upon the blade.

Blair held the weapon up proudly. "I've been busy this night. The merchant riding at her side this afternoon challenged me over something I said. 'Tis a shame, no? Now there is one less suitor to contend with."

Behind Graham, the servants shrank back. Blair enjoyed their reaction.

"Oh dear," Blair said mockingly. "I forgot to clean the blade." His expression hardened. "You don't mind, do you, McNab?" He started to wipe the steel on Graham's leg—and something inside Graham snapped.

He'd learned long ago anytime he provoked his cousin there was hell to pay . . . perhaps not for him but for someone close to him. For that reason, he usually resisted striking out.

But the sacrilege of Blair wiping another man's blood on Graham's leg without any care or concern to the human cost offended Graham to his soul. He caught Blair's arm in an iron grip at the wrist.

"All of you, leave," Graham ordered the servants, his gaze searing into Blair's.

He didn't have to repeat himself. They dispersed quickly.

Blair's face reddened. He attempted to edge the blade closer to Graham's leg. He was strong, but Graham was stronger. He pushed his cousin away with such force, Blair stumbled back. But the shorter man quickly gained his balance and raised the sword, ready to gouge Graham in the side.

Graham refused to flinch. He looked Blair in the eye. "Running an unarmed man through is not something you can brag about," he said. "I believe it is called murder."

"Don't tempt me, coz."

"Then don't anger me," Graham returned evenly. "You are brave with your toys in your hands." He nodded to the sword/walking stick. "But I could still crush you. I have the skill to save life. Conversely, I also understand how to take it. Perhaps you should think on that, *coz.*" He watched his words sink in.

His cousin stepped back. "You wouldn't. You don't have that kind of courage."

"You believe it takes courage to kill another?" Graham couldn't conceive of the concept. "We are far more different than I had imagined," he said sadly.

"Yes, one of us labors and the other is a gentleman."

"One of us saves lives, and the other takes them," Graham answered.

The cocky grin returned to Blair's face. "Then, we are a team," he crowed. He swooped up his walking stick and sheathed the sword. "Except I can dance," he added as a last jibe. He jigged a step or two as he headed toward the door. "Good night, coz. I'm riding with Miss Whitlow tomorrow. We'll wave at you as we pass by." His laughter echoed after him as he disappeared into the hall's darkness.

Graham stared after him and felt trapped. What devil's bargain had he agreed to? At this moment, he could barely recall what Miss Whitlow looked like other than she was passing fair and yet he had entered into that hell-borne wager with Blair for her hand.

Sarah had been right to suspect his motive.

For years, he'd been forced to swallow his pride and watch his cousin threaten and intimidate others. He'd been flattered by Miss Whitlow's marked attention and he had wanted to best Blair. 'Twas his only excuse for accepting such a rash wager.

He was a fool.

Crossing to the wall sconce where three candle stubs flickered and hissed, he snubbed them out with his fingers. The slight burning sting served him right for his own stupidity.

"I'm going to teach you to dance."

Sarah's voice startled him.

He turned to see her standing at the edge of the ring of candlelight radiating from the remaining sconces, her face pale, her silver-gray eyes so wide they threatened to swallow her face. She came forward. Some of the pins had come out of her hair so that it was half up and half down. Her ample bosom over her bodice line heaved with righteous indignation.

He smiled. He couldn't help it. Sarah was a true, loyal friend. Here in his darkest hour, her staunch support touched his heart.

"I'm not teasing," she said, misunderstanding his reason for humor. "You cannot let a man so"— she paused, searching for the right word—"so *vile* as Mister Brock win at anything, including this outlandish wager. I understand now why you accepted the challenge. His type of arrogance cannot be tolerated."

"Sarah, don't worry yourself." Graham walked over to another set of sconces and blew out the candles. "The chances are good Miss Whitlow will not favor either one of us."

"We can't take such a risk. Your future is at stake."

He shook his head. "And I can't let you lose your position because of my own foolishness. You warned me this afternoon I was being silly."

A frown line appeared between her eyes. "You're not giving up, are you?"

He drew a great steadying breath, releasing it before admitting, "You saw me this evening. If I attend the ball, I will be the laughingstock of Edinburgh."

Sarah was in front of him in a blink. "No one would ever laugh at you."

"They should," he admitted bitterly. "I've made a

fool's wager and will pay a fool's price. Such is the cost of being a dupe."

"Not if Miss Whitlow accepts your offer of marriage."

Graham shifted his gaze past her impassioned expression to the night-darkened windows. He could see the reflection of the two of them standing together.

"You said she was attracted to you," Sarah prodded. "The servants agree."

He focused on the determined set of her mouth. "I don't know. She is riding with Blair on the morrow."

He would have moved to put out more candles but Sarah took hold of his arm. "Graham, if Miss Whitlow won't marry you because you can't dance, then she's a ninny and you will have larger problems than the one of working for your uncle for a few more years."

He considered her words. She was right.

"You are going to the ball," she said with conviction. "You will be the most handsome in the room—"

"Most handsome?" he questioned, his teasing an attempt to divert her intensity. His situation was hopeless. Could Sarah not see it?

"Easily," she replied soberly. "You will sweep Miss Whitlow off of her feet, pirate her heart, and save her from such an animal as Blair Brock. Then, you are going to be the grandest doctor in all of Scotland. You will do something worthwhile and powerful with your life and I shall be proud I know you."

A flicker of hope stirred inside him. This afternoon, what with Mr. Fiedler's glowing praise over his ability to be a doctor and then the meeting with Miss Whitlow, Graham had, for a moment, believed anything and everything was possible. Sarah had been right about his motives. She saw his heart more clearly than he. How easy it would be to wrap his arms around Sarah and leave it all up to her . . .

"But I can't dance," he said flatly. He started toward the next wall sconce.

She blocked his path, her hand on his chest. "You will when I am through with you. Every gentleman should know how to dance—and you are a gentleman, Graham.

You are the finest, most noble man I have ever known."
She added in a softer tone, "And my friend. I won't
desert you. I haven't had many friends over the years.
You mean something to me."

Graham covered her hand with his. Instinctively, her
fingers laced with his, a sign of trust. "Sarah, my uncle
will turn you out if he learns of your even offering to
defy him. I will not have harm come to you on my
account."

Her gaze dropped to their joined hands. Almost self-
consciously, she pulled away. "Of course, we must be
careful. No one can know what we are doing." Bowing
her head in thought, the soft golden glow of the candlelight brought out the red in her hair. Funny, he'd never
noticed the strands of color before.

She looked up at him. "Meet me in the schoolroom
at midnight tomorrow."

"Midnight?"

"Aye, everyone will think we are snug in our beds, as
they all will be. Instead, prepare to dance yourself into
a tizzy. I assure you, I'm as good at teaching dance as I
am at needlepoint."

"Sarah—"

She covered his lips with her fingers. "No protests.
You will win the wager. I promise you."

She didn't wait for his response but turned and left
the room, a plucky swing to her hips.

Graham reached up and touched his mouth where her
fingers had been. His lips tingled. Didn't Sarah see the
cause was hopeless?

"I won't be there," he called after her. He couldn't
let her risk her position. "If we are discovered, it would
ruin your reputation."

She turned, walking backward. "Pooh. I'm older than
you are. No one will think anything."

"You're not *that* much older."

She laughed and waved a dismissive hand. "We've
known each other too long to be anything but friends.
Good night, Graham." She disappeared into the hall's
darkness.

*   *   *

The next day, Graham was too busy to think about doctoring or a midnight rendezvous. A new ship was due in by early afternoon and Graham had still not updated the ledgers from the day before or made out the work list for the next week. Uncle Edward assumed Graham would take care of matters and so Graham did.

However, late in the afternoon as he stood along the quayside road, explaining to the ostlers where he wanted the ship's stores unloaded, the beautiful Miss Whitlow rode by on her snowy-white horse. Once again, he was struck speechless by her dewy perfection.

Blair's brutal tactics appeared to have had impact. Fewer admirers trailed behind Miss Whitlow than had the day before. Blair was among this group. He smiled and gaily waved at Graham as he trotted past.

Graham clenched his jaw, struggling with an urge to grab his cousin by the neck cloth and toss him off his horse. From the expressions on their faces, Miss Whitlow's other suitors wished the same thing.

In fact, Graham would be doing Miss Whitlow a favor and saving a life or two if he went to Uncle Edward and forfeited the wager. Then Blair would have no reason to marry Miss Whitlow or combat her other suitors. 'Twas the honorable thing to do, but not the easiest. Graham hated giving in to Blair.

Still, what choice did he have? His mind made up, he turned to walk into the warehouse in search of his uncle when he heard a sound behind him. He glanced back and was caught by surprise. Miss Whitlow sat there on her dainty horse. Her suitors waited on impatiently stamping horses several yards down the street, Blair at their forefront.

He pulled his tricorne from his head, surprised to be singled out. "May I help you, my lady?"

"We have not been introduced," she said, her low voice musical.

Graham bowed. "I am Graham McNab, doctor." He said his title with pride.

"I have heard of you, Mr. McNab. They say you have

the healing touch. You saw my maid last month with Mr. Fielder. When my father paid Mr. Fielder, the doctor said 'twas you who cured her of whatever illness had laid her low."

"I attempt to do my best, Miss Whitlow. God also has a hand."

She gifted him with a radiant smile, her flawless white teeth flashing in the sun. "I've also been informed you will be attending my father's ball. My maid is very close to me, sir. I will save the first dance for you."

Behind her, he could see the frustration and envy on the face of every one of her suitors—Blair more than the others. Nate, who had been rolling a molasses keg toward the warehouse, overheard the honor. He gave a low whistle and hurried off to tell the others, leaving the keg in the street.

Graham didn't know what he felt. Her sudden honor and the jealous scrutiny of the other men left him a bit dazed. Fortunately, Miss Whitlow didn't seem to expect an answer. She put heels to horse and headed on her way. Her suitors fell in behind her, save for Blair. He stared at Graham with undisguised hate.

Graham turned and walked off.

Later, at ten minutes past the hour of midnight, he knocked on Sarah's door, ready for a dancing lesson.

Chapter Five

Sarah didn't discover the reason Graham couldn't dance until the wee hours of the morning.

They'd been dancing most of the night. Dawn threatened and the whole experience had been a frustrating exercise in futility for them both. At first, she suspected he was merely clumsy. She racked her brain for ways to help him understand the timing of rhythm. Of course, they were handicapped since the only music they had was her humming, but she was certain once he understood, he would progress.

His dancing grew steadily worse.

Sarah simplified her strategy. Graham had told her of his conversation with Miss Whitlow asking him to lead her in the first dance. Very well. Sarah would focus on teaching him a single dance he could perform without embarrassing himself.

She decided to stay with the quadrille since most Edinburgh balls traditionally opened with its lively music. Plus, she hummed it the best.

Still her efforts failed.

"Here," she said briskly, tossing back a stray strand of hair from her eyes. She'd taken her eyeglasses off earlier out of fear that with all the dancing and jumping about they'd bounce off her nose. Then, in all likelihood, he would stomp on them.

"Let me demonstrate *one more time*." If she'd said those words once, she'd said them a thousand times. She paused to take a sip of water. "My throat is dry. You hum."

"Me hum?" Graham asked. "I don't know if that is such a wise idea."

"Graham, hum." Her patience and her feet were worn thin by the lack of progress.

He started humming—or attempted to. 'Twas like no tune she'd ever heard.

"Oh . . . my . . . heavens," she whispered in revelation. She wanted to give herself a smack for having been so blind.

Graham was tone-deaf.

He attempted a semblance of the melody she'd been humming and singing over and over for hours, but his was a half beat too slow, too sharp, and too flat.

She listened in open-mouthed wonder.

He stopped humming. His green eyes darkened. "I can't sing either," he admitted defiantly.

Sarah was so relieved she burst out laughing.

"I know I don't sound good, but you don't have to make sport of it," Graham said crossly. " 'Tis humiliating to not be able to sing a note."

Almost joyfully, Sarah threw her arms around him and squeezed him hard. "Don't you understand? Your tone deafness is the reason you can't dance. It's not that you are clumsy or awkward. Or stupid—"

"You thought I was stupid?"

She ignored him. "—You can't *hear* the music."

"I hear music."

"But not in the way I do," she responded. "You *think* you hear it, but you don't or else you could dance."

He digested her words for a moment. She watched as the implications of his tone deafness slowly dawned upon him. "I may never dance."

Sarah shook her head. "You can, but if you can't hear the music, you can't keep the rhythm. You are always a beat behind or ahead."

He looked down at her. "What am I going to do, Sarah? If Miss Whitlow sees what an ox I am, she'll prefer Blair over myself. He'll win the wager."

"She'd be a fool to choose Blair over you for something as silly as dancing," Sarah said, the words coming from her heart.

Something passed in his eyes, an expression she couldn't decipher. It could have been nothing more than the flicker of the candlelight except now, she was aware of his hands resting on her waist, of her arms that she'd impulsively thrown around him, of her breasts against his chest . . . and of a different sort of humming between them. The air suddenly vibrated with the dizziness of it all.

His lips parted, and her heart began to race.

"Sarah?"

She watched his mouth move. Graham's wonderful mouth. Coming up on tiptoe, the better to reach for him, she whispered, "Yes—"

"Whatever we heard came from this room," Blair's slurry voice interrupted, the sound coming from the outside hall.

Graham reacted immediately. He pushed Sarah toward the connecting door of her private quarters and quickly snuffed out the candles, plunging the room into darkness.

"Who'd be up at this hour?" Blair's friend Cullen complained, his tone as boozy as Blair's.

"I heard something," Blair insisted. His voice was so close, she could imagine him turning the door handle at any moment.

Graham grabbed her arm and propelled her into her bedroom. "Get into bed," he ordered tersely. "Pretend to sleep."

She did as he said. He dropped to the floor and slid under her narrow bed. She pulled the covers up to feign sleep, mussing her hair for added effect, just as a step in the other room warned her Blair and Cullen had invited themselves into the schoolroom. Too late, she realized she and Graham had left her door open a crack.

Her heart pounded in her ears. She waited, expecting to be discovered.

"See, Blair? There is no one here," Cullen complained. "Let's return to the study. I've a winning hand."

"Can you not smell it, Cullen?"

"Smell what?"

"Tallow. A candle was burning in here not more than seconds ago."

"Perhaps the governess was working on her lessons or reading a book?" The slam of the books on the floor reverberated in the silence as if he'd pushed them off her desk to punctuate his point. Sarah strained her ears, listening for Blair's reaction.

It came in the menacingly light footsteps crossing the schoolroom's hardwood floor. "The furniture has been moved," Blair whispered. " 'Twas not arranged along the wall like this the other day."

"I have a winning hand downstairs," Cullen said fullvoiced. "I don't want to be up here. No one is here. You could have been imagining the noise."

"I heard something."

"I think your nerves are on end because you are to fight a duel in an hour or so. Relax. You'll easily dispatch that prig Dumfries. 'Course, if you had challenged Major Sutton—"

"You don't think I can take Sutton?" Blair asked, his silky voice suddenly dangerously sober.

"Of course," Cullen said, "but it won't be as easy. 'Tis said he has a good sword arm."

"Aye, but I'm the best in Edinburgh."

"Yes, you are," Cullen replied almost as if by rote.

"Do you doubt me, Cullen?"

"No," came the hasty reply. "I just want to see this Whitlow chit matter settled easily. All this dueling will get people up in arms."

"The matter will be over after I dispatch Dumfries. No one, including the vaunted major, will stand in my way." He raised his voice to add, "Or my cousin."

Silence followed those words. Sarah could imagine Blair waiting to see if there was any reaction to his boast. She held her breath—

And was startled by the sound of a snore coming from beneath her bed. 'Twas too loud to be natural. Graham had done it on purpose.

Blair and Cullen snickered. "Did you hear that?" Cullen whispered laughingly. "The governess snores louder than my horse."

Renewed guffawing met his statement. Practically quivering with indignation, Sarah resisted the urge to grab Graham and drag him out from under her bed.

"Come along," Blair said. "Let us leave the governess to her sleep."

Booted footsteps and the closing of a door signaled they'd left the schoolroom.

Sarah didn't waste time. On her stomach, she leaned over the side of her bed just as Graham slid out on his back. She blocked him from moving farther with a hand on his chest. "They think I snore now," she accused.

He laughed silently, his teeth white in the darkness. "It doesn't matter if you do or you don't. I wanted to divert their attention."

She grabbed a handful of his shirt. "It matters to me."

A gleam appeared in his eyes. "Then I will put about gossip that you don't snore."

She pulled back. "No! Then people, being what they are, will wonder how you came about such information."

"And you'll have to tell them I was under your bed."

At her indignant glower, he laughed and sat up. Their noses were inches from each other in the dark. Sarah's irritation evaporated. They were so close, 'twas as if they breathed the same air.

She did not move away.

Nor did he.

"Have you ever been in love?" he asked.

Sarah pulled back slightly at the unexpectedness of the question . . . and then answered truthfully, "Yes."

"Why did you not marry?"

'Twas a sign of their friendship that she answered with equal forthrightness. "I knew him before my father took ill. However, once Papa was stricken, he didn't want to support a wife and a sick man. He asked me to leave with him, but I could not forsake my duties to Papa."

"No, you wouldn't." She heard admiration in his

voice . . . but for the first time, she wondered how much she'd given up.

At the time, the pain of Robert's defection had hurt her to the point she'd wanted nothing else to do with men or love. Then Graham and his friendship had caught her unawares.

Immediately, Sarah backed away from the direction of her thoughts. She forced herself to concentrate on the wager. "What did you think upon hearing Blair has challenged another?"

He frowned, his expression clear even in the dark. "One day, he will play his game with a man who has more skill than he and he may lose his life."

"What drives him to challenge others? What does it prove? That he can maim, kill, destroy?"

" 'Tis the way of men," he answered grimly.

" 'Tis not your way. You would not be so callous about human life."

There was a beat of silence and then he said, "I don't know. If you had asked me this question a week ago, I would have been more certain of the answer."

"What has changed from this week and the last?" she whispered.

He seemed to edge closer to her. She savored talking to him like this in the dark. 'Twas intimate, the way a husband and wife would communicate, at night when all was quiet and the children were asleep.

"What did I do if not challenge Blair to a duel of sorts?" Graham said, bringing her thoughts to the present. "One that did not offend my moral sense of what is right?"

"And what role does Miss Whitlow play?" she dared to ask and held her breath waiting for his response.

His response was to pull away suddenly. He stood, a silhouetted figure in the dark. "I'd best be going." He moved toward the door leading out into the hall.

She sat up, kneeling on the mattress. "I'll see you tomorrow night? For our dancing lesson?"

He stopped. "Do you still believe there is hope?"

"The ball is in two days. You will dance. I promise."

"Then I will be here tomorrow." He opened the door. "Thank you, Sarah. I value our friendship."

"As do I, Graham."

There was a beat of silence and then he said, "I like your hair down, too." He left.

Sarah sat back on her heels, her hands coming up to her hair. The rest of the pins had fallen or pulled out with her pretending to be asleep. She ran her hands down to where her hair curled at the ends and then, thoughtfully, rose and undressed. Returning to her bed, she paused. The room still held a sense of his presence.

Climbing into bed, she hugged her pillow. She no longer considered the wager a disaster. If it had not been for Sir Edward's greedy desire to keep Graham chained to him, or the young woman's beauty, Graham would have been gone, busy setting up his own practice in medicine.

As it was, the chain of events had snapped her out of her complacency. She had begun to yearn for what other women had . . . and to recognize her friendship for Graham as something deeper, something more meaningful.

Something she still couldn't put words to.

Chapter Six

The next night when Graham arrived in Sarah's room, he didn't greet her with his customary good humor but moved restlessly around the schoolroom, intent on looking at everything but her. She hadn't seen him since the night before.

"I forgot," she said, "I have this gift for you." She lifted Machiavelli's book *The Prince* from her desk. "'Twas the first book you borrowed from me when I arrived here."

Graham turned the volume over in his hands, one finger tracing a line across the leather cover. "This belonged to your father."

"I have other books from him." Although none that she valued more, a fact Graham already knew. "I was going to give it to you the day before yesterday but the news about Miss Whitlow caused me to forget."

He nodded. "I remember returning it to you. I told you I thought Machiavelli's arguments were flawed."

"And I informed you that one didn't argue with a master of philosophy. One either accepted or rejected their ideas."

He lay the book down. "You accepted; I rejected. I thought you the most headstrong woman I'd ever met."

"You had just never met one daring enough to argue with you," she countered but Graham didn't return her smile. Instead, he wandered over toward the windows.

Sarah could no longer endure such distant, unusual behavior from him. "Graham, what is the matter?"

A moment passed while he seemed to process her

question in his mind. Then, "My uncle had his tailor deliver a new suit of clothes cut to my size for the ball."

"Do you not like the cut of the suit?"

" 'Tis fine. My customary blue and brown." He paced the length of the room, turned and walked back.

Sarah placed herself in his path. "Graham, talk to me."

He stopped. "I'm going to concede the wager to Blair."

"What?" Sarah almost choked on the word.

Graham focused on a point past her shoulder. "This morning, he almost killed another man in a duel. Mister Fielder called me in to help."

"The man will live?"

"Yes." His mouth flattened. "But will the next?"

Sarah crossed her arms against her chest, a coldness spreading through her limbs. "You can't let him get away with it. You can't let him bully his way into controlling your life."

"Sarah," he said with a note of irritation.

She confronted him. " 'Tis the truth, no? Men don't need to fight."

He didn't answer, shifting his gaze to stare off into the darkness beyond the windows.

Sarah pressed on. "Mister Fielder lives on the other side of the city. Why did they call him first and not you?"

Graham's eyes narrowed as he turned to her. "Because I was working for my uncle. Because no one realizes I am free to practice on my own."

"They think of you as Sir Edward's man of business and not a man of medicine. I'll make a wager with you. I'll lay odds that if you lose this bet to Sir Edward, he will work you harder than ever and you will never practice medicine. You will spend your time healing servants and ostlers but they are a mere few compared to those you could help. You'll be little more than a slave to your uncle's whims."

"Sometimes I wonder, Sarah, why I've done any of it. I would have been better off to have stayed in Kirriemuir." He referred to the village he'd left years ago in pursuit of his dream of becoming a doctor.

"And done what?" she said without sympathy. She waved her hand in front of his face. "Are you the same man who informed me the day I first arrived here that he was studying to be the finest doctor in Scotland? You had purpose, Graham, and I hate to see people as selfish as your uncle and Blair steal it."

His gaze met hers. "I stole it myself. I was foolish—"

"You were proud," she corrected. "There is nothing wrong with pride, unless it is misplaced like 'tis with Blair." She took his hand and squeezed it tight, attempting to pass on her faith, her belief in him. "My father told me once things happen for a reason." He'd said those words when Gerald had deserted her. "You can't go back and undo the past, Graham. Your only choice is to win this wager. Then you will stop Blair and do what you were meant to do with your life."

He ran the pad of his thumb back and forth along the line of her hand covering his. "What if I'm not so certain I know what I want anymore?" he asked, his words measured and introspective.

Something about his tone set Sarah's heart beating faster. She lowered her gaze to where his thumb still stroked her hand. His fingers were long, his hands strong. Longing rose in her, a longing she refused to acknowledge.

Graham was her friend.

She pulled away. "Let's start our lesson." Her voice sounded husky and slightly breathless. She wondered if he noticed.

He nodded, his hand dropping to his side. "You are wearing your glasses tonight," he observed as if truly seeing her for the first time since entering the room.

She'd forgotten she had them on. "Well, there are no pretenses between us."

"No," he echoed. "Shall we get started?" He didn't act eager.

"Tonight we will succeed," she promised. "Come here, I have a plan. I've been thinking about this." She

pulled him to the middle of the room and turned her
back. "Place your hands on my waist."

"Why?"

She glanced up at him. "Because I'm the teacher."
Her retort earned a smile from him. "Because," she explained patiently, "I hear the music. You hear it too but
you need coaching to capture the rhythm. Hear it
through me. When I move, you move. Then, tomorrow
evening when you dance with Miss Whitlow, pretend I
am standing in front of you." She couldn't help adding
with a quick grin, "You may make a mistake or two,
but men are forgiven such things."

"Even tramping on their partner's feet?"

"It depends upon their appeal in other areas."

"Ah," he said sagely and she could hear laughter in
his voice. The blue devils that had assailed him when he
had first come into the schoolroom were now at bay. Of
course, she was very aware of how close he stood and
of the weight of his hands on her waist.

She wondered if he were as conscious of their closeness as she was. Forcing her thoughts on the business at
hand, she hummed a few bars to warm them up, reminded him to step off on the right foot, and counted,
"One . . . two . . . three—" She started dancing.

And it was a disaster.

Graham's hips bumped hers in the most intimate way
possible. His steps were too long and almost tripped her.
'Twas a comedy of errors.

Graham and Sarah broke apart like two repelling
magnets. For the space of a heartbeat, they stared in
stunned surprise before practically rolling with laughter.
They were laughing so hard, they had to hold each
other up.

She shushed him lest they wake the whole house.

"Shall we try again?" he asked when he could catch
his breath. "I think I almost have it."

Sarah stifled more hiccupping laughs with her hand
over her mouth and attempted to be serious. "Yes, we
are going to try it again and we *will* succeed." She

swiped the tears from her eyes. "The same thing. But not the same way—hopefully."

The pins had come loose in her hair between dancing and laughing. With efficient movements, she pulled her hair back and started to braid it.

"No, leave it," he said. "I told you last night I like it down. You have lovely hair, Sarah."

The compliment sobered her. The air in the room grew close, very close. Sarah feared she was creating meaning where there was none intended and decided the best way to handle the matter was to act as if all were normal—even if her heart pounded against her chest.

She turned her back. "Ready?" 'Twas the only word she could manage with a steady voice.

He came up behind her, standing so close she could feel the heat radiating from his body. This time, he placed his hands at her waist with assured familiarity . . . but she did not move away.

"One, two, three . . . ," she said and then started humming, almost swallowing the tune when her buttocks moved suggestively against his crotch. She wasn't a naive schoolgirl who didn't understand the way of men and women. Graham was fully aroused.

As was she.

They moved, this time in harmony. Once to the right, once to the left. "Now *chassé*," she whispered.

"Do you mean 'fiddle your feet'?" he asked, his voice surprisingly close to her ear. The sound of it vibrated through to the very deepest reaches of her.

She didn't trust herself to answer. Instead, she stopped thinking altogether. She let herself relax in his arms and for a few moments pretended they were more than friends.

They moved as one, performing the whole series of steps four times before she realized she'd been so lost in his nearness that she had stopped humming.

And they had still danced in perfect rhythm.

Graham stopped dancing, but still he held her. She

dared not breathe or do anything that could dispel the magic of this moment.

She closed her eyes, reminding herself he was learning to dance for another woman. He was her friend. He was the man she loved—

She turned, reached up for him and gave in to a sudden moment of madness. She kissed him.

And he kissed back. Without hesitation. As if he'd been thinking the same as herself.

His lips parted covering hers. Graham's mouth. His wonderful, wonderful mouth. She'd not kissed often in her life but kissing him was as natural as breathing.

She needed no schooling. No lessons. All she had to do was listen to her heart.

His tongue stroked hers and pressed closer, wanting more. Wanting, wanting, wanting.

"Sarah." He sighed her name as if it were a benediction. His kisses brushed her eyes, her cheeks, her lips.

His strong, capable hands traced the line of her rib cage, coming up to cup her breasts in his palms. His thumbs stroked the tender skin over her bodice.

His breath brushed her ear. "I've been wanting to touch you here ever since the other night in the ballroom."

Sarah melted into his arms at his words. His lips captured her mouth again. He was moving, taking her with him step-by-step back toward the connecting door of her private quarters.

She wrapped her arms around his neck, this time holding on and not ever wanting to let go. Her back bumped the door frame.

"Sarah," he whispered and pressed himself against her, lifting her slightly so they fit perfectly. One hand cradled her buttocks against the door, the other ran up and down along her thigh, pushing her skirts. Sarah lost herself in his kisses and when she felt his palm rub along the bare skin of her leg above her garters it felt good and right.

She opened her legs, drawn by heat and need. Common sense no longer ruled her brain. Instead, she was overcome by passion. Now she understood why the poets sang its praises and why overprotective fathers and mothers warned their daughters. It numbed the mind and stirred the soul. For the first time in her life, she felt vividly alive . . . and in need, such terrible, yearning need.

Their kiss deepened. Graham moved against her intimately and she was undone. His hands returned to her breasts. Her nipples felt swollen and hard against the soft material of her bodice. He slipped his hand inside her bodice and she cried out from the pleasure of his touch.

She pulled at the buttons of his vest, needing to remove every barrier between them. 'Twas a dance they were doing, one she'd never done, but already she knew the steps in her heart.

Then, Graham's hands came away. He braced himself with his hands against the door frame above her head. "Dear God, what are we doing?"

His question was like being doused with ice-cold water. Her senses returned and she saw herself as she was, leaning against the doorjamb, her skirts up around her knees, her breasts popping out of her bodice.

Graham struggled for control. His lips brushed her forehead and the top of her hair, his breathing labored. "Forgive me, Sarah. I—"

He broke off and stepped back. His dark hair had come loose from his queue to hang down around his shoulders. He pushed it back from his face. His eyes glittered with concern.

Sarah stood, straightened her bodice, and shook down her skirts. Guilt surged thick and hot between them.

Graham walked back into the schoolroom. In the middle of the room, he stopped, hands on hips. "I'm sorry—"

She cut him off. "Please, don't apologize. I was as much a willing participant as you were."

He turned. "How did that happen between us? We're friends." He spoke as if needing validation.

" 'Twas the dancing," she replied tightly. "It does such things to people."

Graham's lips twisted skeptically. "Is that all it was?"

She shot a glance at him. He stood rigid and somber, his stance anything but that of a lover pleased with his actions, and suddenly she had the image of herself standing on the edge of a great precipice. One step—?

"I think you'd best go," she said quietly.

Inside, in her heart, she wanted him to contradict her.

She knew he could not.

Without a word, he left.

Sarah slowly sank to the floor. His whiskers had burned her skin. Her body still yearned. She bowed her head and wept.

Chapter Seven

The next day was the longest of Sarah's life. She hadn't slept well the night before after Graham had left her room and, today, couldn't concentrate on any but the simplest tasks. 'Twas as if she did not know herself at all.

The twins, and the household servants, were excited about the wager and evening ball. The girls squirmed and fidgeted and 'twas all Sarah could do to teach lessons and reply to their numerous requests without pulling her hair out.

She did not see Graham, but she overheard Betty out in the hallway telling Nurse that he was in the warehouse reviewing ledger sheets.

"Is it true the Garrison Commander's daughter was looking for him when she took her daily ride yesterday?" Nurse asked.

"Everyone says so," Betty answered. "He's turned her head. 'Course he's the kind of man who can do that to a lass," she said with a sigh.

"I pray 'tis so," Nurse said. "I'd like to see young Mister Brock get his, and make a wee bit of money on the side."

They laughed and continued on their way. Sarah crossed her arms against her waist, hugging herself close. Miss Whitlow was no fool. She'd recognized in Graham a man worth marrying. Sarah knew she wouldn't let him slip away whether he could dance or not.

Escaping to her room after the twins had finished their lessons, she drew the curtains closed and sat in the dark as if in mourning. Soon, it would be over. Soon, Graham would leave and just as she had years ago when her suitor had left her, she would eventually put the memory of Graham on a shelf.

A knock sounded on her door. 'Twas the twins. They walked in like perfect little ladies but their eyes danced with excitement.

"We saw Graham all dressed in his new finery," Janet said.

"He looks handsome," Jean agreed.

"And he's going to win the wager," Janet said stoutly. "Nurse says 'tis true."

"What of your brother?" Sarah asked, curious.

Janet rolled her eyes. "Blair is handsome but Graham is kind."

"Yes, Graham is kind," her twin echoed. "He has time for us. We irritate Blair."

"Besides," Janet continued with great authority, "everyone knows Miss Whitlow is partial to Graham. Even Father. We heard him shouting at Blair in the library that he must best Graham. The Garrison Commander has been asking questions about Graham's prospects."

"Oh." 'Twas the only word Sarah could manage past the lump forming in her throat.

"Will you come see Graham leave for the ball?" Jean asked. "We are going to watch from the nursery window."

"Um, no, thank you, girls. I need to do a bit of reading. I don't feel well."

They accepted her excuses in the way children do and hurried out lest they miss the opportunity to see their cousin leave for the ball.

Sarah sat still and alone, sensing the passing of time by the beat of her own heart. She closed her eyes and recalled perfectly the taste of Graham's kiss, the warmth of his skin against hers.

Need rose inside her. Wanting. Desire.

Loneliness.

Suddenly, Sarah didn't want him to go without seeing him one last time. She bolted to her door, throwing it open and hurrying to the nursery.

Already dressed in their white cotton shifts and sitting

around a table, the twins looked up in surprise. Nurse was giving them warm milk before tucking them in bed. "Good to see you, Miss Ambrose," she said. "Do you mind watching the girls for a moment while I take this tray downstairs?"

Sarah didn't speak but went to the window. The long shadows of twilight covered the street. Lights from lanterns shone like small jewels around the quay and off the bows of boats. The warehouse doors were firmly locked.

No one walked the streets. They were gone. All gone.

"Is something the matter?" Nurse asked.

Sarah turned. "No, nothing." She remembered Nurse had asked her to watch the twins and added, "Yes, I'll watch the girls for you."

Nurse gave her a concerned look but left the room on her errand. Sarah looked out the window again.

"Were you searching for Graham?" Janet asked. Both she and Jean had risen from the table and come up by her side without her being aware.

Her first thought was to deny it . . . but honesty prevailed. "You said he was so grand, I wanted a peek." She forced herself to smile.

Jean's face fell. "You are too late. He is gone. Blair was handsome, too. Even Father looked his best. He's bought a new wig. Blair has a new one, too."

"I'm sorry I missed them then," Sarah said. She smoothed a hand over their red shiny hair and then gave them each a kiss. "Come now. Let's be tucked in our beds before Nurse returns, shall we?"

"All right," they chimed in unison and scrambled to see who could be the first in bed and under the covers.

Sarah followed them, unable to speak. She'd missed Graham. He would go to the ball and sweep Miss Whitlow off her feet as Sarah had predicted . . . and her world would go on as before. Kissing other people's children. Living in others' households. Sleeping alone in a cold bed—

"Miss Ambrose?"

"Yes, Janet?" she replied absently.

"If you liked Graham so much that you are sad, then why didn't you stop him from going to the ball?"

Sarah didn't know what to say. "Well, because . . . he—" She paused. "Because he had to go meet Miss Whitlow."

"But he seemed sad, too," Jean said. "Janet and I thought so. He looked up at your window as if he wished you were there to say good-bye."

"He did?" Sarah found the information a revelation.

Nurse laughed from the doorway having returned from her errand. "How you two go on." She mugged a face at Sarah. "They are little matchmakers they are. They've thought a long time that you and Mister McNab made a handsome couple—"

"They are friends," Jean corrected.

"Yes, friends," Nurse said jovially, patting the child on the head.

"You can love your friends," Janet said.

"*Ach,* she is much older than he is," Nurse replied pointedly.

Jean rolled her eyes toward the ceiling. "Her age doesn't matter to Graham."

Janet nodded her head in enthusiastic agreement. "Graham loves Miss Ambrose."

Nurse pooh-poohed their comments but Sarah no longer attended to what was being said.

Instead, she stood stunned, feeling as if blinders had been removed from her eyes. "Do you really think he loves me?" she asked no one in particular. Over the years, she and Graham had talked, laughed, and enjoyed each other's company. Now, she realized that even then there had been more than friendship.

Jean and Janet both bounced up to sit in their beds. "Aye, he thinks only of you," Janet said. Jean giggled her agreement.

And Sarah loved him!

The realization rang through her with its truth.

She loved Graham McNab, had always loved him and, yet, had not recognized the fact. No wonder she'd been despondent over his wooing another woman. Last night, her tears had not been over nothing. Her body knew what her mind had not understood.

Raising her fingertips to her lips, she could recall the kiss, the desire, the *passion* between them . . . and he had looked up to her window. He'd wanted her to be there.

"Do you truly believe he loves me?" she asked the girls.

"Oh, Miss Ambrose, you can't put a great deal of weight on what they have to say—" Nurse started but she spoke to air.

Sarah had not waited for an answer. In her heart, she knew the truth even if Graham, like herself, did not yet see.

But she had to catch him first. She had to stop him before he danced with Miss Whitlow. She had to tell him she loved him.

She ran from the nursery to her room. Quickly, she changed into her blue dress. Once she'd been betrayed by love—now, against all reason, she was ready to risk all for love.

She left her room and minutes later was out the door and on her way to the ball.

The Garrison Commander's house was several blocks from Sir Edward's. It took her less than a half hour to travel the distance using several shortcuts she and the twins knew. Darkness had fallen. The evening air was velvety soft. The perfect night for a dance.

The ball was a crush. People were still arriving. Sarah hurried along the line of carriages, heading toward the front door. A gentleman on the steps leading into the house announced to those behind him that things should move along nicely now since the receiving line had been discontinued so Miss Whitlow could lead the first dance.

Boldly, Sarah worked her way up the steps past the others, attached herself to a group of guests, and slipped through the front door. Inside, she flowed with the others toward the ballroom. The musicians were warming up, their chords dissonant.

Because of the purpose of the dance, the snatches of conversation Sarah overheard among the other guests concerned the gentlemen in the room. Every time someone referred to a man's height, her heart leaped to her throat fearing they discussed Graham—and yet, she did not see him.

Then, "Oh, look, Miss Whitlow is being led to the dance floor for the first dance," a matron whispered to another. "Aren't they an attractive couple?"

Fans fluttered. "I believe him more handsome than all the rest," came the reply.

Sarah stopped dead. She was too late. Graham had already led Miss Whitlow to the dance floor. Still, Sarah pushed forward, needing to see him with her own eyes. 'Twould break her heart to watch him dancing with another woman and yet, she could not stop herself. The music started, the chords now sweet and clear.

The tune was for a quadrille. Her prediction had been right.

All eyes were on the couple leading the dance. Sarah's view of the dance floor was blocked by a burly, broad-shouldered man. She moved. He moved. She stood on tiptoe þut could not see around him. At last, frustrated, she pinched the fellow. He jumped and moved out of her way.

Sarah had a clear view now of the dance floor and Miss Whitlow . . . who was dancing with a white-wigged military officer.

Not Graham.

Her gaze searched the room. She couldn't find him. Her heart beat with panic and relief.

Until she saw Sir Edward. Blair stood by his side surrounded by some of his Bully Boy cronies, the expression below his silver-white wig dangerous.

Sarah eased back into the crowd before they could see her and made her way toward the front door. Where was Graham?

She searched a few rooms—the library, the supper room, the den—but he was not there either. By this time, the ball was well under way. People moved among the rooms freely and it was possible she could have passed him a hundred times and not realized it. She never saw him close to Miss Whitlow although Blair led the lady out for the second dance. Several people commented on what a handsome man he was. Sarah could not have cared less.

At last, she admitted defeat. When she caught sight of Sir Edward coming toward her on his way to the supper room, she realized she must leave before discovery.

Outside, she drank in the cool night air and walked home. Fate had intervened. She doubted she would ever have the courage to admit her love now. Perhaps 'twas best because at least she still had her pride.

Bailey met her at the door. He'd been enjoying a cat-nap since he was expected to wait up for Sir Edward. She wished him a good night, picked up a candle, and made her way up the stairs.

'Twas best this way, she told herself. She'd been saved from looking the fool . . . and yet the knowledge did not make her feel better.

All was quiet on the schoolroom and nursery floor. Her footsteps made no sound on the thick runner. She pushed open the door to her room—and stopped short, surprised to see a candle burning.

Graham was there.

He rose from the chair he'd been sitting in as she entered. For a span of what seemed years, they stared at each other.

The twins had been right. He was the image of masculine perfection in his new finery. The marine-blue velvet coat and crisp lace neck cloth set off his broad shoulders and his clear green eyes. He didn't wear a wig like the others, but had pulled his dark hair back in a neat queue tied off with black velvet ribbon.

"Where have you been?" he asked.

Her gaze could not leave his. Wild boars could have been running through the room and Sarah would not have noticed. Her senses were full of him and only him.

"I went to the Garrison Commander's House to find you."

"I left . . . before the dancing."

Sarah's heart beat in her throat. "Why?"

"Because she wasn't you."

Her knees almost buckled beneath her. She feared she was dreaming his words. "But, Graham, she's beautiful and I'm older than you."

Graham's wonderful mouth smoothed into a smile. "Sarah." He said her name softly like the whisper of a benediction. "I've never asked your age."

"But we're friends."

"Aye . . . and we'll be better lovers."

His promise melted all resistance. He held out his hand. "I love you, Sarah. I want to marry you."

Chapter Eight

Sarah couldn't speak. To hear her own heart echoed in his words. She raised her hands up to her mouth, fearing she'd imagined Graham's declaration out of her hopes and secret dreams.

He frowned. "Have you nothing to say?"

'Twas then she realized he was as unsure about her affections as she had been about him. "I love you. I love you so very much," she vowed fervently.

He was in front of her in a blink, taking her in his arms, and raining kisses all over her face. She held the candle out away from them. In her mind's eye, she could see them in this embrace with her hand saving the candle.

She started laughing. He pulled back. "What is funny?"

Sarah blew out the candle in her hand and shut the door. "Nothing." Heedless of the wax, she let the candle, holder and all, drop to the floor and kissed him back with everything she was worth.

They tried to explain themselves between kisses. "I went to the ball . . . ," she said.

"I looked at Miss Whitlow . . . she wasn't you . . . I love you."

"I wanted to stop you . . . I wanted to tell you . . ." Sarah said.

He broke off the kiss and looked down at her. "Then tell me. Let me hear you say it, Sarah."

"I love you."

"Again."

She repeated the words, louder and stronger this time. Graham hugged her close, holding her tight. She hugged back and then slowly realized they were doing a dance. The steps were small, the movements too close for any public dance floor.

They moved toward the bed.

He stopped but she pressed him back until he sat on the edge of the bed. She lifted her eyeglasses from her nose and placed them on the bedside table.

This kind, compassionate, brave man was hers. Let the world take care of itself. She had learned to love again and tonight, she was going to give him her love, all her love.

Lifting her arms, she began taking the pins out of her hair, slowly, one by one.

Then, she unlaced the back of her dress.

Graham's lips parted in surprise before his mouth widened into a grin. He pulled her closer, his lips close to her breast.

"Will you be my wife?" he asked.

Reality intruded. "What of your wager with Sir Edward? Will you be happy married to me and working his ledgers? Can you give up your medicine?"

His eyes met hers. "My life will go on as it has been. My time divided between my uncle's shipping concerns and my medicine. I can live with that. I can't live without you."

Joy and a wave of humble gratitude welled inside her. "You hold my heart," she whispered.

"I shall care for it well," he promised. He slid the dress down her arms. Her nipples were already tight in anticipation. He cupped her breasts with his hands. "My wife," he whispered and kissed the hard buds.

Deep within, Sarah felt an awakening. This was as it should be. She leaned forward, offering herself to him, her man. Her husband.

Graham undressed her quickly, placing kisses where there had been clothes. She tugged at his neck cloth, loosening the knot and tossing it aside. His fine jacket and linen shirt followed.

Soon they were both gloriously naked and yet, she felt no embarrassment. This was the way love should be.

Leaning her back against the bed, he covered her with his body. He was strong and hard in places where she was soft and gentle.

Graham entered her.

Sarah had heard whisperings of this act between men and women—but nothing had prepared her for the sense of completion she felt as he slid deep into her. There was little pain. Another sign they had been destined for each other.

They made love. Graham pushed forward, stretching and filling her, before retreating to start anew. Each stroke of his body against hers was a new experience. This was a dance, she realized, the most wonderful dance of all.

Her body knew what she wanted, what she needed. She wrapped her legs around him, cradling him ever closer. They moved together, reaching, searching, needing and then, without knowing what to expect, she discovered the pinnacle. Graham had taken her there. She was consumed by the brilliance of it all. She cried his name, unable to move, unable to think.

And then, in three slow, deep thrusts, he joined her. His seed filled her and they were one.

A knocking on the door woke Sarah. She came awake in stages but Graham rose up on his elbows completely alert.

'Twas morning. Early morning.

Memories rushed back of their night together. They had not fallen asleep until they had been completely satiated with each other. The memories brought a flood of heat to her cheeks.

The knocking continued, but Graham ignored it. Instead, he ran the side of his thumb along the line of her sleepy smile. "Good morning."

"Good morning," she whispered.

" 'Tis a great day."

She nodded.

" 'Twas a great night," he finished.

She wrapped her arms around him and hugged him

close, reveling in their naked state. She had become wanton, completely wanton. Over the night, she'd discovered herself a carnal creature. She and Graham were well-matched as lovers.

"Miss Ambrose!" The knocking started again. Betty was at the door.

"You'd best answer her," Graham said.

"And tell her to go away."

"Miss Ambrose?" the maid called again.

"What is it, Betty?" Sarah said, smiling as she trapped Graham with her legs to prevent him from leaving the bed. He kissed her breast.

"Have you seen Mister McNab?" Betty asked. " 'Tis an emergency. Master Blair is in the sitting room. He's dying. Bleeding to death. We must find him."

In one smooth movement, Graham rose from the bed and reached for his velvet breeches. Sarah sat up. "He'll be there immediately, Betty," she called. Her hand searched for her glasses.

There was a pause. "He is in *there*?" Betty asked. "With *you*?"

Graham was tossing on his shirt and Sarah saw no reason for pretense in the face of such cheekiness. "Aye. We were having a dancing lesson."

He poked his head out the shirt opening, their gazes met, and he smiled, before calling, "Betty, run to my room and fetch my doctoring bag. I'll meet you in the sitting room."

"Yes, Mister McNab," Betty answered. They could hear her footsteps pounding as she ran down the hall.

"I must go," Graham said, sobering. He tied his hair back negligently with the black ribbon. "I'll talk to my uncle about us later. First let me see to Blair."

She nodded, but then decided she could not stay behind. He left, but she hurriedly dressed, braided her hair, and followed close on his heels.

A clock in the house chimed the hour of eight. Sarah realized it was Sunday. Nurse came out into the hall still in her nightdress. "What is all the shouting?" she asked Sarah.

"Master Blair has had an accident. Keep the girls upstairs."

"Yes, Miss Ambrose." Nurse closed the door.

In the close quarters of the sitting room, Blair lay on the burgundy velvet, down-stuffed sofa, his eyes closed, his breathing labored. The curtains were still shut against the morning light and Blair's face appeared eerily pale against the dark furniture.

Still wearing his dressing robe and nightcap, Sir Edward hovered over him with Bailey close at hand holding the candle. The soft candlelight gleamed on the fresh blood staining Sir Edward's hands. He held them out to Graham. "You must save him. I can't lose him. He's my only son. I'd rather give my own life."

Kneeling, Graham loosened Blair's neck cloth. "Someone, lift the candle so I can see better."

When neither Sir Edward nor Bailey appeared capable of moving, Sarah stepped forward and held the candle high over Graham's shoulders. Betty brought the doctoring bag and set it at his feet. She backed out of the room as if fearing she would be struck with illness, too.

Graham pulled out a pair of sharp shears and cut the shirt off of Blair, exposing the wound.

Blair winced and opened his eyes. Even Sarah could see fever was already setting in. "Have you come to watch me die?" Blair said, his voice low.

Graham ignored the barb. "How did this happen?"

"Duel . . . Miss Whitlow. A garrison officer . . . damn major . . ."

Gently, Graham prodded the deep wound.

Blair didn't even flinch, he was so weak by the loss of blood. Still, he added, "Better swordsman."

"You are lucky to be alive," Graham said matter-of-factly.

"Can you save him?" Sir Edward asked.

Sarah held her breath awaiting his answer, as anxious as the father.

"Aye," Graham answer flatly. " 'Tis fever we must watch for, but Blair is strong. I believe he will overcome."

He reached into his bag and pulled out a leather satchel. Inside was a long needle and heavy thread. "Uncle, prepare a brandy for Blair. It will take the edge off of him while I work. Sarah, open the curtains. Let us have all the light we can."

As she did as he asked, Sir Edward moved over to the liquor cabinet. Sarah noticed he poured two glasses, one for Blair, one for himself.

She returned to Graham, marveling at his calm. Her hands were shaking. "Do you still need the candles?"

"Yes." He threaded the needle. Sir Edward downed his glass and offered one to Blair.

Blair ignored it. Instead, he caught Graham's wrist in a surprisingly tight grip. "Will I be able to use my arm again?"

"You'll be able to use it at writing or working. It will not support your hobby of hacking away at people."

Blair drained the glass of brandy and then motioned for his father to bring over the bottle. Graham set to work.

Sarah held the candle and stayed beside Graham. He did have the healing touch. When he was finished, Blair's wound appeared little more than a neat line of stitching. Graham advised her to return upstairs. "We'll leave Blair where he is because of the loss of blood. I will sit with him."

Sir Edward seemed relieved to have the matter taken out of his hands but later in the afternoon, Sarah saw him pacing outside the sitting room door. For the first time, she pitied the man. Blair was his hopes and dreams for the future. She didn't know what he would do if his son died.

The twins said prayers for their brother and later that evening, Sarah brought them downstairs to their father's side. Through their mutual concern for Blair, Sarah watched a bond that had not existed before began to form between father and daughters.

For three days, Blair fought fever. Graham stayed with him throughout it all. At one point, Sarah heard the rumor whispered, Graham had almost lost his patient, that he'd battled to bring him back from the dead.

The legend of Graham's doctoring skills grew.

At last, Blair recovered. Sir Edward announced a day of holiday. Tight-fisted before, he paid all servants and ostlers double wages in honor of his son's recovery.

And at last, Graham was free to come to her. She was in the schoolroom with the twins. She sensed his presence before seeing him. He stood in the doorway. For a long moment, they stared at each other, ignoring the twins' giggles. He looked tired but happy. He held out his hand. "Come, we are to talk to my uncle."

Sir Edward met them down in his library. "Graham, you have something of import to say to me?" His gaze dropped to where Graham still held her hand. "So, this is how the wind blows."

Graham nodded. "Miss Ambrose has done me the honor of accepting my offer for marriage. Our wager is finished, Uncle. Miss Whitlow married an officer under her father's command. I am free to go."

Sir Edward slowly sank to a chair. "Do you think you can teach Blair what you know of business?"

"Only if he wants to learn."

His uncle nodded. He then walked over to a small chest on his desk. Opening it, he took out ten gold coins. "This is yours, Graham. 'Tis the fee I owe you for saving my son's life."

Graham hesitated. Sarah knew he didn't feel right about accepting money for saving his cousin's life—but she didn't have any reluctance. Surely Sir Edward owed Graham this and more for being his man of business.

"I'd marry you if you didn't have a penny," she said, "but this will help to set up your surgery."

"You're a lucky man," Sir Edward said. He paused. "There isn't a way to talk you out of medicine and into returning to my business, is there?"

"No," Graham and Sarah both answered and then laughed.

"I didn't think so." Coming around the desk, he noticed the Garrison Commander's invitation lying among some papers. He pulled the card out. "Did you ever learn to dance?" he asked Graham. "Could you have won? Blair feared it to be true."

Graham took the invitation from his uncle. "I learned to dance very well." He handed the invitation to Sarah and, together, they left the room.

Sarah and Graham were married four weeks later. The sky was blue, summer was almost upon them, and all Edinburgh seemed to rejoice in their happiness.

They set up his practice not far down the quay from Sir Edward's house so she saw the twins often. Two years later, she gave birth to their first child. 'Twas a wonderful moment for both of them. Graham birthed the baby himself.

Life was good and generous to Sarah and Graham but they never forgot what was important in life. Many a visitor to their home commented on the paper invitation to an Edinburgh ball framed and hanging from the wall like a fine painting.

Across the heading was printed, *A man who can dance can do all things well.*

But handwritten below were the words: *But a man true to his heart is the greatest dancer of all.*

About the Author

Cathy Maxwell's checkered career includes stints as manager of a New England watch factory, a news broadcaster in Dodge City, Kansas, and six years as a naval officer before she started writing. Today, her books routinely appear on the *USA Today* list and *The New York Times* extended paperback bestseller list. Her latest, from Avon Books, is *The Marriage Contract*.

She is also married to a man who can dance.

Forevermore

Lauren Royal

For Terri Castoro,
critique partner and friend forevermore.
I couldn't do it without you.

Chapter One

Village of Cainewood
England
September 1667

They'd sent a carriage to take her to the castle.

In all her thirty-one years, Clarice Bradford had never ridden in a carriage. Gingerly she climbed inside and perched on the leather seat, settling the pink skirts of her Sunday gown.

"I've been in this carriage, Mama. When Lord Cainewood brought me to live with you." Dressed in blue to match her eyes, Clarice's five-year-old daughter bounced up and down on the seat opposite.

"I remember you climbing out of this carriage. That is one day I am unlikely to ever forget." In her short life, Mary had been orphaned by the plague and then abandoned during the Great Fire of London. But in the year since Lord Cainewood brought Mary to her doorstep, Clarice had come to love her like her own. She reached across and tweaked her daughter on the chin. " 'Tis a fine carriage, is it not?"

Mary shrugged, her blond ringlets bouncing on her

shoulders in the same rhythm as the vehicle. "I would rather ride a horse."

" 'Twould not be a very elegant way to arrive at a nobleman's wedding."

A sigh wafted from Mary's rosy lips. "I s'pose not." She nibbled on a fingernail until Clarice pulled her hand from her mouth. "Who is Lord Cainewood marrying?"

"I've not met her, poppet, but if she's marrying Lord Cainewood, she must be a grand lady. I've heard she's from Scotland."

"Scotland. Is that very far away?"

"Far enough." Clarice leaned across the cabin and took Mary's hands in hers. "Can you believe we're going to a wedding at the castle?"

Mary smiled, but 'twas clear she wasn't overly impressed. "I lived at the castle before." Last year, after Lord Caine-wood's brother had swept her from the fire and brought her to Cainewood in the hopes she'd find a home. "For a whole month."

"Well, I've only been in the Great Hall for Christmas dinner once a year. Never anywhere else." The castle was grandly ancient; the very thought of seeing the family's private living space was both exciting and daunting. And the carriage was clattering over the drawbridge already.

"I will show you around, Mama," her daughter proclaimed, displaying nary a hint of the awe that made Clarice's heart beat a rapid tattoo. They must be passing beneath the barbican now, for the carriage's windows were sheathed in shadow. Then it was bright again, and Clarice Bradford found herself inside the crenelated walls of Cainewood Castle.

The carriage door was flung open, and Mary ran down the steps into the enormous grassy quadrangle. "Who are you?" Clarice heard her ask. "And who is this?"

"Ye must be Miss Mary," came a masculine voice. Clarice alighted from the carriage to see a man crouched by her daughter, an infant in his arms. Four stories of soaring, stately living quarters loomed behind him. "And this is baby Jewel. Lord Cainewood is an uncle now, ye ken."

"Lord Cainewood plays games with me sometimes. The babe is lucky to have him for an uncle." Mary ran a small finger down the child's tiny nose. "But Jewel is an odd name. 'Specially for a boy."

"Ah, but Jewel is a lass." A grin appeared on the stranger's face, lopsided and indulgent. "Though she has little hair on her head yet, she's a girl."

"Oh. Will she have hair soon?"

"Aye. A bonnie lass she'll be. Just like ye."

Mary's giggle tinkled into the summer air as the man rose to his full height and caught Clarice's gaze with his.

Something stirred inside her when she met his warm hazel eyes. Since he hadn't answered Mary, Clarice had no idea who he was. He looked to be a wedding guest, though, dressed in a fancy blue suit trimmed with bright gold braid. She'd been told this would be a small family wedding. Judging from his accent, he must belong to the bride's side.

The stranger was tall. Clarice was not a short woman, but he topped her by a good few inches. Straight wheaten hair skimmed his shoulders and fluttered in the light breeze, shimmering in the sunshine, mesmerizing her.

She gave herself a mental shake. This magical fairytale day was sparking her imagination—that was all. She'd never thought to be inside the castle walls as an invited guest to the lord's wedding—she and Mary the only commoners invited—the only non-family invited, come to that. Lord Cainewood had said that since their misfortune had inadvertently led to his marriage, he wanted them with him to celebrate. The sheer wonder of it was going to her sensible head. Making her giddy.

"You talk funny," Mary said to the stranger.

"Mary!" Clarice exclaimed, but she couldn't seem to look at her daughter. Her gaze was riveted to the man's. He didn't talk funny, either. To the contrary, the Scottish cadence of his words seemed to flow right into her and melt her very bones. Lud, she was afraid her knees might give out.

"D'ye think so?" He tore his gaze from Clarice's and

looked down at Mary. "Ye should gae a' folk the hearin', ye ken?" he said in an accent so broad it was obviously exaggerated.

At the look on her daughter's face, Clarice laughed, then clapped a hand over her mouth. Surely laughter wasn't appropriate at a lord's wedding. She schooled her expression to be properly sober. "He means you should listen to people without passing judgment," she told Mary.

The man grinned, showing even white teeth. "I'm Cameron Leslie," he said. "Cousin of the bride." He reached for Clarice's hand. When he pressed his warm lips to the back, her breath caught and she thought she might swoon.

Clarice Bradford had never swooned.

"And ye two must be the mother and daughter I've heard so much about, whose trials set Cainewood on the road to meet and woo my cousin Cait." She released her breath when he dropped her hand. "Though to hear Lord Cainewood's side of it," Mr. Leslie added with a jaunty wink, " 'twas Caithren who did the wooing."

Clarice couldn't help but smile. His cousin Caithren sounded like just what serious Lord Cainewood needed. "I'm Clarice Bradford," she said.

" 'Tis pleased I am to meet ye." He looked down when Mary tugged on one leg of his velvet breeches. "What is it, sweet?"

"Will you pick me up?"

"Mary!" Clarice frowned and set a hand on the girl's shoulder.

But the man handed the baby to Clarice, then reached down and swung her daughter into his arms. "Of course I'll hold ye, princess." His eyes danced with pleasure. "She's charming," he told Clarice.

"I . . ." She cradled the sweet-smelling babe, at a loss for words. Mary was acting inappropriately forward, to the point of burrowing into the man's neck. And Clarice . . . Clarice was *jealous*.

'Twas absurd. The planes of his face were clean-shaven, his skin flawless and . . . young. The man was incredibly young. Early twenties, she'd guess. She could see it in his complexion, the straightness of his lanky form, the angle of his head. This was not a man who had yet suffered the slings and arrows of life.

And Clarice was almost thirty-two years old. Old enough to know she had no business lusting over a young man of any sort, let alone one dressed in the trappings of nobility.

She'd never lusted before, ever. It was quite a heady emotion.

Her daughter was clearly just as smitten.

Clarice startled out of her trance when the whine of bagpipes filled the quadrangle.

"That's our signal," Mr. Leslie said. "I expect I should fetch the bride."

When he set Mary on her feet, the girl reached up and firmly took his hand. "May I come with you?"

"Of course ye may, princess."

"Princess," Mary breathed as they walked away. Bemused, Clarice smiled down at the cooing infant in her arms, vaguely wondering how she'd ended up holding a marquess's niece. And what she was supposed to do with her.

She glanced up to ask Mr. Leslie, but he was already too distant and Mary was happily chatting away. She wondered if perhaps she'd lost her daughter to this man.

Mary had always dreamed of being a princess.

Cameron Leslie was known to be a wee bit quiet. A man of simple needs, he didn't want for much. But when he did find something he wanted, he generally got it.

Right now he was wanting Clarice Bradford. Or his body was, at least. His head told him he couldn't come to that conclusion following a five-minute conversation.

Good Lord, he mused as he climbed the steps to his cousin's chamber, in all his twenty-three years he'd never found himself attracted to a woman as he was to Clarice. Her quiet dignity, her wholesome beauty, something in her large gray eyes. The way she so clearly adored her delightful daughter. A pity his time here in

England was so short. He would like to get to know the lass, but with less than a week before he headed home to Scotland . . .

Wondering how much convincing Clarice would take to spend some time with him, he knocked on his cousin's door and called through the sturdy oak to ask if she was ready.

When the door opened, his jaw dropped. "Cait?" Dressed for her wedding, she looked different from the girl he'd known since her birth. Unbound from its customary braids, her dark blond hair, so much like his, hung straight and loose to her waist. She wore cosmetics and a sky-blue gown trimmed in silver lace. An English gown.

"Good Lord," he said. "Cait, ye look lovely."

"Thank ye." She smiled, her hazel eyes sparkling as she surveyed his own attire, a deep blue velvet suit that he'd borrowed from one of the groom's brothers. No doubt Caithren thought he looked as English as she. She aimed a curious glance at the wee lassie who still held his fingers gripped tight. "And who is this?"

"Her name is Mary, and she and her mother are special guests. She, uh, attached herself to me." Cam lifted his hand, and Mary's little hand came up with it. He gave a sheepish shrug, but his heart swelled, warm and pleased. "She may be walking down the aisle with us."

Caithren knelt, her silk skirts pooling around her. "Good day," she said.

"Good day," Mary returned in a small, polite voice. "I am pleased to meet you, my lady."

"I'm not—" Cait started.

"You'll be a lady within the hour," Cam said with a teasing smile. "Ye may as well get used to it." He knew firsthand how difficult it was to adjust to a new station in life, having unexpectedly found himself to be a baronet after Caithren's brother died last month. He blew out a breath. "I, on the other hand, will never get used to being a Sir."

"Aye, ye will." Cait stood and linked her arm though his. "Shall we go?"

Bagpipe music swelled when they reached the double front doors and stepped out into the sunshine. 'Twas a glorious day to be wed, the quadrangle redolent with the scent of newly-cut grass, the sky blue as Cait's gown and dotted with wee, puffy white clouds. Cameron's gaze swept the enormous castle's crenelated walls and the ancient keep while he mentally compared it to the tiny castle he'd recently inherited in Scotland. Beyond the timeworn tower, the grass grew high and untamed.

"Gudeman's croft," Caithren murmured.

"What is that?" Mary asked.

Cameron knelt down to her. "A place allowed to grow free as a shelter for the fairies and brownies."

"Oh." Mary's eyes opened wide. "Know you stories of fairies and brownies?"

"Many." With his free hand, Cam ruffled her unruly curls. "But they'll have to wait for later." He stood and faced Cait. " 'Tis really the old tilting yard," he said. "They dinna groom it since 'tis long been in disuse."

"I kent that." Her lips curved in a soft smile as she scanned her new home. "Can ye believe this place, Cam?"

He met her hazel eyes. "Ye always were meant to live in a castle, sweet Cait."

"Aye," she said, no doubt thinking of her family's tiny castle at home—Cameron's castle now. "But who'd have ever guessed it would be such a huge, historic one . . . and in England?"

"You'll do fine." Though they'd always been inseparable and he would miss her terribly, Cam knew in his heart she belonged here at Cainewood with the marquess she'd come to love. He leaned to kiss her forehead, then looked up. "There's your man now."

Her gaze flew to her intended, and her face lit at the sight of him. Suddenly Cameron ached for the security this tall, dark-haired man so clearly enjoyed—a woman to love and a place that truly felt like his own. A family. Now that Cait was staying here in England, Cameron felt very alone. A family would be comforting. With several bairns who would grow up and help him make the

Leslie estate into everything he and Cait had always dreamed it could be.

Clarice walked over to take Mary by the hand. " 'Tis time," she said gently, and reluctantly the wee lass released her grip on Cam. The girl looked over her shoulder, her blue eyes lingering on him as the woman led her away.

"Her mother?" Cait guessed.

"Aye. Her name is Clarice Bradford. You'll like her." Cameron's gaze followed the two as they walked toward the gatehouse on their way to Cainewood's private chapel. Clarice's rich brown hair gleamed beneath a pink-ribboned straw hat. Her pink dress was simple compared to those of Caithren and the other women, but it suited her perfectly.

Cameron was simple as well.

He turned to take Cait by both hands. "Are ye ready?" he asked.

"More ready than I ever thought possible." Smiling at him, she squeezed his fingers. "Ye ken, Mam always said it is better to marry over the midden than over the muir."

"I've heard that said, that 'tis wise to stick within your own circle." Unbidden, his gaze flicked over to Clarice. "But I'm not sure I believe it."

"I dinna believe it, either." Caithren's own gaze trailed to her groom, waiting for her by the barbican. "I reckon even mothers are wrong sometimes."

Chapter Two

"A Scots funeral is merrier than an English wedding," the very Scottish bride declared.

The fairy tale wedding was speeding past. Clarice dragged her unfocused gaze from the dining room's diamond-paned windows to the long mahogany table, set with fine china and crystal she'd only heard about in stories. The stack of marzipaned wedding cakes that had sat in the middle was long since eaten.

"Thank you." Dazed, she smiled up at the servant removing her supper plate, which was still piled embarrassingly high with the most delicious food she had ever tasted. She sipped yet again from her seemingly never-empty goblet of spiced wine.

No matter how ridiculous she told herself she was acting, her attention this eve had remained focused on the man beside her. She'd nodded and grinned and drunk to all the loudly proclaimed wedding toasts, and now she was feeling lightheaded. Cameron Leslie—*Sir* Cameron Leslie, as it turned out, for she'd learned that he was not only young and charming and gut-wrenchingly handsome, but also a baronet—had flirted outrageously through it all. When he wasn't slanting her glances or touching her surreptitiously, he was being attentive to her daughter—a sure way to any mother's heart.

Now they all turned to the beautiful bride as she rose with a scrape of her lattice-backed chair. "Whatever happened to that bagpiper?"

Lord Cainewood shrugged. "I think he's eating in the kitchen." His face seemed to radiate a happiness Clarice had never seen. She was thrilled that her and Mary's

suffering hadn't been for naught—while senseless, at
least it had played a small part in bringing these two
people together.

"Well, would somebody fetch him already?" The new
Lady Cainewood moved from the table and shook out
her gleaming silk skirts. "I'll be wanting to dance."

Following the others' lead, Clarice stood and listened
to the bride's instructions. "Hold hands in a circle, lads
and lassies alternating." Clarice found herself between
Sir Cameron and one of Lord Cainewood's brothers,
holding two strange men's hands. Aristocratic men, no
less. Lud, this must be a dream.

"That's it," the bride said. "Now, who has a hankie?"
When one of the men produced one, she handed it to
Sir Cameron. "Ye take the middle since ye ken what
to do."

Clarice didn't know whether to be relieved or disappointed when Sir Cameron released her to do his cousin's bidding. The piper arrived, and Clarice's mouth
gaped open when the bride kicked off her high-heeled
blue satin slippers. Laughing, her two sisters-in-law did
the same.

"Mrs. Bradford?" Sir Cameron tapped her on the
arm. "Are ye not going to take off your shoes?"

She looked at the women's silk-stockinged feet and
then down to her own, clad in wool stockings concealed
by shoes both sensible and flat. Surely she could dance
in them. Lud, she wouldn't take them off, regardless.
Not in front of Lord Cainewood and all his family.

She shook her head, glad when Mary provided a distraction by pulling off her own little brown shoes and
gleefully tossing them into a corner. Laughter erupted
all around when her stockings followed.

"Very well." The new Lady Cainewood turned to the
piper. "We'll have a reel, if ye please."

Around and around they went in time to the rousing
tune, until Sir Cameron came from the center to his
cousin. The circling stopped, and he laid the lace-edged
hankie in a neat square at her feet. They knelt on either
side, and she bestowed him a kiss on the lips. This met

with laughter and Clarice's own startled gasp. But she could sense an affection between the cousins that made her heart warm; she wondered how much they would miss one another.

Lady Cainewood snatched up the handkerchief and took her place in the middle. Around they went again, dancing until she chose her new husband. Their kiss was long and deep. Clarice's cheeks went hot, and she averted her eyes, only to find Sir Cameron watching her in a way that made her cheeks burn hotter. Casually his hand slipped around her waist, making her more uncomfortable, and somehow she thought he was enjoying her discomfort. Or rather, his own power in making her so. When his arm dropped and he reclaimed her hand, she wondered if she had imagined it all. The spiced wine had surely gone to her head.

After much throat-clearing and finally applause, Lord Cainewood went into the center, and the circling resumed. The dancers spun by in a blaze of color. The men wore deep jewel tones, the women mint and plum and the bride sky blue. The fabrics were rich and sumptuous, shot through with silver and gold, adorned with ribbons and lace. The ladies' stomachers were enriched with intricate embroidery, their skirts split in front and tucked up to reveal glorious matching underskirts. Clarice's Sunday gown seemed so ordinary in comparison; when the dance paused for another kiss, she had to stop herself from fidgeting with the plain pink linen.

"Ye look beautiful," Sir Cameron whispered in her ear. She was saved from putting her hand to her cheek when he grabbed it to begin the dance again.

After several more rounds, Mary was picked, and no one was surprised when she selected Sir Cameron. She bestowed on her new love a wet, smacking kiss.

Clarice was the only one who'd yet to be chosen. And it was Sir Cameron's turn again . . .

But he'd no sooner tapped her on the shoulder when the piper quit the tune. Perhaps 'twas just as well—her face was likely as pink as her dress. But she heard Sir

Cameron's groan of disappointment, and it gave her an odd little thrill.

If she didn't know better . . . but no, she didn't believe in love at first sight. Long experience—as a young wife in an arranged marriage, and then a widow alone in the world—had taught her not to trust love at all.

And she and Mary were happy together. Alone together.

But she was at the castle for this one night . . . Just this one night, could she not live out a fairy-tale fantasy? Even ever-so-practical Clarice Bradford was entitled to a harmless fantasy now and again, was she not?

"A kissing dance!" Her red curls glimmering in the light of the dining room's fire, Lady Kendra, the groom's sister, breathlessly made her way to a chair. "I've never heard of such a thing!"

"There is much kissing at Scottish weddings." The bride winked at Sir Cameron, who was still hovering close by Clarice. "A kiss can be claimed at the beginning and end of each and every dance." That news made Clarice all tingly inside. "Now, get up, all ye lazybones. We'll have a strathspey, and a hornpipe after that."

The strathspey was energetic, a sort of line dance with much weaving in and out—no easy opportunity for kisses there. And the hornpipe was wild. After those, the piper played some lively English tunes, country round dances, until they were all worn out. Mary curled up on a chair and promptly fell asleep. Finally, when Clarice was certain she'd collapse, the piper launched into a slow, unfamiliar tune.

Sir Cameron took her by both hands and swept her into the dance. But not before claiming one of those before-dance kisses his cousin had been talking about. He leaned close, and his lips brushed hers, light and fleeting, naught more than a whisper.

Her own lips tingled in response, and the kiss left her wanting more. Clarice Bradford, who had never really wanted a kiss from anyone. Her heart pounded with new and not quite welcome feelings. "Wh-what is this dance?" she managed to stammer out.

"A galliard. All the rage at King Charles's court. Or so I've been told. Kendra taught it to me yesterday."

He danced courtly dances, and with the likes of Lady Kendra. Clarice rarely found herself tongue-tied, but she couldn't think of anything proper or significant to say. Not a word. Besides, she was busy watching everyone's stockinged feet as she copied their steps.

Sir Cameron's hands felt very warm in hers. She'd never danced a dance designed for a couple—all the country dances she knew were done in lines or a circle. She had to concentrate very hard, and she always felt a beat behind. Step forward on the toes with the left foot. Bring the right to meet it and lower the heels. "Just repeat on the other foot," Sir Cameron whispered.

So far, so good. She was almost enjoying herself.

He squeezed her hands. "Now the same, but twice forward. That's right." They came close and then pulled back again. It struck her that the dance was almost provocative, its movements mimicking courtship. Once more her cheeks betrayed her thoughts. She hated that.

"D'ye like it, Mrs. Bradford?"

" 'Tis . . . difficult."

"You're doing beautifully." He gave her that broad smile that made her heart flip-flop, creasing his faintly-stubbled cheeks. Dimples. The man had dimples. Her lips curved at the sight. "Is something funny?" he asked.

"Ah, no. 'Tis just . . ." The dimples made him look even younger. But she couldn't tell him that. "You're doing beautifully yourself, having just learned the dance yesterday."

"I've many to learn before Friday."

"Friday?"

"Jason—Lord Cainewood—is hosting a ball, to celebrate his marriage. All the local gentry are expected, and some from London as well, I'm told." He sighed theatrically. "Three days to learn a host of dances."

She wished she could see the ball. Not attend it, of course, but just see it, perhaps hiding in the minstrel's gallery. She remembered noticing a minstrel's gallery in the Great Hall last Christmas Day. The castle was centuries old and terribly romantic.

But other than the Great Hall, she'd never been inside it before, and odds were she'd never be inside it again. Clarice Bradford did not belong in castles. Which was perfectly all right with her. Tonight was a dream, though, a lovely dream . . .

"And a week from today I'll be gone."

"Gone?"

The music ended, and the single word seemed to vibrate in the beautiful chamber.

Gone . . . Why did the thought make her suddenly sad? She didn't know this man, so surely she wouldn't be missing him.

"Aye, I must get back to Leslie. The harvest approaches." He held onto her hands for a few extra moments, then dropped them. "I should not have been away this long, but I couldn't think of missing Caithren's wedding. And then the ball, just a few days more . . . but after that I must leave."

"Oh." Surely 'twas not proper for her to care about him leaving. She certainly wouldn't admit it.

But he looked like he wanted her to.

Impossible. Wishful thinking was leading her to see things that weren't there. And regardless, he was too young.

When the music didn't resume, Clarice wasn't sure if she was relieved or disappointed. 'Twas past midnight, and the wedding party began stumbling off to bed with a lot of final kisses and good nights. The women even gave Clarice hugs, which rendered her speechless. Titled ladies hugging her.

Lord Cainewood went off to fetch a footman to see her home. Mary didn't wake when Sir Cameron lifted her and beckoned Clarice to follow him through the castle to the double front doors.

Reluctantly, it seemed, he handed over her daughter and leaned against the doorpost, flashing a smile that looked almost shy. " 'Twas a lovely evening."

"Yes, it was. Like a dream, almost." In her arms her

daughter felt limp, warm, and overly heavy. "A beautiful dream of castles and lords and ladies. A fairy tale come true. And now I must return to the real world, but I will carry this memory with me."

"I will remember our dance."

Low and meaningful, his words were like warmed, sweet honey flowing over her. Her own words failed her once again.

He touched her on the arm. "May I see ye tomorrow?"

"P-pardon?" She looked down to where his fingers still rested on her pink linen sleeve. Long, strong fingers, so unlike her late husband's older, coarse ones. Beneath the fabric, her skin prickled and the little hairs stood on end.

"May I see ye tomorrow?" When he removed his hand, she felt a distinct sense of loss. "I thought perhaps you'd like to come out walking."

'Twas impossible! The dream was over, and no matter that her heart melted when she looked into his eyes—there could be no point in seeing him again. "I have work to do tomorrow."

Mary slumped in her arms, and Sir Cameron leapt to right her, his hands gentle, lingering on her daughter as he smiled, then glanced back up at Clarice. "The next day, then?"

"No, I—"

He pulled away, but not before he brushed the hair from her daughter's face. "Ye dinna want to see me," he said flatly. She winced as his eyes faded, his mouth turned down into a grim, straight line.

"No, 'tis not that, my lord—"

"I'm not a lord, Mrs. Bradford. Only a mere sir."

"Oh. Sir. Well. 'Tis just—" She drew a deep breath and tried again. " 'Twould not be . . . seemly . . . for me to be seen about the village with one so . . ." She looked down at Mary's tumbled curls. "Young." There, she'd said it. She looked up.

"D'ye really think I'm too young?" Part of her was mortified that she'd said it—in doing so, she'd as much as admitted she thought he was interested in her. Yet the light was back in his eyes. Clearly he didn't consider this objection insurmountable.

But he knew not about her other objections—ones more deep-seated and not easily brushed aside.

Just then a footman came up and presented her with a short, snappy bow. "Mrs. Bradford? I've been sent to escort you home."

She knew him. John Foster, Mrs. Foster's oldest son. And John Foster knew her, too. Moved to the castle from the village, he was dressed in Cainewood livery and had acquired the manners to go with it.

She could acquire manners too, if she wanted to. But John Foster belonged here, and she didn't. Not here or anyplace like it.

"Shall we leave, then?" she asked, turning to go down the steps.

She didn't dare look back. But she knew Cameron Leslie was watching her. *Sir* Cameron Leslie.

And lud, it felt entirely too good to know that.

Chapter Three

Late the next morning, Cameron paused in front of Clarice's white, thatched-roof cottage. A colorful profusion of carefully tended flowers bordered the pristine raked path through her tiny garden to the unassuming front door. What would she think of the small castle in eastern Scotland that he'd recently inherited? 'Twas no palace, to be sure, but her cottage would fit onto half of one of its four floors.

He sneezed as he approached the door, then almost fell in when it jerked open unexpectedly and Mary launched herself into his arms. "Oh, Sir Cameron," she gushed. "I knew not if ever I'd see you again!"

"Did ye think I'd abandon my precious Mary?" Charmed, he held the barefoot, pink-cheeked lassie tight, shifting her to balance on a hip as his gaze swept the cheerful one-room cottage. Her mother was stirring something in the kettle over the fire, something that smelled fruity and sweet. Not half as sweet as her shy smile when she set down the spoon and turned to look at him, though. "Ah, there ye be," he said.

"Whatever brings you here, my lord?" Clarice blushed prettily and wiped her hands on the apron that protected her simple tan dress, then gestured to the kettle. "I told you I was busy today."

He hadn't forgotten that she'd also told him he wasn't to come at all—he was encouraged that she failed to mention that. "Now, I'm not a lord, Mrs. Bradford. I told ye that yesterday."

"Sir—"

"Please call me Cameron." He set Mary on her feet. "As to what brought me here, I was just walking by—"

"Walking?" Clarice looked a bit flustered, and he was glad for it. Then she wouldn't think to wonder how he had located her house. "You walked all the way from the castle?"

"And why not?" Humming a careless tune, Mary ran circles around him. He smiled at her indulgently. " 'Tis not so very far."

" 'Tis just . . . well, they usually ride down in a carriage." Clarice pushed back some hair that had escaped her brown braided bun. "Or on horseback."

"They?"

"The family, I mean." She reached out to stop her daughter's dance, pulling Mary's small body back against her taller one. Like a shield, Cam thought. "Of course some of those from the village who work there walk, but the family—"

He shrugged, wishing he could set her at ease. "I am not the family."

"But the new Lady Cainewood is your cousin, is she not?"

"Aye, Caithren is kin. First cousins, and all. But I'm a simple man, Clarice—" He stepped closer. "May I call ye Clarice?"

Color flushed her cheeks. Mary squirmed, but Clarice held her tight and nodded.

"Clarice, then. As I said, I'm a simple man. A baronet is yet a commoner, ye ken, and until last month I was not even that, and never thought to be. Until Caithren's brother died—"

She looked down to her daughter's curly head. "I'm sorry."

He waved a hand. Although he would never have wished his cousin harm, he and Adam had never been close. "Until he died, I had no property to call my own. No prospect of any, either. So ye see, I am naught but a simple country lad."

At the word "lad," she glanced up and eyed him

sharply. He wished he could bite back the word. "A simple country *man*, I mean."

She nodded slowly, but 'twas clear she didn't agree. She set Mary free and retrieved her wooden spoon. "Why did you stop here?" she asked again.

"I . . ."

Mary crossed her wee arms. "He said he would tell me a story."

"Did he?" Toying with the spoon, Clarice looked dubious.

"Oh, yes! He said he knows tales of fairies and brownies." The lassie's eyes danced when she looked to Cameron. "Did you not, my lord?"

"I'm not a lord, Mary."

"But you did promise me a story, yes?"

"Aye. That I did."

A small trundle bed sat in one corner, and Mary flounced her way over and perched on its edge. She crossed her ankles and folded her hands in her lap. "Well, tell me one, then. A tale of fairies and brownies. Or one about a princess."

Failing to hide a smile, Clarice turned back to stir her pot of preserves. "Mary wishes to grow up and become a princess," she told Cam. "Though I tell her that is never to be."

"Princesses live in castles." Back and forth, Mary swung her feet off the edge of the bed. "Mama says I will never live in a castle, and I may as well get used to the . . . what is it you say, Mama?"

"The fact." Still facing away, Clarice set down her wooden spoon.

"The fact, yes. That I will never live in a castle, and I may as well get used to the fact."

"Hmm . . . I must say I disagree." As he spoke, Cameron stepped closer behind Clarice, close enough that he could smell her own enticing scent over that of the strawberries. With stunning clarity, a sudden picture invaded his mind: these two, a woman and a child, playing outside his castle.

"Ye could very well end up living in a castle, Miss

Mary. Dinna let anyone tell ye otherwise. Then have ye never heard the story of Nippit Fit and Clippit Fit?"

With a small huff of disapproval, Clarice turned toward him, then jumped back when she saw how near he'd come. He whirled to catch her before she could stumble into the fire, steadying her with his hands on her shoulders.

"Nippit who?" Mary asked, clearly delighted.

Her mother's breath caught. Her gray eyes wide with embarrassment, she slanted a glance to her daughter, then looked back to him.

He didn't think it was his imagination when her eyes darkened and she shivered.

"Nippit who?" Mary repeated.

With an inward sigh, he dropped his hands and turned to the lass, then couldn't help but smile at her cocked head and avid expression. "Nippit Fit and Clippit Fit are not people.'Tis the story of a commoner who became a princess."

"Ooooh. See, Mama?" Mary didn't wait for her mother's answer. "Tell me," she said to Cam.

Looking dazed, Clarice walked slowly to the well-scrubbed table and seated herself before a gigantic bowl of strawberries. Cameron trailed in her wake. "In a country far across the sea lived a prince in a grand castle—"

"Was it pretty?" Mary interrupted.

"Aye." Without waiting to be invited, he pulled out another of the four wooden chairs and sat beside Clarice. " 'Twas full of lovely furniture, beautiful artwork, and rare ornaments. One of them was a wee glass shoe which would only fit the most delicate foot in the kingdom."

Mary's feet ceased their swinging motion. "Like mine?" She stared down at her tiny pink toes.

While Clarice pointedly ignored him and worked at hulling her strawberries, he leaned across the table and craned his neck, pretending to peruse the wee lass's foot. "Why, a dainty little foot like yours exactly. And the prince, he loved dainty maidens, he did, and he decided that he wouldn't marry until the day he found a maiden that fit the shoe." Under the cover of clearing his throat, he scooted his chair a wee bit closer to Clarice's. "That lucky lady would become his wife."

"And then she'd be a princess," Mary said.

"Aye, that she would. So the prince called one of his knights and gave him the task of riding back and forth across the kingdom until he found a lady the glass shoe would fit."

"And did he find one?"

"Patience, Miss Mary. Ye must listen to what happened." Wondering if mayhap he should also practice patience, but unable to help himself, he touched her mother on the arm. "Is that not so, Clarice?"

Startled, she looked up and met his eyes. "Patience, yes." Her gaze flicked to where his fingers rested, and when he didn't remove them, she took a strawberry from the bowl and pushed it into his hand.

Clever lass, he thought, pleased and amused.

"So what happened?" Mary's feet took up their swinging again.

"The knight rode back and forth and forth and back, all around the kingdom, summoning all the ladies to come try on the shoe." He popped the small berry into his mouth. "When word got out that whoever could fit it would be the prince's bride, ye can wager that every lady in the land begged to try it on." He swallowed, and his own shoe met Clarice's under the table.

"And did it fit any ladies?"

"Well, not for the longest time. Try as they might, no ladies could fit their feet into the little glass shoe. Even those who prided themselves on their dainty feet went away in tears." Clarice moved her foot away . . . and then, very slowly, she slid it back. Not daring to sneak a glance at her, Cameron focused on her daughter instead. "Until one day when the knight came upon a house where a laird had once lived—"

"A laird?" Mary's blue eyes looked puzzled. "What is a laird?"

"A Scottish lord, more or less." When she nodded, he

went on. "But the laird had died, and his fortune was gone, so his wife and two daughters worked hard to put food on the table and clothing on their backs."

"Were they beautiful, the daughters? And pleasant, as befits a princess?"

"One of them was bitter and angry at the bad luck that had befallen them. But the younger one was always happy and sang as she went about her hard work. A wee lass she was, a bonnie, sweet thing."

"Like me?" Mary asked. Clarice stifled a laugh.

Cameron's lips quirked as Mary flung herself back onto the bed so that she stared up at the smoke-stained ceiling. "Aye, very much like ye."

"So what happened?"

"When the knight rode into their courtyard holding forth the shoe, the older lass ran forward to try it on. But the younger one didn't."

"Why is that?" Mary queried the ceiling. She raised a hand into the air, squinted up, and traced the path of a distant beam with one wee finger. "Did she not want to be a princess?"

"She guessed her feet were small enough to fit the shoe, but she couldn't imagine herself as the wife of a prince. She thought people would make fun of her and say she wasn't fit to be a princess, so she decided 'twas better to keep back and not even try on the shoe."

"I wouldn't think that," Mary declared.

Clarice looked up from her work. "No, you wouldn't, poppet. But you should. You should learn your place in the world."

"Nay, she shouldn't," Cam disagreed. "Her place is what she makes it, as is yours. We are none of us born to a single destiny—I am the living proof of that."

Clarice's hands worked faster. "Not all of us are so lucky."

"Ye might find yourself lucky someday." His fingers reached out to trail one busy arm.

She froze at the touch. "I *am* lucky. I have Mary." She smiled at the wee lass. "That is luck enough for me—I have no dreams of living in castles."

"Well, I do." Mary rose from the trundle and dragged another chair out to sit across from Cameron. Reluctantly he pulled back his hand. 'Twould not do to court the mother in the daughter's clear sight.

Mary laced her little fingers together on the tabletop. "What happened to the daughters?"

"The knight gave the glass shoe to the older lass, who carried it up to her bedchamber. Some time passed, until, to the surprise of all, she came back down the stairs with the shoe on her foot."

"Did it truly fit?"

"Well, not exactly. She walked with a wee limp and her face was white as a puffy summer cloud. But only her little sister noticed, and she said naught."

Mary shook her head, clearly disapproving of the little sister.

Cameron shared a smile with Clarice. "The knight was so happy to find a lady who fit the shoe, he jumped on his horse and rode to the castle to tell the prince. The next day, the prince gathered his courtiers, and they all rode together to meet and bring home his bride."

"Did he fancy her?"

"Well, there was some excitement, I expect you'll imagine, when the prince's party arrived. Though they were poor, the mother gathered all the food she could find for a feast. The selfish sister helped not at all, but went to her chamber to don whatever fine clothes she could find to impress the prince. When all was ready, the younger sister came not to the table, but hid herself instead. She knew that her foot was the smallest in the house—aye, mayhap in the kingdom—and she worried that if the prince saw her it could ruin her sister's plans."

"But the prince saw her anyway, did he not?"

"Nay, for she hid herself well, behind an enormous black cauldron in the courtyard. The prince and his courtiers had a merry evening with many toasts to the couple. And when it was all over, the bride-to-be rode away with him on his horse, so full of pride she didn't even deign to say her farewells to her sister and their mother."

"Not even to her mother?" When Mary climbed from her chair to hug her mother around the knees, Clarice bent her head to kiss her daughter's curly blond crown.

Cameron was sure he'd never seen such a touching picture as the two of them together. "Not even to her mother." He paused while Clarice drew Mary up to sit on her lap. "But not long after they set upon the road, a wee bird sang from a tree. He trilled, 'Nippit fit and clippit fit, behind the prince rides, But pretty fit and little fit, ahint the cauldron hides.' "

"Oooh . . ." Mary's blue eyes grew wider. "There is the name of the tale!"

"Aye. And the prince cried, 'What is this that bird doth say?' Ye can guess he wasn't truly happy with the bride his knight had found for him. He asked, 'Have ye a sister, madam?' "

"Did she tell him?"

"To her credit, she didn't lie."

"Mama says I must never lie."

"She is wise, your mama. My aunt used to say, 'Tell the truth an' shame the deil.' "

The lassie cocked her head. "The deil?"

"The devil, ye ken? It means ye should always tell the truth. The older sister didn't lie, either, but she told the prince in a whisper, 'My sister is only a very wee one.' "

"Did he hear her?"

"Aye, for he was listening hard for the answer he hoped to hear. 'We will go back and find this wee sister,' he told his courtiers, 'for when I sent forth the shoe I had no mind that the wearer should nip her foot and clip her foot, in order to fit it on."

"Ouch!" Mary yanked a stem off a berry, and, making a proper mess of it, stuffed it into her mouth.

"Ouch, indeed." He reached to wipe some berry juice from her chin. "They all turned around and rode back to the house, where the bonnie younger lass was found behind the cauldron. 'Give her the shoe,' the prince told the older sister, and when she took it off, they all gasped to see that she had clipped off part of her toes to get it on."

A grimace on her face, Mary reached beneath the

table to grasp her own tiny toes. "Did the shoe fit the little sister?"

"It fit perfectly, and she'd no need to cut her toes, either." He grinned at Mary's giggle. "When the prince saw that it fit, he took the older sister off his horse and put the younger one there instead. And they rode to his castle for the wedding."

"A big castle, and a wedding like yesterday." Mary sighed, her eyes lit with memory. "Was it beautiful?"

"I am sure it was."

"And did they live happily ever after?"

"Of course they did. For a hundred years and a day."

"A hundred years?" Clarice handed Cameron another strawberry. "You'll put even more dreams in my daughter's head."

The daughter in question hopped down from her mother's lap and made her way around the table to clamber onto Cameron's lap instead. "There is nothing wrong with dreaming," he told Clarice over Mary's curly head.

"I once was a dreamer," Clarice said softly. And her eyes told him that her dreams were long dead.

"You have dreams," Mary disagreed. "In the night, sometimes I hear you dreaming."

"I suspect those are more like nightmares," Cameron said dryly.

A knock came at the door, and Mary jumped from his lap to answer it, squealing with delight when she saw a small, dark-haired girl. "Anne!" She turned to Clarice, her big blue eyes wide with hope. "Mama? Please, can I play? Oh, please?"

"Run along, poppet," Clarice said. "You can finish your chores later." When the door banged shut, she turned to Cam with a motherly shake of her head, then blushed suddenly. "You must leave," she murmured. " 'Tis unseemly for us to be alone."

When he made no move to depart, she bent her head back to her bowl of strawberries. A spell passed where all he could hear was the liquidy sound of her work, the soft sigh of her breath, and the beat of his own heart in the still room.

"You really must leave," she repeated at last. "As it is, I will be spending all night convincing my daughter she'll not be trying on a shoe and ending up in a castle."

"But, Clarice, I live in a castle. Though it's nothing like Cainewood, more's the pity." He raised her hand and kissed it softly, making her eyes widen. Good Lord, he loved her unique combination of straightforwardness and seeming innocence. "I'm wondering if I could persuade ye to accompany me home to see it."

She tried to pull her hand away, but he held tight. Her cheeks flushed pink. "You're jesting."

"Mayhap." She looked so pretty when flustered, he couldn't resist teasing her a little bit more. "But one never kens what the future may bring."

Her mouth dropped open, and she gave a little huff of disbelief. Taking pity on her, he set her hand on the table and patted it comfortingly. "May I see ye again tomorrow, Clarice?"

"Tomorrow?" she echoed, looking dazed.

He nodded and stood. "I'll not put your reputation at jeopardy by staying here with ye alone," he said, making his way toward the door. "But I will come tomorrow, and together we will decide if I am jesting or not."

Without waiting to see her reaction, he slipped outside, letting loose a resounding sneeze as he made his way through her garden. Whistling tunelessly as he walked back to the castle, he wondered if he had been jesting at all.

Chapter Four

Clarice returned from her morning errands to find Cameron sitting on the low stone wall in front of her cottage, looking altogether too good for her comfort. Beneath a jaunty brown hat, his hair ruffled in the breeze. Her husband's hair had been a coarse gray, but Cameron's was a silky mixture of blonds and browns. Her hand tightened around Mary's as she imagined running her fingers through it.

Breaking from her grasp, her daughter went skipping down the lane, straight into his arms. He stood and swung her in a wide circle, clearly delighting in her high-pitched squeal. Holding a basket heaped with strawberries, Clarice smiled at them from a safe distance.

He stilled and held Mary close, his nose in her blond curls, and Clarice guessed he was enjoying her daughter's charming, childish scent. Though she'd never imagined a man would appreciate a thing like that.

"I've a mind to go rowing on the river," he told Clarice.

"Oh." She looked down at the toes of her neat black shoes. She wasn't about to let on that she'd thought about him all the night and morning. "I hope you'll enjoy yourself."

"I meant with ye." He gave her a lopsided grin, displaying those dimples that made a giggle want to bubble out of her. But Clarice Bradford didn't giggle. "And Mary, of course," he added as he set her on her feet.

Mary's lips parted in a conspiratorial grin that showed lots of tiny square teeth. "I want to play with Anne," she said, more gravely than was her nature. "I told her

I would bring my doll over this morning. Mama made me a most lovely doll,'' she told Cameron.

He noted that Clarice didn't respond to the flattery. "Did you truly tell Anne such a thing?" Her gray eyes looked puzzled before she turned and started toward the cottage. "You knew that today you're to salt and mold the butter."

Mary's cheeks went pink. "I forgot." Cam sneezed as he followed them through the garden. "Please, Mama?" she asked, shutting the door behind them.

Cameron would never have found it in him to deny the wee lass, but Clarice looked resolute. Mary turned to him, her eyes sparkling with mischief. "Would you mind very much taking Mama rowing without me? Only because I promised Anne."

The little minx was plotting to get him and Clarice alone together! He gave her a broad smile, tempted to wink but afraid Clarice might see. "I'll miss ye," he told Mary, "but nay, I wouldn't mind. 'Tis important to keep your promises."

"The butter—" Clarice started.

"I will do it later, Mama. I promise that as well." The blue eyes begged. "Please?" she repeated.

Cameron saw Clarice's features soften. "Very well." She put the basket on the table. "I will walk you to the cookshop. But as for going rowing alone with Sir—"

"We'll be out in the open for the world to see," he hurried to reassure her. "There is nothing unseemly about it."

While Mary skipped to her trundle to fetch her doll, Clarice lifted an enormous pile of colorfully decorated throw blankets, holding them before her as though she hoped they were armor Cam couldn't pierce.

"May I see one?" he asked.

"Certainly." She lifted her chin from the top of the stack and he took one and shook it out. "Crewel work," she explained. "They fetch a pretty penny in London."

"You're very talented with a needle." The designs were lovely. "Were ye thinking to take them to London now?"

Musical laughter filled the room, lifting his heart. "I've never been to London. Martinson—the village black-smith—he visits his sister there twice a year and sells them for me." She replaced her chin on the pile. "I just heard he is leaving next week, so I thought to bring them by. The smithy is beside the cookshop."

"Anne's mama owns the cookshop," Mary put in.

"Ah, I see." Cameron followed them to the door. "D'ye mind if I walk along with ye? I could carry some for ye."

"As you wish." Clarice visibly relaxed when he relieved her of more than half the pile. "But I'm not going rowing."

Half an hour later, Clarice was stepping into a well-used rental rowboat.

Warm sunshine glinted off her braided brown bun as she seated herself on the wooden bench and settled her pale yellow skirts about her. Cameron took up the oars and paddled them into the center of the River Caine, where the gently flowing water took over the work, drawing them downstream.

"A lovely day, is it not?" He set down the oars and swept off his hat, tilting his face to the sun with an appreciative sigh. "I'd wager 'tis raining now in Scotland."

"Do you think so?"

"Aye." He moved to sit beside Clarice, one hand near to where hers was clenched on the edge of the bench. " 'Tis usually raining. Though beautiful for all of that." England was comely, especially here by the river, but the harsh contours of Scotland held more beauty in his eyes than this land's gentle prettiness. "A bonnie place to live, Scotland is." Inching his hand closer, he linked his little finger with hers.

She didn't pull her hand away, but stared straight ahead, feigning interest in a pair of swans that floated on the river. "I am certain Scotland is lovely. But so very far from here."

"Not so far." He twined another finger with hers. "Caithren has already promised to visit next summer."

"But she's from there, is she not? She would want to go home."

"Her home is here now, with her husband. As it should be. But aye, she will want to visit me and see what I've wrought with the land of our forebears." A quick bit of maneuvering, and three of his fingers were wrapped about a like number of hers. Her hand felt cool, her fingers slightly rough from her work.

More evidence, had he not known it already, that she stood on her own two feet and did what had to be done. He needed a woman who would do her fair share of the never-ending tasks around Leslie. His cousin Caithren was like that, and the more time he spent in Clarice's company, the more he found himself thinking she was the same sort of woman.

The sort of woman who would be a helpmate and friend as well as a wife.

He blinked at that thought. "Has the village always been your home?"

"Always. I've never laid my head anywhere else." She shot a swift glance to their joined hands. "I was born here in Cainewood . . . more than thirty years ago."

Cameron didn't miss the falter in her voice. "And you're thinking that's a long time, are ye?"

She pulled away her hand, folding it with the other one in her lap. "I am almost thirty-two. How old are you?"

"Twenty-three."

Her eyes grew hazy, contemplative. "Just as I thought . . ." She drew a deep breath. "I appreciate your attentions, Sir—"

"Cameron. Just call me Cameron."

Clarice hesitated. While she didn't want to anger him by ignoring the request, she didn't want to encourage him, either. Twenty-three! Lud, she was nine years his senior! And a widow with a child. "I appreciate your attentions—'tis quite flattering under the circumstances—"

"And what circumstances might those be?"

She averted her gaze, but the yellow buttercups that

dotted the riverbank looked entirely too cheerful. "I am nearly a decade older than you."

"Ye have lived your entire live here in Cainewood," he said. "I reckon I've seen more of the world."

"What does that have to do with—"

"I assure ye, madam, the difference in our ages matters naught."

For the first time, she sensed an impatience in him that should have frightened her, given her background. But for some odd reason, it didn't. Or not much.

She drew herself up. "How about my feelings, sir? Do they matter?"

"Of course your feelings matter." He captured her gaze with his. "But mayhap you'll find that I can change them."

He was close, so close. Too close. She couldn't breathe. With a straight face, this man—this baronet—was flirting with her. It was insane.

Even more insane, part of her wished he was serious. Her heart fluttered as it hadn't since her all-too-short youth. Apparently the fairy tale hadn't ended yet. But it would, and then she would fall back to Earth, hurt again by a man.

Because that was what men did to women.

Somehow, she managed to find air. "You cannot just wish my feelings different—"

He silenced her with a kiss that stole her breath along with his words, a sweet brush of his mouth that weakened her knees with its tenderness. When he pulled back, she stared at him, silent.

His eyes darkened with concern. "Is something amiss?"

"Your lips are soft," she murmured. She'd never known a man's lips could be soft.

Her husband's sure hadn't been.

"So are yours." Cameron's gentle smile warmed her.

"But—"

"Hush." His mouth touched hers again, more insistent this time. His arms slid around to pull her close, and she scooted along the bench seat until her body was pressed tight to his. She was lost in a whirl of sensation. On their own, it seemed, her hands crept up and stole around his neck, meshing themselves in the silky softness of his straight, shoulder-length hair. As his lips moved over hers, she abandoned herself to the feeling, strange and wondrous as it was.

And improper. 'Twas improper as well. She pulled away, glancing about, relieved to find they'd drifted far enough downstream that no one else was in sight.

"Hush," he said again, grabbing her back to him and pressing his forehead against hers. She stared into his eyes, so very close to hers, sensing an earnestness and an honesty in their murky depths that she'd never seen in a man before.

'Twas only because he was so young. He'd not experienced the way life could bruise and batter, not only the body but the spirit as well.

"Ye liked that," he said, his tone leaving no space for her to argue. "So why are ye trying to escape?"

"I'm not." She tried to shake her head, but only succeeded in rubbing noses. Lud, even that felt good. "I just . . . I only . . . well, you surprised me, is all."

"I told ye yesterday that I want to take ye home with me, Clarice Bradford."

"You were jesting," she breathed, trying not to hope he hadn't been.

His lips grazed hers again, and she closed her eyes, then let out a little whimper when he deprived her of their warm caress.

A low laugh escaped his throat. "Aye, ye like it. And I'm not so sure I was jesting." Before she could react to that, his mouth met hers once more, with a fiery possession that sent the blood racing through her veins. His lips coaxed hers apart, and she was helpless to resist. When his tongue swept inside, hot and emphatic, but still gentle in his way, she paused in shock and then tentatively reached her own to touch it, reveling in the new sensations.

It seemed a long time before he pulled back. As she fought to catch her breath and regain her senses, he caressed her cheek with the backs of his long fingers. "You're an innocent," he murmured. "Are ye not?" His hazel eyes grew murky again. "But ye cannot be. Ye have a daughter, a lovely bright daughter such as I've never seen."

"I did not give birth to Mary," she admitted softly. "She was brought to me an orphan, a year ago, by Lord Cainewood. But I'm not innocent. I was married fourteen years. And . . ." She looked down, her gaze settling on the bottom of the old boat.

He touched her hand. "And ye were nearly raped, is that what ye wanted to tell me? Ye needn't say the words. I've learned from Caithren what happened—your sorry tale that brought her new husband out for justice and into her arms. Lord Cainewood blames himself, as I understand it."

" 'Twas not his fault, though I reckon he may feel responsible. The man was out to hurt him, and mistakenly thought he could do it through me. He thought"— she pushed at one of the oars with the toe of her shoe, then looked up at him—"he thought I was Lord Cainewood's mistress."

He rubbed a thumb under her chin. "You're certainly pretty enough."

She wasn't used to compliments—not from the men in her life. The truth was, she didn't know how to respond to them. So she didn't. "The man would have finished the job he started, except for what happened to Mary."

"Which was?"

"She was in his way. So he slammed her against a wall. When she lay there, still as death, he took off, afraid he'd killed her."

"Which he almost did, from what I've been told."

She nodded gravely. "She didn't wake for weeks. But she's better now."

"Thank God for that."

"I do." From the look in her eyes, he didn't doubt it. "Every day." Her voice came as a whisper. "But the truth is that now I'm healed I don't think of it overmuch . . .'twas nothing that hadn't happened to me before.''

He'd known it somehow, but he wanted to hear it from her lips. "Before?"

"Within my marriage."

He was silent for a long moment; then, with three fingers, he lifted her chin. " 'Tis sorry I am for ye, Clarice. I'm sorry ye were hurt, this last time and the times before. And sorry because . . . I dinna understand. As a man, I dinna think I'll ever understand."

"You understand very well," she said, wonder in her voice.

Cameron moved away, giving her the space he sensed she needed. "Tell me about your marriage."

"I was fifteen." She looked down at her hands clasped in her lap, then back up. "My folks had other mouths to feed. Will needed a wife, children. He was getting on in years—forty-five, he was—and wanted to breed a family to support him in his dotage."

"Your parents married ye off to a man thrice your age?"

"Is that so different from what you're asking?" Her eyes flashed with challenge now, and he admired her for it. He'd never wanted a pliable woman.

He stared at her unblinkingly. "Aye. It is."

A long sigh escaped her lips. " 'Tis the done thing. I was a good daughter. I offered no argument." She shrugged. "I worked my hands to the bone in their home. I thought marriage would be easier."

"But it wasn't."

"Not with Will," she admitted. "All I wanted was a family of my own. But . . ."

"What?" He leaned to touch her clasped hands. "Tell me."

"Will couldn't give me that." Her voice broke, and she paused for a breath. "He betrayed our vows with other women, and he never gave them children, either."

"Marriage doesn't have to be like that, Clarice. Painful and empty and childless." He took her hands in his and squeezed, while words tumbled from his lips, unbidden. "It wouldn't be like that . . . with me."

"Marriage! You're jesting again." But he looked uncertain, surprised by his own words, and she was afraid he mightn't be jesting, after all. "Even were I to take you seriously, and our age difference aside, sir, the fact remains that Mary and I are better off alone. In all my life, I have never been happier than I am now . . . and I don't mean to change my circumstances."

Without a word, he trailed one finger alongside her face, and her cheeks heated even as she tightened her jaw. And her resolve. "No matter what my body tells me, my head knows what is best."

He grasped her hands between his. "Ye speak of your body and your head. But what does your heart tell ye, Clarice?"

Birds twittered in the background while she searched his face . . . a face smooth and unlined, unmarred by the countless frowns and endless anger that had so characterized the only man she had ever been close to.

He'd asked what her heart told her, but she didn't trust it now. "My heart is not at issue here. I—I cannot marry you, Cameron. You're . . . you're a baronet, for God's sake!" She struggled until he let loose her hands. "I cannot marry a baronet."

A new protest. He wondered if it was progress or a step back. "Whyever not? Ye sound like the little sister."

"Who?"

"The little sister, from the story of Nippit Fit and Clippit Fit. She knew her feet were small enough they might fit the shoe, but she couldn't imagine herself as the wife of a prince. D'ye remember? She thought people would make fun of her and say she wasn't fit to be a princess."

Clarice remained silent.

"Dinna sell yourself short, love. Ye are fit to be a queen. 'Tis sorry I am it is only in my power to make ye a mere Lady."

The boat rocked violently when she stood. "This is not a fairy tale, and I am not the little sister. These big feet will not fit into any glass shoes. I am tall, not dainty. Too tall—"

"Ye are not too tall for *me*." He stood as well, to demonstrate, and the boat swung even more. She swayed wildly. Alarmed, he grabbed for her, but she leapt away.

And flailed backward, headfirst into the river.

He dove in after her, clasping her close when she came up sputtering. "Lud!" She laughed, a sound of pure delight that shocked him out of his wits. He'd expected her to be furious. "You're turning my life upside down, Cameron Leslie. Literally."

The water was frigid, and her teeth were already chattering, her lips turning a decided shade of blue. There was only one thing to do.

Kiss the warmth right back into them.

He dragged her against his body, treading water while he pressed his mouth to hers. He was shocked a second time when she cooperated fully. Her arms wrapped around his shoulders; her legs clasped his. He was certain he'd never felt anything as glorious as this willowy, wet woman fused to him, her every curve melding against his body as though they'd been made for one another. They kissed long and deep, until he realized they were slowly drifting downstream—and the boat was drifting faster.

"Hell."

"Wh-what?" Her voice sounded drugged, dreamy.

With a heartfelt groan, he kissed her again, thrilling when her tongue flicked into his mouth of her own volition. He could kiss her forever, except he had a feeling it would swiftly lead to other things.

Not to mention that soon they would be down the river without a boat. He wouldn't mind walking back, but he *would* mind paying for a rickety boat that he wouldn't even hold in his possession. Leslie Castle was bonnie, but the estate itself was cash poor.

"Hell," he repeated, pulling back.

"What is it, Cam?"

Cam. He had to reward her for that with another kiss.

"Hell," he said again a couple of minutes later.

"Do you always curse so much?"

"Only when my boat is floating away."

"Lud!" She looked around wildly. And then, "I cannot swim!"

She hung on to his back as he struck out for the boat. Not too long afterward, he hauled himself aboard and pulled her in after him.

She sprawled on the bench, laughing still. Until she looked down at her wet gown plastered against her front. With a gasp, she crossed her arms over full, round breasts that had shown rosy peaks through the transparent pale yellow fabric.

"Tell me you didn't see that."

"I didn't see that." But he had. Her breasts were beautiful. Everything about her was beautiful. Not only the way she looked, but her beautiful soul. And the beautiful way she felt in his arms.

She shivered. "I . . . I know not what came over me."

" 'Twas the cold," he said, offering her an out. "And the wet." But they both knew that something had changed in the water.

"Yes, it must have been." Her hair had come undone and hung in long, wet tendrils down her back. He wanted to wrap his hands in it. Her arms were still crossed over her chest. "I'm sorry," she said.

"For what?"

"For making you get wet. Ruining your clothes and boots. I hope . . ." She froze, and her face went white. Whiter than even the cold would warrant. "Please don't be vexed with me."

"Why would I be vexed with ye, Clarice?" She looked like she expected him to be angry, and the truth was, that expectation in itself raised his ire. He wanted to kill the man who had taught her to be so wary. Lucky for him, the bastard was already dead. "Ye didn't do it on purpose. And truth be told, I would happily ruin my boots to hold ye again." He moved closer. "May I kiss ye again, Clarice?"

She bit her lip, for all the world looking like she didn't believe him.

He wouldn't push her, not now when she looked so cold and miserable. Moving to the other bench, he sighed and picked up the oars. With strokes made powerful by frustration, the boat was soon slicing through the water toward the docks.

"Tell me, Clarice," he asked presently, "if ye cannot swim, why were ye not frightened when ye fell?"

Her words were long in coming, and when they finally did, 'twas with a kind of wonder, as though she surprised herself with her answer. "I knew you would come after me," she said simply.

Progress, he decided. 'Twould have to do for now.

Chapter Five

"I'm thinking . . ." The horse in the stall before him flicked its tail, and Cameron forced his mind back to the discussion. "I'm thinking if I cross our Highland ponies with some of this stock, then—"

"Why're ye hanging around here, Cam?" Caithren grinned and took her cousin's hand, pulling him out of Cainewood's stables. " 'Tis obvious your head is somewhere else."

"I wanted to study English breeding methods." Plucking his still-damp shirt away from his body, he followed her along the path back to the castle. "And the estate's theories pertaining to crops—why, there are all sorts of newfangled ideas that bear exploring, as long as I've taken the time to remain here in England until—"

"Ye dinna want to talk about crops." Caithren paused on the path, her smile too knowing.

"Nay?" Cameron shuffled his feet in the long trodden grass that led through a meadow sprinkled with yellow buttercups. He sneezed, then rubbed a finger under his nose. "D'ye ken, then, who around here might be considered the expert on sheep—"

"You're not wanting to talk about sheep, either."

He remained silent, cocking one sandy brow.

"You've been distracted all afternoon. Like you'd rather be somewhere else."

He never had been able to hide much from Cait. In an old gesture of affection between them, he reached to tug on one of her braids, then remembered she now wore her hair loose to please her husband. He crossed his arms instead. "How is married life treating ye, Cait?"

"So far I like it." She turned and started ambling over the drawbridge, her long, straight hair fluttering in her wake. "Very much," she called back, laughter in her voice.

Behind her, his boots sounded loud on the timeworn wood. "I'm going to miss ye." They'd been there for each other, always. "I can hardly imagine returning to Leslie alone."

"Ye need someone to share it with." Exactly what he'd been thinking, but he could almost hear the wheels turning in her head. And they weren't running the same direction his did. "There is always Lady Nessa."

"She wouldn't have me when I was plain Cameron Leslie—"

Caithren paused beneath the barbican and turned to him. "But now you're the laird, Cam."

"Exactly." He blinked at her in the shadows. "Whatever feelings I had for Nessa died when she laughed at my proposal. She is sleekit, but cold underneath, ye ken? I'll not be going back to her now." His gaze drifted up to the massive portcullis overhead. The iron-banded gate would kill him instantly should it fall. Indeed, he would prefer such a fate to life with Lady Nessa.

"And the village lasses? I can think of more than a couple who are anything but cold." She grinned and started walking again, backward this time, avidly watching his face. "You've shared a tumble or two with some of them, aye?"

He should have seen something like that coming. He reached for her shoulders and spun her to face away. "I'll not be saying." There were some experiences he didn't share, not even with Caithren. "But there's none of them I can picture spending my life with, regardless." He followed her into the quadrangle and up the winding stairs of the old keep, all the while picturing spending his life with a certain woman who waited in a small white cottage. "I want somebody like Clarice—I mean, Mrs. Bradford."

His statement seemed to vibrate through the ancient stones, and his cousin's feet faltered on the steps. "Ye mean ye want Clarice herself, do ye not?" She resumed her climb, and he could hear the smile in her voice. "Dinna trouble yourself to argue—I saw ye two together at my wedding. Does it not bother ye that she's been married afore?"

"If I were thinking of having her, nay, 'twould not bother me." They went out through an archway onto a long stretch of wall walk that circumnavigated much of the castle. "She didn't have an easy time of that marriage, Cait. Not that I'm planning to take her home with me or anything, ye understand, but 'tis the truth I've found myself wondering if mayhap I could make her happy. And Mary. She's a precious lass, and she's had a hard life."

'Twas quiet, and from up here the view stretched for miles, lush and green. "Ye shouldn't marry someone to right past wrongs," Cait said softly. "Or even to make her happy. Ye should marry for your own reasons. If marriage is what you're implying ye want, ye need selfish reasons, if I may say so."

"I have my own reasons. But they matter not, since Cl—Mrs. Bradford—will not consider my suit. Not that I've been trying to court her. That would be daft, would it not? I'm leaving in four days." He crossed to the side facing the castle. "She thinks she's too old for me."

Caithren was still on the other side, but he could feel her gaze on his back. "What do *ye* think, Cam?"

"I think she's lovely and sweet, and a strong woman who is not afraid of hard work. Life at Leslie isn't easy, as ye well know. 'Tis no Cainewood." He gestured with the sweep of an arm at the immense edifice of the castle and the open quadrangle, continually crisscrossed by servants going about their business. As castles went, Leslie and his lifestyle there couldn't have been more of a contrast. "My wife will not be lying around eating sweetmeats all the day."

When he turned to face her, Caithren's eyes flashed hazel fire. "Is that what ye think I'll be doing?"

He raised one hand in mock self-defense. "I know ye better than that. But the fact remains ye could do naught more than that if it pleased ye. Whereas my wife—"

"Ye *are* thinking of marriage, aren't ye?"

"I think I might love her," he said simply, shocked at his own admission but knowing it was true. "That is reason enough to marry her, aye?"

Cait came over and rested a hand on his shoulder. "Are ye sure, Cam? You've kent her but a few days."

For a spell, he just measured her. "And how long did ye know your new husband before ye decided ye loved him?"

She inclined her head in a thoughtful nod. "Point conceded. Mayhap the Leslies just fall fast." She could hardly say otherwise, since her own romance had culminated in a marriage proposal within less than two weeks. "So then I have a question for ye, Cameron Leslie." She grinned. "Why have ye wasted half the day hanging around here when ye could be courting your lady?"

"She invited me for supper," he admitted.

"Then go ready yourself," she said. "Ye look like a drowned rat." She gave him a shove toward the keep and the stairs, and he was off without another word.

"Just dinna go gathering flowers to impress her," she called after him.

"He kissed me, Gisela." Clarice paced her friend's small cookshop. "Just like that, and then he asked me to go home with him."

"And when he comes tonight, what will you tell him?" Gisela pushed a strand of graying hair back under her mobcap, her words directed to the table where she was counting the strawberry tarts that Clarice had brought her.

"I know not what to tell him. He cannot have been serious, anyway." Drawing a deep breath, Clarice took the empty basket off her arm and set it on the table. "Watch where you're running, Mary!"

"You as well, Anne," Gisela chided her sprite of a child as she watched the two girls race around the cookshop. "You're making me dizzy." She reached out a plump hand to stop her daughter's hectic progress. "Go into the back and fetch Mrs. Bradford two loaves of bread."

"As you wish, Mama." Laughing, Anne streaked past a lace curtain and into the next room, Mary close on her heels.

Clarice sighed. "I'm still wondering how it is I invited him to supper. I was leaving to go home and dry off, and the words just came out of my mouth, all by themselves."

"All by themselves, is it?" When Clarice kept her lips pressed tight, Gisela leaned closer. "You like him, do you not?"

"He's good to Mary. Patient. He told her a story. And her eyes light up when—"

"This isn't about Mary." With a self-satisfied smile, Gisela counted coins to pay Clarice for the tarts. " 'Tis true your daughter could use a man in her life. Can we not all?" Her kind brown eyes sparkled when she laughed. "But this is about you, Clarice, and what you want for yourself."

"I've been happy alone with Mary. After what I went through with Will, I value my independence."

"And?" The money jingled when Gisela scooped it up.

"He's young."

"How young?"

She bit her lip. "Twenty-three."

"A man grown. If it doesn't bother him, why should it you? Other women will be jealous." When Clarice rolled her eyes, Gisela handed her the coins. "And?"

The money clinked in Clarice's hands as she toyed with it, pouring the small pile from one palm to the other. "Scotland. He lives in Scotland. For God's sake, I've never even been to London!"

"And?"

She lowered her head, and her voice dropped to a defeated whisper. "My skin tingles when he touches me. I"—she looked up—"I've never felt like this before."

"I felt like that once upon a time." Gisela's words sounded far away, as far away as where she seemed to be staring. "Then Tim succumbed to the smallpox, and here I am . . . running the cookshop alone. Alone, Clarice." Her gaze focused on her friend. " 'Tisn't good to be alone."

"I have Mary," Clarice said doggedly. *And I'm terrified*, she added to herself.

"For how many years? They grow. They grow and they're gone. You cannot live your life through a child, dearie. 'Twould not be fair to either of you."

Chapter Six

"Delicious." Cameron pushed back from the table. "Another lurking talent I was unaware of. I thank ye for the fine meal."

Her cheeks burning, Clarice rose to clear the plates. " 'Twas nothing compared to what they serve at the castle."

"I've told ye, Clarice, I'm a simple country man. I prefer simple country food."

His words weren't mere flattery—he'd polished off two servings of the stew she'd prepared. She leaned close to access his empty plate. He smelled fresh and faintly spicy, not just the clean scent of the river, but like he'd bathed afterward at the castle, using expensive imported soap. Her husband had worked hard at the mill and rarely bathed—he'd usually smelled of stale sweat.

She jumped back when Cameron released an ear-splitting sneeze. She couldn't help but stare at him. He'd been sneezing ever since he'd arrived.

He shook his head as though to clear it. "Oh, I'll admit that once in a while 'tis nice to eat fancy, but a man could get sick eating like that every day, ye ken?"

"I hope you're not getting sick now," she told him, her heart thudding at the sudden thought. The Black Death had swept through England two years earlier, devastating the population. And its first symptom was sneezing.

His face turned red. " 'Tis just—" He cupped his hands and sneezed into them again.

Unaware of her mother's distress, Mary stared at him

with open admiration. "You have the loudest sneeze I've ever heard."

"Mary!" Clarice admonished, although she'd been thinking the same thing herself before her mind had become fixated on this new concern.

He sneezed yet again, seeming to shake the cottage walls. "My apologies. 'Tis just—" Another explosion had Clarice backing away in an effort avoid this plague. It was all she could do not to grab her daughter and run for the door.

His eyes filled with regret, he rubbed a finger under his nose. " 'Tis the flowers," he admitted sheepishly.

"The what?" Mary asked, nibbling on a nail while Clarice wracked her brain, wondering if her daughter had touched him.

"The flowers." He gestured toward the middle of the table, where Clarice had placed a bowl crammed with cheerful posies she'd picked from her garden. "They make me sneeze."

His words finally got through to her. As he drew breath in preparation for another discharge, Clarice snatched up the bowl, clutching it to her chest and sagging with relief. "Flowers make you sneeze?"

With an obvious effort, he held back. "Aye. I've always been that way—I know not why."

"Lud." And here she'd worried he'd been on the verge of death. Trying not to laugh—at herself or his absurd affliction; she wasn't sure which—she backed toward the door. "Let me just take these outside."

Cameron began to rise, as though he intended to help her. Or to leave.

"Mary," she choked out, "will you please pour Sir Cameron more ale?" She hurried outside, closing the door behind her before she slumped against it, attacked by a fit of the giggles like she'd never before experienced.

Around this man, she seemed to be a different woman. She had to get herself under control. Biting her tongue, she drew a deep breath and used every ounce of her will to keep a straight face as she reentered the cottage.

As she'd requested, Mary had poured more ale. Apparently recovered, Cameron sipped and chatted with her daughter while Clarice bustled about, calming herself and lighting candles to ward off the dark that was swiftly falling. Though she hadn't a clue whether he would stay a spell longer or not, she was hoping the cozy lit room and another cup of ale would keep him there awhile.

To her vast surprise, she found herself craving another kiss. What could it hurt? A memory to keep her warm at night.

He'd removed his surcoat and sat at her table in a thin lawn shirt, the sleeves rolled up to reveal tanned, muscled forearms. That small display of skin was enough to make her remember how he'd looked and felt all wet, with his clothes plastered to his body. Firm and strong, so unlike her husband's aging form. She'd been distracted to the point that she had almost forgotten to eat.

Yet he hadn't so much as touched her all evening. She knew not whether he'd given up, or whether he was simply a gentleman who wouldn't think of pressing his suit in her daughter's plain sight. But she hoped it was the latter.

She was dying for a kiss.

Although the thought of anything more intimate scared the very wits out of her, the truth was she found Cameron Leslie's kisses almost unbearably exciting. But that was because she'd never really been kissed before. A mindless grinding of the lips, yes, but not a real kiss as she'd come to know a kiss this afternoon. The rest she could happily live without. She knew what that felt like, and why anyone would ever call it "making love" was beyond her comprehension. A glossy lie, that, doubtlessly invented by men to keep virgins from abandoning their marriage beds.

"Well, I've got two choices." Refilled ale cup notwithstanding, Cameron rose. "I can either leave, or we can dance."

"Dance?" Whatever was he talking about? Slowly she removed the apron that covered her navy blue dress. A nice dark color. Even if she were soaking wet, he'd not be able to see through it.

"Aye, dance," he said. "I was supposed to practice my dancing tonight, in preparation for Friday's ball. Lady Kendra told me in no uncertain terms that I was to return early, or dance here instead."

She didn't fall for that story, but when he began pushing the table and chairs out of the way, she couldn't seem to find the words to tell him no.

Courtly dancing was for couples, mostly. He would have to touch her. Her hands tingled at the mere thought.

Mary scraped a chair across the floor. "May I dance, too?"

"Of course ye may." He brushed his palms on his plain wool breeches. "We will start with the minuet. I need the most practice in that—"

"We've got no music," Mary pointed out.

"I can count the beats." He cleared his throat and launched right into the lesson. "We count six for each minuet step, but the first movement is only a plié—"

"A what?" Mary cocked her golden head.

"A plié. Just turn out your feet and bend your knees a little."

"Like this?" She pliéd until her bottom nearly touched the floor.

Clarice's heart melted when she saw him bite back a laugh. "Nay, princess. Just a wee bit. Like this." He demonstrated. "Now, that is really naught but a preparation for the step, so we start with the last beat of the previous bar. Six, one, two, three, four, five; six, one, two—"

"I think I feel the headache coming on," Clarice interrupted, putting a hand to her brow. "This is terribly complicated, is it not?"

"You'll do fine. Follow me. Plié, then step forward with your right foot and rise on your toes. Close in your left foot and lower your heels." As best they could, Clarice and Mary executed the steps while he watched. "Good. Now the same on the other side." Counting off, he danced along. "Six, one, two, three, four, five. Smaller steps, Princess Mary. The steps must be tiny to fit in the beats. Six, one, two, three, four, five . . ."

When he took Mary's hands to show her how they would dance together, Clarice wanted to scream. Not that she begrudged her daughter the attention, but lud, she'd been waiting all night to touch him. And she felt downright silly dancing alone.

"Six, one, two, three, four, five. La la la, la la la—"

"What are the words?" Mary interrupted, stopping mid-step.

Cameron blinked. "It doesn't have words." He tugged on Mary's hands to get her dancing again.

"Oh." She stayed stubbornly still and ruminated on that a moment. "I like songs with words."

He shrugged. "I know no words to this one, Princess Mary."

"Then I will sing something else." And without further ado, she launched into a lovely rendition of "The Twenty-Ninth of May."

"Let the bells in steeples ring,
And music sweetly play,
That loyal Tories mayn't forget
The twenty-ninth of May."

The charming dimples appeared when Cameron grinned. "Ye sing beautifully, princess." And finally, while Mary's sweet voice trilled the lilting tune, he dropped her hands and took Clarice's.

Mary made her way to a chair.

"Twelve years was he banish'd
From what was his due,
And forced to hide in fields and woods
From Presbyterian crew;
But God did preserve him,
As plainly you do see,
The blood-hounds did surround the oak
While he was in the tree."

Clarice's feet seemed to glide effortlessly, her body guided by Cameron's warm hands holding hers. Her gaze was locked on his compelling hazel eyes. Her blood pumped much harder than the sedate dance should cause. Lud, what was happening to her? If her daughter weren't watching, she would surely throw herself into his arms.

His smile suggested he just might be reading her mind, and her heart skipped a beat. His hands tightened on hers when she would have stumbled, but he didn't comment on her clumsiness. "She sings of King Charles's restoration, does she not?"

"P-pardon?" The song was the farthest thing from her mind.

"I'm speaking of Mary." The dimples winked, telling her he was pleased with her discomposure. "Her song tells of the Restoration, and Charles hiding in the Royal Oak."

"Oh. Yes." Somehow, probably owing to Cameron's skill, her feet kept moving in time to the melody. He must have been jesting when he said he needed practice; he was a superb dancer. " 'Tis a Cavalier ballad she sings. Cainewood—the whole village—was a Royalist stronghold throughout the Civil War. In support of the marquess, you understand. His family was fiercely Royalist—his parents both died in the battle of Worcester."

"D'ye remember that?"

"Most certainly." Then she remembered something else, and her heart dropped to her knees. "You were too young, were you not? I'd wager you don't remember the Commonwealth. 'Twas no trial to you, was it, that sad period in our history?" For a moment, lost in his eyes and the dance, she'd forgotten their age difference. But it would be there, wouldn't it? Always. Different life experiences.

"Nay. I dinna remember overmuch," he admitted, confirming her suspicions. "I was but a bairn. And though London holds rule over Scotland, ye must remember we are quite far removed from what happens here."

Her voice dropped to a whisper. "We haven't much in common, do we? You're Scottish, I'm English . . ." A profound sense of loss swept through her, and her words trailed off.

"So let the bells in steeples ring,
And music sweetly play,
That loyal Tories may . . . n't . . . forget
The . . . twen . . . ty . . . ninth . . ."

The song trailed off as well. Curled up on the chair, Mary was sound asleep. Their dance ground to a halt. In unison, they both shot her a glance, then their eyes met.

"I want ye, Clarice."

She looked down at her scuffed black slippers. No glass shoe, to be sure. "I was never meant to be a lady . . . indeed, I wouldn't even know how to behave."

With a finger under her chin, he brought her gaze back to his. "Exactly like ye do. You're the best woman I've ever met."

Her smile was quick but sad. "And you're the most charming man *I've* ever met."

"Nay, I'm serious." His eyes searched hers. "You've the kindest heart, the sweetest soul. I wouldn't want ye to behave any other way than ye already do. And no matter what ye say, we have quite a bit in common." Cameron's voice was suddenly lower, husky. "Most importantly, what we have in common is this . . ." And he pressed his mouth to hers. His hands went to the small of her back, pressing her body to his as well. And God help her, she went willingly. Eagerly. Her lips opened beneath his, aching for the sweep of his clever tongue.

When he finally pulled back, she was breathless. Light-headed.

Halfway in love.

"Now I'll hear no more talk of what we don't have in common," he told her. "What we do have in common is much more pleasant, dinna ye agree?"

She nodded, then shook her head. "But there are other things—"

"Aye?" His hands gripped her shoulders, and he kissed her again, short and bittersweet. "I will hear of them, then. We will speak of those things tomorrow."

"Tomorrow?"

"Today ye fed me, tomorrow I'll feed ye." Another kiss. Clearly he meant it to be short, but she kept her mouth fused to his when he would have pulled away, sinking into the caress. With a groan, he capitulated, and for a glorious space of time Clarice was positive there was nothing occupying his mind save for her. The power was heady. When she finally let him release her, she grinned, licking his taste on her lips.

His answering grin was a bit too cocky for her comfort. He dropped his hands from her shoulders and strode to reclaim his surcoat.

"Tomorrow," he repeated, shrugging into it. "A picnic. I will call for ye at noon. And Mary, of course. She may bring her friend Anne if it pleases her."

Her gaze shot to her daughter. Lud, she'd been wantonly kissing a man, and Mary right in the room. Sensible Clarice had lost her senses.

"Dinna worry," he said, reading her mind. "She saw naught." On his way to the door, he paused to draw her close and plant one more kiss that left her reeling. He was outside and down her garden path before she could catch her breath. A final sneeze drifted back to her.

Noon. Fourteen hours from now. Fourteen hours until she would have to tell him the one thing that would send him running from her as fast as his legs would carry him.

This had gone much too far already.

"There's a bonnie loch near Leslie." Seated on the blanket he'd brought—which he'd positioned as far from any flowers as possible—Cameron crossed his arms behind his head and leaned back against the trunk of a tree. "But not nearly as big as this one."

"Hmm . . ." Clarice smiled at the sight of Mary playing with her friend Anne by the lake's edge. "We are fortunate the marquess allows us to enjoy his park." Indeed, 'twas a sylvan scene, blue water lapping softly at green grassy shores. Friendly swans roamed the gently sloped grassy banks, begging crumbs from picnickers. The whole was surrounded by lovely shade trees.

Before they'd eaten, the girls had begged dancing lessons from Cameron. Right there in the open, he'd taught them all a branle, the courante, an almain, and the English pavane. "Lady Kendra's been busy," he'd told Clarice with a grin.

Now, licking the delicious stickiness of roast chicken from her fingers, she turned to the huge picnic basket that Cam had brought with him from the castle. "Lud, there is food left to satisfy the entire village."

He grinned. "I told Cook I needed to feed four ravenous folk."

"Are you telling me you didn't prepare all this yourself?" Sipping wine from a pewter goblet, she sent him a mock glare over the rim.

"Nay." Cameron crossed his long legs. "I suppose ye should know that I cannot cook. 'Tis why I require a wife." Though he'd said it in jest, he was pleased to see that she didn't flinch at his words. Mayhap she was getting used to the idea.

Tomorrow was the ball, and Sunday he'd be leaving for home.

The realization hit with a stab of desperation. He couldn't leave her here. Whatever bond he had felt upon meeting her, since then it had grown. He was more than certain of his feelings now.

He stood suddenly, reaching a hand to bring her up with him, to mold her body against his, to devour her sweet mouth, to convince her, once and for all, that she didn't want to live without him any more than he did without her.

Her goblet fell to the ground and rolled down the mild slope. With her palms flat on his chest, she pushed away. "I cannot do this." Her words came in a harsh whisper. "I'm feeling too close, and . . . you're leaving."

She shot a glance to where Mary played by the water, oblivious.

"Clarice." Fingers on her chin, he gently eased her gaze back to his. "Lord knows, I've tried to be patient, but I want ye. If ye didn't believe it before, mayhap ye will now. Ye have to now, or 'twill be too late." He stared into her eyes, the gray bright with a sheen of tears. "Do ye truly think it matters that you've years to your credit I haven't lived?"

"No," she whispered, for all the world looking defeated. " 'Tis—"

"Ye cannot believe ye dinna deserve a baronet. For God's sake, all that means is I own some land. And with it comes a title of sorts. But I'm not nobility, Clarice, and even if I were, I'd want ye still."

"I know."

Then why did she look like her heart would break? "Would ye be so unhappy then, to leave the place of your birth?"

"No." She shook her head vehemently. "That is not . . . no."

"Are ye afeared, then, to come away with me unmarried? Afeared for your soul? For though the kirk may say it wrong, the truth is I cannot wait three weeks for banns to be called. I must get home. And the thought of leaving ye here . . ."

"No . . . that is not the problem, either. I cannot marry you, Cameron. I cannot. 'Twould not be fair to you, can you not see that? I'm not young anymore, and—"

"I told ye, I care not about such things!"

"Let me finish—"

"A handfasting, then—"

"A what?" She blinked, clearly confused.

"A handfasting. At home, we dinna have too many clergymen, as ye do here. And so it is custom to join hands, and to pledge to each other to live as man and wife for a year and a day. At the end of that time, if no child is conceived, the couple can choose to part ways. When next a priest comes to visit, the marriage is confirmed in the eyes of the kirk. 'Tis simple, no?"

" 'Tis impossible," she whispered.

He didn't understand. "Why think ye so? 'Tis the perfect solution for such as we. A time-honored ceremony . . . tell me true, would ye feel unwed if it were not performed by a member of the clergy?"

She shook her head. "I was wed during the Commonwealth." Cameron knew that during Cromwell's rule, marriage was a civil matter only, not considered to be any business of God's. "And truly wed I was," she added, visibly shuddering. "It took no clergyman to bind me to Will."

Once again he wondered what this marriage of hers had been like. But this was not the time to probe.

"Then what is your objection, if I may ask? I ken ye like me—no, more than that. And I'll not hear otherwise."

"Whenever my husband . . ." Her voice dropped to a whisper, then faded away entirely.

"Aye?"

"I cannot be a true wife to any man," she blurted all of a sudden. "I was married fourteen years. Long years. Yet I never once enjoyed sharing a bed with my husband. He said I was . . . frigid." Her face turned red, but she held Cam's gaze. "I hate that word. But it fits. When it comes to intimacy, I feel . . . nothing. Nothing but pain and revulsion and fear."

Cameron drew a deep breath, let it out. "That was with him. Ye dinna feel revulsion and fear when I kiss ye," he pointed out carefully.

"That is different. I had never been kissed before—" His mouth gaped open, and she held up a hand. "Not really. Not what, with you, I've come to know as a kiss. 'Twas new to me, and yes, wonderful. But I know what the other is like. I know not how other women stand it. I know only that for me, it can never be something I more than tolerate. Barely."

He knew she was wrong. But he also knew that no words would convince her of that fact. " 'Tis sorry I am for ye, Clarice. That must have been hard on your marriage."

"It was. Will always said that a night in my bed was . . . akin to rape. And truth be told, what he did was not all that different from what that other man attempted this summer." A single tear overflowed and traced a path down her cheek. "Will never let me forget, for one minute, what a failure I am as a woman."

"Clarice . . ."

"That is why I was so thrilled to be given Mary." Her gaze strayed to where her daughter chased Anne along the shore, their giggles floating to them on the breeze. "To have a child, at last, and without having to remarry. I . . . I know not if I can go through that again."

A strangled sound escaped his throat, and she looked back to him, her features etched with both determination and pain. "You're young, Cameron Leslie. You have love in your heart, and land and a title to bequeath to children of your body. You shouldn't have to rape your wife in order to get them."

How many times had he pictured those bairns she spoke of running around his castle, growing, working with him side by side? He wanted her for their mother. "Would ye be willing to try, Clarice?"

She shrugged. "I tried a thousand times, with all my heart. I always hoped that if I tried, he wouldn't hit me." More tears ran down her cheeks, and he reached to brush them away, feeling a stab of hurt when she pulled back to avoid his hand. "It never worked, and . . . it never will. Other women speak of a mindless joy, a special bonding. I'll not deprive you of that, not even to secure my own happiness. I'm not that selfish. You deserve better."

He knew she was wrong—that she was warm, not cold, and that with patience, the right man could overcome the emotional scars of mistreatment. She was wrong.

But what if *he* were wrong, instead? What if she knew of what she spoke?

Could he live with that?

She knelt, reaching for the goblet that had rolled away, tossing everything back in the basket. "I want you to leave, Cameron."

"What?" Would she cut out his heart?

"I want you to leave." She stood and shoved the basket into his hands, then tossed the blanket over it. "Now. Just leave me alone, like you should have in the first place."

He stared at her for a long moment, until she turned her back.

"I love ye," he said. Her shoulders remained stiff, unyielding. The words vibrated across the chasm that stretched between them.

A chasm it seemed he couldn't leap. But he would find a way.

Chapter Seven

For the first time in close to a week, Clarice felt like she'd done a full day's work. She'd made some more strawberry tarts and delivered them to Gisela at the cookshop. Her fingers were stained red from picking berries for tomorrow's batch. She'd finished one crewelwork throw and started another, both of which would bring a tidy sum. The house was swept, the linens washed.

Her heart was empty.

She'd known all along that Cameron wouldn't choose to marry a cold woman. She'd been foolish to allow herself to get close. But though she had said from the start that she and Mary were better off on their own—and truly meant it as well—the thought of never seeing him again left her feeling like there was a gaping hole in her middle.

Yet surely she would get over that. 'Twas all for the better. She was terrified at what the marriage bed would bring, and having escaped that once, she'd be daft to go back. She might have lived a fairy tale for a week, but she wasn't meant to live in a castle forever.

She was setting supper on the table when the rattle of carriage wheels started parading down her street. One after the other, the local nobility were making their way to the castle for the marquess's wedding celebration ball.

Mary ran to fling open the door. "Look, Mama! Oh, look at the beautiful coaches! Look, that one has four white horses! And I can see inside. That lady's hair has jewels stuck in it!"

"How lovely," Clarice answered with as much enthusiasm as she could muster—which wasn't much. Of course she'd never expected to attend the ball—unlike her daughter, never even dreamed of such a thing—but that didn't mean she wanted to ogle the guests. She'd prefer to block the entire event from her mind. Just knowing Cameron was there, probably already dancing the new dances, made her heart ache anew.

"Eleven carriages so far, Mama."

"Is that so?" Clarice struggled to pull herself together. "How many if three more arrive?" she forced herself to ask, playing their old game. "How many then?"

Mary's golden head tilted, but she stayed facing away, her gaze glued to the proceedings outdoors. "Fourteen," she finally announced, pride lighting her small voice. "Fourteen, is that right? And here come three more now." She yawned, covering her mouth with one small hand; Clarice had kept her busy all the day long, running, fetching, and helping wherever a girl her size could help. Then suddenly she froze, and her voice sounded puzzled. "Here comes one from the other direction, Mama. Do you s'pose the party is full?"

"I think not."

"But 'tis stopping, Mama, and not turning around. The party must be too full."

Despite her melancholy, Clarice found herself laughing. "I imagine the ballroom is large enough to accommodate half the population of Sussex."

"Cainewood doesn't boast a proper ballroom," came a deep voice, "but they're using the Great Hall. And your mama's right—the chamber is unlikely to be strained to the bursting anytime soon."

"Cameron?" Clarice whispered.

"Good eve, princess." He swung Mary up into his arms and stepped inside, dressed in the blue velvet suit he had worn to the wedding. Lud, he was devastating. Wickedly confident, his grin lit up a place in Clarice's heart, but she steeled herself to caution.

"Good evening, Sir Cameron."

"Clarice." He nodded, a gallant incline of his head. "I hope ye remember the new dances."

"Wh-what?"

"The new dances. I'll be wanting to dance with ye at the ball."

"I'm not going to the ball!" Whatever could he be talking about?

"Oh, aye, ye are. And 'tis started already, so we'd best be on our way." Setting Mary on her feet, he brushed stray curls from her face. "You'll be needing a ribbon for your hair, princess, and ye must put on your best gown."

"Am I going to the ball, too?" Mary's eyes were round as two blue saucers.

"Not exactly. But ye can watch from the minstrel's gallery." The minstrel's gallery. The exact place Clarice had wished she could watch from a few days before. "And there will be one special ceremony I'm hoping you'll want to bear witness to."

"What about a bear?"

"Bear witness. You'll see. Then when ye get tired, ye may sleep in the nursery."

"With baby Jewel?"

"The very same. And her nurse to watch over ye both."

"You've planned everything," Clarice put in, finally finding her tongue. "But I'll thank you not to make promises to my daughter that you cannot keep. I cannot go to the ball. I am no lady, and I've nothing to wear."

"Did ye think I taught ye those dances just so that ye could do them with Mary?" The ostrich plume on Cameron's hat bobbed when he shook his well-groomed head. "I've a gown for ye in the carriage—just wait here while I fetch it."

"Wait here," Clarice scoffed, turning to ladle her soup. "As though I've anywhere to go. Certainly not to a ball at the castle."

But a moment later he was back, a brilliant yellow gown over one arm that reminded her of the buttercups alongside the River Caine. It had an underskirt of golden tissue, and a wide gold flounce all the way around the bottom.

"I had the seamstress add the flounce," Cameron explained, "since you're a wee bit taller than Kendra." An understatement if ever she'd heard one.

Her fingers itched to just touch the sumptuous fabric. "Ye expect me to . . . wear this?"

"Aye. I went to great trouble to have it readied when both Lady Cainewood and Lady Kendra were wanting their new gowns finished at the same time."

"But"—she drew a deep breath—"nothing has changed. Between us, or otherwise."

His eyes were as earnest as ever. "I didn't think that anything had changed. I want to take ye to the ball, Clarice." He held out a matching golden stomacher. "Hurry. 'Tis already started."

Mary snatched it from his hands and shoved it at her mother. "Yes, hurry, Mama. We must bank the fire, lest the soup burn. Will we eat supper at the ball?"

"Aye, delicacies like you've never seen. Your mama and I will bring ye a plate to the nursery."

Mary clapped her hands. "Hurry, Mama!" she repeated. She started working the laces on the front of her dress.

"I'll wait for ye in the carriage," Cameron said over his shoulder as he headed out the door. "Impatiently."

"I feel like I'm in a dream," Clarice said an hour later. "Dancing at a ball in the castle. Ever since the day I met you, I've felt like I'm in a dream. A fairy tale."

He twirled her into the next step. "The dream can last forever, Clarice, if only you'll say aye."

"Oh, Cameron . . ." Tonight, if she had any say in the matter, reality would not intrude. There would be time for sorrow and regret tomorrow. "If only things could be different. I cannot be a real wife to you—not the kind of wife you deserve—"

"What I deserve is for me to decide, for me to choose. And I choose ye. What ye speak of is only one small part of marriage. The other parts are much more important. I choose ye, Clarice. I choose ye and Mary."

She watched his gaze stray up to the minstrel's gallery, where her daughter's small face appeared between the slats. He let go of Clarice long enough to wave, then grinned when Mary waved back.

"Ye said ye were willing to try." They rose on their toes, then moved closer together. "But even without that, what ye have to offer is enough for me." And right there, in the Great Hall in front of all the glittering nobility, he stopped and leaned to give plain Clarice Bradford a kiss.

"Since you're the practical sort," he continued when he resumed the dance, "I'll give ye my practical arguments. I do not wish to marry for lust. That often fades, anyway, or so I've been told. I wish to marry for love, companionship, and the helpmate I ken ye will be." He drew a breath that she might have thought was shaky, if she didn't know him better. "But mostly because I cannot live without ye. Since the moment I laid eyes on ye, I kent ye were meant to be mine. Just like ye are, Clarice. I'll not be expecting ye to change."

"I wish I could believe you," she whispered.

"Why can ye not?" he demanded, displaying the quick temper she'd spotted briefly the day they went boating and again at the picnic. She had to remind herself she'd seen nothing in him to lead her to believe he might hurt her. "What cause have I given ye to doubt my word? Ever?"

"None," she said honestly. "But you walked away. When I told you I am . . . fr-frigid"— she stumbled over the word—"you walked away."

"Ye told me to walk away." The look that he gave her sparked her guilt. At the time, she'd been certain that permission to walk away was what he wanted. But now she wasn't so sure.

"Regardless," he said, " 'tis sorry I am that I did walk away." His hazel eyes looked so earnest, she couldn't doubt him. "I needed to think it through; I'll admit to that, Clarice. I did not ken my own feelings in that very moment. But now I know my heart. I've told ye the truth, and I've never lied to ye before, so I'll thank ye not to accuse me of it now." His hands squeezed hers.

"What ye have to offer is enough. I cannot live without ye, not happily at least."

All at once, rather than seeming too young, he seemed wise beyond his years. And Clarice felt young and untried, frightened of the future yet even more afraid to refuse her one chance at happiness.

"What say ye?" Cameron stopped, right there in the middle of the dance. "Will ye become my handfasted wife, Clarice Bradford? Tonight? For day after tomorrow I leave for my castle, and I'll be wanting to take ye with me. Ye and Mary."

"She'll think she's a princess."

"Nothing will make me happier than she be *my* princess. Except, of course, if you'll be my wife. Lady Leslie. It has a nice ring to it, does it not?" His smile made her heart turn over. "The glass shoe fits ye, Clarice. Ye deserve to wear it."

"The glass shoe would never fit." She glanced down at the hem of the gorgeous gown, thankful it was plenty long to hide her plain black slippers. He hadn't thought to bring her proper dress shoes, and for that he'd apologized profusely, although she suspected he'd wanted to but not been able to find any to fit her big feet. Not that she'd have chosen to wear formal shoes, anyway. She could barely perform the new dances in flat shoes, let alone heels.

"It fits," he insisted.

It sounded impossible, still. She would be living in a castle. Speechless, she glanced around Cainewood's Great Hall. From the polished plank floor, to the tapestries on the walls, to the intricate oak hammerbeam ceiling, the entire chamber spoke of a stately majesty she could never aspire to live up to.

"Leslie Castle is nothing like this," Cameron said, reading her mind as only he could. "Nothing. 'Tisn't ancient like this, but almost new—Caithren's father built it. It boasts naught but fifteen rooms, small rooms, none of them anything like the massive chambers here. 'Tis but a fortified house, really, built to look like a castle."

"Fifteen rooms," she murmured. "*Naught* but fifteen

rooms." Her lips curved up in a wry smile. "I've only ever lived in one."

"Dinna worry—I will hire someone to clean it for ye. You'll not be expected to break your back making our castle a home."

" 'Twas not what I was thinking." Good heavens, she would have a servant? Whoever would have thought it? But of course she would. She would be Lady Leslie.

"Will ye marry me, Clarice? Please. Tonight. Right now." He pulled a white ribbon from his surcoat pocket. "Mary is waiting for your answer."

"Mary?" She glanced up to the gallery, and her daughter waved again. "Mary knows you wish to do this tonight?"

"Well now, while we were waiting for ye in the carriage, she asked again about the bear. She was afraid it would be dangerous." He grinned, displaying the dimples that reminded her he was young. But wise, she reminded herself. So very wise. And entirely too charming. "So I explained to her about bearing witness, and what a very important job that would be. She assured me she is mature enough to handle it."

"Oh." She felt overwhelmed, pressured from all sides. And within herself. She'd been so sure she wanted to be free of men, just she and Mary making a life for themselves. But Cameron would leave on Sunday, and she knew if he left alone, he'd be taking her heart along with him.

She closed her eyes and drew a deep breath. "Yes," she whispered when she opened them. "I will be honored to become handfasted to you, Cameron Leslie. Tonight."

He let out a whoop that had heads turning as he pulled her from the Great Hall.

Laughing, she ran after him, and his cousin, Lady Cainewood, came running after them both.

"Cameron! What are ye up to?"

He stopped in the entry, a three-story stone chamber graced with impossibly tall columns and a majestic staircase. "Getting handfasted, cousin. Right now."

"Without asking me to attend? How dare ye?" His cousin's words sounded stern, but her hazel eyes, so like his, were dancing conspiratorially. "Where? I must fetch Jason."

"Not Lord Cainewood," Clarice begged under her breath. "I couldn't . . ."

"Ye alone, Cait." Cameron started up the steps. "Mary will be the second witness."

Without hesitation, Lady Cainewood followed. When they reached the top of the stairs, Mary came running down the corridor and threw herself into Cameron's arms. "Did she say yes?"

"Aye, princess, she did. Aren't we lucky?"

"Can I call you Papa?"

He froze in his tracks, clearly made breathless with surprise. "I would be honored," he told Mary gravely, his voice husky with emotion. And in that moment, Clarice knew for certain she had made the right choice, no matter how frightened she was of the marriage bed, and moving to Scotland, and becoming a lady. 'Twas the right choice for Mary, and she was more important than all the mental obstacles barring Clarice's way.

He led them all to a chamber and threw open the door. Clarice's breath caught in wonder.

The entire room seemed golden. A carved bedstead was gilded and hung with golden brocade. The rest of the furniture was upholstered and gilded to match. The largest mirror Clarice had ever seen hung over a marble-topped table. She glimpsed herself in it, looking flushed and awed and younger even than Cameron.

"The Gold Chamber," Lady Cainewood explained. "My husband told me 'tis saved for honored guests, and no guest here is more important than Cameron."

Cameron rolled his eyes. " 'Tis the truth I've felt rather ridiculous bumping about this enormous room by myself." He took Clarice's hand and pulled her inside. " 'Twill be much nicer in here tonight with ye by my side."

"Me? In here?" She couldn't imagine. She was afraid

to even stand on the patterned carpet that covered the floor. Her mind boggled at the luxury and expense.

"Did ye think I'd be spending our wedding night alone? Or in your little cottage? Not that it isn't nice," he hurried to add. "Ye keep it quite bonnie. But 'tis one room, ye see, and with Mary—"

"We all see," his cousin put in. "And ye are more than welcome to stay here, Mrs. Bradford, until the day ye leave for Leslie."

Clarice wasn't at all sure she was mentally prepared for a wedding night. "I wouldn't presume, Lady Caine-wood—"

"Ye must call me Caithren. Or Cait, if ye please. We're about to be cousins, after all."

Could it get any more unbelievable?

"Now," Cameron said, "take my hands, right to right, and left to left. In this way our arms make the symbol of infinity, signifying our commitment to be together. Forever."

It sounded too much, too soon. "I thought you said 'twas for a year and a day?"

"Normally, aye. But for us, forever."

When he looked at her like that, she was hard put to refuse him anything. She only hoped this strange cere-mony included a kiss at the end like the traditional one, because she was dying to feel his mouth on hers. No matter that her daughter and his cousin were watching.

He dropped one of her hands long enough to give the ribbon to Mary. "Can ye tie this around our four hands, princess?"

"I'll do it," Caithren volunteered.

"No, I can do it." Proudly Mary stepped up and took the white ribbon. "I learned how to tie last year, did I not, Mama?"

"You surely did, poppet."

Cam reclaimed Clarice's hand. "Then tie it well, prin-cess, for it symbolizes how tightly our family will be bound together. Ye, me, and your mama."

"Wait." Frowning, Mary chewed on a nail. "At Lady

Cainewood's wedding . . . well, should not Mama be holding flowers?"

"Nay!" Cam and Cait shouted together. Eyes wide, Mary jumped, and in spite of the serious occasion, Clarice found herself laughing.

What a marvelous new life she was going to have.

She sobered when Mary came closer, and if the bow was a bit crooked when she finished tying, it didn't matter. "Perfect," Cameron declared.

Then he dropped to one knee and captured Clarice's gaze with his.

"I present to ye, Clarice, my love and my pledge. May I never knowingly or willingly do anything to harm nor grieve ye in any fashion. Accept this pledge as a token of my trust. Like our hands are bound, may our love be as strong. That which is mine is yours, my heart and all my worldly belongings. Will ye share my life with me, Clarice?"

A hush settled over the room, and his hands squeezed hers.

"What am I supposed to say?" she whispered.

"Say aye, my love. Only aye."

She ventured a tremulous smile. "Aye, then. I will share your life. For a year and a day and forevermore."

He rose and leaned forward, his mouth meeting hers in a rush of heat, their bound hands crushed between their bodies. All too soon, he pulled away. "Now, Mary," he said huskily. "Cait? Will ye untie us, if ye please, and bind Mary's hands to ours as well?"

Tears flooded Clarice's eyes as his cousin did as he bid. Soon they were tied together, the three of them, and Cam dropped to one knee again.

"We are bound to ye, Mary, from this day forward, as your parents in our hearts and our souls. Ye have our love, and with it our promise never to harm or grieve ye willingly in any fashion. Like our hands are bound, let our love be as strong. Will ye share your life with us, and be known from this day forward as Mary Leslie, daughter of Cameron and Clarice?"

"What am *I* s'posed to say?" Mary whispered.

Beneath the ribbon bow, Clarice squeezed her daughter's hand. "Just say yes, sweet."

"Yes!" An exclamation of pure joy, the single word echoed in the ancient stone chamber.

And though Clarice had felt like Mary was hers from the day Lord Cainewood brought the girl to her doorstep, in that moment she felt closer to her daughter than she'd ever thought possible. Bound, as Cameron had said, heart and soul. She would never be able to thank him for this precious gift of belonging.

All at once, Caithren was untying the ribbon, and Cameron raised Mary into the air and gave her resounding kisses on both cheeks. Then he handed her to Clarice, wrapping his arms around them both as though he could protect them from the world.

She hoped he could. She was counting on it.

"Am I a princess now?" Mary asked when he finally released them.

"No, poppet," Clarice started.

"Aye," Cam interrupted before she could say another word. "You're *my* princess. And ye always will be, even after ye go off and get married."

"I'm never getting married," Mary declared. "I'm going to live with you forever."

Cameron ruffled her golden curls. "Well, now, 'tis the truth that nothing would make me happier. But we will have to wait and see what happens, will we not? Dinna forget that not last week your own mama was saying she'd never get married, either."

"I must get back to the ball." Caithren sighed, then brightened. "I cannot wait to tell everyone the news."

"Nay." Cameron put a hand on her arm. "This is your night. Yours and Jason's. If you've no objection, I've a mind to take my two women here downstairs for a dance or a dozen—"

"Me, too?" Mary squealed. "Is that why you taught us the dances?"

"Absolutely. We've much to celebrate, the three of us. But in secret, ye ken? No one else will know 'tis not only cousin Caithren's wedding we're celebrating, but our wedding-for-three as well. So lock your lips, aye?"

Mary clapped both hands over her mouth and nodded.

"Good." He took her by the hand and Clarice with his other. "Then let us celebrate."

Chapter Eight

Celebrate they did, dancing the new dances and supping on scrumptious delicacies until the wee hours when the ball finally wound down. The locals headed for home, and guests who'd traveled a distance were each shown to one of Cainewood Castle's hundred chambers. Mary fell asleep on the way up the stairs, and they took her to the nursery and tucked her into one of the small beds that flanked baby Jewel's cradle.

"She looks like a princess," Cameron whispered.

Clarice leaned up to kiss him on the cheek. "Thank you so much for including her in the handfasting. It meant so much to her." She hesitated a moment, still shy with this man—her new husband. "To both of us."

"To all three of us," he corrected her. He bent to kiss Mary's tiny forehead. "Now we've celebrated that, 'tis time for a more private celebration."

Though she told herself she was being ridiculous, Clarice trembled as they walked the short distance to the Gold Chamber. Once more she was awed by the gorgeous room, though Cam didn't give her much time to admire it. The door had barely shut behind them when he set down the candle he'd been carrying and dragged her up against him and into his arms.

His lips on hers were soft, caressing, almost sweet, but she sensed an urgency in him just before they went hot and fervent. He kissed her senseless, plundering her mouth until she was breathless and tingling all over.

"I will make ye forget them," he promised when he finally pulled away. "Your first husband and the other man who mistreated ye."

"I've forgotten them already," she whispered.

'Twas not yet true, he knew, but he would make it true. He lavished her face with little kisses, and her forehead and her neck and her ears. All the while he worked his arms out of his surcoat, and it dropped to the floor with a soft rustle.

Slowly he backed her up, until Clarice felt her legs against the bed. Someone had removed the costly brocade counterpane, and the quilts were folded back in a way that she imagined was supposed to be inviting, but only served to boost her anxiety.

When he eased her down to the sheets, her trembling increased. Best to get this over with. She squeezed her eyes shut tight and drew a deep, shuddering breath. "All right," she forced between gritted teeth. "You can do it now."

She waited a few heartbeats, and when he didn't touch her, she opened her eyes. Cameron stood by the bed, staring down at her, his face an inscrutable mask.

She swallowed hard and frowned at him. "Do you not want to do it?"

"Ye can bet I do." His long fingers worked at the knot in his cravat. "But not until you're ready."

She bit her lip. "I'm ready now. Just . . . just do it."

"Nay." He drew off the cravat and set it on the bedside table. "I'll ken when you're ready. Ye needn't announce it. Especially when 'tis not true."

"I'm ready," she insisted, wanting nothing more than to have this part out of the way. This part wasn't a fairy tale, and she wanted to get back to the fairy tale part of her exciting new life. Tomorrow she and Mary would pack up their things and say good-bye to Gisela and Anne and all their other friends and neighbors, then Sunday they'd be on their way to live in a castle . . .

"You're not ready," Cameron disagreed with staid calmness. His gaze was steady, his voice tender and huskily seductive. "When your breath comes heavy, when ye ache deep inside, when your body trembles with need, not fear . . . then you'll be ready. And I'll not be 'doing it' until I ken ye want it just as much as I do."

"Oh, Cam." Her heart ached at the thought of disappointing him, but she didn't think that was the ache deep inside he was talking about. "I thought I'd explained this to you—I thought you understood. I will never want it as much as you do. I will never want it at all."

"Then we won't do it," he said simply.

Her jaw went slack, and 'twas a moment before her tongue could form any words. "You—you cannot mean that," she finally stammered.

"I dinna lie, Clarice."

"But never . . . do you mean to say that if I don't want it, you will never do it at all?" 'Twas incomprehensible.

"Aye."

She struggled to her elbows to better see into his eyes. He truly looked sincere. And he'd never given her cause to distrust him. She felt a flood of relief, mixed with wonder and a rush of love. "Thank you," she whispered.

Facing away, he sat on the edge of the bed and pulled off one of his shoes. "I dinna think it will come down to never, though," he said conversationally. "I reckon that not too long from now you'll be dying to have me inside ye."

She blushed at the frank talk. "Maybe," she said doubtfully, not wanting to argue. "In a few years."

"I was thinking more like a few hours." His second shoe hit the floor, and he shifted on the bed to look at her. "Or minutes."

Her elbows slid out from under her, and she lay flat, staring up at him. His eyes darkened. Thinking of the way he talked—*when your breath comes heavy, when ye ache deep inside, when your body is trembling . . . you'll be dying to have me inside ye*—made the heat rush to her cheeks and her mouth go dry. She licked her lips. No man had ever talked to her like that. In fact, her first husband had never talked in bed at all—he'd either yelled or taken his pleasure as quickly as he could, in sullen silence.

When Cameron began to lower his mouth to meet hers, a little whimper rose from her throat. Whether from anticipation or fear, she wasn't quite sure.

"Hush," he soothed, and sat up. In a businesslike way,

he removed her shoes. Then his hands streaked under her skirts and plucked off her garters. More slowly, he rolled one and then the other stocking down and off, his fingers tracing delicate paths on her legs. He ran a fingertip along the bottom of one bare foot. It made her toes curl and her breath catch.

Supporting himself on his forearms, he moved over her with a gentle smile. "I promise ye I will not do anything ye dinna like."

He smelled divinely male, and he felt warm, and because she believed him, his weight on her was more comforting than frightening. "Anything?"

"Anything. For now, I will just kiss ye." He cradled her cheek with a hand and skimmed his thumb over her lips. "Ye like kissing, aye?"

"Aye," she breathed. "I mean, yes. Kiss me. Please."

His mouth claimed hers, and she let herself slide into the gentle caress. She trusted him, and he'd said he wouldn't do anything she didn't like.

She definitely liked his kisses.

She still wondered that a man's mouth could be so soft. And when it turned harder, more demanding, she liked that, too. He tasted spicy and sweet, like the wine that had flowed freely at the ball. He nibbled her lips, then traced them with his tongue before delving inside to make her mouth burn with fire. When at last he lifted his head, she found herself gasping for air.

Like he'd predicted, her breath was coming heavy.

His lips trailed down to press a soft kiss in the hollow of her neck. "D'ye like this, my love?"

"Oh, yes." 'Twas a wonder that a kiss, not even on the mouth, could feel so good. It made her all shivery. Her breathing wasn't becoming any calmer.

Between their bodies, his fingers moved to detach the golden stomacher. Beneath it her breasts were laced tightly into the gown's bodice, and he went to work on the bow at the top, then tugged at the laces, and all the while his mouth continued the sensual assault on her sensitive throat. At last he managed to pull the lacing free. He raised himself and spread the bodice wide, then traced a path with his lips to explore the mounds of her breasts through her flimsy chemise.

"So lovely," he murmured, and his words felt warm through the thin fabric. Clarice's heart skittered, then raced faster. She wondered if he could hear it over the ragged sound of her uncontrolled breathing. He hooked a finger in the chemise's lacy neckline and dragged the material down, fastening his mouth on one rosy peak.

Hot. It felt hot and wet and wickedly wonderful. "D'ye like this?" he whispered, his breath ruffling over her sensitized flesh.

In answer, she threaded her hands in his hair and pulled him even closer. Never had she dreamed her breasts would swell and crave a man's touch, a man's lips. Breasts were made to nourish babies, so she hadn't found any use for them. Until now. Swirling his tongue across her tingling skin, he made his way to her other nipple, suckling it until it puckered in response. It made her ache deep inside. Like he'd said it would.

When he drew off her gown, she liked it. When his fingers traced feathery paths all over her body, she liked that too. When he removed his own clothes, she was surprised to find she liked that very much. Her hands explored his heated skin, the unfamiliar contours of his muscles, the smooth planes of his back. She had never voluntarily touched a man before. Touching him gave rise to new feelings, until her body trembled, but not with fear. With need, then, as he'd said it would. She felt like she wanted, yes, needed more from him.

Lud, 'twas just like he'd said it would be.

"I'm ready," she whispered, then drew a sharp breath, shocked that the words had escaped her lips. Surely she couldn't have meant them, couldn't really want him inside her. She knew what that felt like—it hurt. 'Twould ruin all these new and wondrous sensations.

He stilled and rolled to her side. Lifting her hand from where it clenched his shoulder, he brushed his lips over the knuckles. Dark, unfathomable, magnetic, his gaze held hers. "Nay, you're not ready. But ye will be, love."

Relief and disappointment mingled, along with anticipation. Her eyes slid closed when he slipped a hand between her legs and urged them apart. His fingers danced on the delicate flesh of her inner thighs, tantalizing, teasing, and her skin tingled almost unbearably. "D'ye like this?" he asked, and she could only nod her response. "Only what ye like, Clarice. I promise."

When his hand brushed higher, she almost leapt off the bed.

"Hush," he murmured in a soothing tone, taking her mouth in a deep kiss. When she relaxed, he raised his head. "A test, love, to see if ye like it. Will ye trust me?"

She bit her lip and nodded. Slowly he cupped her with a hand. Drawing a deep breath, she nodded again. And his hand moved.

Lud, what sweet torture. Teasingly seductive, his fingers felt exquisite. "I like it," she whispered.

With an ease she never would have imagined, he slipped a finger inside, and a gasp escaped her lips. Half shock, half incredible pleasure. Will had never touched her with his hands, only his fists.

Aroused almost beyond bearing, Cam struggled to hold himself in check. Sweet Lord, she was tight. And frightened out of her wits, he was sure. Once more he was gripped with a fierce urge to murder her late husband. But she gave off other signals as well, signals that made his heart swell with hope and tenderness.

She felt like heaven in his embrace. Her body exuded a heady, musky scent of arousal that drove his own desire to a fever pitch. When he moved his hand, she responded with a blissful sigh that touched a tender place in his soul. Her hips began to shift, her sighs coming between broken breaths as he continued to caress her, driving them both to the brink.

"I'm ready," she breathed in a velvet-edged whisper.

"Aye, you're ready." He moved over her, settling himself into the cradle of her thighs. Poised to enter her, he gritted his teeth and paused. "Are ye sure, my love?"

Her answer was a simple "Yes," her voice laced in wonder. Her hands came around his back and hugged tight. And he slid home, finding sweet glory in the feel of her taking him into herself. He held there, savoring her heat, until, with a tiny whimper that set his heart to singing, she arched under him.

This, Clarice thought, was the real fairy tale come true. They moved together in perfect harmony, a slow, thrilling cadence that made passion radiate from deep within her. Making love. 'Twas the perfect—the only—way to describe it.

Then faster they moved, until she couldn't think at all. Until, in a brilliant burst of fiery sensation, she catapulted out of her old world and into a new one, a world brimming with love and shining promise.

Across the room, the candle sputtered and died. Pressed against him in the darkness, as close as two people could be, she could feel Cameron's heart beat in a rhythm to match her own. She reached for his face and took it between her hands. His cheeks were slightly rough under her fingers, just enough to remind her that, incredible though it seemed, she shared her bed with a living, breathing man.

And it was glorious.

"I love you," she whispered. "I love you for who you are, and who you've magically made me to be."

" 'Tisn't magic, my love. Or if it is," he mused, his words warm against her lips, making her ache anew for the touch of his mouth, " 'tis a magic we can only find together." Reading her mind, he fit his mouth to hers in a way that made the heat pool in her middle.

A long, melting time later, he lifted his head. "Together," he repeated.

"Together," she whispered back. Never had she imagined that word would apply to her and a man. But from this moment forward, it did.

For a year and a day and forevermore.

About the Author

Lauren Royal became interested in the Restoration period at the age of fourteen, when she snuck a valuable first-edition copy of *Forever Amber* out of her great-uncle's library. She lives in Southern California with her family and loves reading, rock music, and hockey (watching it, not playing it!).

Clarice and Mary were introduced in Lauren's first novel, *Amethyst,* the story of Colin Chase, the Earl of Greystone, and Amethyst Goldsmith, a talented jeweler whose father has betrothed her to their dull apprentice. Cameron first appeared in *Emerald,* the tale of his cousin Caithren's romance with Jason Chase, the Marquess of Cainewood. Lauren's next release will be Kendra Chase's story in *Amber,* due in the summer of 2001.

Visit Lauren's Web site at www.laurenroyal.com, where you can enter a contest to win jewelry, try some seventeenth century recipes, and find out how to get free autographed bookmarks. She loves reader mail and can be reached by E-mail at Lauren@laurenroyal.com or "real" mail at P.O. Box 52932, Irvine, CA 92619.

Written in the Stars

Jaclyn Reding

•

Chapter One

*It sometimes happens that a woman is handsomer
at twenty-nine than she was ten years before.*
—Persuasion, *Jane Austen*

Galloway, Scotland
1816

"It is time, dear. You must find yourself a husband."

Devorgilla Macquair Maxwell watched for her niece's
reaction from across the supper table. They were seated
in the oak-paneled dining room at Rascarrel House, a
pink sandstone manor that was not quite house, not
quite castle, but four hundred years of both, set high on
a clifftop above the Solway Firth on Scotland's south-
eastern shore. The brisk February wind whistled and
keened through the stark leafless oaks that lined the
front gravel drive. The air was tinged with the brisk
smell of the waning winter while inside, a fire burned
fitfully in the carved stone hearth, crackling and popping
in the twilight-shadowed room.

Harriet Macquair Drynan, only daughter of Sir Hugh
Drynan, Baron Rascarrel, couldn't help but be taken
aback by her aunt's startling pronouncement. At seven-
and-twenty, it wasn't as if she hadn't expected it. She
had always known the day would come when she would
have to marry, yes, but to hear it so suddenly, so defini-

tively, and over their blancmange pudding, was something of a shock.

"You are certain?" she asked as the footman, whom they called Duff, brought their after-supper tea.

"Aye, Harriet"—the older woman nodded—"I am quite certain for I saw it in a dream."

Devorgilla Macquair Maxwell was every bit as unique as a woman with a name like hers should be. She stood just under five feet in height, could predict the weather by the pattern of the clouds, and always wore black no matter the season. Her age was something of a family mystery, too. Though slightly younger than Harriet's mother, who would have been two-and-sixty that year, Devorgilla had a face unmarked by age, and her hair, the same dark red as Harriet's, a Macquair trademark, was without a single strand of gray. It was as if she knew the secret to some mysterious recipe for youth, thus the fact that she'd admitted seeing something in a dream came as no surprise. It was always something momentous when Auntie Gill had a dream. For as long as Harriet could remember, Auntie Gill had been seeing things others didn't.

Harriet shifted in her chair, pulling her tartan shawl more closely about her shoulders. She wondered why her aunt's words had given her a sudden chill. Her small terrier, a brindly ball of fur called Robbie, lifted his head from where he napped at her feet and blinked at her.

"What exactly did you see in this dream?" Harriet asked, offering the dog a scrap of oatcake beneath the table.

"It was nearly spring," Devorgilla began, "and you were standing in the forest in your mother's wedding gown, oddly, with a red petticoat underneath. Your hair was down and it looked so pretty, so red beneath a circlet of wildflowers. You make a stunning bride, dear."

Harriet nodded, more interested in the details of the dream than in what sort of bride she might make. "Is that all?"

"No, dear. You were surrounded by trees in the forest, rowan trees, twenty-seven of them to be precise."

"Twenty-seven?"

"Yes. They had grown up around you so thickly that there lay only one path out, one small break in the circle of them through which the smallest shaft of sunlight managed to shine. In the midst of that one small opening stood a sapling, its branches just beginning to sprout early leaves. If left to grow, the tree would shut out the light and prevent you from ever making your way through to the outside. And if that were allowed to happen, you would be forever locked in darkness and shadow."

Darkness and shadow . . . Her last words echoed heavily through Harriet's thoughts. "Indeed?"

"I believe the trees were meant to represent one year of your life thus far, with the twenty-eighth—the sapling—signifying your upcoming birthday. The meaning behind the red petticoat, I must admit, escapes me, but with your mother's wedding dress, there can be little doubt as to the dream's significance. This is a sign, just as you have always known it would one day happen. You must wed, Harriet, and you must do it by your twenty-eighth birthday."

In the very next moment, there came a sudden and formidable rumbling of thunder from right above the rooftop. The windows across the room rattled in their aging casements, the wind outside swirled and rushed, tossing sparks about in the hearth beside them.

"By my birthday?" Harriet was stunned. "That is but a fortnight hence! You are absolutely certain?"

"As certain as I can be." Devorgilla looked at her. "As you well know, the visions are never precise."

Harriet cast a wary glance out the window toward the fast-darkening sky. She reached unconsciously for the small golden locket that hung from a thin chain around her neck. Hidden inside was a likeness of her mother, Viola Macquair Maxwell Drynan, the only likeness that had survived of her. Brilliant fiery hair and dark green eyes, everyone who had ever seen it said it was the mirror image of her. And her daughter, it was often said, was the very mirror image of her mother.

Harriet had been scarcely ten when her mother had died, taken by a fever brought on by complications after the birth of her third, sadly stillborn, child. The local physician, Dr. Webster, had warned Viola not to attempt to carry another after the twins, Harriet and Geoffrey, had been born. Their birth had been too much of a trial for her, he'd said, yet Viola had put aside his warnings, following the advice of her heart instead. She'd looked so healthy, so alive, so happy during her pregnancy that everyone soon forgot the physician's dire warning.

Everyone except her sister, Devorgilla.

The dream had come to her too late to have done anything about it. Viola had already been in the latest stages of her pregnancy and Devorgilla had known upon waking that morning that her sister would not live to see the next. Such was the way of it with "the sight." While it may reveal events about to come, there was no earthly way of preventing its prophecy. It was a curse, sometimes, as much as it was a wonder.

From across the table Devorgilla watched Harriet closely, easily sensing her niece's unsettled thoughts. "Your mother loved you very much, Harriet."

Harriet nodded, still looking out the window as she battled against a sudden surge of emotion. She missed her mother more these days, it seemed, than ever. "I know she did, Aunt. It is the one thing about my life I have never questioned. I only wish—"

But whatever Harriet's wishes might be were lost, cut off by the sudden clamor of Robbie barking as he leapt to his feet beneath the table and scampered across the carpet to the far window. He jumped wildly at the low sill.

"Whatever is the matter with him?"

"I don't know," Harriet answered through the canine din. "I wonder—"

She stopped as if she'd heard something, which was impossible given the racket Robbie was making. Still she sensed something, something vague and distant, but slowly coming clear . . .

Harriet looked squarely at Devorgilla. "Geoffrey."

She quickly left her chair and crossed the room, looking out across the lawn at the single iron gate at the end of the back garden. Nearly shrouded in ivy, scarcely visible in the descending darkness, she and her father had closed the gate the day Geoffrey had gone off to war—they had vowed to keep it closed until his safe return.

Devorgilla came to join Harriet at the window. "What is it, dear?"

"Watch the gate, Auntie Gill."

As if in answer to her words, a vague silhouette began to appear through the swirling mist of dusk, a shadowed figure of a man emerging off the lone wooded path through a break in the thicket of the trees. The back of Harriet's neck prickled in anticipation. There could be no mistaking that familiar leisurely gait, that beloved tilt of his head. She reached for Devorgilla's hand.

"Oh, Auntie, he's home. Geoffrey's finally come home to us."

Harriet flung open the window casements, heedless of the gust of chill air that confronted her from outside, and shouted to the dusk wind.

"Geoffrey! Oh, Geoffrey! You're back!"

Chaos instantly erupted where silence and calm had reigned moments before. Everyone within the house rushed for the nearest stairwell and door to assemble en masse to meet the returning young master. Harriet and Devorgilla swept from the dining room with Robbie yapping at their heels, and scampered down the narrow turning stair that led to the back hall where already the Rascarrel butler, Rupert, was waiting at the door.

"Miss Harriet, your coat!"

But Harriet rushed through without a moment's pause, her eyes fixed on that single gate at the end of what suddenly seemed an endlessly long walkway. Tears swelled against her eyes, blurring her vision as the cold evening air stung her nose and cheeks. Still she ran for the gate, gravel crunching under her slippered feet, her hair tumbling from the confines of its neat chignon to fly about her face in reckless ribbons of red.

"Geoffrey!" She launched into his arms the moment

he lifted the latch and stepped through the gate to meet her. "Oh, Geoffrey, is it you? Is it truly you?"

The Honorable Geoffrey Drynan, Master of Rascarrel, the eldest of Baron Rascarrel's two children by a mere matter of moments, was thin and reedy and nearly six inches taller than his twin sister. His hair was not the brilliant red of Harriet's, but more a ruddy brown that tended to fall over his forehead when it grew too long. Blue-green eyes, like the summer waters in Rascarrel Bay, winked above a mouth that was rarely without a grin.

"Hattie Brattie!"

Geoffrey took his sister into his arms and twirled her around, splashing in his tall boots through a stretch of murky puddle and laughing as she squealed like the same wee lass who used to toss snowballs at him from behind the cover of the great garden oak.

"Put me down, you brute," she said, giggling, "and let me look at you."

Harriet skimmed her gaze over her brother from head to toe, over a dark wool coat of indiscriminate color over breeches that were travel-worn and spattered with mud. His face was gaunt and darkened by a rough beard, something she'd never seen on him before. Her father would say his hair was too long, but Harriet didn't care. She was just so happy to see him.

"Oh, Geoffrey." Her breath fogged from the cold, her eyes alight with an excitement that had been too long absent from them. "Why did you not write to tell us you were coming? We could have greeted you properly. We would have had everything ready for you."

"And spoil the warmth of that welcome home, lass? I wouldn't have missed the sight of your bonny face calling out to me from that window for anything."

Harriet beamed. "But Father's just gone yesterday for Edinburgh. He'll not be back for a week, maybe more."

"Well, then, that'll just give us more time to spend catching up for the years we've been away."

"*We . . . ?*"

Only then did Harriet realize there stood someone

else behind her brother, someone poised just outside the open gate. She turned then to look, and when she saw who it was, she nearly lost her breath.

In that first moment, she almost didn't recognize him. The nearly fifteen years that he'd been away had brought a facet of maturity to the eyes that had once boyishly mocked her. But there was nothing at all boyish about him now. Tristan Carmichael, Viscount Ravenshall, stood apart from the others, as if reluctant to intrude upon the tender family reunion. He looked taller somehow, bigger, stronger than she could ever remember him before, his ash-brown hair damp from the misty air and curling slightly at his temple above piercing blue eyes.

For the first few moments, Harriet simply stared, struck dumb by the unexpected sight of him, until Tristan flashed his familiar grin, erasing the years as if they'd never been apart, and banishing any hint of winter's chill. Harriet was horrified to feel herself blushing in response, and quickly lowered her eyes.

When she managed to find her voice again, she smiled softly, and stepped forward to greet him. "Tristan, how wonderful to see you. I'd never expected you'd be back in Galloway again."

"I never expected I'd be back either." He took Harriet's hand and bowed over it gallantly. "It is a pleasure to see you again, Miss Drynan."

"Miss Drynan?" she echoed on a curious smile. "We've known each other too long, Tristan Carmichael, to stand on such ceremony. Harriet—and something more than a formal handshake—will do much better."

"Harriet it is."

Tristan dropped his satchel and took her in a friendly embrace, a thing he had done countless times during their childhood, but that somehow, now, left Harriet keenly aware of the closeness of his arms around her.

He stood so near to her that their breaths mingled on the evening mist between them. She had to lift her chin to look at him. The wooded countryside scent that clung to his wool surcoat brought gooseflesh to her arms that had nothing to do with the cold evening air. Harriet stepped away, absently rubbing her tingling skin. But standing in the midst of that icy darkening dusk, Harriet felt none of the chill, none of the damp of the threatening rain. A thrilling warmth had crept straight through to the deepest part of her the moment her hand had touched his. Fifteen years had done nothing to banish her feelings for him and she found herself staring at him just as she had when she'd been a girl of thirteen.

"Come on, you two," Geoffrey said, interrupting the sudden stretch of time that bound them. "Let us get you inside, Hattie, before you catch a cold that will leave your nose as red as your hair."

Harriet noticed then that Geoffrey was staring at her as she, in turn, was starting at Tristan. She turned quickly for the house. "Yes, Geoffrey, you are right. You both must be half-starved. Auntie Gill and I were just finishing our supper. Come, I'll have the cook fix something to warm you while you both clean up."

If Harriet thought herself startled by the sight of Tristan after all the years apart, he, in turn, was utterly overwhelmed by her. Even now, he found it difficult to tear his eyes away from her, all fiery hair and breathless beauty as she turned and took her brother's hand, leading them down the walkway toward the house where the servants had gathered at the door.

While she laughed and chatted with the others, he took in every movement of her, the gentle sway of her dark green skirts, the pert bounce of the springy riot of rich auburn-red curls that fell down her back to her waist. Her eyes, the color of the stormy Rhinns of Kells, shone gray-green beneath the arched brow that hinted at her keen intellect. Her mouth was sensuous, the bottom lip fuller than the top, and her nose was straight, strong, and nothing at all resembling "pert." That she hadn't long ago become someone's wife could only be called astounding. Tristan watched her and found himself imagining that hair spread upon a downy pillow, twisting about pale shoulders and lush rose-tipped breasts . . .

He'd been away fourteen years, fourteen years in which Harriet had blossomed into a woman of incredible, almost otherworldly beauty. What the devil had happened to the endearing brat sister of his closest childhood friend, the one who had stuck out her tongue and thrown mud cakes at him from the stable loft? Had her hair always been so radiantly red? Her eyes so unfathomably green? Or was it simply that he had been away at war—and away from a woman—for too long?

Later, in the dining room, Geoffrey and Tristan regaled Harriet and Devorgilla with the more fascinating details of their Peninsular campaign over a hastily prepared feast of mutton, ham, assorted cheeses, oatcakes, and hothouse fruits. Time passed quickly, the skies outside grew darker, and the candles guttered lower and lower in their holders, casting a golden glow about the night-shadowed room. Sometime later the rain that had threatened all day had finally come, as if it had simply been awaiting their return, falling softly against the windows across the room as the four chatted away the hours pleasantly together.

Time and again Harriet found her attention straying to where Tristan sat across the table from her. Silently, she studied his face in the candlelight, the clean line of his freshly-shaven jaw, the quiet strength that lay behind his eyes. Had he always been that handsome? What had he been doing all these years past? Had he ever, just once, thought of her . . . ?

"So, sweet Hattie," Geoffrey said, grinning in a way that made her wonder that he could read her very thoughts, "what has my baby sister been up to while big brother was away?"

Having been born but moments before her, Geoffrey had always referred to himself as her "big brother." As a child, Harriet had disliked hearing it, thinking it wholly unfair that he should have been pulled from their mother's womb first before her. Not until that moment did she realize just how much she had missed hearing it while he'd been away.

"Things here have been," she said on a weary sigh,

"much the same as they always have." She struggled for something to tell him. "Old Angus's granddaughter had triplets last fall and Father has bought another painting. Oh, and Uncle Neil and Aunt Phyllis went on holiday to Bristol."

"And what of you, Hattie? What have you been up to all this time I've been away?"

Harriet glanced at her brother and gave a shrug. "I ride. I walk about the firth when I can. But with the weather so poor, I've not had much else to do but read and watch the winter pass through the windows."

Lackluster response! Oh, how she wished she had something more to say, some tale of adventure to share with him as he always had her, some new and exciting *thing* to tell him just this once . . .

"Actually, Geoffrey," Devorgilla piped in from the far end of the table, "Harriet does have some news of her own."

"She has?"

Everyone, including Harriet, turned to look at her.

"I have?"

"Yes, dear." Devorgilla looked at Geoffrey. "Your sister has decided to marry."

"What?" Geoffrey nearly erupted. "Why wasn't I told of this? What the devil do you mean you are getting married? To whom?"

Harriet lifted her chin, more than just a little pleased that for once, she had been able to astonish him. "Well, that particular detail has yet to be determined."

"I was thinking perhaps one of our local lads might do," Devorgilla suggested. She glanced at Tristan across the table. "Surely one of them would do well enough for a husband."

"Such as who?" Geoffrey spouted. "Wills Littlebrown?"

"Good heavens, no!" Harriet exclaimed.

Devorgilla nodded. "Yes, he does have a bit of a bucolic quality about him, doesn't he? I should hate to think of what your children would smell like." She thought. "It is unfortunate that so many of our young men were lost to the wars or have yet to return from the Continent. Still, is there no one else?"

Harriet shrugged.

"Angus Blackburn?"

Harriet scowled. "Too hairy."

Devorgilla thought again. "Seamus Armstrong?"

"The man's teeth are rotting from his mouth!"

"Well, I'm afraid the only others I can come up with are either already married, yet in the schoolroom, or well past the prime of their lives." Devorgilla looked at Harriet. "You can think of no one else?"

Harriet gave it a moment of serious thought then finally shook her head. "I shall have to go to Edinburgh."

Where in heaven had that idea come from? Harriet had never even considered leaving Galloway. But now that she'd said it, she found she liked the idea. Immensely.

Geoffrey, however, did not agree. "Harriet, you cannot simply *go* to Edinburgh for a husband. You've never been any farther from home than the summer fair at Dumfries."

"Precisely my point. In the city, I will be better able to weigh my options."

"Your options? Just what do you think to do? Purchase yourself some poor fool halfling at the nearest corner market?"

Harriet frowned at her brother. "It is done in London all the time, Geoffrey. They call it 'The Season.' Need I remind you that our own mother did that very thing when she met and married out father?"

"It's true, Geoffrey," Devorgilla interjected. "Your mother met your father one afternoon at a bookshop in Edinburgh. Within a fortnight, they were wed."

"But that was different," Geoffrey sputtered. "Mother knew what she was doing!"

Harriet gasped. "I beg your pardon? I am nearly the same age as Mother when she wed."

"Actually," Tristan finally broke in, silencing them both, "there is someone Harriet could marry from right here in Galloway."

Everyone silenced. They all turned at once to look at Tristan.

He'd been so quiet, and Harriet had been so distracted by Geoffrey's bluster, she'd nearly forgotten he was there.

"There is?"

Geoffrey added, "Who?"

Tristan answered, "Me."

Chapter Two

"There are secrets in all families, you know . . ."
—Emma, *Jane Austen*

Tristan's godfather had once told him that when a man proposed marriage to a woman, it was like standing before the world utterly naked. Not until that moment could Tristan truly appreciate the wisdom of that man's words.

The room had fallen ominously silent. No one moved, not so much as to take a sip of tea. Even the rain outside seemed to have stilled as if awaiting Harriet's response. Tristan stared at her, searching her face in the glow of the candlelight for some clue, some indication of her reaction. But instead of the joy and excitement that every man hoped to see on the face of the woman he asks to wed, on Harriet Tristan saw only dismay.

"Me? Marry you?" she finally said, already shaking her head. "But you said you never planned to marry, Tristan. You were going to live the life of the blithe wayfarer, remember? Traveling the world for the rest of your days?"

They were words he'd spoken after the deaths of his parents fifteen years before, casualties of a slick road, a high cliff, and a stormy night. He had been grief-stricken, insensible. He'd been young. He could never have known then how they would come back to haunt him.

"Harriet, when I spoke those words, I thought to leave Galloway forever, yes. But much has happened since I had to go to live in Edinburgh with my godfather. I've been to university, I've traveled the world, and for nearly a decade now I have been a soldier at war, surrounded by nothing but war's destruction. It is enough to change any man. I long now for a quiet life. A stable life. It isn't by mere coincidence I returned with Geoffrey. I have roots here in Galloway, a family home not a mile away, responsibilities to the viscountcy that have too long been neglected."

As he sat there watching a range of emotions play across Harriet's face, none of them favorable, Tristan tried to figure out how he could have been so mistaken. Was it possible that what had happened, that *thing* he had felt the moment his eyes had met hers, that incredible awareness, had only affected him? Had she not felt it, too?

He'd felt certain she had. Her face, her voice, her eyes, everything had told him Harriet had been just as overwhelmed at seeing him as he had her. He hadn't planned for it to happen that way. On the journey home, the idea of marriage had been a vague, in-the-future prospect, something he would get to *someday*—until the moment he and Geoffrey had arrived at Rascarrel House, and he saw Harriet racing down that walkway toward them with her skirts and radiant hair flying out behind her. All at once, like the melting off of the moor mist with the morning sun, Tristan had seen her—and he'd known.

After too many years of foreign lands and foreign faces, Harriet was familiar, stirring his blood just as unexpectedly as the first glimpse of his Scottish homeland from the ship that had carried him and Geoffrey back from war. He had known her more than half his life, knew the sharpness of her mind, the fire of her wit, the infectious ring of her laughter. Harriet was life. Harriet was home. Harriet could be *his* home, if only she would say yes. Which she wasn't doing.

But she also wasn't saying no.

"Of course you'll need time to consider . . ."

And then she said it.

"No." Harriet looked at him, her expression filled with gloom. "Time will not change anything. I already know my answer. It is impossible, Tristan. I can never marry you."

Tristan felt as if he'd been punched in the gut. Hard. He blinked. "But did you not just say you needed to marry?"

"Yes. I do need to marry, and as quickly as possible."

"So it is just me you don't wish to marry."

Harriet looked at him, her eyes dark with torment. "I never said I *didn't want* to marry you, Tristan. I said I *can't* marry you. They are two very different things."

Tristan was falling fast into confusion. "You are saying you would like to marry me, but for some incomprehensible reason you cannot? That you'd rather wed a complete stranger than wed me? What sort of reason could be so compelling as to keep you from wedding the man you want?"

"It"—Harriet stammered, glancing from Geoffrey to Devorgilla—"it is your age."

His age?

Tristan stared at her, stunned. Of all the things she could have said, all the reasons she could have given, it was the very last thing he would have expected to hear. "What the hell does my age have to do with anything? I'm the same age as you."

"Yes, I know that. To the day. Nearly to the hour actually, except that you, like Geoffrey, were born before me. I remember you used to tease me about it when we were children. Which is precisely the problem."

"That I teased you? Oh, good God, we were children, Harriet—"

"No, the problem isn't that you teased me, Tristan. The problem is that you are older than me and nothing in the world can change that."

Tristan shook his head, gone beyond confusion now to absolute befuddlement. "I don't understand. Is there some law that prevents a woman from marrying a man who was born the same day as she?"

She shook her head. "Oh, Tristan, can't you see? It is all because of this accursed red hair!"

Tristan could only stare. "What in bloody hell does your hair have to do with this?"

Devorgilla broke in, a calming presence amidst the simmering storm of bedlam. "It is a long story, Tristan."

"A very long story," Geoffrey added.

Looking around at the faces of the others, Tristan saw one thing clearly. Something was going on to which everyone else in the room was privy but him. "And I have all night to hear it."

Devorgilla looked at both Harriet and Geoffrey, then nodded solemnly. She took a sip of tea, then quietly started to speak.

"It began more than four hundred years ago, on a small island off the western coast where my ancestors once ruled. The chieftain of the clan, Alain of Macquair, had a beautiful daughter, his only child and heir, known across the land as *Maighdean nan MacGuadhre*—the Maid of Macquair. She had hair the color of flame, eyes the deepest green of the Hebridean sea. When it came time for her to wed, Alain pronounced that only the best of warriors would do, for through her the clan of Macquair would continue—"

Geoffrey broke in then. "Tradition claims the Macquairs were descendants of the great MacAlpin, the oldest and most purely Celtic of the Highland clans, of royal descent from the dynasty of Kenneth MacAlpin who united the Picts and Scots into one kingdom. Such a lofty lineage made the choice of husband for this heiress a most vital decision. Thus the chieftain, Alain, contrived a series of contests whereby only the most worthy of men would succeed to win his daughter's hand."

Devorgilla nodded. "Now, as you might guess, warriors from clans far and wide came to compete for this exalted prize, for besides her beauty, the heiress also brought a vast dowry. With each contest, mighty warriors fell, until there were but two remaining. One was another great chieftain like Alain, older, experienced, who had seen many battles and whose strength and bravery were renowned across the land. The other was a young lad, barely twenty, younger even than the lovely maiden but madly in love with her and willing to fight to the death to win her hand.

"Alain, of course, thought the warrior the more fitting husband for his only daughter and so concocted a final contest that would best be won by strength, thereby giving his choice the upper hand. But the young lad had something the warrior did not. He had great cunning, and through this cunning, he bested the warrior against the odds. Everyone was stunned, but when he came forward to claim his prize, Alain refused the lad, sending him off and vowing to wed his daughter to the warrior instead. This angered the lad's mother, a sorceress, who set upon the Macquair with the *Droch Shùil*." At Tristan's questioning glance, she added, "The Evil Eye."

Harriet suddenly spoke, repeating the sorceress's prophecy. *Yon Maid of Macquair, and any after, with fiery hair and eyes as green as ice, shall watch her chosen husband perish, and any man after him, unless she should take to husband a man of honor, a man of cunning, and of an age that is younger than she . . . else the ancient clan of Macquair shall vanish forever."*

A flash of lightning suddenly rent the night sky outside the dining room window. Thunder rumbled. Robbie whimpered under the table as Devorgilla went on with the tale.

"This was the mother's way of teaching Alain of Macquair that age and experience do not necessarily the best man make. Her son truly loved the maid, and she him, and true love must never be denied. Still, Alain scoffed at the ominous curse and arranged for the wedding of his daughter to the warrior regardless. But, on the day of their wedding, as the warrior groom came to meet his bride at the altar, he was seized by a sudden tremor, and fell dead at her feet. Thrice more this came to pass, until no one would court the Macquair maiden for fear of losing their lives. No one, but the valiant young lad who had rightfully won her hand."

"So the chief saw the error of his ways and let the lovers wed?" Tristan finished, guessing the end of the story.

Devorgilla nodded. "Fearful of becoming the *last* Macquair chieftain, and the one responsible for this noble line's downfall, Alain did finally consent to the marriage of his daughter to the younger man. Upon their marriage, he even named the lad the next Macquair chieftain to assuage the sorceress's anger at the wrong he had done. Thereafter, the lovers lived a long and happy life together. But the curse which had been cast lived on, and for the generations afterward, the prophecy has held true. Those red-headed Macquair maidens who married younger husbands lived long and happy lives blessed by healthy children. Those who did not suffered heartache and tragedy because of it."

Tristan had begun to wonder if he'd somehow traveled back in time several centuries, back to the days of witches and wizards and dark magic spells. "This all makes for an interesting story, and it is easy to see how it has come down through the years, but this is the nineteenth century, not the ninth. These sorts of things just don't happen any longer."

"Aye, they do, Tristan Carmichael." Devorgilla's expression darkened dolefully in the muted light. "For I was one such unfortunate Macquair maid."

"Auntie Gill!" Harriet exclaimed. "In all these years, all the times we've talked of the legend, you've never said anything to me about this."

"I had no need, child. There is no point in dwelling on tragedy." She turned back to Tristan. "When I was sixteen, I believed myself in love with a neighboring landowner, a man much older than my tender years. I had believed that since Harriet's mother, my sister, Viola had already wed, I was free to wed the man of my heart. My mother warned me against it, but I refused to listen and betrothed myself to my suitor. All was well until, on the eve of our wedding, my love took a sudden tumble down a narrow flight of stairs, breaking his neck in the fall. I have never forgiven myself for being so foolish."

"This is why you never wed?" Harriet asked. "Why you wear mourning to this day?"

Devorgilla simply nodded.

The room fell silent for several moments as each of them reflected on the tale. The fire burned sluggishly, casting shadows on the wall while outside, the rain began to fall anew.

Suddenly Harriet spoke out, "Oh, would that I had been born bald instead of marked by this red hair!"

Devorgilla smiled. "I remember your mother Viola once saying something very similar to our mother when we were young girls. I will tell you now what she said to us then. 'Tisn't a blemish, dearest Harriet. Your hair is a blessing, for it is you who has been given the honor of preserving the Macquair heritage for another generation."

"Perhaps I should just not wed at all, like you."

"You cannot do that, Harriet. Once your mother had you, it became clear who the next Macquair maiden would be. I am too old now to bear any children. The Macquairs are one of the last great ancient Scottish clans. So many like the MacAlpin have been adopted into other clans, their own history lost to the shadows of time. If you were to disregard the prophecy and your special place in it, history hundreds of years in the making would come to naught."

But Tristan remained skeptical. "Truly though, just how much could Harriet possibly be risking by choosing a man her same age?"

"It doesn't matter," Harriet answered him. "It isn't a risk I am willing to take." She stared at him, and her eyes grew misty. When next she spoke, her voice trembled. "Because I love you, Tristan. I think I have all my life, at least since the day you rescued me from that tall tree I had climbed."

A single tear escaped to trail softly down her cheek.

The torment she felt was reflected on her face in the candlelight.

"You saved my life that day, Tristan Carmichael, and it is for that reason I will not be your wife—because doing so could very likely take your life away."

Chapter Three

I like this man;
pray heaven no harm come of it!
—Lady Susan, *Jane Austen*

Tristan awoke before dawn the following morning after a restless night spent more awake than asleep, his twilight hours plagued by images of flame-haired Macquair maidens and a witch's evil eye.

He was downstairs before most of the house had yet begun to stir. Rather than trouble one of the maids with an early breakfast, he quickly saddled one of the horses in the Rascarrel stables and headed off through the morning mist for the forest shadows to the west.

Just a mile. It was all the distance that separated him from the place he'd been born, where he'd been raised, and then ultimately inherited. In the years Tristan had been gone from Ravenshall, its upkeep had been seen to by a steward he'd never met named Whitmore who sent monthly reports to him by way of his godfather in Edinburgh. He scarcely knew if the place had prospered, or fallen to neglect in his absence. But as he came through the trees and caught a glimpse of it—his first glimpse in nearly fifteen years—his breath left his body in a rush, fogging to the cold of the morning.

After all this time, it still hadn't failed to stir him.

Surrounded on all sides by dense pine forest and rugged woodland landscape, Ravenshall Tower lay hidden from view of the main coaching road like a slumbering pastoral giant, unseen, but not forgotten. Never forgotten. It was a place that had been a part of the Galloway landscape longer than most of the ancient gnarled trees that grew around it. Dutch gin, French brandy, and Brus-

sels lace were known to be smuggled from the beaches
and into the caves that ran beneath the tower even to
the present day.

Tristan stood for some time, watching the single
square tower keep reflected in the morning light on the
waters of the quiet burn that stretched behind it. He
loved that the very walls still came alive as they had
when he'd been a lad, the native pink Galloway sandstone that formed it winking and shimmering as if made
of diamond dust in the mellow sunlight.

The foundations for the ancient tower had been laid
at almost the same time Edward I had been snatching
the Stone of Destiny from Scone Abbey in the late thir-
teenth century. It had been at various times wrecked
and rebuilt, added to and passed through several notable
families, until it had come to the Carmichaels early in
the previous century after the Jacobite uprising of 1715.
Childhood had been happy there, days spent with Geoffrey poking about the same dense woods and hidden
caves the smugglers used by night. They had explored
every tree, every bit of shoreline, vowing never to
leave—until the day the coach carrying Tristan's mother
and father had plunged off a cliffside, forever changing
his life.

At the age of thirteen, Tristan had inherited the viscountcy and had become the sole heir to all that Ravenshall encompassed. And with that, he'd had to leave
his home, Geoffrey—the friend he held closer than a
brother—and everything he loved, to attend university
nearer the home of his godfather and guardian. Afterward, he'd traveled. Then the war had come. Somehow,
fourteen years had passed, bringing Tristan to stand
again before the home he'd been taken from all those
years ago, the home he'd thought never to see again.

The home he had hoped to make again—with Harriet.

Tristan spent the next hours meeting with Whitmore
and getting acquainted with the overall workings of the
estate, which proved to have grown profitable in the
years of his absence. As he walked through the quiet

hallways and chambers shrouded by dust cloths, the house felt emptier than he could have ever imagined it.

"Shall I have the maid air out a bedchamber for you tonight, my lord?" the steward asked as they toured what had been his mother's rose garden on the sunny side of the tower. He could almost still picture her standing amid the vibrant blooms.

"That won't be necessary, Whitmore," Tristan replied. "I'm for Edinburgh this afternoon to see my godfather. I will write to let you know when I intend to return and permanently settle in."

Truth be told, Tristan no longer knew when that might be.

Thanking the man for his fine work, Tristan hoisted himself into the saddle to return to Rascarrel for his belongings and to bid his friend good-bye. He had just come into a clearing at the edge of the wood when he suddenly caught sight of Harriet riding in the distance ahead.

Her red hair was tucked up beneath a tall derby hat, the dark skirts of her riding habit draped over her horse's flank as she cantered off across the dew-kissed field toward the firth's northern shore. Morning mist swirled about her, making it look almost as if she were floating on a cloud. Maybe, he thought, maybe if he tried once more to talk to her, this time alone, he could convince her to change her mind and become his wife.

By the time he caught up with her, Harriet was nowhere to be seen, just the mare she'd ridden standing alone and riderless on a remote height overlooking the firth. Tristan left his own mount to graze upon a tuft of grassland, and took the narrow pathway of natural stone steps leading down toward the rocky stretch of shoreline below.

The Solway Firth was the border Mother Nature had created between England and Scotland, and from where he stood, on a clear day, Tristan could see all the way across to Cumbria. Many a sailing vessel had come to grief on her shifting sands and unpredictable surging tides. At this particular point on the bay, vast crags spilled out into the water, winds collided and surged, making it far too treacherous a landing point for even the smallest vessel—thereby leaving it the most secluded spot in all of Galloway.

Tristan followed the path of Harriet's bootprints to a small opening no higher than three, maybe four feet nearly hidden beneath an overgrowth of gorse. He carefully pushed aside the thorny brush, ducking his head to enter, and arrived at a natural cave no doubt carved out of the tumbledown wall of rock thousands of years before.

Only the smallest finger of sunlight shone inside, enough for Tristan to make his way back into the darkness. He stopped when he reached a rock wall and could go no farther. But Harriet wasn't there. He was about to call out to her when he heard a sound, a splash that seemed somehow to come from behind the cave wall.

Tristan felt around in the darkness until he found a small opening in the rock wall that led to a second chamber. It was high enough for him to stand and lit by two small openings in the rock overhead, allowing the morning sunlight to pour inside. At the foot of the chamber, carved out of the granite by nature's hand, was a small crystal spring fed by fresh waters from some underground source. Over the centuries, it had formed a pool that twisted and turned, weaving its way for some distance inward along the cave floor. Even now, in the waning of winter, the air inside the cavern was comfortable, not cold. The waters of the pool would be warm as well, he suspected, softened by the natural minerals of the earth like a Roman bath.

Tristan watched in silence as Harriet threaded her way easily across the surface of the water, her arms cutting in gentle strokes, her hair, the darkest red, floating softly behind her. She moved with the grace and ease of a swan, beautifully poetic, and he was utterly mesmerized by her. When she turned suddenly and began floating on her back, Tristan found himself holding his breath as the peaks of her breasts rose just above the surface. In the light beaming down, they were palest white, tipped in rose beneath the sheer wet fabric of the shift she wore.

Tristan was taken by an image then, an image of himself standing naked with Harriet in that glistening underground pool, water dripping off of them both as they wound arms and legs together. He would make love to her here hidden away from the rest of the world outside. Together, they would forget that anything else existed but them.

He watched as Harriet kicked her feet, gliding to the pool's edge. She pulled herself up with her arms to sit with her feet dangling, threading a toe across the rippling water as she wrung out the dripping weight of her hair. The sunlight shone down through a cleft in the rock above her, lighting her glistening skin. The steady rise and fall of her breasts beneath the damp shift nearly did him in.

Tristan hadn't realized that he had stepped from behind the cover of the wall until he heard his own voice echoing to his ears. "Harriet . . ."

"Tristan!" Harriet scrambled to her feet, taking up a tartan blanket she'd brought along to cover herself. "How . . . how did you find me here?"

"I saw your horse alone up on the height while I was riding nearby. I worried you might have been injured or gotten lost, so I followed your footsteps into the cave."

The water dripping off of her was creating quite a puddle beneath her feet. She nodded, her initial uneasiness fading. "Well, thank you, but as you can see, I'm quite fine."

"Yes. Yes, you are."

He could see her skin grow flushed in the sunlight. He watched as she snatched up the pile of her clothing and retreated behind the shelter of a rock wall to dress. He should leave, he knew, but he didn't. Instead Tristan made his way down toward the edge of the water where moments before she had been sitting, limned golden by sunlight. Even standing beside it, he could feel the warmth rising from the water's surface. The heady scent of her wet skin, earthly and floral, surrounded him.

"How did you ever find this place?"

Harriet came back around to face him. She wore a new shift, dry and falling nearly to her ankles. Her hair was still damp as it twisted about her shoulders. "It was many years ago. I was out riding and just happened upon the opening quite by chance. I remembered you and Geoffrey talking about all the caves you had explored together as lads, about the smugglers who'd hidden their contraband in them. You would never let me come with you to explore them. I was curious, so I came inside and found this place instead. I couldn't believe it. It seemed carved by some sort of nether magic. I've been coming here ever since. It is unlike anything I've ever seen. Even in winter, the water is warm and the strongest blustering wind cannot bring a chill inside."

Tristan took a step closer. Harriet shifted. "And the walls—look at them," she said in effort to divert his attention away from the curve of her neck. "See how they shimmer in the sunlight? They are filled with rough amethyst." She gave a nervous laugh. "You'll probably think this is silly, but when I was a young girl, I used to imagine this was a secret fairy haven. I wondered that if I went into the water, perhaps I could find my way to some mystical underground kingdom."

Tristan took another step toward her, his voice dropping softly. "And did you find it, Harriet, your fairy kingdom?"

Harriet lowered her eyes. "See, you do think I'm silly."

"No. Truly, I don't. *I think you're beautiful.*"

Harriet looked up at him and their gazes locked. Neither moved nor said a word. Neither had to. Each already knew what the other was thinking. Seeing her now, her hair hanging in dripping red strands, her skin aglow in the shimmering light from above, Tristan was more certain than ever that it was Harriet he wanted, needed, in his life. He wanted to spend his days looking at her, watching her grow old with him, listening to her thoughts about worldly things and even otherworldly things. He wanted her to be his wife and bear their children. He wanted to tell her the things he told no one else, things he kept hidden away deep inside himself. He wanted to share all of the rest of his adventures with her.

He wanted to love her.

And looking into those eyes, the greenest depths of emerald, Tristan knew that Harriet wanted those things, too. If only he could somehow convince her to cast aside the shadow of that damnable legend and follow the advice of her heart.

Without a word, Tristan reached for Harriet, took her fully against him, and lowered his mouth to hers for a kiss.

Harriet felt quite certain the earth had ceased its spinning and everything else outside of that cave somehow melted away to a blur. The touch of his mouth, the strength of his arms, made Harriet lose herself to the singular pleasure of the racing of her own pulse beat. It was the first time in her life she had ever been kissed, and she gave herself over to it, trembling with sensation as his thumb traced along her chin, opening to the pressure of his mouth against hers.

She tasted him on her lips and tongue. She dropped back her head and arched into him even more. She felt him moan softly against her, his kiss becoming one of urgency, hunger, awakening her senses and sapping her strength until she felt sure her knees would buckle beneath her. It was the most incredible thing she had ever known.

When his mouth left hers to drag across the taut column of her throat and he lifted his hand to gently cup her breast, her knees did buckle and she clung to him, never wanting to let go. The kiss was more than she could have ever imagined, and Harriet knew from that moment on, her life would never be the same again.

But then, just as quickly as the gift of his kiss had come, like a bolt out of the blue, a voice sounded in Harriet's head, shattering the magic of that fleeting moment.

Yon Maid of Macquair, and any after, with fiery hair and eyes as green as ice, shall watch her chosen husband perish, and any man after him, unless she should take to husband a man of honor, a man of cunning, and of an age that is younger than she . . . else the ancient clan of Macquair shall vanish forever.

Shall vanish forever . . .

Forever.

With a gasp, Harriet pushed away from Tristan. She covered her mouth with her hand and backed several feet away, staring at him in sudden speechless terror.

He looked stunned. "What is it, Harriet? What is the matter?"

"Did you . . . hear that?"

"Hear what?"

Harriet didn't respond. Instead she looked up out of the cleft in the rock above her head. Sunlight no longer shone inside, glistening the walls with its amber and amethyst light. Somehow, in the space of that one moment, in the measure of that one brief kiss, the skies outside had darkened with a brewing storm, the wind whipping in off the firth and whistling through each tiny crevice around them like the keening of a thousand distant voices.

Forever . . .

"We should not have done that." She looked at him, her expression grave. "It wasn't wise."

"Wise? What the hell do you mean, Harriet? I kissed you, and it was . . . wonderful, and then suddenly it was gone." Tristan took a step closer. "What happened just now? Why do you look so—frightened?"

Harriet shook her head, holding out her hands as she skirted to where the rest of her clothing lay. Tristan took a step toward her.

"No, Tristan! Don't come any closer to me." She took up her stockings, hurriedly pulling them on. "I should not have done that. You should not have done that." As she tied off her garters, she looked up at the sky, seeing something there that he did not, and pleaded, "It was a moment of weakness, nothing more!"

"A moment of weakness?" Tristan looked at her. "Harriet, who are you talking to?"

She jerked on her skirt. "No one."

She was hurriedly fastening the waist of her skirt, hastening to jam her arms into the narrow sleeves of her redingcote. Finally, when she had twisted her hair into a wet knot beneath the cover of her hat and was making to leave, Tristan reached out and took her by the arms, shaking her. Her hat fell and the wet weight of her hair tumbled down her back anew.

"Stop it, damn it! Don't you see this is craziness? You love me. I love you. Did you hear me, Harriet? I said I love you."

Harriet's eyes dulled more gray than green as she shook her head in dismal defeat. "No, Tristan, you cannot love me. Don't you see? It can never be. *We* can never be. I thought you realized that last night."

"The only thing I realized is that you've been listening too long to old wives' tales. It is time you started living in this century, Harriet, not in those centuries already past."

"No . . . Tristan, I cannot involve myself with you! It is foolish . . . , dangerous . . ."

"Why? We are two people who want nothing more than to spend the rest of our lives together. Whatever could be wrong with that?"

Harriet didn't respond, just pulled away and made great work of fastening the buttons on her boots. When she straightened, Tristan took her by the arms again, refusing to let her go.

"Deny it, Harriet. Deny that the kiss we just shared meant nothing to you. Deny that it made you feel more alive than you've felt in a long time." He could see the beginnings of tears glistening in her eyes. He wished he could banish them. "You cannot deny it, Harriet. Because it would be a lie."

Harriet dropped her head forward to rest against his chest. She mumbled into his waistcoat, "Why, oh why, couldn't you have been born just one day later, Tristan?" Harriet lifted her head to look at him, bringing a single corkscrew tendril falling down her cheek, twisting just beside her ear. "You must accept it, Tristan, as I have. No matter what my heart feels, or how much I loved kissing you just now, any attachment between us is impossible. I am going to Edinburgh, as I had originally planned, and I am going to find the man who will be my husband. We will forget that any of this ever took place. It is the only choice I have."

Tristan stared at her through eyes dull with despair. Suddenly it was as if a vast chasm stood between them with no possible way across and he realized he had lost her even before he'd truly found her. "You can try all you like to convince yourself of it, Harriet, but I know that I will never forget what we just shared. Nor will I ever forget what we could have been."

And with that Tristan turned and walked out of the cave—and out of Harriet's life.

Chapter Four

*. . . If the adventures will not befall
a young lady in her own village,
she must seek them abroad.*
—Northanger Abbey, *Jane Austen*

Edinburgh

Harriet's first glimpse of the Scottish capital city was that of an ancient stone fortress perched high upon a mountain of rock reaching nearly to the clouds. Besieged, destroyed, and rebuilt several times over, a castle had stood on the site for the past eight centuries at least, playing host to the likes of Mary Queen of Scots, even Robert the Bruce.

Beneath this lofty cragged crown ran a mile-long stretch of road called the High Street, wide enough for five carriages to ride abreast, lined by tall stone buildings with slate roofs, some six, even ten stories high. Like a formation of watchful soldiers, they towered above the small coach carrying Geoffrey, Devorgilla, and Harriet past the city gates—Robbie perched eagerly in Harriet's lap, wagging his wiry tail at every passerby.

High above their heads, tall chimneys puffed out billowing clouds of coal smoke that had given the city its nickname of "Auld Reekie." Ladies leaned out windows. Boys and dogs chased one another around the Mercat Cross. Everywhere they looked, there was something of interest to be seen.

For Harriet, who had never gone farther than an afternoon carriage ride from home, the city was like a vast world of adventures just waiting to be had. From almost the first moment after they'd departed Rascarrel the day before, the sun had come out with glorious ceremony, banishing the dull, colorless clouds that had plagued the

skies nearly endlessly over the past weeks. Spring was
approaching. Harriet decided to take it as a sign that
she was doing what she was meant to, coming to Edinburgh to seek her future. If only that thought could
somehow ease the bittersweet memory of Tristan standing before her in that cave, telling her the words every
girl longed to hear.

I love you.

How angry he'd been that last time she'd seen him.
He had left for the city without even saying good-bye,
refusing Geoffrey's offer to accompany them in the
coach, opting instead to ride to Edinburgh alone on one
of the horses from the Rascarrel stable. Didn't he realize
she was doing this for him? Couldn't he see that if she
had her choice, they would be traveling to Edinburgh
together to share the happy news of their betrothal with
her father? Every waking moment, since the moment
Tristan had returned with Geoffrey to Rascarrel, Harriet
had fought the battle of her head against her heart. It
would be easy, so, *so* easy to throw caution to the wind
and marry Tristan. Everything in her heart told her to
do just that . . . but then she remembered the words of
her aunt, of how she had spent her life haunted by the
memory of the man she had loved, who had died for
loving her. Harriet knew she would rather spend four
lifetimes without Tristan than endure one waiting every
day for some peril to befall them. She could only hope
that someday he would realize the sacrifice she made
for him.

When they arrived at the Rascarrel town house on
Charlotte Square, no one was more surprised to see the
children of Baron Rascarrel standing on the doorstep
than Baron Rascarrel himself.

As a young man in his twenties, Hugh Drynan Baron
Rascarrel had been a gent of the city, an artist struggling
to pay the rent painting portraits of wealthy patrons
while dreaming of the day when his true heart's work,
landscapes of his native Galloway, might find their own
niche among the exhibitions at the renowned galleries.

It had been a bright spring day much like the present

one when he'd gone to a local bookshop seeking inspiration nearly three decades before. Turning a corner, he'd collided, literally, with a woman he thought must surely be a fairy nymph. All fiery red locks and sparkling green eyes, she had cast a spell about him with her smile. Like a dream come true, this vision with the name Viola Macquair Maxwell had asked him if he'd like to take a walk with her around the park.

A fortnight later they were wed. It made no matter to Sir Hugh if Viola had chosen him for his age or the color of his breeches. He'd been utterly captivated.

Now in his early fifties, his graying hair brushed forward in the style of the day, Hugh Drynan's interests in art had turned from that of creating to collecting. His was said to be one of the finest collections in the kingdom, so fine, in fact, he'd recently received a request from the Prince Regent to view it.

"Harriet?" the baron asked upon seeing his only daughter standing smiling on his doorstep when he'd only just left her a few days earlier in Galloway. "Has something happened?"

And then he recognized the grin of his long-absent son behind her. "Geoffrey! Lad, you've come back!" He threw out his arms to them both.

"This is a surprise," he said as he ushered the party of them inside. They withdrew to the parlor where the baron immediately began to quiz Geoffrey about the wars, the Continent, Napoleon, anything to fill the gap of the past years apart while Harriet went off to the kitchen to brew them all some tea.

". . . and there I was in Brussels," Geoffrey was saying as she brought in the pot and set it on the table, "enjoying a nice bit of French brandy at the Duchess of Richmond's ball when I looked across the room and spotted Tristan of all people dancing with the duchess's daughter. We spent the rest of the night catching up. It was like he'd never been away. And then, suddenly, within hours we were marching to battle, fighting side by side. It was all over nearly as quickly as it had begun, and we were coming home."

The baron nodded. "Good lad, Tristan Carmichael. Glad to hear he's made a life for himself after the tragedy of his parents' accident. Where is he now?"

"He's here in Edinburgh actually. Come to see his godfather. He's planning to reside in Galloway eventually, once things there have been settled."

"Settled?" questioned Sir Hugh. "Is something the matter?"

Geoffrey glanced quickly at Harriet, who was setting out the cup of tea she'd just poured. She frowned at him. "You might as well know, Father, for you'll no doubt hear about it later. Tristan has asked me to marry him."

"Splendid!" The baron beamed. "I hope you said yes."

"Actually, no. I refused him."

"What? Why . . . ?" And then he realized. "Oh, yes, the prophecy." He knew the story well, but it had been a blessing to him, not a curse, for it had brought him the gift of twelve years with his beloved wife.

Sir High looked closely at Harriet. "You love Tristan. You have since you were a wee lassie."

Harriet stared at her father, dumbfounded that he should know something she'd thought only known to her.

"You were devastated when he left Galloway, Harriet. A father can sense these things about his only daughter."

Actually, it had been Devorgilla who'd told him, but Harriet need not know any better. "But certainly a man born the same day as you should be safe enough."

"That is the same thing Tristan said, but what if it is not?" Harriet left the tea tray and crossed the room to the window, blowing on the brew in her cup to cool it as she watched the traffic pass by. "What if some misfortune were to befall him? We would never know until it is too late. And I would never forgive myself if Tristan came to harm because of me."

The baron nodded, unable to argue against his daughter's unhappy logic. "She makes a good point." He let go a sigh. "Chin up, my dear. I'm sure all will work out in the end. It always does."

Harriet, however, found little comfort in his words.

After they shared a makeshift supper of cold ham and crusty bread, Geoffrey and the baron went off to the nearest pub for a celebratory tankard of ale. Devorgilla excused herself, claiming a headache from their journey, and retired above stairs for a nap. Harriet was thus left alone for the afternoon to sit and ponder how best to find herself a husband in less than a fortnight.

Where on earth to begin?

The knocker on the front door sounded at almost the same moment. Harriet went to the hall and opened the door onto the greeting smile of an older woman carrying the most enormous muff Harriet had ever seen. Only after Robbie began barking at the thing, and it hissed, did Harriet realize it was a cat.

"Good day to you!" the lady's melodious voice rang out. "I am Lady Harrington. Lord H and I hold the house there on the corner just across the square. We had despaired of meeting anyone new this season at all, but then I saw your coach, saw that you had baggage and meant to stay, and I knew I had to come right over to meet you."

She was like a swirl of new spring air, all floral and brisk and lively. Harriet invited the woman inside, cat and all, asked the kitchen maid to bring tea, and settled in for a visit. In truth, she was grateful for the diversion. All Harriet had been able to think about was the fact that Tristan was there, in that same city, possibly even on that same street, and she could not see him. In fact, as angry as he had been the last time she'd seen him, he likely would never want to see her again.

For all her formidable figure, Lady Harrington was quite fashionable with her salt-and-pepper close-cut curls graced by a stylish bonnet. Lucinda, as she asked Harriet to call her, spent a pleasant hour chatting about the comings and goings of most every family in the neighborhood, how Lord and Lady So-and-so's son had lost a fortune at the gaming tables the week before, or that the Earl of Whatever's mistress lived in a flat in the small house off the lane. She seemed to know everyone's business and Harriet soon found herself likening her to a vibrant butterfly, flitting about from flower to flower, making certain to stop at each one lest she should miss out on something important.

"Have you children of your own?" Harriet asked when she finally managed to get in a word.

"I have two daughters, Wilhelmina and Rosalind, now grown and moved away." The viscountess sighed. "I devoted my life to seeing them both successfully wed, one to an earl, the other to a marquess, no less. They are my finest accomplishments."

It soon became apparent that now that her daughters were wed, Lady H was quite at loose ends with what to do with herself. As such, she was always on the lookout for new opportunities to employ her matchmaking expertise.

"So, my dear, I saw you arriving with a handsome young man this morning."

Harriet poured them each a fresh cup of hyson. Her only experience in female socializing had been with Devorgilla or the occasional call to the vicar's wife, so she fell into conversation with the fascinating viscountess quite easily. "Yes, we are very excited because my brother, Geoffrey, has just returned from the Peninsula."

"The Peninsula! I declare, how exciting!" The viscountess chuckled to herself. "For a moment, when I first saw him, I thought he might be your husband."

Harriet handed Lady Harrington her tea. "Oh, no, my lady. I am not married."

"Betrothed, then?"

"No, ma'am."

"Significantly attached?"

Harriet simply shook her head.

The viscountess's eyes lit up like a bonfire. "My heavens! How can it be that such a lovely girl hasn't yet found her way to the altar?" She answered before Harriet ever could. "But, of course, that must be the reason for your visit to the city, isn't it? To find yourself a husband?"

Harriet chewed her lip. Was her desperation so obvious? She looked at Lady Harrington. She'd only just met the woman but something about her told Harriet she could confide in her. "I'll admit I had rather hoped to meet some eligible gentlemen . . ."

"I knew it!" The viscountess clapped her hands with delight.

"But I've a slight problem," Harriet confessed.

"What, dear? No dowry?"

"No, I am well dowered."

"A scandal from your past then?"

"Indeed no. It is just that . . . for reasons I cannot go into now . . . I have less than a fortnight in which to find myself a husband."

For anyone else, this might have been a deterrent. But for Lucinda, Lady Harrington, Matchmaker Extraordinaire, it was little more than a challenge—a challenge she was all too eager to accept.

"Well, then, we'll have to act quickly. And I know just the person to help you."

"You do? Who?"

"*Me!* I am acquainted with every family of good breeding in town, and even some of not-so-good breeding, if you know what I mean." She fished inside her beaded reticule, taking out an ivory-covered tablet and pencil. "I shall make a few notations . . . tell me, dear, do you prefer light, or dark?"

Harriet was lost. "Tea?"

"No, dear, suitors! Do you prefer your gentlemen blond-or dark headed?"

"Oh, well, dark, I suppose . . . but not too dark. Sort of an ash brown."

The viscountess nodded, scribbling. "Tall, or closer to your own height?"

"Tall."

"Of a good build?"

"Yes."

"A well-established man who has his own fortune . . . preferably titled . . ."

". . . and with eyes the color of the bluest sky."

At the viscountess's curious stare, Harriet realized

she'd just described Tristan. "Truly, my lady, I don't think I would know until I saw the man for myself."

"Indeed. And I know just the place to do it."

Harriet looked at her, waiting.

"The Annual Assembly. It is hosted by the Society of Edinburgh Ladies, of which I am a founding member. 'Tis this coming Friday at the Assembly Rooms on George Street, just down the street from here. Invitations went out weeks ago, but I will make certain you receive one this very afternoon."

Harriet brightened. "Oh, Lady Harrington, could you? That would be wonderful! I honestly didn't know what I was going to do. I'm afraid I haven't much experience with this sort of thing."

The viscountess smiled. "Tut, tut, dear. Just leave that to me. By week's end, you'll have more acquaintance-ship than you ever dreamed possible."

She stood then, taking up her cat muff from where it lay snoozing on the settee. "I'm off now. Other calls to make, you know. The days just don't have enough hours in them." She started for the door to leave. "Now, if you are in need of a gown for the assembly, you must go posthaste to Madame Angelique's shop on Rose Street. She is without a doubt the finest modiste in town. Comes from France, of course. All the good ones do. Her girls can measure you up and deliver something splendid in time for Friday evening. Just tell Madame I sent you. Oh, and don't forget to ask her to include your red petticoat, dear, just in case. You never know if you might need it."

Harriet stopped at the door, her hand yet clutching the handle. "Did you say 'red petticoat'?"

Auntie Gill's dream . . . hadn't she said she'd seen Harriet wearing a red petticoat under her mother's wedding dress?

Lady Harrington laughed. "Why, yes, dear, I did. It is a necessity for every young Edinburgh lady this year. Do you not know about the tradition?"

Harriet shook her head.

"Oh, sweet child, this is a leap year, you know, the

best of all times for making marriages. If you should
have any difficulty in winkling a proposal out of our
young men, on Leap Year Day—February the twenty-
ninth—all you need do is don your red petticoat and
you can ask the man yourself!"

A lady . . . can propose to a man?"

The viscountess bubbled. "Oh, yes, and it's perfectly
legal, but only on Leap Year Day, mind you. It is an
ancient custom, written into law some five hundred years
ago, and thankfully never written out. And if the man
in question should dare to refuse, besides being possessed of a complete lack of decency and common sense,
he is liable to pay a fine or make some sort of offering
to you, a new silk dress, a pair of gloves, something in
return. I've only seen that happen once though, dear,
and she wasn't nearly as lovely as you are. Just something to bear in mind, when you visit Madame Angelique
for your gown. Farewell to you for now! Ta ta!"

Harriet stood at the door and watched the colorful
matron make her way along the paved walkway toward
the corner of the square. She hadn't made it twenty
yards before she spotted someone else of her acquain-
tanceship and was flagging them down with her lace-
edged handkerchief.

"My lady . . . !"

Harriet shut the door and leaned her back against it,
reflecting a moment or two on all she had just learned.
Leap Year Day—February the twenty-ninth. Auntie Gill
had seen a red petticoat in her dream. She had thought
the dream had signified Harriet's approaching birthday.
But what if instead the dream was a sign of a day—
a day when a lady could legally propose marriage to
a man?

Chapter Five

*To be so bent on marriage—
to pursue a man merely for the sake of a situation—
is the sort of thing that shocks me.*
—Lady Susan, *Jane Austen*

The doorway of Firkin and Sons Bookshop was tucked away on a quiet corner lane off Thistle Street, flanked on one side by a clockmaker, a tearoom on the other, just west of St. Andrew Square. Devorgilla and Harriet had spent more than an hour at Madame Angelique's choosing fabrics and getting measured for their gowns, which would, as Lady Harrington had promised, be ready in time for the assembly.

Afterward, the two ladies walked the few blocks from the modiste to the bookshop, Robbie pulling eagerly on his leash in front of them as fashionable coaches and decorated sedan chairs passed by on the busy street. While Devorgilla ducked into the confectioners' shop for a batch of her favorite candied almonds, Harriet tied Robbie to the small iron boot scrape outside the door before heading inside to Firkin's.

The bell above her head tinked softly as she entered the tidy shop that was surrounded floor-to-ceiling with shelves filled with neat rows of books of various size and color. Atlases littered the top of a broad table in one corner and newspapers were set out near plumply stuffed armchairs for those wishing to catch up on the day's events.

Harriet stood for a moment just inside the door, trying to imagine how her mother must have felt when she had stood at that same place, for that same reason, all those years before. Had she been frightened? Excited? Had she ever known the heartache of loving a man she could not have? What had made her choose Sir Hugh on that spring afternoon? Harriet reached for her locket and closed her fingers around it, drawing courage from its presence in her hand as she stepped inside the shop and slowly looked around.

"Good day to you, madam." A slim, scholarly-looking fellow in spectacles came forward from where he'd been sorting through a stack of books to greet her. "Welcome to Firkin and Sons, one of which I am." He smiled at his own jest. "Is there something in particular I might help you find?"

Yes, please, if you wouldn't mind, Perhaps you could direct me to the nearest unmarried young man . . .

Harriet smiled at him, shaking her head. "I just thought to browse a bit."

The clerk grinned, nodding. "Well, we have just about anything a lady'd be looking for here at Firkin and Sons. Popular novels over here: Austen, Edgeworth, others. Poetry in the far corner. We even have those little etiquette guides the younger misses are so fond of."

"Etiquette guides?"

"Aye, madam. You know the ones that tell you the proper way to dress and talk and how to catch a gentleman's eye?"

Harriet's interest was instantly piqued. "Indeed? And where did you say I might find those?"

"Toward the back of the shop there, madam. By the fashion journals. You can't miss them."

Harriet nodded, thanked the man, and departed immediately in the direction he'd indicated. She came at last to a small alcove set apart from the main area of the shop. A pretty little carved bench was set against the wall and Harriet stood, scanning the shelves until she happened upon a title in shining gold leaf:

A Reflection on Refinement by A Lady of Quality.

Curious, Harriet took the small book and opened to the first page.

All Manner of Useful Advice on Propriety, Beauty, Grace, and Accomplishment For the Cultivation of Fe-

male Etiquette By A Lady of Rank and Most Esteemed Grace and Virtue.

What followed was ten chapters of detailed instruction on most every topic of female interest, from fashion to deportment, coiffures to proper speech. It was all the things young girls were expected to know and practice in the sphere of society, all the things they were taught from a tender age by their mothers . . .

. . . all the things Harriet had never learned.

Harriet lowered onto the bench, reading through the first few pages.

A lady's posture should always be that of a graceful willow, elegant and straight, without the slightest hint of a slouch.

Without even realizing it, Harriet straightened her back, drawing her shoulders back, her chin higher as she flipped the page to read on.

A true lady of elegance never looks into a man's eyes directly. Instead she gives brief glances from out of the corner of her own eyes before casting her gaze downward demurely so as to draw attention to the softness of her cheek, the grace of her hands . . .

By the time she finished reading the first chapter, Harriet was convinced that the "Lady of Quality" who had written the book was nothing short of a genius. This book, and the assistance of Lady Lucinda Harrington, were everything Harriet needed to find herself a husband.

Harriet took some coins from her reticule and paid the clerk, then quickly left the shop, intent on spending the rest of that afternoon studying each page. She'd completely forgotten her initial purpose in coming to Firkin's in the first place, to see if she might be as fortunate as her mother had been when she'd found her father. But as she approached the door to leave, Harriet had to stop when she found her way suddenly blocked.

"Hello, Harriet."

His eyes were dark, blank, his expression guarded. Still her breath caught at the sight of him. She wondered if he were still angry with her.

"Tristan . . . hello. What are you doing here?"

"I thought I'd look for something good to read. Any recommendations . . . ?" He glanced at the book she held before her. "Ah, *A Reflection on Refinement.* I see you are arming yourself before heading off to the battle-field—I mean, the ballroom."

Harriet frowned at his acid tone.

"I thought this book might prove helpful."

Tristan shook his head. "You'll have a far better chance catching yourself a husband by being yourself, Harriet, than by following whatever advice you'll find in that absurd tome."

She gave a small *harrumph*, reaching down to quickly untether Robbie. He was obviously still angry with her, and now ridiculed her attempts to secure her safe future. "And of course, your vast experience in finding a husband qualifies you to make that observation. I thank you for the advice, Tristan, but I'll take my chances with someone who's donned a corset at least once in their lifetime. Good day."

She turned and walked swiftly away, tugging for Robbie to follow.

Chapter Six

There is nothing like dancing after all . . .
One of the first refinements of polished societies.
—Pride and Prejudice, *Jane Austen*

Harriet spent nearly every waking moment of the next few days preparing for the assembly.

Among the first things she did was hire a ladies' maid, something she'd never had the need for before, though they certainly could have afforded the luxury. She had grown up dressing herself and arranging her own hair in its customary chignon simply because she preferred it, but according to Lady Harrington, the services of a ladies' maid in town were not just a luxury. They were a necessity.

Her name was Delphine and she was French (as all good ladies' maids are). They spent the entirety of a day just trying out a variety of coiffures, making note of those that best complemented Harriet's features, and still other notes of those that did not. They experimented with cosmetics, Balm of Mecca, some lip rouge, but Harriet found she preferred to forgo the paint, thinking it made her look too like a French porcelain doll. The services of a dancing master were engaged, and within just a couple of days, Harriet had learned the steps of at least a dozen new dances.

She accomplished more in the space of those few days than she had in a month at home. It seemed an extraordinary amount of preparation for one simple night out, but if it helped her to find a husband by the end of the month, then Harriet was all for it.

On the night of the assembly, Harriet sat at her dressing table staring in the mirror while Delphine fixed her hair, her stomach twisting in worrisome knots. Her gown had not yet arrived from Madame Angelique's, and the hour was growing quite late. What if her gown wasn't ready in time? What if she completely forgot how to dance the quadrille? What if she got so nervous, her stomach so upset, over the importance of this one night, she threw up on her best possibility for a husband?

At the sound of the front door knocker, and the footsteps of the footman approaching her chamber, Harriet breathed a sigh of relief. At last, her gown had arrived.

The box from Madame Angelique's was pink and pretty and tied with a bright red ribbon. Harriet slipped the silk creation on, waiting while Delphine quickly arranged her skirts around her, then turned to see the finished product in the glass.

A moment later, bedlam erupted.

"Auntie Gill!"

Devorgilla hastened up the three flights of stairs to Harriet's bedchamber to find her beloved niece standing in the middle of the room with tears rolling down her freshly powdered cheeks.

"Whatever is the matter, Hattie?"

"Look at this!" Harriet turned to the glass once again. "I cannot go to the assembly looking like . . . like . . . I mean, good God, I'm half undressed! My ankles are showing. Not only that, my breasts are showing!"

The gown was cut in a Grecian style with a high waist over straight, unadorned skirts meant to drape closely to Harriet's figure. Short capped sleeves decorated with knots of ribbon set off the elegant line of her shoulders. The color, a pale blue-green, was a perfect complement to Harriet's hair and eyes. The neckline, cut square and deep, showed the shape of her bosom quite nicely.

Devorgilla came into the room. "Harriet, dearest, the gown is stunning, truly! It becomes you very well. I promise you will look as elegant as a swan."

"A swan with half its feathers plucked."

Devorgilla took Harriet's hands and turned to face her. "My dearest Harriet, you are like a daughter to me. Before she died, I promised your mother that I would watch over you. Do you honestly believe I would allow you to go out on this, the most important night of your life thus far, dressed inappropriately?"

Harriet stared at her, mute.

"Well, do you?"

Slowly, tentatively, she shook her head.

"Of course I wouldn't. Now listen to me. Up until the past several days, you have lived your life sheltered from the rest of the world. You have never been to the city, have never moved about in elegant society. The time has now come to stop hiding your light, Harriet Mac-quair Drynan, and let it shine for all to see!"

Wearing that dress, there wouldn't be much of her that wouldn't be seen . . .

Still, Harriet knew that her aunt was right. At home in Galloway, she could wear her serviceable woolens and linens. But if she wanted to catch the eye of a young man, she would need to stand out. And, besides, what else could she do? She had nothing else appropriate to wear to the assembly, and she simply couldn't afford to miss the opportunity of this night.

By the time Delphine put the finishing touches to Harriet's coiffure, she no longer resembled herself in any manner. Her scalp stung from all the tugging and pulling it had taken to create this work of art, but as she looked on it in the mirror, Harriet had to admit it had all been worth it.

Her hair had been curled and twisted and pinned into a style that left tight corkscrew ringlets of red hanging about her neck and dangling down against one cheek. A pretty bit of matching ribbon provided the finishing touch. The end result, the gown, the hair, the white silk gloves that reached to her elbows, all of it came together perfectly, even if she was showing more of herself than she'd ever dreamed decently possible. But just when she'd thought the preparations complete, Devorgilla returned to Harriet's chamber, dressed for the assembly, and carrying a small velvet-covered box.

"My dear, these were your mother's. She charged me with the responsibility of giving them to you when the time was right. I do not think there can be any more appropriate time than now."

Harriet opened the lid carefully. An elegant pearl necklace set with a stunning single emerald pendant lay inside with a matching pair of earrings alongside. They were the finest things Harriet had ever seen.

"Oh, Auntie Gill, they're beautiful."

"Not nearly as beautiful as you will be wearing them," Devorgilla said, unfastening the clasp as she set the circle of them around Harriet's slender neck. The emerald slid to rest just above the curve of her breasts. The earrings sparkled and flashed, glowing with facets of green fire in the lamplight as Harriet stared at her reflection in the mirror. Suddenly, the memory of her mother struck her with a wave of long-hidden emotion.

"I can still remember how beautiful she was," she whispered softly.

"And you are every bit as beautiful, dear. Now, then, enough of those tears else Delphine will have to powder your cheeks again. Are you ready to go?"

Harriet took a deep breath, squared her shoulders, and nodded.

Sir Hugh beamed at the vision of his daughter descending the stairs before him wearing the heirloom wedding present he had given his wife three decades before. "Oh, sweet Harriet, how very much you look like your mother the first time I saw her." He gave her an affectionate peck upon her cheek.

Harriet noticed then that her brother was staring at her queerly. "Geoffrey, is something the matter?"

He shook his head as if clearing his thoughts "Oh, I'm sorry, miss, did you say something? I was just waiting for my sister to come down. Did you perhaps forget her upstairs?"

He grinned and Harriet took a playful swing at him with her new beaded reticule. "It is a bit of a masquerade, is it not?"

Geoffrey only shook his head, his tone no longer teasing. "Masquerade, no. One of the finest paintings in our father's collection unveiled, yes."

Harriet blushed beneath his compliment. "Does this mean I need never hear myself referred to as 'Hattie Brattie' again?"

Geoffrey laughed. "Some things, my dear sister, will never change. Even when you are wed with a gaggle of children squirming at your feet, you will always be my own sweet *Hattie Brattie*."

Harriet wouldn't have it any other way.

It was a fine night for February, the air crisp but not too cold, so rather than hire a coach, the foursome decided to walk the short distance down George Street to the Assembly Rooms. The stars winked overhead against the fullness of a winter's moon as they made their way by the light of the gas lamps, a perfect night for Harriet's first venture into society.

As they approached the pristine columned façade, lights from the tall windows facing the street cast wavering shadows of light on dark. Faint strains of music and the murmur of conversation spilled from the doors leading inside while coaches lined up at the front to let off their passengers.

After checking their cloaks, they made their way through a crowded hallway to the equally crowded assembly room beyond. Harriet faltered, feeling as if every pair of eyes in the room were suddenly trained upon them. Her hesitation, however, was soon put at ease when she spotted the colorful advancing kaleidoscope of Lady Lucinda Harrington bearing down on them from across the room.

"Oh, my dear, my dear! You came! I'm so delighted. And may I say you look positively stunning in that gown. Madame Angelique has outdone herself." She glanced at the others. "And this must be your charming family?"

"Yes, my lady," Harriet replied and quickly dispensed with the introductions.

Geoffrey soon made for the far corner where a group of young gentlemen had congregated near the drinks table. Harriet's heart gave a jump when she spotted Tristan among them, looking resplendent in his suit of formal black. She wondered why he'd come to the assembly, if he would ask her to dance. She wondered if he would like her new gown.

They moved off into the crowded room and Lady Harrington began to introduce them to others of her acquaintance, an earl and even a duke among them. As they approached the entrance to the ballroom beyond, the baron's attention was taken by a painting he spotted hanging in the upper gallery. He bid them to go on without him so he might take a closer look. Flanked by her aunt on one side and Lady Harrington on the other, Harriet officially made her entrance into society.

"My dear," Lady Harrington whispered to her, "with any luck, there will be a goodly assortment of eligible young gentlemen present tonight, sons of some rather influential men. Thankfully, as your brother can attest, the lads have begun making their way back across the Channel and should be eager for the company of our young ladies."

Harriet nodded, straightening her posture the way she'd been practicing in the mirror, and glided elegantly across the floor.

Lady Harrington gestured across the room. "That young man there by the potted palm is the eldest son of Lord Stanbridge, an earl. He's set to inherit twenty thousand across as well as a substantial fortune in Argyllshire when he weds." She nodded, eyes wide no doubt for effect.

Harriet studied the man from across the room. He was blond, angelically so, with a smile that seemed to come easily. He wore his suit of clothes well, but he wasn't as tall as Tristan, or nearly as handsome.

"Do you happen to know his age, my lady?" Devorgilla asked discreetly.

"His age you say?" Lady Harrington thought. "Hmm, well, I believe he is five-and-thirty. Two-and-thirty at the very least.

"Indeed." Harriet quickly crossed him off her mental list of candidates. "Has he perhaps any younger brothers?"

The viscountess looked at Harriet quite as if she'd just asked for her family's secret pudding recipe. "I do not believe so," she answered a bit uncertainly. "I believe he is the only child."

She brightened a moment later. "Now there's another favorable candidate just coming into the room."

Harriet looked, spotting a tall figure turned out like Tristan in formal black. Favorable, indeed, he had the look of a rogue, and Harriet noticed several of the young ladies nearby whispering about him. His eyes raked the room, catching Harriet's gaze. He smiled, flashing white teeth, and nodded to her.

"Ooh, and he's definitely taken notice of you, dear. Anthony would be quite a catch. A viscount in his own right. Although his earlier years were a bit risqué, his father did the right thing in sending him off to the Continent to fight against Napoleon. He nearly fought at Waterloo, too, except that by the time his regiment made it there, the battle had already been won."

Harriet nodded, thinking that Tristan *had* fought at Waterloo, and quite courageously if Geoffrey were to be believed. "Has this Anthony yet reached twenty-eight?"

Again the viscountess looked puzzled. "Yes, I believe he has. Very recently, though."

Harriet turned, dismissing the roguish viscount who'd almost made it to Waterloo as well. She looked around the rest of the room, and soon focused on the figure of a man standing nearest the garden doors. He was dressed neatly, not too ornate, and his boots displayed an admirable polish. According to the instructive pages of *A Reflection on Refinement,* this was considered a well-regarded quality in a man. His sandy-colored hair and dimpled smile gave him a somewhat boyish appearance, which caused Harriet to consider him all the more closely.

"That young man there, standing by the doors. Do you know him, my lady?"

The viscountess smiled somewhat wistfully. "Why, yes, dear, that is my husband's nephew, Sir Duncan Harrington, Baronet." Her voice dropped to a near whisper.

"But I'm afraid I must save you the trouble and the time. He wouldn't do for you for a suitor. You see, his father has left him quite without financial prospects, which is why my husband and I have taken him under our protection. We are hoping to convince him to pursue a career in the law."

"Oh, money is of no matter to me, Lady Harrington. My father has scads of it."

Lady Harrington stared at her, stunned. "He has . . . I mean, it isn't?"

"Oh, no, not at all," Harriet assured her. *On to other matters.* "How old is he?"

"He is six-and-twenty, dear. Just turned."

Harriet brightened. Things were finally beginning to look up. "I should like to meet your nephew sometime."

It took Lady Harrington a full half-minute to respond. "You wish to meet him? Duncan? My nephew? Oh, my dear, why of course!"

She turned to face the room. *"Dunnn-cannn!"* Her voice rang out clear as a town crier, causing everyone in the vicinity to turn and stare. "Do come and meet our charming new neighbor!"

Standing with Geoffrey by the drinks table, Tristan caught sight of Harriet as she was making her way across the ballroom. In the first moment, he was taken aback—she looked absolutely stunning. He almost didn't recognize her, and probably wouldn't have if Devorgilla hadn't been walking beside her. Her radiant hair was pinned up high on her head, showing off the elegance of her neck—and the deeply-cut décolletage of her gown—to advantage. And in the next moment, as she smiled and extended her hand toward a buff-breeched buck who scarcely looked old enough to shave his chin, he realized what she was up to.

Tristan quickly excused himself from the others and circled the room. As he approached, he could hear Harriet laughing, but it wasn't the laughter Tristan knew so well and loved. Instead it was . . .

. . . *a twitter.*

"Oh, Sir Duncan, you are quite funny!"

She'd obviously been spending all her time since he'd seen her last reading that damnable book. Even her voice wasn't her own, but a softer, lighter version, aimed to charm. She was practicing the advice from the book to the extreme, as if the more she adhered to that misguided feminine wisdom, the more attractive to the opposite sex she'd become.

Harriet began to flutter her eyelashes like a nervous butterfly when Tristan came to join their little gathering. He whispered quietly to her, "What's the matter, Harriet? Something in your eye?"

The fluttering stopped, superseded by a most chilling glare. "Lord Ravenshall, good evening. Have you had the occasion yet to meet our neighbor, Lady Harrington, and her nephew, Sir Duncan Harrington?"

"Oh, no, Miss Drynan," Sir Duncan piped in. "The honor is all mine." The man was looking at Tristan with an expression akin to awe. "Lord Ravenshall's bravery on the field of battle is legend among the Scottish regiments." He bowed his head reverently. "My lord."

Tristan fixed the buck a bland stare. "A pleasure, Harrington."

"I heard tell that you were virtually unstoppable at Corunna—"

"What a pity we won't be able to hear of it in more detail," Harriet interjected. "I believe it is time for our dance now, Sir Duncan."

Duncan glanced once at Tristan before nodding. "Yes, of course. If you would please excuse us, Lord Ravenshall." He bowed his head to the others. "Aunt Lucinda. Miss Maxwell."

Tristan watched as Sir Duncan led Harriet to where the dancers were gathering. He recognized the look in the young man's eye as one far too familiar—and far too predatory—for his liking. Harriet, on the other hand, had no earthly idea of what she was doing. Which only indicated to Tristan that he would need to keep his eye on her.

Looking around quickly, Tristan spotted a young lady

standing alone against the near wall. He approached, bowing before her.

"This may seem a bit forward, miss, since we haven't yet been formally introduced. I am Lord Ravenshall. Might I beg the honor of this dance, Miss—?"

The pretty blonde immediately blushed under his attention, fluttering her lashes in exactly the same way Harriet had moments before. Just his luck; another student of *A Reflection of Refinement.*

"I am Miss Blum," the blonde tittered. "Miss Flavia Blum, and I would be honored to dance with you, Lord Ravenshall."

Tristan offered her his arm and walked her to the line of dancers just forming in the center of the room. He could see Harriet standing with her conquest several couples forward in the line. The music began, and the dancers followed suit.

They had made only a few steps into the dance before Harriet turned and noticed Tristan dancing with Miss Blum. She must have been startled to see them, so startled, in fact, she misstepped, treading on her partner's toes. Tristan found a small sense of satisfaction in the wrinkle that creased her pretty brow.

"So, tell me, Miss Blum," he asked, turning his attention to his partner, "are you from Edinburgh?"

The shy coquette blossomed under his attention, unleashing the charm she'd been tutored in since girlhood. Tristan, for his part, played the role of interested suitor from top to toe, smiling at her, peering into her eyes, looking for all the world as if no one else existed except the inimitable Miss Blum.

In truth, as he chatted politely with her, Tristan found himself comparing her garnet earrings to the color of Harriet's hair, found himself longing for a glance from that familiar pair of green eyes. Harriet, however, seemed to deliberately avoid looking his way. She was enticing her partner with shy glances and charming smiles, and more than once Tristan caught Harrington's gaze slipping downward to the lush display of Harriet's breasts.

By the time the music stopped, ending the dance, Tristan felt quite certain he might throttle the randy young buck. He bowed to his partner, asked for another dance later on, then crossed the room to the garden doors, knowing if he remained spectator to Harriet's flirtations another moment, all sense would abandon him and his fist would end up in Harrington's face.

He was only outside a few moments when he heard the door opening behind him. He already knew who it was and said without turning, "Have you given up on the dancing already, Harriet?"

The crispness in his voice cut sharper than evening's chill.

"What are you doing, Tristan?"

"Enjoying a moment of solitude on a peaceful winter's night."

"You know what I mean, Tristan. I saw you. In there. With *her*."

Tristan turned. "I really don't believe I owe you any explanation, Harriet, especially after I've been made to watch you pushing your half-bare bosom under another man's eyes all night."

Her tone changed immediately, from one of anger to one of regret. "I was afraid you would not like the dress. I had no idea it would be this . . . this, *scant*. I knew I shouldn't have worn it, but I had nothing else suitable."

She thought he disapproved when instead the only thing he'd rather see her in other than that dress was nothing. Tristan looked at her. Standing as she was, sketched by moonlight, Harriet looked more beautiful than he could possibly imagine. "Why are you doing this?"

"Tristan, you know I have no choice—"

"You have every choice, Harriet. All you need do is say you will marry me and we can end this madness tonight."

Tristan took a step toward her and Harriet could feel the warmth of his body standing now just inches from her own. She looked up at him in the moonlight, waiting, hoping . . . hoping he'd kiss her just one more time. If he would, she told herself, it would be enough to last her a lifetime without him.

Tristan didn't keep her waiting long.

The kiss was soft and tender and achingly sweet, the sort of kiss that made one feel as if time virtually stood still. Harriet's breath caught and she let go a blissful sigh, losing herself in the true magic of being held in the strength of his arms. When he deepened the kiss, drawing her farther into the garden shadows, she gave herself over to him yet more, never wanting the kiss to end.

It was Tristan who slowly, reluctantly pulled away from her a moment later.

"Harriet, stop this senselessness." His voice was a rough whisper wrapping over her. "Do not deny what is between us."

The pulse of her heart was drumming to her ears as she lost herself in the depths of his blue eyes. How? How could he not be the one for her when everything about him felt so right?

Harriet closed her eyes and leaned into him, whispering, "Kiss me, Tristan, kiss me again . . ."

And he did, this time without the softness, the tenderness of before, but with a desperate hunger that had him taking her by the arms and locking her against him, his mouth seizing hers, tasting, seeking, begging, and she gave, oh, she gave, dropping her head back and opening to him utterly and completely—

—until the sky above them split with an ear-shattering crack.

They parted, looking up at the darkness above them. A moment later, it began to pour as if the floodgates of heaven had burst.

Harriet squealed, covering her head with her shawl, and the two of them ran for the ballroom door. Blessedly, the attentions of everyone else inside were taken up with a musical trio who were in the midst of performing a Mozart sonata. No one noticed that they had been alone together on the garden terrace. No one saw them slip quietly inside. No one except Devorgilla.

Harriet caught Devorgilla's eye from across the room.

When she saw her aunt's responding frown, she quickly looked away.

Tristan and Harriet stood for several minutes at the back of the assembly, watching the performance. Neither looked at the other.

Finally, Harriet whispered, "We shouldn't have done that."

Tristan drew in a slow breath. "Harriet—"

"Do you not see, Tristan? Whenever we are together, something like this happens. Remember in the cave, how the wind started howling the last time you kissed me? And now this, a perfectly lovely evening and then suddenly, a raging downpour. Someone or something is trying to tell us we cannot be together. It is a sign."

"Bloody hell, Harriet, it isn't any sign. It is the weather. Believe it or not, it does rain in Scotland."

"Yes, I know that. In fact, truth be told, I have spent more time here than you have."

Tristan mumbled. "That's your problem."

"I beg your pardon?"

"Nothing. Applaud, Harriet, the performance has ended."

Any attempt at further conversation ended when the others in the room broke into applause. The crowd began to disperse. Harriet turned, only to find that Tristan had vanished.

Insufferable man . . .

But even as she thought this, she still felt the touch of him on her lips, the taste of him on her mouth, the feel of his hands against her skin . . .

Chapter Seven

*Where so many hours have been spent
in convincing myself that I am right,
is there not some reason to fear
I may be wrong?*
—Sense and Sensibility, *Jane Austen*

The morning sun rose on a gloriously clear sky tufted with clumps of white clouds, prompting Harriet to take Robbie out after breakfast for a walk in the gardens behind Charlotte Square. She'd slept later than was her custom, having stayed at the assembly well into the wee hours the night before. After their interlude on the garden terrace, Tristan had vanished and hadn't returned, leaving Harriet nothing else to do but spend the rest of the evening taking stock of the other gentlemen present.

It hadn't proved a productive enterprise. She must have seen, and considered, and then ultimately discounted well over a dozen different gentlemen as potential husbands. No matter who she saw, from duke on down to baronet, they all of them somehow fell short of her requirements. Too old, too arrogant. This one fond of drink, another fond of gaming. Except for Sir Duncan, who was perfectly pleasant, had danced with her three times, and had fetched her numerous glasses of ratafia. After everyone else she'd seen, he remained her best prospect for matrimony.

But he still wasn't Tristan.

Tristan was tall and dark and had a way of looking at a girl that just made the rest of the world fade away in a shimmering mist like that which hovered above the Galloway hills at sunrise. He was exciting, alive. Sir Duncan was kind, politely so, and utterly proper, but he was the sort of man who would never dream of so much as holding a girl's hand without first asking permission.

What was she going to do? She had less than a week remaining before her birthday. Only a few days after that, she would be returning to Galloway. Her time was fast running out. There was always Leap Year Day, she supposed, if matters didn't improve, but she really didn't relish the idea of running around the streets of Edinburgh in her red petticoat, proposing to every man she encountered under the age of eight-and-twenty. There had to be something else she could do, some place she could go. She'd already tried the bookshop, but had ended up meeting Tristan. Then the assembly—and again, Tristan. Perhaps a walk through the park, Harriet thought with hope, would prove her salvation.

But the park soon proved just as fruitless. Harriet circled the green once, twice, but only came upon nannies with children, or romantic couples of which the men were already plainly spoken for. One such couple, an elder pair, both greeted Harriet with a nod and a smile as they strolled arm-in-arm along the graveled walkway. Harriet found herself stopping on the path to watch them and admire the obvious devotion they had in their eyes for one another. It was the sort of devotion rooted in having spent years—even decades together. She wondered ruefully if she would ever know such happiness.

As they vanished from sight through the trees, Harriet tried to imagine her own life decades from then. Would she have someone to grow old with? Someone who would care for her in sickness, someone to share in the joy of a morning walk through the park with her? What if her marriage was a loveless one? What would she do when she no longer had her family around her? Both Auntie Gill and the baron were getting on in years, and Geoffrey would likely meet someone and fall in love with her and would spend the rest of his life surrounded by the children created of that love. Whenever Harriet tried to imagine such a happy scene for herself, a life surrounded by children and love, there was only one man she pictured beside her—

—the one man Fate wouldn't allow her to have.

Harriet was sitting on a bench lost deeply in thought, shaded by the winter-bare branches of an oak, when Robbie, who'd been sniffing at the ground by her slippers, shot up suddenly, bounding off for the opposite side of the park. His leash slipped hopelessly from Harriet's fingers before she could stop him.

"Robbie, no! Stop!"

He paid her no heed as he dashed beneath the cover of an evergreen and disappeared.

Harriet took up a handful of her skirts and ran as quickly as she could toward the trees where he'd gone, calling his name as she searched for his familiar brindly shape in the bushes. All she could hear was the distant sound of his barking. And then, a moment later, she could hear nothing more.

She came around a turn and was met by an empty expanse of green echoing with the nearby sounds of the streets. What if she lost Robbie in the city? He'd never been to Edinburgh before, wouldn't know his way around the twisting narrow alleys and wynds. He could easily dart into the street right as a carriage was driving by. He was so small, so fast, the driver would never see him.

"Robbie?" she called again. Her voice had grown desperate. "Where are you?"

"Good day," summoned a voice from the other side of a rather large oak. "I think perhaps the chap you're looking for is over here."

Harriet circled around to find a man who looked to be in his forties leaning against a vast granite boulder. A tall brown-and-white deerhound stood beside him, quite obviously the object of Robbie's attention, since Robbie, himself, stood right beside them, his pink tongue hanging out as he blinked at Harriet with his bright dark eyes.

"Oh, yes. That is him." Harriet bent down to retrieve his trailing leash. "I am so sorry we disturbed you, sir. I was lost in thought and he bolted before I ever had a chance to stop him. He never behaves this badly." She glared at him crossly. "That was very naughty of you, Robbie."

Robbie lowered his pointed ears in a gesture of repentance, but only for a moment.

The man, who was dressed as a gentleman in a brown frock coat and buff-colored breeches, simply smiled. He had light-colored hair, sort of a silvery sand, that was cut short and fell somewhat scattered about a high forehead. His rounded cheeks were rosy from the cold morning air, and his pale bluish-gray colored eyes beneath bushy brows had a weary sort of look about them.

"It was no trouble at all," he said. "Maida here didn't mind having some canine company."

Harriet reached to pet the other dog's slender snout. He was a beautiful creature, dwarfing Robbie beside him, with an elegant arch to his neck as he lifted his head to oblige her stroking fingers. "Well, I thank you for catching Robbie for me, sir," she said. "Naughty or not, I don't know what I would do without the little beast." She turned to the man. "By the way, sir, my name is Miss Ha—"

"Harriet," came a sudden unexpected third voice. "I would never have expected to see you here today."

Harriet turned about just as Tristan slipped from behind the cover of a tree. Harriet's heartbeat leapt at the mere sight of him. He looked incredibly handsome in nankeen breeches and coat with his dark hair ruffled by the breeze. He held a stick in his hand as he approached them, which he tossed a few yards away for Maida to fetch. Robbie bounded off behind the other dog.

"Tristan," she finally said. "What are you doing here?"

"Just taking a bit of the morning air with my godfather and Maida."

"You two are acquainted?" asked Tristan's godfather.

"Aye, sir. Harriet is Geoffrey Drynan's sister."

The man offered his hand in greeting. "Miss Drynan, I've heard much of you and your family over the years and am glad to finally make your acquaintance."

"As am I, Mr. . . . ?"

"Scott." He held up a small, leather-bound volume. "You're from Galloway. Tristan and I were just discussing your local poet, Robbie Burns." Harriet's dog scampered back to them at the sound of his name. "Would it be a fair guess to say that this little one was named for our fine poet?"

"Actually, no," Harriet replied. "I do enjoy Mr. Burns's poetry, although, truthfully, I much prefer novels. No, my Robbie is named for Rob Roy."

"Ah," he nodded. "The MacGregor."

"Yes, sir. One of my mother's ancestors actually knew the man. They haunted the hills of the Trossachs together, outwitting the government troops who sought to take the MacGregor in."

"He must have passed down many tales."

"Actually, according to my aunt, who knew the man when she was a child, he used to say that the exploits of the MacGregor written by the likes of Defoe and others had been so greatly exaggerated, that people no longer knew where fact left off and fiction took over. The Highland Scots, who knew the MacGregor, are the ones who keep the real legend of Rob Roy and his now vanished way of life for the succeeding generations."

"Indeed, it would be fascinating to talk to some of them." After a few moments, the man stood. "Well, I'd best be off. The skies to the north are fast growing dark and I've some work to finish while the day is yet light." He bowed his head to Harriet. "It was a pleasure meeting you, Miss Drynan." He stooped to scratch Robbie between the ears, "Likewise to you, Little Mr. Mac-Gregor. Tristan, I will see you later for supper at the house. Charlotte will expect you at seven."

At Tristan's nod, he stood and turned, calling to Maida who walked without a leash, never running ahead or falling behind, but staying close to his side. They made a genteel picture as they walked away together, and Harriet and Tristan watched them go until they'd faded from sight through the trees and they could hear the *thunk* of his godfather's walking cane no more.

"Your godfather is a very pleasant man, Tristan. I

enjoyed meeting him." And then she realized they were alone again together. She turned, looking at the sky. "It is getting late. I probably should be going."

"May I see you and Robbie home?"

Harriet looked at Tristan. After the events of the previous night, she knew she shouldn't accept his offer. She shouldn't even be with him there in the park as it was. Whenever Tristan was near, her thoughts became clouded, distracted, just like the sky overhead. But there was something about this man that made her feel truly alive, somehow more aware of her own femininity. And for this reason, Harriet found herself taking the arm he offered her. A walk home from the park would do no harm, she told herself. Her life, the one without Tristan in it, could wait one more day.

They strolled quietly together, Robbie tugging before them, each lost to their own thoughts as the breeze whistled around them, stirring leaves on the narrow garden pathway. Harriet glanced once at Tristan, studying his profile in the daylight shadows, and couldn't help but think back on the elderly couple she had seen earlier that morning. No matter what she did, it seemed, wherever she went, he always seemed near. If she wasn't destined to love him, to spend her life with him, why then did Fate persist in throwing them together? Was it to torment her, remind her each day that she couldn't be his . . .

. . . or was it perhaps to test her instead?

By the time they reached Charlotte Square, the skies above the city were dark with scudding clouds. The temperature, Harriet suddenly realized, had dropped dramatically since she had left the house earlier that morning. The wind had risen and now whipped across the secluded square, cutting through the thin fabric of her new spring spencer jacket.

She shivered as they approached the door to the Drynan town house.

"You are cold," Tristan said. "The weather is changing."

Harriet turned to stare at him. She blinked against

the wind. "It seems a common occurrence whenever we are together."

He frowned at her. "Harriet, I refuse to believe that a storm is brewing simply because we've spent a little time in each other's company. Do you really think that our walking together can change the pattern of the weather? That is the most ridicu—"

Just then, a single tiny bit of white floated past his nose. He looked at her. "Was that . . . ?"

"Yes, Tristan. It was a snowflake."

As they stood a few moments more, several others drifted by. Soon the snow was falling in windy swirls of white.

"It has been known to snow in February before," Tristan muttered.

Harriet shook her head in despair. "This is hopeless, Tristan. Don't you see? Someone is trying to tell us we shouldn't be together. If we were to ignore these warnings and marry against the wishes of those powers we cannot see, it would end up . . . it would create a natural disaster. I've been thinking about this ever since the assembly last night, Tristan. Even before that. I'm sorry, but for your sake and for mine, I cannot see you anymore."

She turned for the steps to leave, but stopped when she felt Tristan take her arm. "Harriet, don't—"

Harriet shook her head, closing her eyes tightly against the tears threatening to spill. She didn't look at him. "Tristan, please, I must go. I have an early supper engagement this evening and need to get ready."

"Sir Duncan Harrington, I presume?" His voice had grown clipped.

She turned to look at him. His expression was hard, angry. She didn't want to hurt him any more than she already had. "Yes. Lady Lucinda has invited my family to dine. We have accepted."

"Bloody hell you are . . ."

Tristan took the steps between them easily, closing in on Harriet and forcing her back against the stair railing until she could retreat no farther. She was so startled by his sudden advance, the closeness of his body to hers, she could but stare. His face was inches away, his breath hot against her cheek, his legs pinning hers beneath her skirts. He took her chin, forcing her to look at him. His eyes were filled with a dark unreadable emotion, his look so intense, Harriet knew then he was going to kiss her.

And he did, a moment later, seizing her mouth with his.

Harriet's senses swirled like the snowflakes on the wind that suddenly howled around them. She moaned and dropped her head back, dropping her arms to her sides, too overwhelmed by the feel of him, the taste of him, the power of him. Snowflakes fell freely against them as his tongue stroked hers, overtaking her, body and soul, with a kiss that made her his forever . . .

. . . a kiss that would be their last for all time.

They both knew it, and when Tristan pulled away a moment later, Harriet dropped her head forward and rested her temple against his chest. She didn't immediately open her eyes, but just stood there, feeling the beating of his heart, matching her every breath to his, reluctant to let go of that magic, clashing, crazy moment, because she knew when she did, it would be the last time Tristan would ever hold her like that again.

His eyes captured hers when she looked up at him, scorching her with gleaming blue fire.

"Will you think of me, Harriet," he said roughly, "of that kiss, when it is Sir Duncan who is holding you?"

Harriet swallowed hard. She couldn't answer. Tristan answered for her.

"Just remember, Harriet, a lifetime without passion in it will seem like two lifetimes." He released her suddenly as if he couldn't bear to be near her. "You needn't worry about any natural disasters any longer. I'll trouble you no more."

His words were so harsh, and so very *final*. Harriet knew something vital had just changed between them, and she couldn't help feeling as if she'd lost a most precious thing. Unable to say a word, she stood and watched helplessly as Tristan turned from her and walked away, snow dusting her eyelashes and melting against the warmth of her falling tears.

Supper at the Harringtons' began pleasantly enough, with Lord and Lady Harrington, Sir Duncan, Harriet, Devorgilla, and Sir Hugh all in attendance. The meal was excellent, salmon steamed with fresh herbs, roast mutton with vegetables, and bannocks fresh off the griddle. There was even a delicious lemon syllabub for dessert. Afterward, they withdrew to the parlor for cards and conversation.

Lord Harrington and Sir Hugh were comfortably established with a bottle of port by the hearth, discussing the politics of the day, leaving Harriet partnered by Devorgilla, and Lady Harrington partnered by Sir Duncan, to play at whist. Everything started off smoothly. Harriet and Devorgilla had taken the first round, and were well on their way to taking the second when the viscountess unwittingly changed the course of the evening by asking one simple question:

"Harriet dear, I've been wondering ever since the assembly, how is it you are acquainted with a man as notable as Lord Ravenshall?"

Harriet looked up suddenly from her cards. For the briefest of moments, she wondered if Lady Harrington had perhaps seen her with Tristan at the door of the town house earlier that day. She studied the viscountess's face in the lamplight, searching for a sign, any indication, and finally decided she was letting her imagination get the better of her. She answered calmly, "We are actually neighbors in Galloway, my lady. He and my brother were childhood friends and then served together on the Peninsula. I have known Lord Ravenshall all my life."

"I see . . ."

After that, conversation was about little else *but* Tristan, his military heroics, his sterling reputation, his potential as a prospective husband. Even when Tristan wasn't there, Harriet thought to herself, he still was.

"I declare," said the viscountess, "when word got out

the other night that Lord Ravenshall had returned to Edinburgh, I think every mother in town immediately set out to get their unmarried daughters in front of him. Can you imagine? He is quite the prize. Even when he was at university and living here in town, the viscount could turn any woman's eye from the age of six to sixty. If Wilhelmina and Rosalind weren't already wed, you can wager I'd be finding a way to get that man on his knee before one of them as quickly as possible." The viscountess quirked a brow over her cards, "Although from what I understand, he's already shown a marked interest in one lady in particular . . ."

Harriet blanched. Oh, God, Lady Harrington *had* seen Tristan kiss her . . .

"He has?"

"Oh, yes. And I must say Flavia Blum would make the viscount an ideal wife. She comes from a very good family, impeccable background. Why, she has . . ."

Flavia Blum? Was that the name of the young blond woman Tristan had danced with at the assembly?

"But he's only just met her," Harriet said more to herself than to anyone else.

"Well, I saw them dancing together at the assembly and the viscount couldn't take his eyes off her. I even commented on what a striking couple they made. Everyone agreed. I wouldn't be at all surprised if Lord Ravenshall proposes to dear Flavia before society quits town for the summer. They say he's come back to Scotland to settle down, assume his responsibilities, even set up a nursery . . ."

An image of a child with Tristan's blue eyes flashed to Harriet's thoughts. The idea of his creating that child with another made Harriet feel sick inside.

"Time will certainly tell, of course," Lady Harrington went on. "My guess is, if it does happen, it will be sooner than later. In fact, I understand from Flavia's mother, whom I chatted with just this afternoon, that Ravenshall is to take her on an outing to Arthur's Seat on Wednesday. He asked her just today."

Harriet nearly dropped her cards. Tristan was courting

Miss Blum? She thought back on his words, the look in his eye when he'd left her standing on the doorstep that morning.

I'll trouble you no more.

Had he left and gone straight from her to see Miss Blum?

"Is something the matter with the cards, dear?" Lady Harrington broke Harriet from her troubling thoughts. "You look positively bewildered."

Harriet shook her head. "No, no. I was just wondering . . ." She looked at the viscountess. "What is this Arthur's Seat?"

"Oh, it is really nothing more than a large hill that rises behind Holyrood at the far end of the High Street. They say it was formed from an extinct volcano and gives a stunning view of the town. Some have said it resembles a crouching lion." She smiled. "In my youth, it was the place where young lovers would go to spend time alone together."

"Indeed?" Harriet had only half heard that last bit, her attention still taken up with thoughts of Tristan taking the blond Miss Blum on such an intimate social outing. "I should like to see this Arthur's Seat."

"You would?" Lady Harrington smiled. "I'm sure Duncan would love to take you."

Sir Duncan's cheeks grew suddenly flushed. "You wish me . . . to take Miss Drynan to Arthur's Seat?"

"I would be most interested in seeing these volcanic formations," Harriet agreed.

"But—"

There came a thump from under the table that brought Duncan to staring at his aunt. "Of course, Miss Drynan, I should be happy to take you there. Tomorrow?"

Harriet thought for a moment. "I'm afraid I have an appointment with the modiste tomorrow that is sure to take some time. Then I had planned to catch up on some letter writing, and an afternoon at the lending library before we leave for Galloway at week's end. So that would rule out the next few days at least . . ."

"Can you go on Wednesday?" Sir Duncan asked.

Harriet smiled. "Why, yes. Yes, I think I can."

Devorgilla shot Harriet a look from across the table. Only she seemed to have caught on to the fact that Harriet had just deftly arranged their outing for the same day Tristan was taking Miss Blum. "Oh, but Harriet, have you forgotten? Wednesday is your birthday."

"Your birthday? How marvelous!" said the viscountess. "It is the perfect day for an outing then."

"Oh, but I'm afraid I cannot chaperone you that day," Devorgilla went on, doing everything she could to foil Harriet's plans. She knew the more time Harriet spent with Tristan, the more dangerous things could become. "I've already committed to tea with an acquaintance of mine."

"Oh, well, I can chaperone," Lady Harrington piped in. "Thankfully that odd bit of snow from this morning didn't stick, and the weather is already showing promise of a warm turn. By Wednesday, it is sure to feel more like spring. I'll have our cook prepare us a picnic basket to take along. We'll make a day of it."

Harriet looked at the viscountess and smiled. "I'm looking forward to it."

Chapter Eight

Why not seize the pleasure at once?
How often is happiness destroyed by
preparation, foolish preparation?
—Emma, *Jane Austen*

By midweek, the weather had turned positively spring-
like. The sun shone brightly, the birds trilled in trees
that had begun to sprout early leaves virtually overnight.

Lady Harrington, however, awoke on Wednesday
morning the victim of a fierce head cold.

"Oh, my dears," she said after a flurry of sneezes and
sniffles. "I just do not think it would be wise for me
to go."

She was tucked upon a chaise in the Harrington parlor, the very picture of misery, a blanket wrapped
around her legs, and a handkerchief laced with camphor
pressed against her red and stuffy nose. Miss Tibby, her
cat muff, lay curled and snoozing on the pillow beside
her.

"No, of course you will not go," Harriet agreed. "We
wouldn't dream of allowing it, would we, Sir Duncan?"
The viscountess sneezed again. "Do try some elderberry
tea for that, my lady. It is quite restorative."

Lady Harrington smiled her thanks before sneezing
again.

Duncan said to Harriet, "I'm afraid we'll have to post-
pone our outing till another day."

"Nonsense, Duncan!" Lady Harrington trumpeted
from behind her handkerchief. "Dear Harriet is leaving
Edinburgh only a few short days from now. Who knows
when she'll ever return? You . . . *she* might never get

this opportunity again. I shall simply send our maid Mildred along with you in my stead. *Millll-dred!*"

Within a quarter hour, they were rolling down Princes Street, picnic basket—and Mildred—at hand.

Visible for miles around the city, the misshapen peak of Arthur's Seat grew from a verdant carpet of turf strewn with grazing woolly sheep to a lofty series of crags at its towering summit. Hidden among the primitive formations were picturesque lochs and even an ancient ruin, where only the distant sounds of the city echoed on the wind.

"Shall we take our picnic now, Miss Drynan?"

They had been walking about for nearly an hour without any sign of either Tristan or Miss Blum. Perhaps they'd missed them, Harriet thought. Perhaps they had come earlier that morning, or better still, perhaps Miss Blum had caught Lady Harrington's same head cold and had to cry off.

"This looks like a nice spot," Sir Duncan said. "It affords a stunning view of the city."

Harriet had to agree. They stood upon a high bluff secluded by tufts of heather and gorse overlooking the whole of the city of Edinburgh. From their vantage, she could clearly see the High Street running through its center, looking from this distance like a vast herringbone with its countless narrow wynds and lanes branching off on either side. At its head, the maiden castle fortress rose like Olympus through the hovering mist.

They enjoyed a pleasant meal of cold chicken, oatcakes, and fruit the cook had packed for them while chatting quietly about the view, the pleasantness of the weather, other trivial things. It was indeed a splendid day, the sun shining its warmth from a blue sky stretching as far as the eye could see. Afterward, Sir Duncan offered to read a bit of poetry aloud from a book he'd brought with him while they stood on the heights appreciating the vista before them. But as he serenaded Harriet with delicate words about love and longing and loss, she scarcely heard him. She was far too occupied with searching the lower pathways for any sign of Tristan and Miss Blum.

She told herself she simply needed to talk to him, to tell Tristan he was making a mistake. Tristan was angry with her, she knew, reacting to her rejection of the other day, and had sought out Miss Blum because of it. Harriet didn't want to have been the one who had spurred him to rushing headlong into a hasty marriage he would regret for the rest of his life. What could he possibly know of this Miss Blum person? He'd danced with her *once*. He could not possibly have discovered her views on the world, her true character in the space of a single quadrille.

It, of course, never occurred to Harriet that she was doing much the very same thing with Sir Duncan.

"Miss Drynan?"

Harriet suddenly realized that Sir Duncan had finished reading. "Oh, I'm sorry, Sir Duncan. I must have gotten lost in my thoughts."

He looked at her strangely. "Miss Drynan, I would be much obliged if you would call me simply 'Duncan.'"

She smiled politely, peering beyond his shoulder to where their carriage was parked below, and where Mildred the maid was chatting with the coachman. "All right, Duncan. And you may call me Harriet."

Duncan was silent for a few moments. "Miss Drynan," he said, then corrected, "*Harriet,* I have been thinking of you often since we met at the assembly."

"And I you, Duncan. I have enjoyed spending time in your company."

Was that a footstep she heard? Harriet craned to see if anyone was approaching on the path below.

"I know we've only just met and scarcely know each other. I don't pretend to hide my financial troubles, but I wondered if . . . I wondered . . . oh, Harriet . . ."

Duncan suddenly seized Harriet around the waist, pulling her abruptly against him and pressed his lips tightly to hers in a kiss that was fraught with desperation, nervousness, and uncertainty. It didn't send her senses swirling the way Tristan's kisses did. In fact, truth be told, Harriet was so shocked by the gesture, she didn't immediately react. She just stood there, eyes wide, and waited for Duncan to release her.

Which he did, a moment later, when they heard the sound of someone clearing his throat behind them.

Duncan jerked away, his face coloring like a tomato. "Lord Ravenshall, I . . . I mean *we* were . . ."

Oh, God, Tristan.

Harriet was at once stunned, horrified, and humiliated beyond imagination. How had this happened? She had been watching for Tristan for hours, and he chose that very inopportune moment to show himself? She focused on the toe of her half-boot, wishing she were dreaming.

"Sorry to interrupt," came Tristan's chill voice, confirming for Harriet that this wasn't any dream. "Miss Blum and I had thought to check the view from here. We didn't know anyone else was about."

Harriet glanced upward. Tristan gave her one long, hard stare, his face set as rigid as the walls of stone that surrounded them. He made to turn. "We'll just be going on our way."

"No!" Harriet quickly spoke out. "Do not leave so soon, please, stay and join us for a little while." She yanked a bottle from the picnic basket. "We have wine . . . and shortbread. Let us drink a toast to . . . to your birthday, Tristan. Happy birthday."

Tristan stared at her. "And happy birthday to you, Harriet."

"You both share the same birthday?" asked Miss Blum. "How odd . . ."

Tristan hadn't wanted to come there at all that morning. Had he his choice he would be anywhere but there at that moment. It had been by a bad stroke of luck that he had run across Miss Blum and her mother moments after he had left Harriet at the doorstep the day he'd met her in the park. He'd been angry, upset, at his inability to make Harriet see reason. Mrs. Blum had sensed a moment of emotional weakness in him and had seized it, mentioning an outing to Arthur's Seat that left him no possible way of escape.

When he'd climbed that bluff only moments earlier, it had been to lose his thoughts to the incredible view he knew he'd find there. Instead he had found Harriet locked in another man's embrace, and it had taken every ounce of willpower he possessed not to explode. Tristan looked closely at Harriet as she sat on the blanket. Her face was flushed and her eyes were wild and her hands even trembled as she poured them each a glass of wine. Somehow he read in her eyes a plea . . . a plea for him not to leave her there alone? Could she have been as startled by Harrington's kiss as he'd been to come upon it?

He turned to the silent blonde standing beside him. "Miss Blum, would you like to stay?"

"I don't mind," she answered. "That was a bit of a climb." She looked at Sir Duncan, "As long as you're certain we aren't intruding."

"Not at all." Harriet answered for him, making space on the blanket beside them. "Here, please sit awhile."

She held out her hand to Miss Blum. "How do you do, Miss Blum? I've heard much about you from Lady Harrington. I am Harriet Macquair Drynan, but please call me Harriet." She went on chatting nonstop. "Have you ever been to Arthur's Seat before, Miss Blum? It is beautiful here, isn't it? You can see for miles around. I was wondering though how it got its name, Arthur's Seat."

Tristan decided to join them on the blanket. Sir Duncan was looking rather glum, and he found he liked that. "Legend has it that Camelot was built on its crest and slopes, and that the Kings of Fairydom lived within the caves that pierce the hill. Some try to discount the tale, of course, but there was actually a prince named Arthur who lived in Scotland in the sixth century, around the time of the earliest records of settlements around Edinburgh."

The conversation, and the wine, freely flowed. After a while, the foursome decided to walk together along the narrow mountain path, circling above Dunsapie Loch nestled far below the rocky heights. They stopped to observe some seabirds that had flown in off the firth before continuing upward toward rockier ground.

Tristan was pointing out a few of the more distinguishable landmarks on the horizon to Sir Duncan and Miss Blum, discussing the city at various times throughout history. He didn't realize until he turned sometime later, and noticed the vacant space behind them, that one of their party was suddenly missing.

"Harriet?" he called, scanning the area nearby.

She didn't answer.

"Is something the matter?" Miss Blum asked beside him.

"Harriet must have wandered off a bit in her explorations," he answered. "Do you remember where you last saw her?"

"I thought she was inspecting that formation of rocks over there." She pointed to where now there stood no one.

"Do you suppose she has gone back down to the bluff where we picnicked?" suggested Sir Duncan.

No matter her enthusiasm for wandering, it wasn't like Harriet not to answer when someone called. Which only meant one thing: she was too far away to hear him.

"I suppose it is possible," Tristan answered, trying not to worry. "Sir Duncan, why don't you take Miss Blum back down the hill to the carriages. The skies have begun to darken and it looks as if a storm is brewing." He ignored the fleeting thought that once again, when he'd been with Harriet, the weather had taken a sudden turn. "We don't need for another one of us to get lost."

"Do you fear Miss Drynan is lost?"

"I don't know. I don't think so. In any case, I am very familiar with the area up here, so I will more easily find her. If it should start to rain before we return, please see Miss Blum home safely."

Sir Duncan reluctantly agreed. He really had no other choice.

When they'd gone, Tristan took a moment to think. He tried not to consider all the many perils that could befall a young lady alone up on these heights. There were sheer cliffs easy to slip from and pathways that wandered aimlessly for well over a mile. He remembered, too, when he'd been a lad, hearing tales of the gypsies who'd been known to lurk about the Dasses and the brush beneath Salisbury Crags. Harriet could easily be dragged off, if not by a gypsy, then by any other convenient fiend.

"Harriet!" he shouted to the now gusting wind.

Tristan glanced at the gathering clouds that were moving in swiftly from the firth. His uneasiness grew. *Little idiot. What was she thinking wandering off like that?* He started backtracking the way they'd come. It took him at least a quarter hour to circle the bog. Just as he came back around to the bluff where he'd first happened upon Harriet with Sir Duncan earlier, the rain began to fall.

"Harriet, damn it, answer me!"

He turned and stared through the rain at the great rock face of the ancient peak before him. She could be anywhere up there among the countless crags and crevices and—

—*caves*.

Tristan turned and headed at once for the far path.

Harriet was lost in more ways than one.

She had allowed her curiosity to get the better of her, stupidly wandering off amid a place where each rock had begun to look like the next. Somehow, before she realized it, she'd gotten separated from the others. She was now sitting in the shelter of a secluded cave, watching the rain fall outside. She was freezing, her teeth chattering against the damp inside the cave. It had been so warm and pleasant that morning, she hadn't bothered to bring a shawl. Thankfully, she had offered to carry the blanket after their picnic and so wrapped it around her shoulders to ward off the chill. She wasn't too worried. She knew that once the rain stopped, she would find her way back down eventually. The city was, after all, plainly visible below. The question was what would she do when she got there? The twenty-ninth of February was but a day away, her last chance—maybe her only chance—in which to secure herself a husband. But *who*?

Sir Duncan was younger than her, yes, and everything that was amiable and kind. He seemed interested in the things she had to say, asking about her childhood at Rascarrel, the books she liked to read. He wasn't given to any falsehood, freely admitting that his estate in Aberdeen was badly in need of repair. He'd admitted, too, that he hadn't the funds to see to it. She knew if she asked him to marry, he'd likely accept, even if he didn't love her. He was dependent upon his uncle and aunt, and to refuse Harriet and her dowry would be foolhardy.

So why not simply marry him?

The answer was clear in Tristan's words echoing on the keening wind.

Will you think of me, of that kiss, when it is Sir Duncan who is holding you . . .

The truth was, in that urgent moment when Sir Duncan had so earnestly kissed her, Harriet had thought of nothing else but Tristan.

He had been right. Duncan's kiss had not been the sort that would fill her days with excitement, looking forward to the moment when she might steal another. His had been a kiss of routine, of "this-is-what-I'm-supposed-to-do-so-I'll-do-it." And while she might spend hours cataloging Sir Duncan's good points, assigning him qualities he himself probably wouldn't admit to, in the end, Harriet still found herself thinking about, longing for, Tristan.

And she knew she always would.

Just a single look from him sent her heart racing to the clouds. When she looked at Sir Duncan, all she could think of was the fact that if they were to wed, she would thereafter be known as Lady Harriet Harrington.

That thought alone was enough to make one think twice.

Tristan knew her so well, so completely. He knew her thoughts without her ever having to speak them. He knew her dreams unlike any other. But could she risk the danger of the Macquair prophecy? Somehow history had to be mistaken? In her heart, Tristan was the man she was meant to know and love, whether he was born one minute, one hour, before her or after. All her life, Harriet had been told the story of the Macquair maiden, of the young lad who had unjustly been denied the hand of his beloved bride simply because of his youth. But wasn't this the same injustice, the denial of true love because of the technicality of a single day?

Surely her sorceress-ancestress could not condone her curse preventing the happiness of another pair of true lovers. Harriet looked outside the cave opening, peering solemnly at the glowering sky, high above the dark rolling clouds, where all the mysteries of the universe lurked and said aloud in a voice strong and clear, "Guide me, spirit of the Macquairs, maidens who came before me. Send me a sign, some indication of the course that I should follow."

A flash of lightning severed the sky, illuminating the whole of the mountain peak. A moment later, a vision of Tristan appeared before her.

It was all the answer she needed.

"Harriet, thank God. Where in the hell have you—"

Tristan never finished his thought. Harriet stood and crossed the distance to meet him, throwing her arms around his neck and pulling his mouth to hers in a kiss that sealed their fates forever.

He didn't speak. He didn't have to. He only took Harriet up in his arms, looking deeply into those gray-green eyes he knew and loved so completely, and carried her back inside the cave. He laid her on the blanket and kept on kissing her until the two of them were naked and wrapped in one another's arms. The rain outside fell harder, the wind building and howling with each kiss they shared. Inside that cave, a destiny written centuries earlier was finally realized.

Lightning flashed against the darkness of the sky and thunder that rivaled the trembling of the earth crashed above them the moment Tristan joined their bodies as one. Harriet no longer cared for she was at the very place she belonged. A deluge could unleash its fury on the rest of the world outside that cave, but nothing was going to prevent her from loving this man for the rest of her life. She twined her fingers through his hair. She nestled further into the circle of his arms. Forever after, the sounds of the storm would be their own passionate serenade.

A tempest the likes of which Edinburgh hadn't seen in decades rocked the Scottish capital city throughout the night. Streets flooded, trees were felled, while in a cave high above the turmoil, two lovers endured another fury . . .

. . . that most beautiful fury of all.

Chapter Nine

There is one thing . . . which a man can always do,
if he chooses, and that is, his duty;
not by manœuvering and finessing,
but by vigour and resolution.
—Emma, *Jane Austen*

When morning dawned, Harriet awoke in the arms of
the man she knew she was destined to love. The sun
was shining, birds trilled in the trees. Peace and harmony
reigned over the land. The world had not ceased its spinning overnight. The oceans had not risen up in protest.
Everything was precisely as it should be.

They dressed slowly, undressed again, and then
dressed again an hour later. Together they descended
the heights of that incredible mountain and walked hand
in hand through the city streets all the way to Charlotte
Square. A tender peace filled Harriet, a complete and
utter happiness with all that her world had become. No
longer did she question her future, no longer did she
struggle in search of her destiny. Her destiny, she knew,
stood right beside her.

The peace and the calm, however, were to be shattered the moment they walked through the front door.

"Harriet!"

Geoffrey's booming voice, coupled with that of her
father rose up to greet them. Harriet and Tristan looked
at one another before they stepped into the doorway
to the parlor where it seemed all of Edinburgh society
had converged.

Sir Hugh, Geoffrey, and Devorgilla took up the far
corner, while Sir Duncan and Lady Harrington, complete with her cat, huddled on the settee. Tristan's godfa-

ther, Mr. Scott, stood at the window and had no doubt seen them approaching off the square. All the party lacked was the presence of Miss Flavia Blum to make it complete.

"I expect you will do the honorable thing, Ravenshall," Sir Hugh said before Harriet could utter a single word. Devorgilla kept silent, sitting in the corner chair by the window. Her face, however, was openly ominous.

"I have every intention of it, sir," answered Tristan, setting his arm more closely about Harriet's waist.

Lady Harrington stood, her eyes fixed on Harriet as she crossed the room. Her face was a mask of non-expression.

"Lady Harrington, I—"

"Tut, tut, dear," the viscountess said. "I am just relieved to see you are safe." She smiled. "Everything else is just as it should be." She turned to her nephew. "Come, Duncan, we must go home and inform Lord H. that our friend is safely home, and leave this family to their privacy."

Duncan shot Harriet a nervous glance as he crossed the room.

"Duncan," she said, stopping him, "I am sorry if I led you to thinking my feelings for you were more than those of friendship. I truly have enjoyed meeting you. I hope that this won't mean an end to our acquaintance."

He shook his head. "Not at all, Harriet. Like a pair of gloves, a person knows when something doesn't fit. We weren't a right fit. We might have managed, as some people do with a pair of gloves where the fingers are just a little too long, but two people should never end up together because of desperate circumstances. It makes for a lifetime of regrets."

Harriet smiled at him, startled by his unusual wisdom. She realized then there was more to Sir Duncan Harrington than she'd ever allowed herself to see and she hoped, truly hoped, he would find his "right fit" someday.

After they'd gone, Harriet turned to her father. "Father, I have something to tell you."

"And I have something to tell you, too, Harriet Macquair Drynan. I'll have no more of this nonsense of younger husbands. Tristan is a good man. The only man good enough for my daughter. What does it matter if he was born February the twenty-eighth or not?"

"If I may interject a moment . . ."

Everyone turned at once to where Tristan's godfather still stood at the window.

"Right before you two arrived, moments before really, Harriet's aunt was telling me the story of your family's legend, of this curse prophesizing that Harriet must marry a younger man—"

"It doesn't matter, sir," Harriet broke in. "I have every intention of spending my life with Tristan." She looked at her aunt. "Please, Auntie Gill, you of all people must understand. What is life without love? Without happiness? It isn't a life at all. Somehow I just know I am meant to be with Tristan. I know he isn't younger than I am, but he's close enough."

Devorgilla looked at her, tears filling her eyes. She nodded quietly as if to say what would be . . . would be.

"Truth be told, Miss Drynan," Mr. Scott said, then, "Tristan really is younger than you are."

"What?" It was a collective response that came from everyone else in the room.

"Tristan was born on February the twenty-ninth, a Leap Year Day. I know this well. I was there, and if you seek out the Ravenshall parish register, Tristan, you will see that I speak the truth. Your parents simply decided to celebrate the occasion on the twenty-eighth, to avoid the confusion that would come about with every fourth year."

Tristan stared at his godfather, clearly as stunned as the rest of them. "They never told me that."

Mr. Scott simply shrugged. "After a while, years of always celebrating the occasion on the twenty-eighth, no doubt they simply forgot about it. It wasn't as if that one day was going to make any difference." He chuckled. "Of course, they could never have foreseen these particular circumstances."

Harriet was grinning as she turned to face Tristan. "So you really are younger than I am."

"It would seem so, my love. By a day."

"So all this trouble was for nothing?"

"No, not for nothing." He took her into his embrace. "If anything, it proves that what is destined to be, will be. We were both willing to risk anything, even the wrath of an ancient sorceress's curse, to be together." He smiled at her. "Otherwise, I might never have known if you truly loved me, or if you had married me simply because I happened to be younger than you."

"Tristan . . ." Harriet said.

"Yes, my love?"

"Happy birthday." She reached up to give him a kiss. She giggled when she stepped away a moment later. "Now let me go fetch that red petticoat . . ."

Epilogue

*A heroine returning, at the close of her career,
to her native village, all in the triumph of recovered
reputation and all the dignity of the countess.*
—Northanger Abbey, *Jane Austen*

Ravenshall Tower, 1818

Harriet strode into the breakfast parlor, her eyes glued
to a letter she'd received from Lady Harrington in that
morning's post. Tristan was there, as was the nursery
maid who was feeding their daughter Viola her morning
porridge. Harriet stopped to press a kiss to the little
one's sunshine-kissed red curls before lowering into the
chair beside her.

"Lady Harrington has invited us to a wedding, Tristan." She looked at her husband. "It seems Duncan has
asked Miss Blum to be his wife, and she has accepted."

Tristan nodded over his toast and jam. "A fine couple,
although, actually, I'm surprised it took Lady H. this
long."

Harriet set aside the letter. It was then she noticed
the package sitting beside her breakfast plate. "What
is this?"

"That, my dear, arrived for you by courier just a little
while ago," Tristan replied as he poured her a cup of
her favorite tea. He took her hand and kissed it. "It
comes to you from Edinburgh."

Harriet narrowed her eyes on him. "Why do I sense
you already know something about this?"

Tristan simply took a bite of his toast, saying nothing.

Harriet took up the package and untied the string that
held it. Inside was a small, leather-bound book wrapped
in a brown paper cover. Printed on the front page, its

title read: *Rob Roy, by the Author of Waverley, Guy Mannering, and The Antiquary.*

She looked at Tristan. "Who is this from?"

"Why don't you read the inscription inside and find out?"

Harriet scowled at him, then turned the page to where the following words had been written.

To Dearest Harriet, My gratitude for the suggestion.

It was signed simply, *Walter Scott.*

Harriet blinked. She read it again. *Mr. Scott, Tristan's godfather?*

Harriet looked at Tristan, stunned. "Walter Scott? Your godfather, Mr. Scott, is the author, Walter Scott?"

He nodded. "Aye, one and the same."

"But why did you never tell me before? We've spoken of him often. He was present at our wedding, for heaven's sake . . . yet you've never told me his first name!"

Tristan grinned, his blue eyes twinkling as he looked at her. "Did you think your family was the only one to have its secrets?"

Author's Note

In the Scottish capital city of Edinburgh, in the middle of the Princes Street Gardens, there stands a monument over two hundred feet tall erected in memory of Sir Walter Scott. There are two hundred and eighty-seven steps to the top, and carved into the monument are sixty-four niches in which statuettes of many of his characters can be found. Beneath its gothic arches stands a white marble statue of Scott with his faithful deerhound, Maida, sitting at his side.

Scott's novels are steeped in the traditions and customs of Scotland. Although this story is purely a work of my imagination, his authorship of what are now called the Waverley Novels was indeed, as I indicated, unknown for many years. It is a mystery that Scott himself seems to have enjoyed prolonging; he didn't officially reveal himself as the author until 1827, at a public dinner in Edinburgh held at the same Assembly Rooms in which Harriet first searched for a husband.

I recently had the privilege of visiting Abbottsford, Scott's country home located south of Edinburgh, after I'd already finished writing this story. It is an incredible place. In his lifetime Scott acquired such items as Rob Roy's own broadsword, dirk, and pistol, which are displayed on the walls. I spent hours there, imagining Scott sitting at the very desk where he wrote his wonderful stories, the hallways echoing with the laughter of his children and the barking of his numerous dogs.

As I walked through the last room on our tour, I happened to catch a glimpse of a portrait of Scott's wife, Charlotte, that hung on a wall in the dining room. Her name was engraved on the plate beneath it, along with the dates of her birth and death. As I stood admiring her image, I noticed something I had never realized before, but that gave me that shiver of wonder authors sometimes get when everything about a story suddenly falls into place.

Scott was born in 1771.

His wife, Charlotte, was born in 1770.

Sir Walter Scott was married to a woman who was older than he.

About the Author

From the time she read *Harriet the Spy* at age seven, Jaclyn Reding knew she wanted to be a writer. The leap from child spy to novelist was fostered in years of concealing paperbacks behind her high school textbooks, and in her college studies of English history and literature. Jaclyn believes there is no better career than that of a writer. "Accountants," one of which she is married to, she says, "don't get paid to daydream, can't go to work in their pajamas, and certainly aren't allowed to write off their fifteenth rental of a Jane Austen video on their tax returns."

Born in the Midwest, Jaclyn makes her home in Arizona with her husband, young son, and various other domestic creatures. In addition to writing, her passions include playing her flute very badly, haunting antique bookshops, and making a spectacle of herself by cheering very loudly at her son's hockey games.

You can visit her on the Web at:

http://www.jaclynreding.com

The Demon's Mistress

Jo Beverley

Chapter One

London
April 1816

Glorious spring sunshine beamed through the open curtains, and the raised window let in courting birdsong. Nearby, people chattered amid their busy lives, and wheels rattled as a horse and cart hurried down the back lane.

The golden light danced on the disheveled hair and ravaged classic features of a young man lolling in the faded armchair beside the window. It glinted off half-lowered lashes and golden stubble that suggested a night without sleep or orderly waking, and dug deep into a jagged scar down one cheek that told of more dangerous adventures in the past.

His legs, in breeches and well-worn boots, stretched before him, and a half-full wineglass tilted in his lax, long-fingered hand.

On a round table by his elbow stood a decanter with an inch or so of pale amber wine, and a plain, practical pistol.

He raised the glass and sipped, seeming intent on the garden outside the window, but in fact Lord Vandeimen's gaze was directed at nothing close or visible. He looked at the past, both recent and far, and with increasing, slightly fretful curiosity, at the future.

Switching the glass to his left hand, he placed two

fingers on the cold metal of the pistol barrel. His father's pistol, used for the same purpose nearly a year before.

So easy.

So quick.

So why was he waiting?

Hamlet had had something to say about that.

In his case, he decided, he was pausing to enjoy this particularly fine wine. After all, he'd spent nearly all his last coins on it. He must be careful not to drift away under its influence and waste this moment of resolution. One bottle hadn't put him under the table since he was a lad, though.

So long ago, those days of wicked youthful adventures. Was it really less than ten years since he'd been a carefree youth, running wild on the Sussex Downs with Con and Hawk?

No, not carefree. Even children and youths have cares. But blessedly free of the weightier burdens of life.

The three Georges. The triumvirate.

His drifting mind settled on the day they'd tired of having the same patriotic name and rechristened themselves. Hawk Hawkinville. Van Vandeimen. It should have been Somer Somerford, but Con had balked at such a effete name. He'd taken a variation of his second name, Connaught. Con.

Con, Hawk, and Van. They'd grown up like brothers, almost like triplets. Back in those days they'd not imagined a time when they'd be so apart, but Van was glad the other two weren't here now, With luck, they'd hear of his death when it was history, the pain of it numbed. They hadn't seen each other since Waterloo.

Con had returned home directly after the battle, but Hawk and Van had lingered awhile. Hawk was still with the army now, tidying up Europe. Van had been in England for four months, but he'd carefully avoided his home and old friends.

He drained the glass and refilled it, his hand reassuringly steady. It was strange that Con hadn't hunted him down. Any other time, that would have worried him, but not now. If Con didn't care, that was good.

No friends. No family.

Once, in another life, there had been so much more. When he'd left at sixteen to join his regiment, mother, father, and two sisters had waved farewell. Ten years later, all were shades. Did they watch him now? If so, what did their ghostly voices cry? Wouldn't they want him to join them?

"Don't protest to me, old man," he said to his ghostly father. "You took the same way out when you were left alone. And what have I—? Oh, devil take it!" he snapped, slamming down the glass and seizing the pistol. "When I start talking to ghosts, it's time."

Impelled by some mythical urge, he picked up the glass and poured the remaining wine to stream and puddle on the waxed floor. "An offering to the gods," he said. "May they be merciful."

Then he put the long barrel cold into his mouth and with a final breath and a prayer squeezed the trigger.

The click was loud, but a click didn't kill. He pulled the gun out and stared at it with wild exasperation. A flick showed him the problem. The flint of the old-fashioned pistol had worn and slipped sideways.

"Shoddy work, Van," he muttered, desperately trying to think whether he had a fresh flint anywhere in his rooms, his hands trembling now. If he had to go out and find one, the moment might pass. He might try again to pull his life out of the pit.

He knew he didn't have a fresh flint, so he poked out the old one, sweat chilling his brow and his nape, and tried to fix it so it would work. He'd drunk enough to make himself clumsy. "Plague and tarnation, and hell, and damnation, and—"

"Stop!"

He looked up, dazed, to see a figure standing in his doorway, draped in white, crowned in white, hand outstretched, looking like a stern Byzantine angel . . .

Smooth oval face, long nose, firm lips.

A woman.

She swept forward to grip the pistol barrel. "You must not!"

He kept a hand tight on the butt. "What the devil business is it of yours, madam?"

An elegant woman in high fashion, including a turban-style hat with a tall feather. Where the pox had she come from, and what business was he of hers?

Her steady eyes held his. "I need you, Lord Vandeimen. You can kill yourself later."

He dragged the pistol out of her gloved hands. "I can kill myself anytime I damn well please, and take you with me!"

She straightened, looking down her long nose. "Not with only one pistol ball."

"There are many ways of killing, and I'll save the pistol for myself."

He saw her pale and suck in breath, but when she spoke it was steadily. "Give me a few minutes of your time, my lord. Then, on my word, if you still wish it, I will leave you to your purpose."

Such scorn. Such judgment in those blue-gray eyes. If the pistol had been working, he might have shot her to wipe away that scorn. He immediately put the weapon down.

She snatched it and retreated a few wise steps, pistol clutched to her creamy gown. Then she looked down at it, shuddered, and placed it on his open desk by the papers he'd carefully prepared.

Curiosity suddenly wiped out anger and urgency.

This woman knew him, but he had no idea who she was. Not surprising, since he hadn't been moving in fashionable circles.

Her gown was in the height of fashion, as was the long, pale cashmere shawl that looped over both elbows and almost trailed the ground. He knew enough of women's furbelows to price that shawl at a sum that would reroof Steynings.

It wouldn't fix the damaged plaster or the rotting wood, but the roof would be a start.

"Well?" he asked, linking his hands, ready to enjoy this interlude at the gates of hell.

She subsided into the chair that matched his, then jumped when it sagged down beneath her.

"It hasn't collapsed under anyone yet," he remarked. "Am I to know your name, or is this all cloaked in hoary mystery?"

Color blossomed in her creamy skin, making her look less like a plaster saint, and much more interesting in a fleshy way. He suddenly wondered what she'd look like far gone in sex, which was another thought he'd not expected to have again.

"My name is Maria Celestin."

His brows rose. The Golden Lily. The wealthy widow who had just emerged from mourning, causing every red-blooded fortune hunter to seethe with desire. Someone had suggested that he pursue the woman as the solution to his woes.

She'd have to be insane to marry him, however, and he'd no mind to marry a madwoman.

He knew the age of the Golden Lily. Thirty-three. That explained her composure and steady eyes. He knew her bloodlines. She'd been born a Dunpott-Ffyfe and married down to some upstart foreign merchant.

"And your purpose here, Mrs. Celestin? If you are seeking consolation of the flesh, I regret that I am neither in the mood nor the state to oblige."

"Then it is as well that I am not, my lord."

She didn't blush. Perhaps she'd heard the same too often. Distressing to be cliché.

She too had linked her hands in front of her, and now she'd grown accustomed to the chair she was trying to be elegant and composed. She wasn't, though. She was wound tight as a watch spring like a raw recruit on the brink of battle.

Gad, he hoped she wasn't here to fight for his immortal soul.

"You lost ten thousand at Brooks' last night, my lord."

It stung, but he hoped that didn't show. "And how did you find out about that, Mrs. Celestin?"

"There were many people there. Word is out. You cannot possibly pay."

He looked down at his hands before gathering enough will to meet her eyes coolly. "My estates, decrepit though they are, will probably settle the bill."

"I will pay that debt in return for your services for six weeks."

He hadn't expected to feel shock again. "You *do* want consolation of the flesh."

Now she did blush, though her tone was chilly. "It seems an obsession of yours, my lord. Unfortunately for you, I am not at all interested." She even dared to look him over, briefly, with patent lack of interest. "What I require is an escort and a bodyguard."

"Hire a dragoon, madam."

He began to rise, ready to throw her out, but something in her steady gaze pushed him back into his chair. Whatever this was about, she was deadly serious.

"A dragoon would not serve, my lord. To be precise, I wish you to pose as my affianced husband for the next six weeks, in payment for which I will give you ten thousand pounds. What is more, if you fulfill our agreement to the letter, I will give you a further ten thousand pounds at the end. You can drink it, game it, or use it to rescue your estates. That will be up to you."

The little beat of excitement that started in his chest was a betrayal. He was as good as dead, dammit. He didn't want this now.

He was lying.

It was the chance, the new beginning he'd been hunting for months. He wouldn't show hope or excitement. He wouldn't reveal his need to this madwoman.

"Tempting," he drawled. "I have learned, however, that if a bargain appears too good to be true, it probably is."

Her neatly arched brows rose. "What trap do you foresee? That I hold you to our mock betrothal? Do you object to marrying a fortune?"

"Not at all. Why don't we simplify everything by marrying now?"

"Because you drink too much, and game too wildly, and, it would seem, choose the easy way out."

He knew he was turning red. "I see. So, what benefit do you find in your strange arrangement that is worth twenty thousand pounds?"

She rose with admirable smoothness, rearranging her fabulous shawl so it didn't drag on the floor. He was suddenly aware of full breasts and round hips beneath the elegant vertical flow of her ivory gown. Inappropriate for an almost-dead man to note such things but she was, in a chilly way, a very attractive woman.

"My purposes are none of your concern, my lord," she said in a voice one might use to a greengrocer. "I merely require you to engage yourself to marry me, and to act for the next six weeks as if that were true. This does mean," she added pointedly, "that you will have to act like a man I might wish to marry."

"Ah," he said, belatedly rising. The room wavered slightly, and he hadn't drunk enough for that. He wondered if the pistol had worked, if this was some heavenly illusion.

"What dreams may come. . . ."

The smell of spilled wine soured the air, however. Surely heaven could do better than that. "You will expect me to resist excessive drink and gaming, madam? Gad, will I have to squire you to Almack's? They'd never let me in."

"Almack's is boring. Balls, routs, breakfasts, masquerades . . ." She gestured vaguely with a hand covered by fine cream kid in color remarkably like her fine cream skin. "I will require you to escort me to most events I attend, to stay by my side for the usual amount of time, and to be well mannered and sober. When not by my side, you will do nothing to shame my choice."

"Alas. I must avoid my favorite opium dens and wild wenches?"

"You must avoid anyone hearing about them." She looked him in the eye, despite being six inches shorter. "You are in love with me, Lord Vandeimen. For six weeks, and a payment of twenty thousand pounds, in the eyes of the world, you adore me."

"Do I get to kiss you, then?" he asked, advancing on her, suddenly furious at this demanding woman who thought she could buy him, body and soul.

And probably could.

He found himself looking down the barrel of his pistol, held in her steady, but tense, hands. "You will never, ever, touch me without my permission."

He smiled at the pointless threat. "Why not pull the trigger?" he drawled. "That will achieve my end, and save me from the sin of self-destruction."

Her eyes widened, and for the first time he saw overt fear. She'd put herself in a situation she didn't understand and couldn't control, and had the wit to know it.

It was about time she learned some other lessons.

Glancing to one side to distract her, he snatched the pistol. She gasped and stepped back, pale becoming pallid.

He was tempted to seize her, press the useless pistol to her lush breasts, and claim the kiss he'd threatened. Disgusted by that, he snapped, "Leave."

She looked at him, breathing rapidly. "You are rejecting my offer?"

He wanted to say yes, but the same impulse that had sent him to the tables ruled him here. "No. You've bought six weeks of my life, Mrs. Celestin. I accept your terms. However, I'll need an advance on the second ten thousand if I'm to put on a show worthy of you. I am literally penniless."

Now she had what she wanted, she attempted her former manner, but she couldn't hide her fear. Not a foolish woman, at least.

"I'll deposit eleven thousand for you at Perry's Bank," she said, a touch of panic fluttering in her voice. "One thousand is advance on our final settlement. Arrange your affairs, my lord, and have a night's rest. We can meet formally tomorrow at the Duchess of Yeovil's ball. Do you have an invitation?"

He glanced at the messy pile of cards and envelopes on the desk. "Probably. Even a ruined lord is a lord."

She too looked at the pile, lips suddenly pursing. What was it? A powerful urge to organize? Was she a meddle-some, managing woman? He almost set limits on their bargain, especially that she keep her fingers out of his affairs, but why fool himself? He'd come this far and would go further if necessary.

He'd sell himself to her in any way she wanted for nine thousand clear and a fresh start. She didn't need to know that, however.

"Is that all, Mrs. Celestin?" he asked in a bored tone, pistol still in his hand.

She jerked slightly, nodded, and after a hesitation where she clearly felt there was more to be said, walking rapidly out of the room.

Maria paused for a moment on the landing, a faint shudder passing through her. Athena, but she'd almost been too late. A few more seconds . . . ! And then she'd pointed his pistol at him, threatening to kill him.

She pressed a gloved hand to her mouth. Was any-thing more absurd? She'd never held a pistol before in her life, and then he'd dared her to kill him as if he wanted it! He was so young, so full of promise. Was self-destruction too deeply rooted to be pulled out?

Then he'd taken the weapon from her. So easily. She should have expected that from a man known as Demon Vandeimen. She should have expected that uncivilized edge anyway. He'd survived a long and bloody war. Of course he wasn't safe!

She hurried out of the house. Her liveried footman leaped forward to open the carriage door and assist her in to sit beside her aunt.

Harriette Coombs, round in face and body, was merry by nature, but knew when to worry. Like Maria, she was a widow, but she had enjoyed thirty years of happy marriage instead of ten years of mixed blessings. She had three children set up in the world, whereas Maria had none.

Maria sometimes felt that except for wealth, she had nothing. No, not true. She had Aunt Harriette.

"Home," she said, and as soon as the footman shut the door, the coach began to roll away from the most difficult thing she had done in her life.

"Well?" asked Harriette.

"I was almost too late! He was . . . No one answered the door. Some instinct made me enter anyway, and he was . . . He had a pistol in his hand, ready to fire!"

"By my soul! You promised him the money, dear? He will be different now?"

"I did, but—" It had all been done in urgency and on impulse, and now reaction was setting in.

"He looked so terrible, Harriette. Haggard. Clothes all awry. The room stank of wine and he was drunk. I was going to pretend the money was an old informal debt, but I knew I couldn't do that. He'd probably have gamed it away tomorrow!"

"So what did you do?"

Maria bit her lip, unwilling to even put her ridiculous plan into word. "I . . . I bought him. For six weeks. For six weeks, Lord Vandeimen is to be my besotted, impeccably behaved, husband-to-be and escort."

Harriette's eyes widened, but she said, "Very clever, dear! If he has any honor at all, he will have to behave well, and it may give him a chance to change."

"Will it work?"

Harriette patted her hand. "You've done the best you can, dear. It will expose you to talk, though."

"Oh! I'll look like—"

"A widow after tender meat."

"A tender wastrel, even. People will think me a complete fool. Or a predatory harpy. Harriette, he's eight years younger than I am!"

"I was eight years younger than Cedric."

"It's not the same." Maria sucked in a deep breath. "I have to do it, though. Maurice swindled his father out of that money. Ruined him, and pushed him to suicide. I have to put it right, at any cost."

She leaned her head back against the satin squabs.

"Did I mention that he is beautiful? Hair the color of primroses. Classic bones. Lips so perfect they could have been carved. A mess, of course, after the wild life he's led recently, and scarred. But still, Lord Vandeimen is the most beautiful young man I ever stood face to face with."

And the world would think her turned idiot because of it.

Harriette squeezed her hand. "Don't worry, dear. While you're pulling him back from the brink, I'll look around for a suitable young lady for him, one with a strength of character and a generous dowry."

Maria smiled. "Thank you. I don't know what I'd do without you."

She firmly ignored a betraying stir of dissatisfaction with that plan.

Chapter Two

Van woke when the clock persistently chimed. Damn it, he'd drifted into a daze or a doze. He sank his head into his hands. Wine and a sleepless night had given him a tantalizing dream. Twenty thousand pounds. If only it were true.

He suddenly looked around the room. Had it been a dream?

His pistol still lay on the table, but then, he'd taken it from her and put it there. She hadn't conveniently left her shawl, or a glass slipper.

The Golden Lily. Could his imagination really have conjured up a flesh-and-blood woman of such distinctive appearance? That long, sleekly curved elegance and smooth oval face. That creamy skin which flushed so delicately when another woman would have been beet red, and gone waxy with fear.

Hell. He'd deliberately frightened her!

But no one was mad enough to offer twenty thousand pounds for nothing. It must have been a dream.

But what if—?

He was trying to sift truth from fantasy when someone tapped tentatively on his door. His heart suddenly raced. Was she back, but more cautious now?

"Yes?"

The door creaked open, and his valet, Noons, peered around it. His ex-valet.

Disappointment swept through him like a chill. "What the devil are you doing here?"

Wizened Noons smiled tentatively. "Begging your pardon, my lord, but I went as you ordered. But I got to thinking about how you'd manage alone. You know you're no hand with your clothes, my lord. I'd be more than happy to stay with you until things come right again. And then stay on," he added hastily. "Begging your lordship's pardon . . ."

Van closed his eyes. If his pistol had worked, poor Noons would have returned to find the body, and after he'd dismissed him specifically to avoid that.

Or no. Mrs. Celestin would have. Bad planning, Van. Very bad. You should at least have locked the door.

He opened his eyes to see that the weatherbeaten creases on Noon's face were crumpling even further. The man thought Van would dismiss him even again.

Making an impulsive decision, he surged to his feet. "I was just going to set the Runners to find you, Noons! Our fortunes are reversed. I have hopes of a rich widow, but I can hardly go a-courting without you to turn me out well, can I?"

He'd go to Perry's Bank. If the money was there, he'd have a start. If it wasn't, he'd complete what Mrs. Celestin had interrupted. Somehow without hurting Noons more than he had to.

Misery switched to blinding joy in the valet's face. "My lord! My lord! Oh, this is such good news! I was so afraid . . . I won't tell you what I was afraid of—"

His eyes, glancing around, had found the pistol.

Van thought of lying about it, then shrugged. "It misfired. Faulty flint." Then he saw the look on the valet's face.

Noons retreated. "I'm sorry, my lord. No, I'm not sorry! I couldn't bear what you might do when I was out of sight. And see, I was right, wasn't I?"

For a moment, Van wanted to throttle him, but then he forced a smile. "Yes, by gad, you were right. For six weeks, at least."

"Six weeks, my lord?" Noons gingerly picked up the pistol and put it out of sight in a drawer.

"Never mind. First order of business is to tidy me up so I can visit my bank."

"Bank, my lord?" Noons glanced at the empty decanter in concern.

"A small loan to enable me to go fortune hunting. So, work your magic."

Three hours later, rested, shaved, and turned out to Noons's satisfaction, Van looked in a mirror. He wished the signs of dissipation could be polished away like the scuffs on his boots.

If the Golden Lily had been real, however, he'd polish up. Though he often felt like Methuselah, he was only twenty-five. His body must still have some repairing powers.

He rubbed a finger down the scar on his right cheek. That wouldn't go away, but that, at least, was honorable.

He put on his hat and went out to test whether his visitor had been an apparition or real. A strange mission, almost like a trial. If he returned with no money and no hope, he would have to execute himself.

With that in mind, he paused by a gunsmith's shop and counted his few coins. Yesterday, he'd paid Noons and his bills, then taken the rest of his money to Brooks'. He'd come home and bought that one bottle of good wine. Now he had just over a shilling.

He left the gunsmith with a flint, a sixpence, one penny, and a farthing. All he possessed in the world.

Oh, he could tease things out by selling bits and pieces, but after last night's disaster, that would be stealing. Despite his words to the real or imaginary Mrs. Celestin, his estates would not completely cover his debt. Everything he owned, even to the clothes on his back, belonged to the men holding his IOUs.

The only hope lay at the bank. With the careless acceptance of fate that had carried him to hell and back for nearly ten years, he walked on briskly.

As he approached Perry's, however, his steps slowed. Somehow, passing through busy streets, greeted by the occasional acquaintance, he had begun to slide back under the damnable seductiveness of life. It shouldn't be difficult to stroll into the bank and ask whether an account had been set up for him there, but it had become the moment that would dictate whether he would live or die.

He hovered, seeking alternatives, but he knew there were none.

He'd inherited neglected estates drowning in debt. He had no skills but soldiering, and the war was over. Even if it wasn't, he couldn't go back. He knew now how Con had felt. Con had sold out in 1814, then returned for Waterloo, but after the break, he'd lost the habit of war, the crusty, protective shell. He'd come through the battle without serious physical wounds, but damaged in other ways. Van had known that. He should have found Con and tried to help. He'd been too wrapped up in his own problems.

In some ways Van had enjoyed war, enjoyed the constant test by fire, but he'd never become hardened to death. Each death around him had spurred him to fight more wildly, as if picking up the banner of the fallen without caution or consequences.

A clear form of madness. He'd been aware of that, and yet it had gripped him. No question of stopping, of backing away, with all the ghosts cheering him on.

But that drug had gone, drained to the last, overdosing drop at Waterloo. Once gone, there was nothing left. He could not fight again. He could not help a friend.

Why did a person live? What was the point? He'd carried on only because of another set of ghosts, his family preaching his duty to continue the line, to repair Steynings and restore it to the home it had once been.

He'd turned to gambling. He had luck and he stayed sober, so he generally won. Paid his way, in fact. He'd never made enough to change anything, however, in part because he couldn't bring himself to fleece the innocent or those who couldn't afford it.

Tiring of it, he'd made a bargain with the devil. He'd gamble the night away without restraint or caution. If he emerged a winner, he would settle in the country and work at restoring his home. If he lost, he'd put an end to it.

He'd lost. True to his bargain, he'd stayed through

the night, even though the debts had mounted, actually welcoming the growing total that would remove any ambiguity.

He mourned that moment when he had known exactly what he must do, so like the absolute of a forlorn-hope charge in battle. Then, with a muttered curse, he took up his last forlorn hope and walked into the bank.

It was oak-paneled and sober, looking respectable and solid, as a bank must. Was it her bank? If she was real, if she had deposited the money, would everyone here know his account had been set up by the rich Mrs. Celestin?

He had no reason for pride anymore, but it still stung.

A neatly dressed clerk came forward, bowing. "How may I assist you, sir?"

Van gathered generations of wealth and arrogance as armor. "Lord. Vandeimen. I have an account here, I believe."

For a wretched heartbeat he thought the clerk was staring at him in puzzlement, but then he smiled. "Yes indeed, my lord. Permit me to take you to Mr. Perry, my lord."

Van wondered if he staggered as he followed down a corridor and into the handsome office of the owner of the bank.

Reprieve.

He had six weeks more of life!

He still felt dazed as he emerged, guineas in his pocket, wealth established, debts paid. Poor Mr. Perry had been disappointed to find that most of the fortune trusted to his care was to promptly leave it. Van still had a thousand pounds in the account, and nine thousand more if he could satisfy his employer.

The Golden Lily.

He took a deep breath of spring air, appreciating it like a fine wine. He blessed the warmth of the sun on his face.

But as he strolled back to his rooms, wariness grew. For twenty thousand pounds Mrs. Celestin had to want more than his adoring escort. What? He'd swallowed the hook, so now he'd be reeled in.

Despite her rejection, perhaps she was after coupling. He fought back a laugh. If so, he'd be the most overpaid whore in London, no matter what her tastes!

In fact, he rather liked the idea. He'd like to warm that damnable, cool composure, see her flush and become disordered, unruly, wild . . .

Madness. She was probably all cool composure in bed, too.

When a ragged crossing-sweeper hurried to clear some horse droppings from his path, he dug out the sixpence, the penny, and the farthing, and dropped them into the lad's hand. With the boy's enthusiastic thanks loud in the air, he strolled on, a sparkle starting inside him.

With difficulty, he recognized mischief and challenge. How long was it since he had felt that way? Despite his employer's command that he not touch her without permission, surely in six weeks of adoring companionship, he could find out whether she was cool in bed.

Even a servant deserved amusement.

As he passed the gunsmith's on the way home, however, he remembered the flint, and fingered it in his pocket. It comforted him. If the strange Mrs. Celestin demanded anything intolerable, he had the easy way out.

The next night, Maria entered the Yeovil mansion in a state of unusual turmoil. Few would guess, for it was her nature to conceal her emotions, but she knew, and she knew why.

He'd paid his debts. Everyone gossiped about that as much as they'd gossiped about his ruinous night at the tables.

Where had the money come from? they'd asked.

Had he gone to the moneylenders? If so, poor man.

Would he lose again? Then what?

A sad case, both men and women agreed. Hero in the war. Fine old family. No hope, though. Father ruined the properties, and the son doesn't have the heart to start from scratch. Shame for such a promising young gentleman.

A promising young gentleman.

On hearing that, Maria had thought of the slack-lidded, stubbled man in the rumpled clothes, and the way he'd taken that pistol from her. Promising? Of what? Perhaps it was the fact that he was still a gentleman that had prevented him from shooting her.

If he was a gentleman, he'd work off his debt to her. He'd be here tonight. That terrified her almost as much as him not being here. If he was here, she'd have to deal with him.

For six weeks.

He did terrify her, and only the smallest part was a fear that he'd attack her. Instead it was fear of the energy and intensity he'd given off. She'd wanted to back away. To be safe.

Worse, she'd wanted to press closer, to inhale that energy, to absorb it, surrender to it. She'd surrendered to her physical nature once before, and lived to regret it.

She would not make a fool of herself again.

Harriette knew how she felt. Harriette was the one person who knew everything, and now her aunt glanced sideways and smiled—the sort of chins-up! smile given to someone before a trying experience.

They greeted the duke and duchess—the duchess was Maria's cousin, twice removed—and their daughter, Lady Theodosia, who was being launched here. Then they moved into a reception room, and on into the glittering ballroom.

It was, of course, a most sought-after invitation, and therefore well on its way to being a "crush." It might be hard to find her quarry. Or for him to find her. Maria felt an absurd temptation to climb on one of the chairs set around the walls, both to see and be seen.

"I don't see him," said Harriette, who was indeed stretching on tiptoe.

"Don't make a fuss," Maria hissed as she smiled and obeyed the beckoning Lady Treves. A pleasant lady, but she had a handsome, hopeful son, and so was destined to be disappointed.

So many hunted her fortune. She hadn't lied to Vandeimen about that, or that she'd pay a fortune to be able to attend these events without a swarm of what she thought of as her wasps. She saw two of the more persistent ones buzzing toward her now.

Ten proposals she'd had so far. Ten. And she'd only been free of mourning for a few weeks.

Of course it wasn't just the money, she acknowledged as she greeted Lord Warren and Sir Burleigh Fox. She was a Dunpott-Ffyfe. Marrying Maurice had not done her credit any good, but he was, after all, dead, and had left her a very wealthy widow with excellent bloodlines. A jam pot for wasps.

She smiled and chatted, trying not to favor any particular man and parrying the more clumsy attempts to flirt or flatter. Where was Vandeimen? Why wasn't he here?

She froze in the middle of an idle comment to the duchess. What if he'd paid his debts and gone home to shoot himself?

"Maria?"

"Oh! So sorry, Sarah. Of course I'll be a patroness of your charity for wounded soldiers. The government should have done much more. And after all, Maurice made a great deal of money from supplying the army."

She'd be paying conscience money—to the soldiers who'd worn shoddy boots and uniforms, and to Lord Vandeimen who'd been ruined. Military charities were Sarah Yeovil's passion, however, because she had lost her younger son at Waterloo. She was dressed tonight in dark gray and black.

Maria remembered Lord Darius as a charming young rascal, always up to mischief, but her mind was presently fretting over another young man of about the same age. Was Lord Vandeimen lying in a puddle of blood?

She itched to invade his rooms again, to prevent disaster, but she stayed where she was and smiled. If he was dead, he was dead, and discovering it would not repair matters.

"Tattoos, Mama?" queried Lord Gravenham, the duchess's older son.

Maria paid attention and tried to guess what they were talking about.

"Sailors have them," Sarah said earnestly. "So if they drown, their bodies are more easily recognized. If soldiers had tattoos, it would serve the same purpose."

"It would do no harm," said Lord Gravenham, but Maria suspected he was thinking as she was. There'd been more than ten thousand corpses to deal with after Waterloo, most thrown into mass graves to prevent disease. One of them had been Dare's, but in a situation like that, who was going to note tattoos for identification?

"I had the idea from Lord Wyvern," Sarah was saying. "A friend of Dare's," she added to Maria. "One of this Company of Rogues they formed at Harrow, though of course he wasn't Wyvern then. Just plain Con Somerford. Such good friends, and such good men . . ." She pressed a black-edged handkerchief to her eyes and took a visible moment to collect herself. "He and two friends had tattoos done before going to war. On the chest. A G for George."

"That's a very common name, though, isn't it?" Maria said, trying to cover the moment and show an interest. "For true identification, it would need to be more distinctive. A full name?"

"They were all called George."

Maria flashed Lord Gravenham a look, wondering if Sarah had finally slipped over the edge.

"So of course they needed something else," Sarah went on. "Wyvern has a dragon. It fits the title he's inherited, though at the time he could not expect to. The other two men were a George Hawkinville—a hawk, and George Vandeimen, a demon. It goes with the sound of his title, of course, and it's the family name too. But not a wise choice." She shrugged. "But then, they were only sixteen. I'm so glad to hear better news of him."

"Vandeimen?" Maria asked, and it came out a little

high. "The one who lost his fortune?" He had a *demon* on his chest?

"I was saying to the duke that we should do something. He and the others were so kind to Dare last year. Professional soldiers, you know. But Vandeimen's affairs seem to have sorted out. So, can you help me there, too, Maria? I will have to hire people who can do these tattoos, and obtain the cooperation of the Horse Guards . . ."

The orchestra struck a louder note, alerting all that the dancing was to begin. Sir Burleigh hovered. Maria promised support for the foolish tattoo fund and gave the persistent wasp her hand.

She loved to dance, though she knew she did it with grace rather than verve. They called her Lily because of her pale complexion and habit of wearing pale clothes, and Golden for her outrageous wealth. She knew they also called her the Languid Lily, and shared scurrilous jokes in the men's clubs about whether she was languid in bed.

She would love to be able to sparkle, and perhaps she had as a rompish sixteen. The years had taught her control and discretion, however, and they reigned even in the dance.

In the bed—well, that was a private matter.

Then as she turned in the dance pattern, she saw him.

She missed a step, and with a hasty apology she concentrated on the dance. When she glanced back across the room, Vandeimen was gone.

He was here, though. She couldn't have mistaken that tall lean grace and primrose hair, made more brilliant by dark evening clothes.

He was here.

Alive.

Ready to fulfill his bargain.

With a sudden beat of the heart she knew it had begun.

Chapter Three

When the set was over, Maria felt flushed, an unusual occurrence for her. She plied her fan as her wasps gathered, all seeking the next chance at the jam pot. Maria playfully put off choosing.

Where was Vandeimen?

Had she imagined him?

Then she saw him, in company with Gravenham. Beside the marquess's mousy solidity, Vandeimen seemed a wild spirit, despite his perfect, tidy appearance. His primrose hair shone in the candlelight, and his scar, doubtless honorably gained, suggested wickedness, especially with the lingering marks of dissipation.

"Mrs. Celestin," Gravenham said, "you have enraptured another of us poor males. Here's Vandeimen begging me for an introduction. Now mind," he added, "I wouldn't agree if you were a sweet young innocent, but I judge you well able to deal with rascals such as he."

Maria appreciated Gravenham's subtle warning. It showed that Vandeimen was in danger of losing his place in accepted circles.

"A rascal, my lord," she said to Vandeimen, offering her hand. "How intriguing."

She managed a cool manner, but was alarmed that she hadn't thought of this essential detail. Of course he couldn't just walk up to her. He had to find someone respectable to introduce him.

He bowed gracefully over her hand, perfectly judging the distance. A slight inclination would be cool. To actually touch his lips to her gloves would be scandalously bold. Just over halfway was within bounds, but hinted at interesting ardor.

She kept her light smile fixed and prayed not to shiver. This perfectly turned-out young man with deft social skills was not what she had expected.

"Then perhaps I might persuade you into the dance, Mrs. Celestin?" he said straightening but still holding her hand. "Some opportunity there to be rascally."

"Really? I was not aware of that."

"How dull your partners must have been." He tucked her hand into the crook of his arm. "Come, let me brighten your life."

He stole her from under the noses of her wasps, and she wasn't sure whether to be outraged or wildly amused.

"My partners have not been particularly dull," she said, as they joined a set.

"Good. Then you won't be shocked."

She wasn't sure about that. What did he plan?

She did know about rascally dancing. If she let her mind slide back to her folly with Maurice, she could remember times when he'd used the dance to full advantage. After all, where else could a slightly disreputable man get close enough to a lady to tempt her to folly?

The music started and they began the steps. For the moment it was just a dance, giving her room to think.

She hadn't anticipated him planning to kill himself.

She hadn't anticipated him being dangerous.

She hadn't anticipated the need for introduction.

She hadn't anticipated his perfect management of the situation, or how he matched the steps of society as skillfully as he matched the steps of the dance.

She should have expected all of it. Heavens, social duties were part of an officer's life. And yet, she had failed to anticipate his social skills.

What else had she neglected?

That he would be wary.

As she met his eyes in the dance, she recognized that. Of course her quixotic actions must appear suspicious. As they joined hands and passed, she wondered what he feared. What did he think she wanted for her twenty thousand pounds?

And what—even more fascinating—would he be willing to do for it?

She danced back toward him, wicked thoughts stirring despite every attempt to bury them deep in her mind. They linked arms in an allemande, and turned, eye to eye, bodies moving in harmony.

A sudden awareness rippled through her of exactly what she could demand from him in service—for six long weeks. She knew her rare color was building, and spun off to the next gentleman with relief.

She'd never thought of such a thing when she'd planned this. Never! She must immediately put it out of her mind. It would be both foolish and wicked. She was supposed to be rescuing him, not exploiting him, and he was eight years her junior.

She fiercely concentrated on the present, on the weaving steps of the dance. She couldn't help but watch, however, as he danced with other women in the set. She was not alone in her reaction. Each one, young or old, responded with a brightening of the eyes, a widening of the smile.

He was a flirt. A handsome, instinctive flirt whom women could not resist responding to. She'd not anticipated that, either. She'd known the world would assume she was buying youth, but not that she had been charmed out of her wits and money.

The idea was so repulsive that she wanted to cry halt now. He could have the money and go to hell or heaven—

Then he was back to partner her. As they stepped together, first one way then the other, he said softly, "Am I supposed to fall madly in love with you, or is this a more considered affair?"

Mouth dry, eyes locked with his, she said, "Madly in love. Why not?" If she was going to be thought a fool, she'd rather be thought a mad one.

His eyes held hers, and then, as the dance moved him on, they lingered for a speaking moment. Fascinated, she realized she was doing the same thing, and hastily looked at her new partner, Sir Watkins Dore, to see an understanding smile.

"A handsome rascal," the middle-aged man remarked, "but penniless and with a taste for the bottle and the tables, dear lady. A word to the wise."

From there on, Maria passed through the dance unable to block the mortifying awareness that everyone thought they were witnessing a powerful attraction between an older woman and a charming young rascal.

She couldn't blame Vandeimen. He was following her instructions to the letter. Though smiling and polite, he had somehow muted his effect on the other ladies, and turned it all on her. Often her eyes collided with his intent ones. It was hard for her not to believe that she had suddenly become the center of his universe.

When the dance ended and she curtsied as he bowed, she knew all eyes were on them. It was excruciatingly hard not to say something cutting, or behave in a chilly manner to show that she was not a gullible fool. As it was, she let him place her hand in the crook of his arm, and strolled with him.

"Everyone's watching," she said, though she knew she shouldn't. She was in control of this adventure, wasn't she?

"I'm sure you are watched anyway, the Golden Lily."

"I'm used to that, but not to this." How absurd to feel that she could talk honestly to him like this. Of course, apart from Harriette, he was the only one aware of their purpose. "I'm probably not looking as dazzled as I should."

"I'll be dazzled for both of us." When she glanced sideways at him, she saw how his smiling eyes were intent on her. "Some wariness on your part is doubtless realistic," he added. "You are too wise to actually marry me, after all."

She smiled at the joke, but it pressed on an old wound. Her feelings were too like the lunatic infatuations she'd succumbed to when young, culminating in Maurice. She had a weakness for dashing, handsome, dangerous men, but she was no longer young and silly. Had she learned nothing?

Cool air startled her back to the immediate, and she realized he had led her out onto a small balcony. They were still in view, but it gave some protection from being overheard. It also must cause more talk.

What point in balking, though? She was about to be society's favorite topic of amusement for six long weeks. It was a price she would pay to right a wrong.

"Thank you for coming," she said, wafting her fan and gazing out over the lamplit garden below.

"You thought I wouldn't pay my debt?"

A sudden chill in his voice made her turn to him. "I didn't mean it that way. You were . . . The need to—"

"Madam, you have bought me—body, mind, and most of my soul—for six weeks. I will go where you command, speak as you wish, act as you instruct, so long as it does not offend the part of my soul I have retained."

Oh dear. Pain and wounded pride. She must remember that though war had aged him in many ways, he could still be tender in others.

"Excellent," she said coolly, returning to the safe contemplation of the garden. "You are playing your part well, my lord, so please continue to act as if you were intent on winning me." She glanced back with a carefully calculated smile. "I doubt that will hazard your immortal soul."

They confronted each other for a moment in silence, and she nervously broke into chatter. "The lamps in the garden are pretty, are they not? I wonder if there is a way to explore there."

Her gloved right hand rested on the iron railing, and he covered it with his left. A hand brown from years of sun and weather, strong with sinews and veins, long-fingered, marked by many minor scars. A hand that looked older than he was. A fine hand perhaps meant by nature for softer ways, for music, for art, for gentle love . . .

"I would know that I had little hope," he said, curling his fingers around hers and lifting her hand from the railing, turning her toward him. "A penniless man with dilapidated estates, and eight years younger than you."

"True . . ."

He brought her hand between them, chest high, and in the process angled his body so that he shielded her from the crowded room. "The only reason you would consider my suit is for my looks and charm. Poor Mrs. Celestin," he added with a glint of edged humor, "you are going to have to succumb to looks and charm."

"I would hardly be the first widow to do so. I'm sure I can play the part." She returned exactly the same sort of edged look. "It's not as if I am actually going to place my person and my fortune in your hands, after all."

"Just the additional nine thousand pounds."

"*If* you behave yourself." She looked him up and down. "You do, at least, have both looks and charm, and conduct yourself well in society. It would be even more galling to make a fool of myself over an *unappealing* wastrel."

He stilled, his scar seeming to slash more darkly across his right cheek. She instantly recalled the man she had first met, the one who had disarmed her, and surely come close to hurting her.

He dropped her hand. "I can become unappealing anytime you want, Mrs. Celestin. I would advise you not to push me too far. A man ready to die is equally ready to consign nine thousand pounds to the devil."

The small balcony was suddenly confining, and he blocked the way out. She desperately wanted to look away, or to try to push out of this confined space. As with an animal, however, to show fear was to lose control. She met his angry eyes. "What of the eleven thousand, my lord? You owe me service for that."

His nostrils flared, and she suddenly saw in him a stallion. A young, magnificent, abused stallion on the edge of going bad. Dear heavens, who did she think she was, to try to keep together something so riven through with cracks?

"I'm sorry," she said quickly. "I spoke thoughtlessly. I chose you for this because you are a gentleman."

"But why did you choose anyone, Mrs. Celestin? What is the purpose of this extravagant charade?"

She'd hoped to put this off until she'd thought of a better rationale, but clearly she had to say something now. With great effort, she spoke lightly. "One person's extravagance is another's whim, Lord Vandeimen. I have a mind to enjoy this season, and I am pestered by fortune hunters. You are my guard against them, that is all."

She must have presented it correctly, for she saw his tension ease in scarcely perceptible, but significant, ways.

"You must be very, very rich."

"I am."

"Then of course, I am completely at your service. Command me, dear lady."

Shockingly, the requests that came to mind were all indecent. She sank back on what she had said before. "Do as you would if you were intent on sweeping me out of sanity and into your martial bed."

He looked at her for a moment, then raised his left hand and rested it on her naked shoulder. Warm. Roughened from the practice of war.

No, not practice. Real, deadly war. How many deaths had those intent blue eyes seen? How many had his elegant hands delivered? How much suffering, during battle and after? She had lost no one of importance to her except a baby brother, half remembered, and Maurice, who had died miles away on a hunting field, and by then not truly grieved.

They called this man Demon. A terrible label for a noble soldier and hero, but she could only think of how very familiar he must be with death. No wonder he'd seemed indifferent as to whether she shot him or not. He probably cared for nothing at all, and was wounded too deeply for that to change.

Was he going to kiss her, here in full view of everyone? She should prevent that, but for the moment, she was paralyzed.

With scarcely a pause, however, he brushed his hand across her bare shoulder, sending shivers down her spine, until his fingers moved into the loose curls at the edge of her hair. He could be tidying a curl or brushing away an insect. He played there for a moment, eyes holding hers, then lowered his hand to his side.

Fear still held her, but underneath surged something even worse. Lust.

Triumph glinted in his sudden smile.

Ah.

She sucked in a deep breath. He was going to do what she had paid for, but for pride's sake he was going to try to seduce her at the same time. Not surprising, though yet again, something she had not anticipated.

She certainly had never anticipated that it might be so terribly possible.

Already a part of her was crying, *Why not? Why not? You could lie together with him tonight!* Deep muscles clenched at the thought.

She often lay in the quiet night remembering a man's body on hers, in hers. She didn't wish Maurice back, but memory of hot intimacy always left her feeling aching and hollow.

She was staring at him. Carefully, slowly, she turned her head to look past, unfurling her fan. She couldn't afford to give him a weapon like that, and it would be wrong to use him. She must remember her purpose— to heal him and set him free with the money Maurice had stolen.

"The next dance is starting," he said. "Shall we be partners again? It will create just the storm you want."

Storm. An apt name for the tumult inside her, but she agreed. She had set her course and would pursue it, even through a storm of embarrassment, scandal, and yes— frustration.

She was no blushing ingenue. She could control herself and her demon. She went calmly with him to form an eight.

She completed the dance almost hectic with emotion. Beneath dissipation, dark memories, and that nasty scar, was a young man, a devastatingly attractive young man, who was doing his best to bewitch her.

And his best was very good.

She'd struggled to pin her mind to higher thoughts—to his experiences in the war and his need of gentle nurturing at home. Beneath that logical and noble mind, however, quivered a body that wanted to tear his clothes off, press to his heat, inhale and taste him, and bring him nurture and release of another kind entirely. His very youth, his pain, his sensitivity, his leashed resistance to her rule, were all exciting her more than she could have believed possible.

Before he even suggested an outrageous third dance, she accepted an invitation from another man. It didn't matter who, but it was Mr. Fanshawe, a pleasant gentleman who doubtless would like to marry her money, but who didn't make a nuisance of himself about it.

As they strolled, waiting for the next set to start, she made herself seriously consider Mr. Fanshawe as husband. She did want to marry again, and he was comfortable, undemanding, and her own age. He was the sort of man she had expected to choose, but now the prospect made her want to yawn.

She knew why, but that was only a temporary insanity.

The music started and she let the dance sweep her up, enjoying as always the neatness of fluid movements up and down the line. When she extended her hand to dance round and past the next gentleman, she almost faltered.

Vandeimen!

She recovered, smiled, and danced on. Idiot! Nothing to stop him joining the same line. If he was playing the part of ardent suitor, of course he would. Her hand still tingled from his touch, however.

It must not be.

She wove back down the line, approached him again, joined hands, stepped around, and onward.

That was how it would be. Swirled together by fate, six weeks of linked hands, and then onward and apart. He would have a new chance at life, and she would have a clear conscience.

She did wish it had been possible to do it impersonally, but while she'd been coming up with elaborate schemes, he'd plunged suddenly into darkness and she'd known she had to act. She'd been right, too. Frighteningly right. She still shuddered at the thought of being moments too late.

When it was his turn to dance down the middle of the long line with his partner she saw that he was partnering a flushed and dazzled young thing burdened by a pudding face and frizzy mousy hair. He'd either chosen or been dragooned into partnering a wallflower, but his smile for her was bright and warm, and he was creating a brief heaven for her.

Beneath the wastrel lay a good man. She shouldn't be surprised, and she certainly shouldn't feel a proprietary pride. He wasn't hers, and that was exactly where he should look for a bride. Among the innocent and fertile young.

Fertile. She grasped that painful thorn. In ten years of active marriage she had not conceived, and it hadn't been Maurice's fault. He had four bastards that she knew about.

Vandeimen needed children to rebuild his line.

What a betrayal that she even needed to remind herself of that! Beneath the dark and the scars, however, Vandeimen was a good man, and she was glad of it.

Women teasingly divided potential husbands into three groups— heaven, purgatory, and hell. Maurice had promised heaven but turned out to be purgatory, which she gathered was all too common. Vandeimen, she suspected, was a purgatory who would turn out to be heaven for the right woman.

But not for her.

For supper partner, she chose Lord Warren. He was a widower with two sons, so the fact that she was unlikely to have children didn't matter to him. He was sensible, honest, and persistent in pursuit, but would make an excellent husband. He held a minor position in the government. Perhaps being a political hostess would amuse her.

She concentrated on his interesting conversation, and that of the other people at her table, but then a burst of laughter made her glance across the room. Vandeimen was at a table with a group that glittered with youth, life, and high spirits.

His natural milieu.

"Noisy, aren't they?" Lord Warren said.

Maria turned back to him, pulling a slight face, grateful that she hadn't revealed a touch of wistfulness. "They're young."

"Indeed. My eldest is not much younger, and he and the rest can destroy tranquility in a moment."

She sipped her wine to hide another reaction.

If she married Lord Warren, she would become stepmother to sons not a great deal younger than Lord Vandeimen. Only eight years divided them, but the way the world worked they were almost different generations.

She conversed with Lord Warren and the other older people at her table, trying to block the sounds of lively chatter and bursts of laughter from across the room.

It was a relief to rise to return to the ballroom. As she strolled out with Lord Warren she decided she would leave the ball soon. She'd done enough for one night. Vandeimen could come up with other modes of pursuit tomorrow.

Then he rose fluidly from his table to put himself in her way, smiling, seemingly relaxed. Gorgeous.

"Mrs. Celestin, you expressed an interest in exploring the gardens. Miss Harrowby had just suggested a stroll out there. Would you care to come?" He gestured to the French doors that stood open to the warm night.

She froze for a moment. It was bold. It was almost impolite, though Warren would expect to hand her over to a new partner soon. If she accepted, it would be a clear sign to all that she was encouraging him.

Everyone was watching.

She smiled at her escort. "If you don't mind, my lord . . ." then moved her hand from his arm to Vandeimen's.

Glances shot around the young people carrying many messages, and whispering began behind her in the room, but in moments she and a number of other couples were heading into the lamplit dark.

Chapter Four

"Am I a chaperon?" she asked as they walked outside and a breeze touched her skin. That surely explained the slight shiver.

"I do hope not."

The next shiver was not due to the breeze.

The other couples melted into the shadows, so only the ghostly pale of the ladies' dresses, soft talk, and laughter revealed their presence.

"I feel like a chaperon," she said, trying to remind him of her advanced age. "Who is partnered with whom, and are the pairings acceptable?"

"Don't fuss. I doubt anyone is going to be ravished." He turned to her and added, "Who doesn't want to be, that is."

"Who would want to be?"

"All the men."

It startled a laugh from her, and he grinned, looking much younger. *Oh, Maria, do you know what you're doing?* When he guided her farther from the house, however, she did not resist.

Though the garden was not large, paths wound around bushes and trellises, creating illusions of privacy. Illusions only, as giggles, conversation, and the occasional squeal could be heard all around.

It was a sleeping garden, but someone had planted nicotiana and stock that perfumed the air, and the paths were studded with creeping herbs that released scents as they walked. The sultry air increased her awareness of folly. This was not necessary for her plan, though it fit neatly with his.

He was going to try to kiss her, perhaps even to ravish her, to prove that he was master. One of these matters of male pride that she recognized without understanding them at all.

The question was, what was she going to permit, and why?

He paused beneath a tree. "Would this be too early for me to beg for your hand in marriage?"

Ridiculously, her pulse began to race. "It would seem impetuous."

"So. Be a wild, impetuous woman for once."

The tone stung, and an overhead amber lantern laid harsh lines on his face, deepening the jagged scar.

"I eloped with Celestin," she said, and relished startling him.

"Your family didn't approve?"

"He was foreign and self-made."

"You must have loved him very much."

After a heartbeat, she said, "Yes, yes I did."

It wasn't a lie. Wild, impetuous love had driven her into Maurice's arms—carefully created wild impetuous love as unreal as this mock devotion.

"Then have another adventure." He took her hands. "Agree now to marry me. We'll put the notice in the papers tomorrow and shock all London."

She realized that he was speaking as if they might be overheard, and they might. She was vaguely aware of a couple nearby talking softly but earnestly about the meaning of freedom and love.

Ah, youth.

"Well?" he asked.

No point in hesitation. "Very well."

He smiled. Even with the amber light it seemed warm. "You've made me very happy."

"Have I?"

"But of course. Now I get to kiss you. But not here," he said before she could protest. "That amber light is doing terrible things to your looks."

That disconcerting thought allowed him to tug her into

deeper, untinted shadows. Then she got her wits back. "You do not have permission to kiss me."

"Are you going to scream?" He pulled her into his arms. "Wouldn't that rather spoil the show?"

She braced her hands against his chest. "Stop this!"

Shockingly, however, his strength and hard body weakened her, as such things always did. Maurice had not loved her, but he'd been a good lover when he'd bothered, and he'd given her what most excited her.

He would turn up in the middle of an ordinary day, seize her arm, and march her to the bedroom. She'd been practically in orgasm before he had her clothes off, and he'd made sure she whirled into that madness two or three more times before he went on with his busy day, leaving her languid.

Satiated.

Conquered by her flesh.

And it had been a conquest, a matter of pride to him to succeed in everything. She'd known it, but never had the strength to resist.

Zeus, she didn't need those memories now. Despite hot skin and aching thighs, she said, "Force a kiss on me, Lord Vandeimen, and our arrangement will be at an end. It will make you a thief of the money you've already spent, and I assure you, you won't see a penny more."

She couldn't see his expression, but his arms neither tightened nor slackened. "You threatened me once before, Maria. Didn't you learn that I don't care enough? Send me to hell if you want. I'll have my kiss."

He knocked up her bracing arms and cinched her close, then captured her head and kissed her.

Ravished her.

Shock and remembered hungers opened her mouth and pressed her closer, betraying her utterly. It had been so long, so long, since a man had held her, kissed her like this. She'd told herself she was glad to be free of it, and known that she lied.

She found she'd thrust her hands beneath his jacket, and was clawing at his long, tight back through silk and linen. She stopped that at least, but her heart thundered and that betraying ache had become throbbing demand.

His lips released hers and slid down her neck.

She should stop him now. She should. Instead, she was fighting not to fall to the ground and tear his clothes off.

He pushed his thigh between hers. She heard her own sound of need, and finally dragged herself out of his arms. "St—"

His hand came hard over her mouth.

He was right. She'd been about to scream.

"Hush," he said softly, "hush."

No apology, just soothing sounds he might make to a frantic animal.

Animal.

Oh, God.

She closed her eyes, excruciatingly mortified to have reacted like that to the cynical attentions of a man more suited to be her son than her lover. Then she was in his arms again, being held quite gently, her face pressed to his shoulder, however, just in case.

Oh, to wipe out those foolish moments! To take frosty leave of him and never see him again.

You can, whispered a voice. *Just give him the money and cut free.*

She couldn't. He needed more than money. He needed a clean break from corruption, and a helping hand back to ordinary, sane ways. The fact that he'd stolen that dishonorable kiss showed he was still deep in the pit. She suspected that soon he'd be ready to shoot himself over it.

She moved her head slightly to take a clearer breath, and he let her. His head rested against hers, however, and his arms were no longer imprisoning. Despairingly, she sensed that he was relishing this embrace. How often had he simply been in someone's arms?

His mother and two sisters might possibly have held him if he needed it. Mother and younger sister had died of influenza. His older sister had died in childbirth round about the time of Waterloo. His father had shot himself not long after, and perhaps the other deaths had been part of it. It had mostly been the debts, though, and they had been Maurice's fault.

There must have been women abroad, but had they been the sort to just hold him when he needed holding? The sort to whom he could confess fear and doubt? The sort to let him weep?

Did he ever allow himself to weep?

Her own eyes were blurring, tears ached in her throat, and she realized her hands were making stroking movements on his back. Motherly, she told herself. He probably could do with a mother substitute.

She wanted to burst into wild laughter.

She fought for composure and looked up. "I believe we are engaged to be married, Lord Vandeimen."

She couldn't really see his features, but that meant he couldn't see hers either. The silence stretched too long, however, before he asked, "I should send the notice to the papers?"

She heard surprise. "Yes."

After another silence he asked, "And then what? Do we go through the form of drawing up marriage settlements?"

"Why not? They will make a model for when I truly commit to marriage."

He moved slowly away, then linked her arm with his and drew her back to the path and the amber light.

"I apologize for what happened," he said, looking fixedly ahead. "You are being nothing but kind, and I attacked you, frightened you. Since you are kind enough to continue with this arrangement, I give you my word it will not happen again."

Maria stopped herself from protesting. This was how it must be, and if he hadn't recognized her reaction for what it had been, that was a blessing.

"Then we have everything settled. Now I would like to go home. You will escort me and my aunt?"

"Of course."

But he paused beneath a bright lamp and deftly tidied her appearance, straightening her pearl necklace, adjusting her sleeve, and tucking a curl back into a pin.

Every brushing touch was flaming temptation, but she concentrated fiercely on the fact that he was being clever again. There'd be enough talk without them reentering the house in disarray.

Presumably tidying up after garden embraces was part of the skills of a military officer.

"Were there many social events in the Peninsula?" she asked, and to keep the balance, reached up to adjust his cravat, thankful for her gloves. Even so, the sense of his skin, sleek over his firm chin, or the muscles and tendons of his neck, could drive her wild.

Heavens, but she wanted him. Rawly and demandingly wanted him.

"Sometimes," he said, raising his chin for her. "In Lisbon, mostly. And Paris. And Brussels."

The Duchess of Richmond's ball, from which the officers had slipped away, many not to be seen alive again. Yes, doubtless he had experience at partnering respectable young ladies at balls, and occasionally slipping out for a kiss—or even more—in a garden.

Neglected wives and hungry widows. She knew how men saw these things. Maurice had told her that men, too, thought of women as heaven, purgatory, or hell, but in two different ways. They assessed brides that way, but they also used the terms to assess lovers.

In a potential lover, hell was diseased, or married to a suspicious, vengeful man, or tainted in some other way. No wise man chose such a lover, but she could hear Maurice laugh as he quoted that the way to hell was often paved with good intentions.

Purgatory was what most men had to put up with to get sex they neither had to pay for nor marry for.

Heaven was an attractive married woman with a strong sexual appetite and a safe husband. Some widows fit into that category if they emphatically did not want marriage.

She realized that in some ways she was heaven. She was even barren. A distinct advantage.

She gave the starched cloth a final twitch, then they linked arms to reenter the house. She knew the people lingering in the supper room were watching, as were those they met as they went in search of Harriette. Probably everyone knew by now that the Golden Lily had gone into the garden with wild young Lord Vandeimen who desperately needed money.

She caught a few disappointed grimaces from the wasps and their families, and a few looks of concern, or even pity from others.

It was hard not to shout out an explanation.

Of course I'm not bewitched by this young fool! I'm saving him. In weeks I'll be free, and so will he!

Thank God for Harriette. Maria found herself blank of conversation, but Harriette chattered to Vandeimen without any inhibition at all.

By the time they climbed into their carriage, Harriette had opened the subject of his family and offered condolences on his losses. Along the way, she uncovered the fact that he'd had little contact with the remnants of his family, and hinted that he really should change that.

Maria watched anxiously for signs that his patience with this interference was snapping, but he seemed, if anything, bemused.

Harriette progressed next through the war, gaining a brief account of his career before moving on to her favorite subject, the Duke of Wellington.

Vandeimen seemed indulgent. "If you want stories of the great man, Mrs. Coombs, you'll have to hope my friend Major Hawkinville returns to England soon. He was on his staff."

"Really! Then I do hope to meet him."

"My aunt has a *tendre* for the duke," Maria teased, both pleased and disconcerted by the way Harriette could deal with Vandeimen while she could not. Of course Harriette was over fifty and had sons older than this dangerous creature.

She noted his casual mention of Major Hawkinville, who must be the friend the duchess had mentioned. Who was the other? Lord Wyvern. Ah, yes. She'd heard gossip about the recent death of the mad Earl of Wyvern, and the passing of the title to the sane, Sussex branch of the family. Vandeimen needed friends. Perhaps she could find them for him.

At last the carriage drew up in front of her house, and the first battle was over. "Norton can take you on to your place, my lord," she said.

He had climbed out to help them down. "No need. And it's somewhat out of the way."

"All the more need," said Harriette firmly. "Your place is too much out of the way, young man, and did not look at all comfortable." She turned to Maria. "I think he should move in with us."

"Harriette, that's impossible!"

"Why? We have one unused bedroom, and I and the others can be chaperon if anyone thinks it's needed. Well, my lord?"

He looked between them. "Others?"

After half an hour of Harriette, the poor man looked like someone swallowed by the ocean and spat out drenched and exhausted.

"Other guests," Maria said, unable to help a sympathetic smile. "My late husband's aunt and uncle have lived here for years. They are somewhat invalid, but still present in the house. There is also my young niece Natalie, and my aunt, of course."

As she spoke, she realized that having him in her house would make it hugely easier to control his way of life. With him off in Holborn she'd be in a constant fret as to whether he was drinking, gaming, or priming his pistol.

"It would be an economy, and my poor valet would be ecstatic to return to civilization . . . If you are sure you don't mind. It will cause talk."

"We will cause talk anyway, and it will be a great deal more convenient to have you nearby. Please, let Norton take you to your rooms, and tomorrow, move in here with us."

He bowed. "Your wish is my command, as always, O ruler of my heart." There was a distinct edge to the last part, and she wondered if he understood her purpose.

Not a stupid man. Why had she assumed he would be?

Because, she thought, as the coach carried him away, so many of the cavalry officers she'd met had been. Dashing, courageous, but not of sparkling intellect. She rather gathered that those who were clever found themselves seconded to other duties.

"Well done," said Harriette as they entered the hall. "Everything set."

"I think him moving here is a bit extreme."

"Truly?"

Maria shrugged. "There's a lot of work to be done. But he has friends. That's a hopeful sign." She explained what the duchess had said.

"Tattoos?" said Harriette with a grimace. "What were their mothers thinking? But it will certainly be easier for Lord Vandeimen to meet his friends here."

Maria looked around at pale walls, marble pillars, and discreetly tasteful classical statues—or copies of them, to be precise. Maurice had made every effort to impress, and this house had been his principal point of impression. She had been another. Sadly, all his impressions had been imitation. Even the pillars were faux marble.

He'd taught her many lessons, including that most people had two or even more faces. She'd already seen a number of faces to Lord Vandeimen, but she suspected there were more.

The six weeks loomed in front of her and she hurried to the peaceful sanctuary of her bedroom, but even there uncomfortable memories stirred. She'd enjoyed Maurice's demanding visits to her bed. Once she'd realized the truth, however—that she was merely part of his strategy for entering and using English society—her hunger had shamed her.

As her maid stripped off her finery, she remembered the many lonely nights when she'd longed for him to come to her. She'd often thought of going to him, but never found the courage. How could she? His care for her sprang at best from mild affection, and at worst from a need to keep her pacified so she wouldn't crack his illusion of perfect success.

Begging for more had been unthinkable.

Though he'd been discreet, she'd known about his mistresses. They had all been lively, colorful women. Not like her.

She knew about his bastards, too, because he'd told her about each one, and the provision he was making. The allowances had been specified in his will. Another inherited burden.

And then there was Natalie.

Natalie's mother had been Maurice's aristocratic Belgian cousin, Clarette, but she was also Maurice's child. When her official parents had died, she had come to live with him. The truth was never spoken, but Tante Louise and Oncle Charles knew that Maurice and Clarette had been in love since their teens.

Natalie was a delightful girl, but Maria had resented having a reproach at her infertility under her roof. Now she'd invited a demon there.

She smiled wryly as she dried her hands and applied cream. No danger in that. If she hadn't been able to go to her husband demanding sex, she certainly could not invade her hired escort's rooms with that in mind.

Chapter Five

The next morning, Maria sat at the desk in her boudoir trying to pretend that she was working on her accounts, but with every sense alert for his arrival. She'd sent the coach and had no reason to believe that he wouldn't come as arranged. Still, she felt she would not have a moment's peace until he was here.

Safe.

Oh, what nonsense, but that's how she felt.

A laugh escaped, and she rested her head on her hand. She wanted to wrap the man in flannel cloth and protect him, like a mother with a delicate child. Was anything more ridiculous?

And yet, it wasn't ridiculous to see him as delicate, if by that she meant fragile. It was her task to make him robust again—without giving in to other, baser, desires.

A carriage? She shot to her feet and peered out of the window. It was. Her carriage. At last!

Heart suddenly racing, she made herself stand still and take a deep breath.

You make him strong again, Maria, and then you let him go. You mustn't permit anything to happen that might entangle him with you.

Her throat actually ached, which was an alarming warning.

If he even shows interest in you it will simply be a game, a game to prove he's your master rather than your debtor. Have some pride!

That worked better to bring her to her senses. She glanced in the mirror to be sure she was her usual cool and elegant self. Her simple morning gown was white with a narrow, pale blue stripe. A fichu ensured modesty, and matched the white cotton cap tied beneath her chin with pale blue ribbon. She looked a perfect, respectable widow, and thus armored, went down to greet her guest.

She almost collided with Natalie rushing toward the stairs.

"I just wanted to see," the girl whispered, flashing her dimples. "I looked him up in the library this morning. He was mentioned in dispatches *four times*! He must be very brave."

"Yes, I believe so." Instinct made Maria speak coolly even though she knew she should be acting besotted. She looked her sixteen-year-old "niece" over and reset a hairpin to hold up escaping curls. "Since you're presentable, why not come down and be properly introduced?"

Excited delight lit up Natalie's face. She was not one to hide emotions. Every one showed, and usually at twice normal intensity.

Being short with mousy hair, Natalie couldn't claim beauty, but she had enough vivacity and character to become a raging success when Maria let her loose on the world. She was sixteen now. Next year there would be no putting it off. Such a daunting responsibility.

She heard the door below open, and voices, and continued down, aware of Natalie by her side as if excitement gave off noise. Pray heaven she wasn't as audible. At the bend in the stairs, where the hall came into view, she paused.

He was wearing a brown jacket and buff breeches that could be the same ones he'd worn two days ago, but now they were neat. He looked so perfectly comfortable in them that she felt she was seeing him for the first time. She was caught by the fluid grace in the way he moved, and the effortlessly genuine smile he tossed as reward to the footman who had carried in his trunk.

Such a beautiful young man . . .

She collected herself and moved on, reaching the bottom of the stairs, then crossing the hall, hand extended. "Lord Vandeimen, welcome to my home."

He turned, still smiling, and bowed over it. "It was kind of you to invite me, Mrs. Celestin."

His eyes flickered to her side, and she said, "My niece, my lord. Natalie Florence."

He bowed, and Natalie dropped a curtsy, dimples deep with excitement. Oh Lord, Maria thought, don't let her fall into an infatuation with him. I can't cope with that on top of everything else.

Then she realized he was chatting with Natalie in a very easy way, and if he had dimples they might be showing too.

Oh Lord, don't let him fall in love with Natalie!

But then, like a cold wind, she realized it was all too likely. They were going to bump into one another all the time. And what would be wrong with it? In a year Natalie would be ready for her season, and if Lord Vandeimen courted her then, it would be completely appropriate.

It would make her his secret stepmother!

See it that way, she sternly directed.

He turned back to her. "The notices have gone to the papers, my dear. I should perhaps seek a private moment for this, but why shouldn't the world witness our happiness?" He produced a ring from his pocket and held out his hand.

A quick glance showed Natalie standing there, hands clasped in vicarious ecstasy, showing no sign of jealousy. Yet.

Maria hadn't anticipated this. She hastily twisted off the rings Maurice had given her, and held out her hand. He pushed the new ring onto her finger—with a little difficulty.

He gave her a rueful glance. "I estimated it for the jeweler, but I think it will have to be stretched a little."

"Easy enough." She looked at the ring, which was surprisingly modest. The small diamond in the center was surrounded by pearls. She didn't mind the simplicity, but she'd expected a pretentious statement. Perhaps she'd been remembering Maurice. The ring she'd just taken off held a very large blue diamond.

"The smaller stones were rubies but I had them changed," Vandeimen said. "Since you have a taste for pale colors."

She hadn't liked Maurice's ring, which had been tastelessly ostentatious, but she didn't much care for this one either. Not because of the value, but because it was insipid. Was that how he saw her?

She looked at him in buff and brown, and at Natalie in a boldly striped dress with a sky-blue sash.

Perhaps it was time to change. But not for the next six weeks. For this business, insipid was good. Very good.

"It's lovely," she said. "Now, let me show you the house and your room, my lord."

She shooed Natalie back to her lessons—she wanted no fledgling love affair for the next six weeks, at least—and led him upstairs.

When Van was eventually alone in his bedchamber, he shook his head. When had he last been in such elegantly opulent surroundings? Had he ever?

Steynings in his youth had been a fine country house, but it had been a country house, a home. The houses of his best friends had been even more so. Hawkinville Manor was an ancient, rambling place, Somerford Court a rather ugly Restoration construction, but wonderfully welcoming. Army living had thrown him into everything from pigstys to palaces, but they'd all been the worse for wear.

This house must be less than twenty years old, and appointed with great wealth and fairly good taste. He didn't exactly like it—he'd never been in a place before where everything seemed so shiny new—but it was an extraordinary setting.

"Good reminder that it isn't your setting, Van," he muttered, exploring his new quarters.

Noons had already put his scant belongings in the drawers, and a table held glasses, a number of full decanters, and bowls of fruit and nuts. A richly marqueteried breakfront desk contained heavy writing paper, and everything else needed. The glass-front shelves above held a selection of books that seemed to be chosen with care to meet every possible taste.

By her?

It hadn't been wise to agree to move in here, but last night he'd not been able to resist. Comfortable living tempted him, but he also wanted to get to know Maria Celestin, to come to understand what was going on here, and the way he felt.

Hades, he'd almost ravished her! It hadn't felt like that at the time, but it was obvious from her reaction that he'd completely misjudged it. Of course he had. He was a hired servant, nothing more, and he'd attacked her.

He'd gone over and over it in the night.

There'd been pride involved, yes. He'd wanted to master her. Revolting thought. It had spun out of control, though.

Something about her drove him wild. It wasn't just her coolness, either. Today, when she'd come down the stairs, the way she moved had practically rendered him breathless, even if she had been in a shapeless pale dress and a concealing cap.

Last night she'd worn an elaborate turban. At their first meeting she'd been in a toque. He felt almost rage that she hid her hair so much. Soft, dark blond curls had ruffled out around her cap, and when she'd turned to her niece he'd seen escaping tendrils against her long, pale neck.

Did it curl all over? How was it arranged? How long was it? Naked in bed, would it flow long, loose, and pale around her?

Stop it, Van.

He pressed his fist to his mouth.

Stop being an animal. She's a mature, respectable widow who would not even let you touch her except for this eccentric plan of hers.

He was rough from war. Broken in fortune. Broken in spirit. What was he doing now, after all, but marching to duty's drum, left foot, right foot, like the most wretched dullard in the infantry?

In six weeks he'd have enough money to continue the march, that was all, and doubtless he'd never see Maria Celestin again.

They attended two routs and a soirée that night. Maria wanted first reaction over with. She had to endure some sly comments about his youth and good looks, and about his moving into her house, but people mostly seemed to accept the situation, though with amusement.

She left Vandeimen to decide how to behave, and he managed to project a kind of reverent adoration that made her want to scream. Bad enough to be thought an older woman made foolish by lust. Even worse to be treated like a revered saint.

But then, partway through the evening she began to wonder if he was doing it deliberately to try to counteract the more sordid aspects.

If so, it didn't work.

"My dear," said Emily Galman, a thin, predatory woman Maria had known since her first season, "a tiger on your leash! I shall study you for teeth marks."

Her quick dark eyes already were.

"Divinely handsome," said Cissy Embleborough, who'd also made her curtsy at the same time, but who was a friend. "I'm not sure I'd find him comfortable, though."

"Comfort isn't everything." Maria immediately wished the words unsaid.

Cissy laughed. "True. And it may come in time."

It was three days later that she encountered Sarah Yeovil at a private exhibition of medieval art. "Maria," Sarah said, drawing her into a quiet corner, "are you sure this is wise?"

"Wise?" Despite the mild words, there was something ferocious in Sarah's manner.

"He's such a disturbed young man. Are you being fair?"

"It isn't—"

"A woman of your age should be wise for both, not . . . not *use* someone!"

Maria knew she was coloring. "I'm not using him, Sarah," she said, praying there wouldn't be a scene. "I'm *marrying* him. And if you think he doesn't want to—"

"Of course he wants to," Sarah hissed. "You're rich as Croesus. But what else can you offer him? You're old and barren."

It was so cruel that Maria froze. But then she realized that Sarah was thinking of her lost son, a man of the same age. She was reacting as if Maria had trapped Dare. She hadn't trapped anyone, but the thought of herself and Dare, whom she'd known when he was a gap-toothed child, made her shrivel with shame.

She longed to explain, but she didn't want to reveal Maurice's sin to anyone. Perhaps she was more like him than she'd thought, always trying to keep the facade in place.

"We suit," she said rigidly. "He's excellent company."

Sarah was hectically red. "You met him less than a week ago! Gravenham should never have introduced you."

Maria had to stifle laughter at this reversal of Gravenham's discreet warning, but she ached for her cousin's pain.

"You must release him," Sarah said. "You know he cannot draw back."

Nor can I. "But we suit very well."

Sarah stared at her as if she were a worm, and walked away.

Maria let out a breath, praying that her cousin not make this a public estrangement.

Vandeimen came over. "You look upset."

She forced a smile. "The duchess still mourns her son. She sometimes says things she doesn't mean."

"We all mourned Lord Darius. He had the gift of merriment."

She looked at him. "She said you and your friends were kind to him."

"A despairing sort of kindness, though his *joie de vivre*

was a gift just then, before Waterloo. But you don't want to speak of war. Come, the abbey choir is about to sing 'Palestrina.' "

She went, mainly because it would remove any need to talk for a while. She suspected that was his idea, too.

To her, it was as if something pleasant had suddenly been spoiled. It surprised her that it had been pleasant, but she had begun to enjoy the season in the past few days. Her wasps had flown after other jam pots, but the true magic was that she'd enjoyed Vandeimen's company.

He was unfailingly courteous and an excellent, efficient escort. He wasn't a wit, but he held up his end of a conversation. He knew how to acceptably flirt with the ladies and joke with the gentlemen. People were slowly looking past the shocking match and his reputation, and beginning to accept him as simply a gentleman, which he clearly was.

Now, however, the thought of Dare rose up to corrode everything. Her family had regularly visited Long Chart, the Duke of Yeovil's seat, and she could remember Dare still in a toddler's skirts. She'd only been eleven, but that picture stuck because he'd managed to escape his nurse and climb a tree, causing pandemonium.

He must have been eight when he'd recruited most of the children in the area to dig a moat around the castle folly in the grounds. The duke had been impressed enough to complete the job, but at sixteen and on her dignity, Maria had thought him a grubby menace.

She'd last met him when he was a lanky, grinning youth passing through London on his way to Cambridge. She'd been married a few years by then, a matron and mistress of her own home. She'd also been veteran of awareness that she'd been duped by an imaginary love, and suspicion that she was barren. She had faced a difficult, dutiful life, whereas he had been practically bouncing with anticipation of a limitless future. She'd felt old then, and she felt old now.

Listening to the angelic voices of the choir—she'd probably been dancing at a ball when Dare's voice broke, when Vandeimen's voice broke—she reminded herself that this engagement was completely imaginary.

She glanced sideways at her youthful responsibility, at the strong, clear lines of his profile, and the vibrant health of his skin. In only days, the marks of dissipation had disappeared, but it would take longer for the inner wounds to heal.

She'd begun to let him choose where they went, and he seemed to prefer the more cultural events. He'd chosen this one and was enjoying it. He'd been at war for so long that much of society's routine pleasures must be fresh to him.

Her personal reaction to him was her problem—hers to control and hers to conceal.

As the days turned to weeks, control never became easy, but she managed it, helped by the fact that he kept his word. He never again tried to kiss her, or to touch her in any way other than courteously.

The worst times were those spent quietly together—lingering over breakfast, or sitting in the Chinese room, or strolling in the summer garden. Sometimes they talked, but often they were each involved in reading or even thought.

It was too much like husband and wife, and she liked it very much. She told herself that he was on best behavior for the six weeks, and she knew it was true, but she still thought that they rubbed together surprisingly well.

Vandeimen could listen as well as talk. Maurice's breakfast table conversations had mostly been monologues on whatever issue of the day interested him. She had been his attentive audience.

He could endure a silence. Maurice had seemed to feel obliged to throw words at any lingering silence as if it were a rabid dog.

He liked to read. They did not have a great deal of time for reading, but he appeared to enjoy it. He picked seemingly at random from her excellent library—again chosen by Maurice for effect.

Oh yes, he had become a pleasant part of her life.

Thank heavens Harriette was their buffer. She went

nearly everywhere with them, treating Vandeimen like another son, and gave off relaxing warmth like a good fire. The healing was all Harriette's work.

But then, one day, Maria realized that her aunt's healing powers were not working.

They were chatting before dinner when Harriette said something about Vandeimen's home. He snapped at her and left the room.

As the door clicked shut, Harriette pulled a face. "I shouldn't have pressed him for his plans, but—"

"But why not?" Maria asked. "We have spent four of our six weeks. It's time he made plans to restore Steynings."

"My dear, have you not noticed that he never speaks of the future?"

Maria sat there, hands in lap, searching back over four weeks. "Never of the future, and rarely of the past. He talks easily of the present."

"Because the present offers no threat."

"Threat? I thought it was going well."

"Oh, he seems whole," said Harriette with a sigh. "He is healthy, polite, even charming. But it's like a lovely shell around . . . around nothing."

Nothing? Maria suddenly felt as if she were trying to inhale nothing, as if there was no air. "But I can't hold him beyond the six weeks."

"No, you probably can't. So you must find a way to get beneath that shell."

"If there's nothing there?" It was a protest of sorts. She'd fought so hard to keep apart.

"Something must be *put* there. What about those friends of his?"

"Con and Hawk? He seems willing to talk of their boyhood pranks."

"Precisely. Where are they? He needs old friends, friends who will make him face the difficult past and plan the difficult future."

"You think he's avoiding them? Oh, heavens. He never goes to manly places such as Tattersall's, or Cribb's, does he? Or to clubs or coffeehouses. I've been pleased, thinking it safer. But it keeps him from his friends."

"Or his friends are avoiding him," said Harriette. "Find out. Find them."

A footman announced dinner and Maria rose, flinching under those instructions. She didn't want to get involved like that. She feared getting too close.

As she left the drawing room she wondered what to do about the theater party she had planned for the evening. She had invited guests to her box at Drury Lane to see Mrs. Blanche Hardcastle play Titania. There was no reason not to go, except that she and Vandeimen had never been apart in an evening, and she worried what he might do.

What did he do when alone in his room?

He wasn't drowning his sorrows. Though she hated to, she'd questioned the butler, and the decanters in his room were being used sparingly. She knew, however, that he wouldn't need to be drunk to kill himself, and he probably still had his pistol.

She'd have to stay home tonight, though if he lurked in his room and shot himself, she couldn't see how to stop him.

He appeared however as they crossed the hall, ready to escort both of them into dinner. Of course, she thought as she placed her hand upon his arm. He would always punctiliously give the service for which he had been paid.

She ate a dinner for which she had no appetite, wondering if she could use his powerful sense of duty and honor to save him.

Harriette, bless her, picked up conversation as if nothing had happened, and talked about plans for the garden.

The play was doubtless excellent, and ethereal Mrs. Hardcastle with her long silver hair was perfect as the fairy queen, but Maria paid little attention. She sat in her box seeking ways to put Vandeimen in contact with his past, his future, and his friends.

As Sarah had said, they had been born neighbors in

Sussex and all called George. A patriotic gesture, he'd explained, in response to the actions of the French sans-culottes against their own monarch.

"We were lucky, I suppose," he'd said. "We could have all been called Louis. That would have been too much for our staunchly English fathers to stomach, thank God."

They'd been christened on the same day, in the same church, and been playmates in the nursery years. As lads they'd been inseparable, and in the end, they had all joined the army at the same time. Their talents and incli-nations had differed, however, and their military careers had swept them apart. Con had chosen the infantry, Van and Hawk cavalry. But then Hawk had been seconded to the Quartermaster's Division.

They hadn't seen a great deal of each other during their army years, but he didn't talk about them as if they were estranged. So why weren't they in touch, at least by letter?

Lord Wyvern was probably busily involved with his new estate in Devon, but he could still write.

Hawk was Major George Hawkinville, heir to a manor that went back to the Domeday Book. His father, Squire John Hawkinville, was still alive, living at Hawkinville Manor. Her gazetteer had described it as "an ancient, though not notable house in the village of Hawk in the Vale, Sussex."

The same gazetteer had described Vandeimen's home as "a handsome house in the Palladian manner," and Somerford Court as "Jacobean, adapted and adorned, not entirely felicitously, in the following centuries."

The main word used to describe Crag Wyvern in Sus-sex was "peculiar."

Wyvern had been a second son, but Vandeimen and the major were both only sons. Strange that they had joined the army.

Major Hawkinville was still at his duties abroad, ap-parently, but Wyvern must know of the heavy losses Vandeimen had suffered—mother, two sisters, then fa-ther—so why was he doing nothing to help? If only one of these friends was here to help hold Vandeimen together . . .

The curtain fell, signaling an intermission, and she must leave her thoughts to smile and talk as her footman served refreshments. Everyone was enchanted by the play and delighted with the Titania.

"Mrs. Hardcastle's hair is naturally white, they say," said Cissy Embleborough, "though she's still under thirty. And she always dresses in white." Cissy leaned closer and whispered, "They say she was mistress to the Marquess of Arden until he married last year. So not quite as pure as the white suggests."

Maria had never imagined it.

Her guests were the Embleboroughs, including Cissy's son and daughter. Natalie was here, too, and Harriette, of course. Maria was mostly able to let talk flow around her. She noted Vandeimen doing the same thing. Did he generally do so, or was this part of his dark mood? She suspected she had been very unperceptive these past weeks.

There was a knock on the door. Her footman opened it and turned to announce, "Major Hawkinville, ma'am."

Maria stared at the tall man in uniform, feeling as if she'd performed a conjuring trick. Then she thought to look at Vandeimen. He was already on his feet. "Hawk!"

There was joy there, but a great many other things too.

Chapter Six

He was smiling, and it was a heartaching flash of boy-
ishness she'd never seen before.

Now he was grasping his friend's hand, and she had
the feeling that he'd like to embrace him. They weren't
estranged, and whatever magic had brought the major
here, it was good magic.

Everyone was watching them, doubtless sensing an
important moment, then Vandeimen turned to her.
"Maria, I've spoken of Major Hawkinville, an old friend
and neighbor. Hawk, my lovely bride to be, Mrs.
Celestin."

She held out her hand. "I'm very pleased to meet
you, Major."

He was hawkish, though a second later she wasn't sure
why. No hooked nose, no yellow eyes. His face was lean,
his hair a soft brown, and worn a little long with a wave
in it. He was, above all, elegant, making even Van look
a little rough around the edges.

He took her hand and actually raised it to his lips.
She felt their pressure through her glove. "How unfair of
Van to steal you before I had a chance, Mrs. Celestin."

She started to smile, amused by his flirtation, but then
she caught a hard glint in his deeply blue eyes. Hawkish
indeed. But why was he turning a predatory eye on her?

"You are still in the army, Major?" she asked, to fill
the silence, though it was inane, given his scarlet and
braid.

"Easing my way out, Mrs. Celestin."

"They'll be reluctant to let him go." Vandeimen's
smile said that if there'd been any ambivalence, it had

gone. "We chargers and marchers are two-a-penny, but organizers like Hawk are treasured more than gold. Quartermaster Division," he added in explanation to everyone. "Got the armies to the field, with weapons and supplies intact. To the right field at the right time, even, if they were really good."

The teasing look between the two men suggested it was an old joke.

"And tidied up afterward," said the major, "which is why I get home a year late and find all the loveliest ladies taken."

He flashed Maria another look, but then turned to Natalie and to Cissy's blushing, seventeen-year-old daughter to express relief that some lovely ladies were still available.

Maria picked up conversation, but she was puzzling over the man's animosity. Was it Maurice? He'd made a great deal of money supplying the army with clothes and equipment. Perhaps he'd clashed with Major Hawkinville at some point.

Was it the age difference? She wouldn't have expected another young man to be outraged.

Or perhaps she was misreading a dark mood that had nothing to do with her.

The bell rang to warn of the end of the intermission, so Maria invited the major to stay. He accepted, and she settled to the next act plotting how to keep him by Vandeimen's side as long as possible. She could bear his antagonism if she must.

At the next intermission, they all strolled in the corridor. Maria wasn't sure how, but she ended up partnered with the major, while Vandeimen escorted Louisa Embleborough, a young miss suitable for either of these handsome heroes.

"Jealousy? Already?"

She looked up into those very blue, very chilly eyes. There was no doubt. He was antagonistic toward her. She'd like to confront him directly about it, but that might drive him away. She made herself answer lightly.

"Not at all, Major. I know how devoted Lord Vandeimen is to me, and *I* trust his sense of honor."

His eyes narrowed, but then changed, so that she couldn't be sure what she'd seen. "Perhaps it is I who am jealous, Mrs. Celestin. You are exceptionally beautiful."

Ah. Blatant fortune hunters she could deal with. Smiling, she said, "No, I'm not."

"You must allow me to know my own mind, ma'am. Beauty is not the same in every eye."

"Strange, then, that some people become acknowledged beauties."

He looked around and discreetly indicated a young brunette surrounded by men. "I don't know who she is, but I assume she is a toast."

"Miss Regis? Yes, she is much admired."

"I'm sure she is perfect to many, but I cannot admire a turned-up nose, and her smile is far too wide." He looked back at her. "Your mouth, however, is perfect."

Her not-too-wide smile was making her cheeks ache. Did he know she didn't want to send him off with a flea in his ear?

"Perfect," she echoed. "How lovely. What else about me is perfect, Major? I'm thirty-three years old and must hoard any compliments that still come my way."

"You're barren," he said. "And that is not a compliment."

Her breath caught. "And you are an uncouth swine, but you probably can't help that either."

They were both smiling, hiding their battle from those around.

'Van's marrying you for your money. If he needs money, I'll find a way to get it for him."

"Are you Midas, then? He lost ten thousand in one night." She watched in satisfaction as his smile disappeared. "Now, escort me back to my box."

At the door he halted, smile absent, hostility unmasked. "He deserves better than to marry for money, Mrs. Celestin. And he needs a family."

She agreed with him, but she couldn't let that show.

"I want his happiness, Major Hawkinville. For that reason, you are welcome to call at my house. You will understand, I'm sure, if I try to avoid you."

She went into the box alone.

Van was finding shy Miss Embleborough hard work, but he kept an eye on Maria and Hawk at the same time. He might not have seen a great deal of his friend over the past ten years, but he could still read him. He was in a hawkish mood.

Doubtless he thought Maria a heartless harpy and was riding to the rescue. As the bell sounded and people flowed back into their boxes, he managed to pass Miss Embleborough on to her brother, and paused with Hawk outside the box.

He closed the door, leaving them alone in the corridor. "You can't fight with Mrs. Celestin without picking a fight with me, you know. And I always win."

He said it lightly, but Hawk would understand that he was serious.

"Only because you've always been a madman." The tense look eased, however. "I probably did go a bit beyond the line."

"Why?"

"She said you lost ten thousand in one night. What the devil have you been up to?"

Van hadn't wanted any of his friends burdened with his problems. "My father left debts."

"And you decided to add to them?"

"I was trying to recoup them. You know I've always been lucky. Hawk, why were you picking a fight with Maria?"

After a moment, Hawk said, "I suppose it's mostly because of her husband."

"Celestin? You knew him?"

"Only as a name. He was one of the worst suppliers of shoddy goods and short measure, but we could never pin anything on him. Very clever use of middlemen. It galls me to think of all that money on a woman's back."

"Will it help to think of me benefiting from his ill-gotten gains?"

Hawk laughed. "Zeus, yes! Can't think of a better use at this point." After a moment, he added, "Look, don't throw a punch, but is it worth the money to marry a woman so much older?"

Van thought of explaining. He didn't mind revealing his follies to Hawk, but he didn't want to put Maria in a worse light. Then he recalled an amber light, and a ravishing kiss that hadn't been repeated . . .

"So," Hawk said, smoothing over the silence, "at least you'll be able to restore Steynings to all its former glory."

If Hawk thought this was a love affair, all the better. "That's the idea. Look, I'd better go back in. Come 'round tomorrow and we'll have more time to catch up. Have you seen Con yet?"

"I'm fresh off the boat. Heard about your engagement and set off—"

"—to save me, like George and the dragon? I don't think poor Maria should be seen as a dragon."

Hawk grinned. "And you're no trembling maiden. As for tomorrow, perhaps you'd better come to me. I'm staying at Beadle's Hotel in Prince's Street."

Clearly the disagreement between Hawk and Maria had been unpleasantly sharp. "Very well. Have you heard from Con at all?"

"No. Haven't you?"

"No."

"Have you tried?"

Van shrugged. "I didn't want to clutter his life with my problems. Since Waterloo, since Lord Darius died, he has enough."

"Perhaps your clutter would have been a distraction."

It was a reproof, and perhaps warranted, but Van said, "He'd have felt obliged to lend me money, and his family's never been wealthy."

"What about the earldom?"

"I still wouldn't want to dun off him. Forget it. Perhaps you should have come home sooner instead of play-ing around Europe."

"Playing around—?" Hawk sucked in a breath.

Van knew he should apologize. Hawk had been clean-ing up the bloody mess left by the battle, by mounds of corpses, by destroyed property, by allies turned to ar-guing among themselves over responsibility and repara-tion and even what to call the battle.

The apology stuck, though, and after a moment Hawk said, "Come over and we'll talk tomorrow." He strode off, never looking back.

Van leaned against the wall and closed his eyes, the sweet image of a pistol floating in front of him. He'd trained himself into a demon of destruction. Perhaps there came a point of no return.

He'd thought some things endured, particularly his lifelong friendships with Hawk and Con. But if Con needed his friends, he'd not found one in him, and now he'd lashed out at Hawk.

Perhaps there was no going back. He could reroof Steynings and bring the land into good heart again, but he doubted he could recreate past happiness in a house empty except for ghosts.

He might be able to do it with Maria's help.

He couldn't tell if this feeling was love, frustrated lust, or an insane kind of dependency, but he realized that his bleak mood, his bitterness, his attack on Hawk all grew out of the rapidly approaching end of his service to Maria.

And she insisted that he not touch her in any inti-mate way.

He knew what he ought to do. He ought to prepare to bid her a courteous farewell, leave to restore his home, then pick a young lady like Miss Embleborough to marry and have children with.

He'd rather shoot himself.

Maria entered her house on Vandeimen's arm as usual, and as usual they all took a light supper and chat-ted. She thought he looked strained, and hoped desperately that he hadn't fought with his friend over her. She silently berated herself for letting Major Hawkinville goad her, though how else she could have reacted, she didn't know.

Perhaps she should write an apology, though she'd done nothing wrong. It galled her that he, too, saw her as an aging harpy prepared to suck the blood from a younger man. Did everyone? Sarah Yeovil hadn't spoken more than the briefest word to her since that medieval affair.

And in a couple of weeks it would all be over.

If she were a weaker woman, she'd sink into tears.

Persistent Harriette was using Major Hawkinville's appearance as a lever to open up discussion of Vandeimen's friends and his home. He looked strained, but he was still in the room and talking, though saying little to the point.

She found herself watching him through a prism of his friend's eyes. Major Hawkinville hadn't seen Vandeimen for nearly a year, she assumed, and he had been disturbed. That was why he had attacked her.

She remembered the incident before dinner, and Harriette's words. A glossy shell with nothing inside.

That was not true. There was a lot inside, all of it tangled, dark, and dangerous. And now, for some reason, he was pushed to a brink.

When they separated to go to their bedrooms she tried to persuade herself that her concerns were only tiredness—hers or his. As her maid undressed her, however, and combed out her long hair then wove it in a plait, she worried.

When she climbed into bed, she knew that tomorrow she must insist that they travel to Steynings.

It was duty that drove her. She must correct the terrible wrong that Maurice had done to his family. By now, however, it was more than duty. She had to rescue him. She could bear to let him go, but she could not bear to let him fall back into the pit.

It was as if she saw a wonderful person through crazed glass. His honor showed in the damnable fact that he'd never again tried to kiss her. His cleverness showed in the way he managed to exhibit devotion and passion in public without ever doing anything improper.

His natural kindness showed in many ways. He never made fun of anyone. He would dance with clumsy shyness as if with a beauty, talk with a bore as if with a wit, smooth over rudeness so it was almost unrecognized.

He even spent time with Tante Louise and Oncle Charles, and no one would deny that they were a sour old couple who constantly carped at each other and the world.

She began to see, however, lying there in the dark, that all his kindnesses came from dogged duty, the same sense of duty that had driven him into the next battle, and the next, and the next.

Dogged? He had been a madman, an enthusiast, hadn't he?

Now she wondered, wondered if it had been more a case of never doing things by half measures, and whether that was what he was doing now, bleakness still in his heart.

And what exactly was he doing now, this very minute?

She tried to tell herself that he too had gone to bed, but something was screaming that he hadn't. That he might have his pistol in hand again. After a struggle, she climbed out of bed and reached for her wrap.

Oh no. Definitely not. She was not going to look for him in her nightgown!

Feeling more foolish by the moment, she put on a shift, dug through her drawers for one of her light corsets that hooked up the front, then for her simplest round gown. She wound her plait around her head and pinned it in place.

When she looked at herself in the mirror, she saw a woman blatantly well past the blush of youth in a plain gown, with plain hair and no ornament. She turned toward her jewel box, but then stopped herself. To decorate herself would put a wicked twist on this errand.

Grabbing her candlestick, she went out to make sure that her demon was not bent on something hellish.

The house was still. Surely everyone except herself was sensibly asleep. She knew she couldn't sleep until she had made a thorough check, however.

The ground floor was peaceful. She went back upstairs and checked the drawing room. Nothing.

She paused in the corridor, accepting what she'd always known. Whatever Vandeimen was up to, he was in the privacy of his bedroom, and she could not invade there.

Yet she could not let this rest.

She allowed herself to creep down to his door and listen.

Silence.

There, see. He was asleep.

Then she heard something. A movement, no more, but it suggested that he wasn't asleep.

He could be ready for bed.

Even naked.

She stood there, watching candlelight play red and black on the gleaming mahogany of the door panels, hearing only silence. Then, with a sigh and a wince, she gave a tiny tap on the door.

A voice. She couldn't tell what he'd said, but she turned the knob and peeped in.

He was sprawled on the floor in breeches and open-necked shirt, head and shoulders supported by the chaise near the empty fireplace. The room had been in darkness, and he raised a hand to shield his eyes for a moment.

"Devil take it, it's the angel again," he muttered, lowering his hand and staring at her. An empty glass was almost falling out of his other hand, and a half-empty brandy decanter sat on the floor nearby.

She almost berated him, but stopped herself. That would do no good. She closed the door behind her, thinking, thinking.

It had all been illusion these past weeks. He was still the half-drunk man who'd been about to kill himself, and she still had to save him.

Chapter Seven

"What's the matter?" he said in a voice turned lazy by drink. "No one's going to know except Noons, so I'm not breaking the rules."

A chair sat opposite the chaise on the other side of the fireplace. She went cautiously toward it, but then at the last moment she turned to the table of decanters. She put her candlestick there, took a glass and the decanter of claret, and sat on the floor in front of the chair, facing him.

She filled the glass, then placed her decanter on the floor in mirror image of his and took a drink. "There are certainly times when getting drunk seems like an excellent idea."

Guarded eyes rested on her as he sipped. "You mean there are times when it doesn't?"

The bleakness hit her, but she tried not to show it. She didn't know what she was doing here, but she knew she mustn't fall into emotion. "Did you get drunk before battle?"

"Not on purpose." He shifted slightly, relaxing. He was, at least, willing to talk. "Some did. They tended to die. Perhaps happier than the ones who died sober. Or even the ones who lived . . . I was caught in the bottle once or twice . . ."

He eyed his almost empty glass and the decanter, and then went about filling it with notable care.

Maria sipped her wine. This was the first time he'd mentioned the darker side of war. Was that good, or bad? Was it war memories that chained him in the dungeons, or the loss of his family, or both? She couldn't wipe one away, or bring the other back. She had to try to give him reason to live.

"Why did you join the army?" she asked, as if making idle conversation. "You were an only son."

"Still am. Last of the line as well. All the hopes and expectations of the Vandeimens rest upon these paltry shoulders." He toasted her and drank. "You have a lot of hair."

Instinctively, she touched the tight knot of plait, but she stuck to her purpose. "So, why did you join the army?"

The eyes half-glimpsed beneath lazy lids suddenly shot wickedness. "Let down your hair and I'll tell you."

Perhaps she should rise and leave now, but she knew she couldn't abandon him here like this. She could call his bluff, but she suspected that Demon Vandeimen never bluffed.

She raised her hands and pulled out the pins, letting the braid fall heavily down her back. "Don't think to play your games with me, sir. You'll neither win nor escape by pretending to desire me."

"Pretending? You can come over here and feel if you want."

Her breath caught and she couldn't help glancing at his crotch. She hastily looked up. "So, why did you join the army?"

"That isn't really down," he complained, but then said, "The others were. Why not?"

"The others?" Her mind was stuck on his earlier words, however. He was aroused? Now? By her? A responsive beat began between her thighs.

"Con. Hawk." He knocked back an irreverent amount of her very good cognac. "Con was a second son and willing to do his duty. Defeat the Corsican Monster. Save the women and children of England from invasion, rape, and pillage. Hawk saw a way to escape his family. As for me . . . what more could a sixteen-year-old who fed on excitement and challenge desire?" Those dangerous eyes met hers again. "I feed off excitement like a vampire feeds off blood, dear lady. Do you want to come over here and let me drink your pale, angelic blood?"

"No," she lied, beginning to burn with raw lust. She should leave . . . "And my blood is as red as yours, I assure you."

"All the better." He put down his glass and shifted to begin crawling over to her. In another man it might have been clumsy, but she immediately thought of a wolf, a lithe and lethal wolf. She wanted to flee, but she knew that would be disastrous. And part of her wanted to stay, even to bleed . . .

He knelt beside her on all fours and raised a hand to her neck. "So pale, so pure . . ."

"I'm a widow." Despite fingers stroking her neck, she used a cool tone, trying to deny all this, trying to summon the strength to flee.

His eyes were close now, intense, pupils large in the dim light. "You shouldn't have chained me, dear widow, if you didn't need me."

Need. She did need him. It had been so long, and here was that danger that always drove her wild.

It was real danger now. Not her husband, who had only pretended because it excited her, and that excited him. It was this wild and wounded young man with heat and sex rising off him like steam.

A wise woman would get up and run.

A decent woman would save him from himself.

Mouth dry with fear and longing, she whispered, "Do you need a woman, Vandeimen?"

"I need you."

"Then take me."

He kissed her with brandy-soaked heat and greedy passion, and she kissed him back as fiercely, sprawled against the seat of the big chair. It had been so long, too long, and he tasted like hell and heaven combined.

Then she was flat on her back, her legs up over his shoulders and him in her, deeply, fully, in her. He reared up, hands on the floor on either side of her head, eyes triumphantly on hers.

Magnificent. Beautiful. Virile.

Lethal—and she loved it.

She clutched his arms, moving, then firing off into her own particular hellfire heaven.

When she opened her eyes, swooningly pleasured, she was still locked in position with him, wishing she could see behind his closed eyes and set face.

Was he in heaven or in hell?

He shifted, sliding out of her and away, letting her legs come down, head turning from her.

"Don't," she said quickly, "say you're sorry."

He knelt between her legs, sweaty, rumpled, troubled, but he looked up at her. "You liked that?"

"Is it unladylike? In these things, I am not a lady."

She saw that he was hunting for evasion, for polite lies. She had no way to convince him with words, so she simply waited, lewdly disheveled, on the floor.

"What else do you like, then?" The unvarnished hunger in his voice made her want to smile, but she was afraid a smile might be misunderstood.

"A bed for a start. I'm too old for carpets all night." She put in the reminder of her age deliberately. She wanted this, but honestly.

She stretched out a hand to be helped up, but he went to his haunches, put his arms under her, and rose to his feet. His raw strength started the thunder of excitement again. Oh, she was a wicked woman to like this so, but she did.

He staggered slightly as he carried her to the bed, but it was drink not weakness.

Was she taking advantage of a drunken man?

He wasn't that drunk, and he was getting as much from this as she.

He placed her on the bed carefully enough. "Will you undress for me?" he asked. "As I watch?"

It stirred a little qualm. "If you'll remember that I'm gone thirty, and can't rival a sweet young thing of eighteen."

"Does it matter?" He leaned against a bedpost, prepared to watch.

His comment could be taken many ways. She chose

to ignore it. Even this was exciting her—the demand that she do something a little difficult and daring.

Did he understand her all too well?

Eyes on him, she loosened the drawstrings of her gown and pulled it off over her head. He was still watching. She had nothing on now but her shift and corset. Heart seeming to beat in her throat, she undid the front hooks of her corset, one by one.

He suddenly moved to brush her fingers away, to undo the last hooks and peel it open, almost reverently. She didn't want reverence. She pulled his shirt out of his unfastened pantaloons. "Strip."

With a laugh, he obeyed. She thought she moaned at the sheer beauty of his body. An anatomist could study muscles from him without dissection, but they were all sweetly smoothed by flesh—ands scars. Dozens of slashes, some puckered from rough healing.

For every one, she suspected, there was an internal scar. Scars, once formed, were permanent, though time did soften them. What of the scars that marked his heart and his soul?

She saw the dark stain of a tattoo on his chest, and remembered the duchess's comment.

"Rumor says that's a demon," she said.

"Rumor tells the truth, for once."

He came toward her and she saw that it was a demon, pitchfork in hand, amid red flames.

What was she doing here in a bed with a mad young demon?

He stripped off her corset and tossed it aside, then pushed her down on the bed in her shift. With a sudden grin, he ripped the garment open down the front.

Mad. Demon. And he understood her. It frightened her that, but thrilled her at the same time.

While her heart still raced, he spread the garment wide so she lay on it and leaned down to suckle her left breast, deep and firm.

"I love that," she breathed, even though her body's surge must have told him. "I love it. Teeth too, if you don't draw blood."

He looked up, bright-eyed. Whatever else, he was alive now, alive in this moment. Every inch of him. "And what if I do draw blood?" he asked, sending another mad shiver through her.

"You'll spoil this." Deep in her mind, however, an imp stirred with curiosity. No. She couldn't want that.

He kissed her breast softly—both a tease and a promise. "You're a remarkable woman, Maria."

"I'm a hungry one, too."

He laughed and returned to the ravishing of her breasts while she used nails to torment his skin. Without drawing blood.

Then he spread her legs and pushed into her again, and she rose eagerly, hungrily, nearly in orgasm already.

He moved in and out once with tortuous slowness. "It'll be longer this time." He made it into a thrilling warning.

She opened her eyes. "Will it?"

His wolfish smile was answer. "Do you like it long?"

Her head was buzzing, and the world swirled. "I don't know," she whispered. "My husband never went very long. He was over thirty when he married me."

"You've had no one else?"

She could protest the implication, but just said, "No."

"Am I better then?"

She laughed because it was only part tease. Deliberately, she challenged the demon. "I don't know yet."

He shifted and put one hand firmly over her mouth, while beginning deep, even strokes. She looked up, excited by that mild restraint. It implied that she had no right to object. That he could do anything with her, even draw blood.

And perhaps he could.

As she'd thought, Maurice's demanding sex had been a very safe game. Now she might be in the jungle with the animals. It excited her as nothing before.

She moved to wrap her legs around his waist, but he said, "No. Keep them down."

It could be a request. It sounded like a command.

Then he stilled and lowered his head to her breasts

again, sucking painfully strongly, arching her, breaking a muffled cry from her. His teeth. She felt his teeth, pressing so carefully, but so lethally.

Her heart pounded with sudden terror and violent lust. His silencing hand felt like a gag, but when she tried to fight it off, it tightened. He raised his head and looked at her, a glint of triumph in his eyes before he lowered again to her breasts. Mercy on her, it was that contest again. What might it drive him to do?

Instead of biting, he licked. Slowly, lazily, he licked all around her breasts when she wanted to scream at him for more.

She lay there, pinned to the bed, resentfully enduring this meaningless tonguing, resenting even more that he'd assessed the game as a whole and was winning a Pyrrhic victory simply by being gentle. She was full with the burning hardness of him, and apart from an occasional twitch, he wasn't moving at all.

He looked up again, claiming the mystery. She could hate him, but she didn't. She realized that she was hot, hot all over, boiling with need, excited by being entirely in his power and that she'd never before had time to know what this felt like.

Desperately intolerable.

He took his hand from her mouth and began to thrust. Deep rhythmical thrusts that truly did feel as if they could go on forever. He was watching her as if she was more interesting than his own pleasure. She watched back, desperately fighting dissolution under those competitive eyes.

Losing.

"Bastard!" she hissed, and surrendered.

When she swam out of the hot darkness he was still thrusting.

"Zeus, no," she muttered, but he didn't stop. Why did she think she could say no to this? And did she want to? Soon her body ripped off into madness again.

It happened one more time but that time he was with her, or far, far away from her. When he collapsed on her, she had to fight the urge to push him off and run away.

No more.

She couldn't take any more.

But of course, there would be no more. It was not physically possible. Was it? What did she really know of this?

Maurice's lovemaking had been strong, and when he demanded that daytime sex she'd been excited before he'd entered her, and exploded quickly. He'd always stroked her to more pleasure afterward as if in a kind of payment. She'd didn't know why, and had never asked. He'd seemed to enjoy watching her fall into pleasure.

She'd never experienced anything like this, however. Ravished expressed it perfectly. Ravished, razed, and conquered. Aching, burning, and drained, and ashamed about how much she was already grieving the loss of it.

There was no doubt. Lord Warren would never do this to her . . .

She woke exhausted, parts of her body still sore. She gently touched her nipples and almost flinched. When she tried to move away from him, however, she found he was lying on her hair.

When had it been freed of her plait?

During that other ravishing sometime in the night, as hot, as fierce, as strong as before. Could she walk?

She had to.

The light through the partially open curtains suggested very early morning, but she must be back in her room when her maid came.

She looked back at him and saw his eyes open, watching her. Blank eyes. Guarded eyes. With a suppressed groan she knew she couldn't let him feel the slightest regret about what had happened. And there wasn't any. She just didn't want more at the moment.

Or most of her didn't want more.

Parts of her were shameless hussies.

"Good morning," she said softly.

"Is it? Good?"

"It promises to be a lovely day." But she realized they were going to have to talk about sex. It was not something she had ever imagined doing. She reached up to touch his stubbled cheek. "I fear you must have a low opinion of me this morning."

By a sudden release of tension, she knew she had found the right words. He moved his rough chin against her hand. "You really enjoyed that?"

"Oh yes. But," she added quickly, "I couldn't take more now."

Too late she realized that the "now" promised things she wasn't sure about, but she couldn't retract it.

"I liked it, too," he said.

She tapped his cheek in playful rebuke. "You like challenge, Lord Vandeimen. How silly that sounds. May I call you Van?"

"Of course. Or," he added with a grin, "Demon. You called me that a time or two."

She knew she was coloring. "I'm sorry."

"Don't be. It's one of my names. I'd rather you not call me George." But his lids had lowered over his eyes.

"What is it?" she asked. "Better to be honest."

He looked at her. "Was this what you wanted all along? What you're paying for?"

"No!" Then she calmed herself. "No. I promise."

But it reminded her why she'd started this, and that he didn't know the truth. She didn't want to tell him now, to spoil this strangely beautiful night, but she must. For the sake of the fragile connection between them, she must.

She eased her hair free of him, then laid her hand on his shoulder. "Van, I have to tell you something. I don't want to, but I must."

She felt the tension, even though her eyes could not detect it. "Yes?"

"I know your father lost most of his money and shot himself . . ."

His brows twitched, but he didn't say anything.

"The money was lost in an investment involving rubber production."

"You do know a lot. Why?"

That was a more dire question than he suspected. She

tried to find words to soften it, but there were none. "My husband was the principal in that scheme."

She left it there, not trying to explain or excuse because there was no explanation or excuse, searching his still features, braced even for violence.

He moved slightly, freeing himself of her touch, lids lowered so she could no longer read his eyes. "And your part in this?"

"None! I knew nothing about it until after Maurice's death. I found it in his papers, his accounts . . ."

She noticed his chest rise and fall with his breaths wondering what else she could say to hold off disaster. But then he looked at her. "Is that why you sought me out? Why?"

Panick gripped her. If she told him, he'd know he didn't owe her anything. He'd leave!

So be it.

She licked her dry lips. "When I realized what Maurice had done, I knew I had to put it right. From pride, however, I didn't want anyone to know what a scoundrel my husband had been. I tried to think of cunning schemes. I followed your doings anxiously, and even thought of finding someone to deliberately lose a fortune to you at cards."

"Why didn't you?" But he was looking lighter, if rather dazed.

"I didn't know how. That's how I heard about your disastrous loss, though. It was so unlike you. I'd heard that you nearly always won. I knew I had to act." She reached out again to touch him, and he didn't move away. "Thank God I did."

He collapsed down on his back. It broke contact again, but she didn't mind. He was staring at the ceiling. "I wish your husband was alive to be killed," he said, almost idly. "But it wasn't entirely his fault, you know. There were too many deaths in the family. They broke my father's spirit. In the end, he was probably glad of an excuse to go. I should have dragged myself away from war to help him."

She took a risk and lay down beside him, close to him.

He moved his arm and gathered her in, and she almost melted with relief. She'd told him, and it hadn't destroyed everything.

"You were doing your duty," she said.

"Doesn't duty to family come first?"

"If it did, there'd be no more wars."

"And that would be a good thing."

She rolled closer, put her arm across him. "Speak of war if you wish, Van, but don't torment yourself. Sometimes there are dragons, and they have to be fought. Doubtless Saint George left family behind to worry."

"Saint George. We all wanted to be Saint George the dragon killer, so none of us could be. And Con ended up getting a tattoo of a dragon. I never did understand why."

"So much worse than a demon?" she teased, licking over his grimacing devil, then blowing.

He rolled over her, smiling. "To us it was. To us the dragon was everything bad, from the head gamekeeper to the French. But he insisted."

"It links in to the title he has now."

"But he never expected to inherit that . . ." He took a handful of her hair. "This is beautiful."

"It's mousy brown."

"Not at all. It makes me think of young deer and the soft mystery of the forests. It's very English hair." He buried his head in it for a moment, then looked at her again. "If we couple again it will be on my terms. Gently."

"You don't like it like that?"

"I like it. But I want to cherish you gently to heaven one day, my lady."

"This is only for the six weeks!" It came out harsher, blunter than she meant, but she meant the warning. To herself as much as to him. "In fact, as you now know, you owe me nothing."

"Are you saying that I owed you this?"

She colored fiercely. "No. But the money is yours. You don't have to pretend to be engaged to marry me."

"I keep my word. I am still yours to command, my lady."

A number of lewd suggestions flashed through her mind, but the saner parts of her body protested, and anyway, she still needed to help him heal. That had been the main purpose all along, and now she knew what must happen next.

"Then we visit your home for a few days," she said. "Just us."

He stared at her. "Why?"

"Why not? If I were really to be your bride I would want to."

"But this is mere pretense."

She tried not to show that the flat words stung. "Why not?" she asked again.

"It's been virtually uninhabited for a year and before that it hadn't been kept up too well."

"Then it's time you assessed what needs to be done."

He rolled away to lie on his back again, but this time it was hostile. "I know what needs to be done."

Her mouth dried, but she had to continue. His fierce resistance showed that it was important. "You will soon have the money to care for it. You need to start making plans."

He did turn back to look at her then. "Is this a command, O ruler of my heart?"

At the biting edge, she wanted to say no, to let him escape, but she said, "Yes."

He rolled away from her, out of his side of the bed, shocking her with his beauty because her mind had not been in that place. Every muscle, every bone, was angry.

He turned. "Didn't you want to get back to your room?"

She was tempted to clutch things around her and scuttle, but this was another of the demon's damned battles. She climbed out of her side of the bed stark naked. Not trying to cover herself, but glad of her curtain of hair, she asked, "When can you be ready to leave?"

"In moments if necessary. How do we travel? Horseback?"

She winced at the mere thought, and knew he'd said that deliberately. "Curricle?"

"I don't have one."

"I do. You can drive if you want."

"I don't know how." At her look of surprise he said, "It's not something you do in the army in wartime. I can ride twelve hours at a stretch, though, if I have to."

She wondered if it was only her lustful side that caught an ambiguity there, and leaped toward it even as most of herself recoiled. She turned to look for clothing, even if it did lose her points. Her shoes. Her corset. Her dress . . . Where was her shift?

Still in the bed. She turned and he had found it. He tossed it to her. She realized she was going to have to hide it and hope her maid didn't notice the loss. She looked at him again. He was slightly erect.

She scrambled into her dress over nothing, and tugged the laces tight beneath her breasts. Without her corset she had to push them up first, and she glanced anxiously at him.

Anger had been replaced with a hint of a smile.

"What are you laughing at?"

"You're beautiful, even if you're not eighteen. And that comes free of charge. And I like to make you turn from a lily to a blush-pink rose. The journey will take four to five hours. Can you drive that long?"

It astonished her that he asked instead of stating it. Warmed her. "Probably not. We'll travel post."

"Where will we stay?"

Even thawed, he was making this trip entirely her concern, dissociating himself while being obedient to her commands. She would not be weakened by that.

"There must be an inn."

"The Peregrine, where I am known. We are engaged to wed, but an unchaperoned journey is still slightly shocking."

"Only slightly. I'm not a delicate young miss, and we'll have separate rooms. I'll order the post chaise and a hasty breakfast, and we'll set out in an hour."

She left with that, creeping back to her room feeling like a naughty child. No, like a wicked woman.

She was wicked to have let it go this far when it could never go further, but at least she had told him the truth. She felt lighter for that, happier, cleansed of deceptions and sins.

As reward, she'd steal the two remaining weeks for herself before saying farewell forever.

Chapter Eight

They sped out of London as true daylight broke, alone. She'd announced that they did not need their personal servants. She very much wanted to be alone with him, and it wasn't for lustful reasons. She hungered to know him better.

"You never really explained how you joined the army," she said as they passed through Camberwell Toll Gate. "Didn't your parents object?"

"Somewhat. I think they recognized the madman in me, though."

"You're not mad."

He smiled. "I feed off excitement as a vampire feeds off blood," he said again, making her instantly hot and needy. The glint in his eyes sent off warning signals, but it was so much part of him that she rejoiced.

"I can't cure you," she said calmly.

"I don't want to be cured. I think you're something of a madwoman yourself."

Oh no. She was not going to talk about sex in broad daylight. "So your parents let you go."

His smile acknowledged her retreat. "Bought me a commission in the regiment of my choice. Waved me farewell." The smile faded. "And I more or less forgot about them."

He leaned back into his corner and stared into nothing. "It was all so exciting, so new. New friends, new places, new challenges. Then when it ceased to be new, ceased to be pleasant, it had swallowed me whole. I always assumed they'd be there, frozen like waxworks, when I was ready to return."

Maria inhaled a careful breath, thinking carefully about what to say. "Did you never return home?"

"Not in the last five years. I could have. I should have . . ."

"Your family understood, I'm sure. They must have been proud of you. And later, their spirits guided you to safety."

He turned sharply at that. "Pap. Good men with adoring families died all the time."

Shame flooded her for speaking such an empty platitude, but all she could think to say was another. "They must want you to be happy."

"I am attempting to live, and live well."

It was like trying to read a foreign script. "Why is it so hard, Van? Do you not want a good life?"

"Do I deserve one? For some reason you see me as something worth saving. I'm not so sure." But then he turned to look out of the window, and she knew he wanted to be left in peace.

She granted him that, for now. She felt as if she were cracking open the cage of a seething demon, here in a confined space. She remembered, an eon ago, feeling inadequate and unprepared. Back then, she'd had no idea of the true challenge. Back then, however, she hadn't cared as she cared now.

After the first change of horses, she broke the silence. "Tell me about getting a tattoo."

His brows rose, but he answered. "It hurts."

"I suppose it must. Does it take a long time?"

"Ours did."

"Do you ever regret having a devil engraved on your chest?"

It was meant to be a light question, but he said, "I have wondered if I was inviting a dark fate."

"That's not possible!"

"It's surprising what's possible."

"Did your friends' designs have any mysterious power?"

"Hawk was always hawkish, but he's become more so.

Con . . . It was strange that he chose a dragon. I've never been sure what it meant to him."

"A taste for sacrificial virgins?" she suggested.

He laughed, fully, eyes bright. "I have no idea. We've been out of touch too long."

She risked a probing question. "I gather he came home after Waterloo. Why haven't you seen him?"

That killed the laughter, but he shrugged. "I came home in January, and he was hunting in the Shires. When I visited Steynings he wasn't in the area."

"You could have written, arranged a meeting."

"Perhaps I didn't want him involved in my mess."

That made her heart ache, but it was hopeful that he was speaking of these things. Perhaps the physical act of moving toward home was moving his mind. Had their passionate night had any part in this? She'd like to think so.

Over the hours they chatted about childhood, and families—but only the sunnier aspects—and about the easier parts of their adult lives. It was clear that his childhood had been happy, his family loved, and that one of his greatest problems since returning to England might have been loneliness.

At the fourth change she suggested that they stop for refreshments, but he looked around almost like a dog sniffing the air, and said, "No. Not long now."

She'd been noting the mileposts to Brighton, forgetting that his home was not in the town. They were six miles away and must be close to Steynings.

He spoke to the postboys, giving instructions, and not far from the inn they took a side road. She read the signpost. Mayfield, Barkholme, and Hawk in the Vale.

"Hawk in the Vale?" she guessed.

"That's the nearest village, yes. It's pronounced Hawk'nvale."

"Like your friend's name."

"Almost. The family's been there about as long as the village."

He was looking out of the window, but it was no longer a means to escape conversation. She knew he was seeking signs of home. They reached the top of a rise, and he pointed to the left across rolling hills to a white house on a hillside. "That's Steynings."

She relaxed. Perhaps he'd just needed to come here to embrace his home and his purpose. Perhaps their talk along the way had helped as well, and their night of passion. Whatever had worked the miracle she sensed that he was finally, truly, coming home.

Her face suddenly ached with unshed tears, but she made herself be happy. Soon her task would be over, and she could go on with her life with an easy conscience.

"How long until we get there?" she asked.

"An hour, likely. It's not far, but we're off the good roads."

"It's a handsome house."

The house had disappeared behind trees now, and he turned to her. "Built new by my Dutch ancestor who came across with William of Orange and married into the English. Then fancied up in the Palladian style by my grandfather." He flashed her a slight smile. "Around here, we're the *nouveau riche*."

"The Hawkinville name was in the Domesday Book, I assume."

"Lord yes."

"And Lord Wyvern?"

"That title's only a couple of hundred years old, and it belongs to Devon, not Sussex. But the Somerfords have been here for five hundred years or so. Typical English blue blood. Saxon, Norman, Dane, and a bit of everything else that's come by in the last thousand years. Like the Dunpott-Ffyfes."

"True."

They share a smile that might be the most honest one ever.

Eventually the coach slowed to turn into a village. "Hawk'nvale," he said with soft satisfaction.

It lay in a gentle valley, with a broken row of old cottages set along the river. Each had a narrow garden running down to the water. That style marked a truly ancient settlement dating back to the times when rivers were more important than roads.

The large church set on a rise across the village green had a square Anglo-Saxon tower that marked it as at least eight hundred years old. To either side, like curved arms, lay newer buildings, so that the whole village embraced the green.

Surely it stood ready to embrace a returning son.

They drew up on the modern side of the village, in front of the stuccoed Peregrine Inn and climbed down.

"This is New Hawk," Van said, looking around. "Down by the river is Old Hawk."

"Where does Major Hawkinville live?"

"Wherever he puts his hat. But his father's house is in Old Hawk, of course. The walled place with the tower inside."

It was so much part of the older section of the village that her eye had ignored it. Now she saw a walled conglomeration of buildings surely going back in parts to the days of the ancient church. "Ancient, but not handsome," she remembered.

"Did it actually hold against the Normans?" she asked in fascination.

"The wall's not that old, but the tower probably saw William the Conqueror go past. It's a fascinating old place, but getting impossible to live in comfortably."

A tall, cheerful man strode out of the main doors to greet them. He seemed glowingly happy to see Van. Van, smiling, introduced him as Smithers, the innkeeper.

The healing was happening, she was sure.

Mr. Smithers regaled her with stories of the Young Georges' impish youth as he led her to her room. It proved to be as up to date as her own at home. A maid brought water and she freshened herself. When she went down, she was directed to a private parlor where Van had arranged a meal.

She was glad of it, but would have been as happy to go directly to his home. To complete this healing journey. He wasn't in the room yet, so she looked out of the window at the green, watching people cross, sometimes stop to chat. This had the feel of a good place.

She heard laughter, and returned to the door of the parlor to look out. Van stood in the middle of a group of men of all ages and types, a few maidservants hovering as well. It was clear they all were delighted to see him home again, and were at ease with him. He looked more relaxed than ever.

And younger. Much younger.

He was home.

She'd done her job.

All that remained now was to set him free.

After the meal they hired the inn's gig and drove to Steynings Park. Though she was sure he could manage a gig, he insisted that she drive.

The neglect soon became obvious. The road worsened, the hedges were untrimmed, the ditches at the sides of the road appeared clogged. All the kinds of things that didn't get done without someone in charge.

"Have you not been here at all?" she asked.

"Once. There was nothing I could do."

She could have pursued that, but let it go.

When they came to the walls of the estate it was as well the iron gates stood open because the gatekeeper's cottage was deserted. From a slight sag, she suspected the gates couldn't be moved without a mighty struggle.

"That isn't a recent problem," he said as if she'd remarked on it. "My father felt it was unseemly to have closed gates, as if the local people weren't welcome."

"I like that."

"He was a very likable man. Very generous and trusting."

And thus used by Maurice. Thank heavens Van didn't hold that against her.

Weeds tufted the long drive, evidence not just of neglect but that little traffic had passed this way. The drive took them straight up to the square house with the two curving Palladian wings on either side.

The windows were dirty, and a sad air of neglect hung

over the place, but there was no sign of serious decay. He directed her down the side of the house to a separate stableyard at the back. A middle-aged man came out lethargically to take the horse.

Van greeted the man as Lumley, but there seemed little fondness there. Probably the few staff remaining in the house were short on wages and tired of neglect.

Van assisted her down. "Let's do the guided tour, but even at its best, Steynings wasn't a jewel. I suppose some architects must be better than others."

As they toured the house, she saw what he meant. In places the proportions were not quite right, and some doors were inconveniently placed. All the same, it was a pleasant home, and ghosts of happier times lingered in pictures on the walls and arrangements of cloth-shrouded furniture.

She looked at one excellent portrait of his Dutch ancestor. "You never thought of selling this?"

"All or nothing."

Victory or death, even in financial matters. Infuriating in one way, but she couldn't help admiring it.

They ended up in a small drawing room, where the cloths had been removed and tea set out. She sat to pour. "I don't see that much needs to be done here other than cleaning."

He roamed the room restlessly. "There's some leakage from the roof. Brickwork needing pointing. Possibly dry rot in one section of the basement. Not obvious things, but if neglected the place will crumble about somebody's ears one day."

She passed him a cup. "The nine thousand will cover it?"

"Oh yes. And the servants etcetera."

It seemed invasive to quiz him on his affairs, but he needed to focus on them. "And the estate? Is it profitable?"

A look suggested that he thought it was invasive, too, but he answered. "Slightly. Times are hard now the war's over, but we'll make do once some money's been plowed in. Drainage, fencing, marling. All the things tenants put off. I should have been here helping, shouldn't I? I should have sold the damn pictures and plowed in the money."

She sipped, deliberately calm. "Why didn't you?"

She thought he wasn't going to answer, but then he said, "Now, I'm not sure." He looked around the room as if it represented the whole house. "I couldn't bear to peck away here like a crow pecking out the eyes of the dead—"

He stopped, and she could find no words to invade that silence.

He suddenly put down his cup and saucer and said, "Come upstairs. There's something I want to show you."

They'd toured all the main rooms, but she rose and went with him up the wide stairs and along a short corridor. He opened a door and invited her in. She entered and looked around curiously at what was probably the master bedchamber, shrouded in white cloths.

Then she saw his expression. "No, Van."

It was instinctive and she didn't entirely mean it, but she knew she must.

He came close to rest warm fingers on either side of her face. "Why not?"

Her wretched body was already shimmering with excitement but she knew she had to do what was best for him. He was running away into something simple. "The servants . . ."

"Aren't likely to come up here unless ordered to." He unfastened her bonnet ribbons and tossed it aside, then her cap, then began on her hairpins.

She whipped herself out of his hands and retreated clutching her wanton hair. "No!"

He simply stood there, temptation incarnate, by his need as much as his beauty. "Why not?"

She struggled to push back loosened pins, to recreate order. "We didn't come here for this."

"We didn't come for tea, either. We've just had tea."

"Is that what it is for you? Like tea?" It was nonsensical, but she threw it as a weapon.

"I don't much like tea." Then he sobered. "Is this one of the games you like, or do you really not want to?"

It made her feel ashamed, and confused, and uncertain, and she wanted to soothe him in the one way that seemed to work . . .

"Marry me, Maria."

At the shocking words, she retreated another step, shaking her head. "No, Van. No. That was never part of this."

He became still. "So. It was just an amusement for you."

"No!"

"Then what? Why not? Am I wrong in feeling there's something special between us?"

She lowered her hands and felt a heavy hank of hair tumble down her back. "Not wrong, but not right either. I'm eight years older than you."

"Well then," he said, "will you mind if I marry Natalie?"

She just stared. Eventually she managed to say, "If she's willing—"

"She's nine years younger than I am."

She could have slapped him. "That's not the same thing!" Then she braced herself to say the words that always hurt. "More importantly, I'm barren."

She saw it hit him, shaking her head. "Are you sure?"

"Of course I'm sure." She snared the fallen hair, coiled it, and fixed it in place. "I've never shown any sign of conceiving." She fired a fatal arrow. "And it wasn't Maurice's fault. Natalie is his daughter."

His sudden pallor made his eyes an even more brilliant blue. He bent abruptly to pick up the hairpins that had fallen from her hair, and when he rose, he was merely sober. "What if I don't care?"

"You have to care. It's your duty to care."

"Maria, I love you."

She shook her head. "No. You can't."

He came over to her, pins in his extended, beautiful, scarred hand. "I thought that too. That I couldn't love. I thought I was dead except for an inconveniently beating heart. Then you burst into my room that day and brought me back to life."

She took the pins trying not to show how the mere brush of her fingers against his warm palm shuddered her. "I don't regret it, but I will if you persist with this."

Red flushed his cheeks, but he didn't look away. "Are you denying what burns between us? Can you say it means nothing, that it's on my side only?"

He'd put the blade in her hand, and all she had to do was wield it—deny her love, agree that it meant nothing . . .

She tried, but the sacrilegious lie stuck in her throat. Her lips moved, but no sound came out, and heaven only knows what he read in her face.

She turned sharply to the mirror, stabbing pins into her hair, striving for courage to cut him free.

She heard the door close and turned to find that he'd gone.

Van went downstairs in that state of shivering light-headedness that had always swept over him after battle, when he'd realized that yet again he was miraculously alive and intact. But this battle had only just begun.

She hadn't said that the fire burned on his side only.

Was it willful folly to believe she'd stuck on a lie rather than a hurtful truth? All he knew was that this was demon Vandeimen's most crucial battle and he'd fight, fight to the end.

He stood in the silent, slightly musty hall stirring again the dreams that had built here for him this afternoon.

He'd begun to dream of a freshly-painted hall, the plaster cornice repaired in that corner, the parquet floor perfumed and gleaming with wax. Now his mind put flowers in the vase on the table, and potpourri in the china jar. Then laughter trickled from upstairs and children ran down and out, out into the grounds to explore as the triumvirate had, to be Robin Hood in the woods and pirates on the river—

The vision shattered and he sucked in a deep breath. Yes, his idyll had contained children and it would hurt to let that part of the picture go, but children weren't as important as Maria. Anyway, they could bring children into their lives as she had Natalie. Heaven knows, there was no shortage of orphans in the world.

Natalie. Oncle Charles and Tante Louise had gossiped maliciously about Natalie, so that had been no surprise. He hadn't made that other connection.

He burned with the need to act, to charge wildly into battle, but where was the enemy here?

He went over to the china potpourri pot his mother had loved and lifted the lid to find that it still contained dusky petals, doubtless put there by her own hands. Having been covered for so long, a faint perfume stirred like a ghost of summers past.

Tears stabbed, and he looked up, swallowing, fighting, until the danger past. There could be summers here again, and children even if they were not of his blood. There could also be Maria.

There had to be.

It wouldn't be the first time he'd led a forlorn hope.

He heard a sound and turned to see her coming down the stairs, gloved and hatted, composed except for something bruised in her eyes. He would cut off his arm rather than cause her pain, but he could not let her run away without a fight.

He met her at the bottom of the stairs, blocking her way.

He saw her flinch, but she met his eyes. "We should return to London. We can make it before dark."

"Of course, but let me say something first. We can have children." He overrode her protest. "We can give a home to orphans as you have to Natalie."

"You have bastards you need to house, Lord Vandeimen?"

It was harsh as a swung saber, but attack had never daunted him. "Not that I know of. Fight with me, Maria, instead of against me."

She met his eyes, lily-pale, steel-cold. "We are not on the same side in this."

"Maria—"

"No!" She sidestepped to walk around him and he grabbed her arm.

She whirled, furious—and afraid.

Instinctively his fingers loosened, but then he tightened them again. "All I want to make clear is that if you are barren it is not an insurmountable obstacle."

"Your title would die."

"So, it would die. It's an upstart Dutch transplant only five generations old. It's not worthy of human sacrifice."

Her lips tightened and she suddenly looked older, older than her years. All he wanted was to cherish her and he was bruising her in mind and spirit.

She opened one gloved hand and he saw his ring in it. "I'm sorry, Lord Vandeimen," she said, looking at some vague point behind him, "I find we would not suit."

"Dammit, Maria"—he sucked in a breath—"We have a contract and it has nearly two weeks to run."

Her eyes clashed with his. "I'm ending it now. As soon as we return to town I'll have your nine thousand pounds transferred to Perry's."

"A contract has two parties. I say it will hold until the end."

"Hold to it if you want. I will not wear your ring, and you will not live in my house. I will not see you again, Lord Vandeimen. In fact, if you have any honor at all you will stay here and get on with restoring your home!"

It hurt, like blows, like blades raining down on him, but he kept hold of her arm and spoke steadily. "And leave you to return unescorted? I think not. But you're right, we should leave."

He let her go then, and stalked out of the house before he gave into temptation to shake her, kiss her, or ravish her.

He suspected she'd succumb to angry ravishment, and that would be the cruelest blow of all.

Chapter Nine

Maria sank down onto the lowest steps, shaking with fury and pain. It was like trying to hack off one of her own limbs, and he was making it harder and harder. Why wouldn't he simply take the money and go?

The last thing she wanted to do was to follow him, to travel with him back to the village and then on the four-hour journey to London, but what choice did she have? Like so many other wounds, it could be endured and survived. She pulled herself to her feet and gathered strength to walk out to the stables.

When she arrived there the gig was ready and he was sitting with the reins in his hands. She climbed up beside him in silence and they set off.

"Maria—"

"Van, don't. Please." She gripped her hands together and realized that she still had his ring clutched in one. It would be a grand gesture to toss it away, but she couldn't do that. She couldn't do that any more than she'd been able to cut him free cleanly with cruel words.

He steered around a deep dip in the drive then picked up speed again. "I amputated one of my men's arms once," he said, eyes ahead. "It was mostly off anyway, but he was bleeding to death and we were stuck in the remains of a village in the sierra. I tied it, hacked off the remains, and cauterized it with my saber heated in the cooking fire." He turned to look at her. "He begged, too, but he's alive today and home on his family's farm in Lincolnshire. He married a childhood sweetheart and has a baby now."

She didn't know what to say other than to beg again,

and she believed what he was saying. He wouldn't stop because she begged, because he believed that what he was doing was right.

They turned out of the generously open gates onto the country road. "Are you sure about Maurice?" he asked quietly. "About Natalie?"

She could weep for clung-to hopes, but answered flatly. "Yes. He had four other bastards that I know of, currently aged two to ten. I can list their names if you want. He never concealed them from me, and he left provision for them in his will."

"List their names."

"What?" She stared at him.

He glanced at her, seeming almost calm, almost as if none of this mattered at all. "You said you could list their names. I asked you to."

Feeling as if they'd slipped into a land where nothing made sense, she said, "Tommy Grimes, Mary Ann Notts, Alice Jones, and Benjamin Mumford."

He nodded, but said nothing. The children should have been a winning blow, and yet Maria felt uneasily as if she had put a sharp weapon into his hands. She needed a shield. She would marry Lord Warren. He wouldn't expect a passionate heart, and marriage would distract her. After all, she'd have the care and guidance of his sons, not much younger than Van.

But she'd never again burn in the fire of her demon's passion.

Human sacrifice.

Oh yes, he had the right of it there, and was it right to sacrifice Lord Warren in her cause?

When they arrived back at the inn, she hurried up to the privacy of her room, leaving him to arrange for the coach to be ready. As she waited her mind circled that incident he had mentioned, the amputation.

How old had he been then? He'd said sierra, so in Spain. At least two years ago, perhaps longer, and he was only twenty-five now. She could imagine the inner terror, the sweating hands, the threatening vomit. She was also sure of the courage and willpower that had kept his hands steady, had done what had to be done as quickly and deftly as possible.

Love poured through her again, carried on respect and admiration. She wanted him in so many, many ways. But she loved him enough to cut him free and cauterize the wound despite his protests. Then perhaps one day she would be able to speak calmly of his happy life along with a sweetheart and a baby.

Van made the arrangements, and considered four hours in the coach with Maria. He couldn't. He couldn't trust himself not to argue, or worse, try to persuade by force or seduction. The demon was writhing inside him, calling for the fight to the death, for all or nothing.

He asked the innkeeper about a horse to hire and found that a Mr. Slade kept three fine horses at the inn and rarely rode them. Slade, apparently, was a wealthy iron founder who'd retired to the village and built the overlarge, stuccoed house that stood out in the village like a tombstone in a garden. Van was surprised Squire Hawkinville had permitted it.

Slade was a convenience for him, however. At the price of a few moments being oozed over by Slade he had the use of a bay gelding for the journey to London. It would cost more later. The iron founder was clearly delighted to put a local lord under an obligation. It was worth the price. He'd pay any price for Maria's comfort—except to let her go.

By the time they arrived back, the light was going and a misty drizzle completed a miserable day. Maria had spent the journey planning ways to force Van to accept that their arrangement was at an end, but she'd been constantly distracted by the sight of him on horseback.

He rode superbly of course, one with the fine horse, and completely in control. He mostly rode alongside, but occasionally he raced ahead then circled back exhilarated, smiling. Until his eyes met hers and settled again to cool purpose.

He was going to fight, and she shivered at the thought.

She was drowning in guilt, too. He was a cavalry officer, and she'd never thought to offer him a horse. She put that aside as a minor sin past redemption, and focused on amputation.

As soon as she was out of the coach and he was off the horse, she said, "Your indentured servitude is at an end as of now, my lord."

He paled so the scar stood out starkly on his cheek, but said, "Not here, Maria," and turned to tip the postboys and to arrange for one to ride his horse to the livery stables.

She was left burning with embarrassment. She'd spilled her words in the open street. She hurried into her house feeling not like a resolute matron, but like a guilty child. She almost fled up to her room, but he'd follow her there. She knew he would. She couldn't deal with this in such an intimate setting.

Surely she had the right to throw him from her house!

Harriette came down the stairs. "Maria? What are you doing home? Is something the matter?"

"I've decided my arrangement with Lord Vandeimen is at an end. He will be leaving."

"Will I?" he said behind her, and she turned. Her footman was hovering, looking uncertain. If necessary, John would throw him out. If he could, that is. A brawl in the entrance hall of her house? How had matters come to this?

"Maria." It was Harriette, and she had the door to the reception room open. "We need to talk."

Maria wanted to refuse, but if she did, Harriette would speak her mind in front of the servants. She stalked into the room and shut the door. "Don't interfere, Harriette."

"You cannot be so impossibly inhospitable."

"There's no longer any need for him to be here."

"He's healed?"

Maria was struck by uncertainty. It was only last night that he'd taken to deep drinking. So much had happened since that it seemed an age ago, but it had only been last night.

"He's ready to begin restoring his home," she said. "That's what you wanted, isn't it?"

Harriette eyed her. "I think he's making you uncomfortable, and that's why you're trying to cast him out. What's he done?"

Maria circled the room then admitted it. "He proposed to me."

"Ah. And you said?"

"No, of course. It will not do."

"Why not?"

"Put aside age and the fact that I bribed him into this, I'm barren."

Harriette's face sagged. "Oh my dear, I had forgotten. It would have been wonderful."

"No it wouldn't. I'm too old for him. He's too . . . demanding. Controlling."

"Oh no. You're made for each other. I've thought it almost from the first. You laugh with him, and blush with him. He makes you young again. He's steady with you, at ease with you. You anchor him. Be that as it may," she added briskly, "you are not throwing him out of here so suddenly, especially if you've just hurt him—"

"I haven't hurt him."

"Any rejected proposal is hurtful. He's staying for the remaining days."

"Whose house is this?"

"Yours, but you'll do as you're told. You don't want to have to wonder whether he's digging out his pistol again, do you?"

"He wouldn't . . ." Maria glared at her aunt. "You're a conniving old woman."

"I'm not so old as that. In fact," she said with a naughty grin, "if you don't want him, perhaps I'll set my cap at him. I don't mind a bit of control in the right places."

She walked out of the room leaving Maria gaping. She sank into a chair and leaned her head against the back.

Twelve days. Only twelve days. That could be endured.

And twelve nights, every one of them temptation.

*   *   *

Maria retreated to her room that first night, but she could hardly hide forever. She emerged after breakfast the next day braced for persuasion, even seduction.

He had gone out.

Feeling deflated instead of relieved she set out to have a normal day, the sort of day she'd enjoyed before meeting Demon Vandeimen, the sort of day that would fill the rest of her life.

His absence crept with her like a gray ghost.

When she visited Crown and Mitchell to consider one of the new kitchen stoves, she turned to him for an opinion. When she found that a book she'd been waiting for was available, she anticipated sharing it with him. When she flipped through her pile of invitations, she thought of which would most please him.

She didn't want to attend social events. People would notice the absent ring. After a moment she pulled it out of her pocket and slid it on her finger again. It was still small and pale, but precious. She was entitled to keep it, and she would.

She would never wear it again, but she slid it off and put it back in her pocket. A guilty weakness, but it would be something to remember him by through the rest of her life.

Van went to Beadle's Hotel, and was taken up to Hawk's rooms.

Hawk closed the door on the nosy maid. "Trouble?"

Trust Hawk to see that instantly. This was his private parlor, comfortably if plainly decorated. Van had the irrelevant thought that it would have been luxury during their campaigning years. And that, despite danger and death, life had been simpler then.

He'd come here to get Hawk's help, but putting the situation into words felt like sealing it in reality. "Maria's decided she doesn't want to marry me."

"Ah. I'll be honest and say that I'm not sorry."

"Why?" Van could have said other, more bitter words, could have thrown a blow even, but restrained himself. "You met her once, and spoke a few words. What the devil reason do you have to try to come between us?"

So much for restraint.

Hawk stayed calm, but Van saw him shift slightly, balancing to be ready for attack. He couldn't believe this. Was everything in his life going to fall apart?

"I haven't tried to come between you," Hawk said calmly. "Though I could. I wasn't going to speak of this, but perhaps it will help you accept your lucky escape. I said that her husband engaged in shady dealings. I had other suspicions, which I confirmed by making some inquiries yesterday."

"You've been making inquiries about Maria?" Van could feel the words in his mouth like ice, like fire. "How dare you?"

"Of course I dare. I couldn't let you marry a woman like that without—"

"A woman like that?"

Hawk stepped back, raising a hand, his eyes fixed on Van as on a predatory animal. "Hear me out before you hit me."

Van sucked in a deep breath. "Speak."

"Celestin had his fingers in many rotten pies, including highly speculative investments. He was leading partner in the investment that ruined your father. He got out intact—he generally did—leaving your father to bear the loss. He as good as put the pistol to your father's head, Van. I don't know what game his widow is playing, but—"

"Is that it?"

"What?"

"Is that your evidence?"

For once, Hawk looked unsettled. "Yes."

Van felt muscles unbunch, sinews release. "She told me. Why should she be blamed for her husband's dishonor?"

"She obviously knew about it."

"She found out after Celestin's death, from his papers and accounts. And I believe her on that, Hawk."

Hawk didn't look relieved, but he said, "Then for your sake, I'm glad. Except that apparently she has cast you off."

With matters so on edge between them, Van didn't want to expose Maria any further, but it wouldn't make sense otherwise, and he needed Hawk's help. "The engagement is a pretense. Maria hired me to play her husband-to-be for six weeks. She said it was for protection from fortune hunters, but as I discovered, it was to return the money my father lost in that investment."

"So it was all pretense anyway," Hawk was saying, looking brighter. "Your six weeks must be nearly up and you'll be able to restore Steynings. All's well that ends well."

"Except for the fact that I love her. I took her to Steynings yesterday and realized that the place will mean nothing to me without her by my side. I asked her to marry me, and she said no. I'm not willing to accept that answer."

"I'd say you don't have any choice."

"I can fight. That at least I can do well."

"Perdition, Van, if the woman doesn't want you, she doesn't want you!"

"I love her, and I think she loves me too, though she won't admit it."

"Will you try to throttle me if I say that we are easily misled about such things? If she loved you she would marry you."

"She thinks the age difference matters. But more important, she thinks she's barren."

"Ah. She has no children. More honor to her, then. The line dies with you."

"So it dies! What the devil difference will that make to the world? But I'll never persuade her to marry me as long as she believes it true." He collapsed into a chair. "Thing is, Hawk, I'm not sure it's true. I don't want to raise false hopes, but I want you to put your inquisitive talents to some use, for once."

Hawk stayed standing. "You're being damn rude for someone wanting a favor."

The sudden chill shocked Van back into his sense. "Gad, so I am." He looked up at his friend. "Have you ever been in love?"

"I don't think so."

"It can blast away common sense as well as manners. That's why I need a cool head to look into Maurice Celestin's intimate affairs and bastards." He tried a smile. "For old times' sake?"

Hawk pulled him out of the chair and into a brief hug. "For past, present, and future, you idiot. But I warn you," he added, eyes steady, "I'll tell you everything I find—good or bad."

Van met his eyes. "Can you not see how wonderful she is?"

"I see a handsome woman with strength of character. She claimed to have saved your life, and it's probably true. But that means you were vulnerable to her maturity and strength of character. Van, when she first came to London to flirt at Almack's, we were pretending your gamekeeper was the Sheriff of Nottingham, and that Con's father's bull was the Minotaur."

Van laughed. "Zeus, that poor bull! But you're as bad as she is, Hawk. It doesn't matter. Trust me on that—it doesn't matter. Just find out the truth about Celestin's bastards."

"And if she really is barren?"

Van smiled. "Then I'll try to win her anyway."

Maria found she lacked the courage to go out. She had no taste for gossipy company or idle pleasures, and no courage to face questions about her missing ring and missing fiancé. She would have to one day, but not yet, especially not with him still in her house.

Every day Van took an early breakfast then left the house, returning in time for the evening meal. She joined him for that meal because it would be petty to leave him and Harriette to eat alone. And anyway, she hungered for the last few scraps of the feast—the sight of him, the sound of his voice, his expression whenever their eyes met, the ache in every muscle, every bone at the memory of their lovemaking.

When she and Harriette left the dining table he did not linger, but nor did he join them for tea in the drawing room. He retired to his room for the night, but always with a look that said as clearly as words, "If you join me again, you will be welcome."

Every night, it was another Waterloo not to take up that invitation.

She counted the days till this torture would be over, and counted the nights as the beginning of an eternity without him.

Then the last night came, the last good night, the last look across the dining table. He'd announced that tomorrow he would to return to Steynings and begin his work there.

She rose, but lingered, one hand on the back of her chair as if glued there. The final cut. She couldn't bear it. She must.

From courtesy, he was standing too, separated from her by the wide table and a tasteful arrangement of spring flowers. She'd had plenty of time for flower arranging.

"I hoped you would change your mind," he said quietly. "I have been tempted to force you. Perhaps I would have failed anyway, but I managed to stop myself trying. But I have words I could say, things I could show you that might make a difference."

Maria glanced to the side and realized that Harriette had already left. Her heart rose up, beating fast. "I don't see how." It was weak, but it was all she could manage. Now the absolute end was here, she couldn't quite face it.

"Things and words might not matter," he said. "It all comes down to love. I love you, Maria, in the deepest truest way. I am sure of that. But I don't know whether you love me enough to take the chance."

A breaking heart was proof, wasn't it? A breaking heart clearly wasn't visible. "What words, what things?" she whispered from a dry mouth.

"Misty words and butterfly things. It's the love that counts. Come to me, Maria, and speak of love, and perhaps we can fight side by side. If not, there really is no point, is there? And whatever happens, I will leave tomorrow unless you ask me to stay."

He walked from the room then, lean, lithe, beautiful. Her beautiful, beloved young demon, whom she shouldn't want at all, but wanted more than breath itself. She stood staring at the flowers choking back a scream of, *What words? What things?*

She gripped the chair harder. She mustn't weaken now. Truths were truths. Words couldn't wipe away the years between them. No *thing* could make her womb fertile.

But then she turned and ran upstairs. Ignoring Harriette waiting in the drawing room she ran down the corridor and flung open the door to his room. "What words? What things?" she cried. "Why are you doing this? There is no way to change what is!"

He quickly shut the door, then stood barring it. "Why? Because I'm Demon Vandeimen, of course, and you are my last forlorn hope. Do you love me, Maria? Or does the fire only burn on my side?"

She stood looking at him, fighting, fighting . . . "I love you, Van. But don't you see that—"

He swept her into his arms and carried her to the bed. She melted even as she cried, 'No, Van. This won't change my mind!"

All the same, she was ready, ready to be taken in a violent storm that would sweep away reality for a brief while.

But he laid her down gently and sat beside her on the bed. "This isn't part of the battle. Let me love you, Maria, one last time. Tell me what you want tonight."

You, now—hot, hard, and fast. But this would be the last time, so she said, "Show me the gentle love you promised once, Van. And pay no attention if I weep."

He smiled and began to undress her, cherishing each revelation with touch and kiss so that every inch of her body felt worshiped. The lust stirred and the fire burned, but the gentleness encircled it so she could only lie and watch as he stripped off his clothes to join her, skin to skin in the bed.

She was afraid that it wouldn't work this way, that she'd be left softly quivering with need, that she'd disappoint, but he swept her up with tenderness, with worship, up into a slow, sweet crescendo of heaven that she'd never even known existed . . .

She did weep, though she did not mean to, wept deeply in his arms, against the devil on his naked chest, because gentleness, she found, went deeper into the soul than hard passion, and the thought of its loss was like ripping roots from her heart.

He stroked her hair, seeming to know these were tears that should be allowed to fall. "Say again that you love me, Maria. Please."

Impossible to deny it now. She swallowed. "I love you, Van. But it doesn't change anything."

He pushed her back and smiled at her, a blissful smile that made her want to weep again, but bitterly. "Don't try to deny facts, please," she begged. "When I married Celestin, already somewhat on the shelf, you were a scrubby schoolboy!"

He shook his head. "Let's look at things first."

Chapter Ten

He slid out of the bed, picked up a leather folder from the table, and came back to sit up beside her.

Puzzled and wary, she eased up by his side. "What is it?"

"My drawings." He undid a tie and opened the portfolio. "Are you a connoisseur? I hope not." He began to turn sheets of paper to show rough sketches of army camps and assorted buildings. Tolerable, but nothing special.

What had this to do with their age difference?

Then as he turned the sheets, she reached out to stop him. "That's Major Hawkinville."

It was a quick sketch of a man in shirtsleeves at a desk laden with papers, but it captured him perfectly.

"Before Waterloo. That was an organizational nightmare." He flicked through a few more sheets. "That's Con."

She saw a man with strong features and short dark hair standing in classic soldier pose staring into the distance, a long cloak concealing most of his uniform. He almost looked like a statue.

"He looks tired," she said. "After battle?"

"Before Waterloo. He didn't want to be there. None of us did, of course, but he especially. He left the army in 1814, so he'd been away for nearly a year. He'd grown used to living in sunlight, and came back to join us in the shadows. I think he's still in the shadows, and I haven't tried to help."

He moved on and showed her a series of drawings of boys and men. Some were quick sketches, others highly

334

worked pencil portraits. All were of distinct individuals. Not a professional standard, no, but drawn by a skilled amateur who had captured his comrades-in-arms in many moods.

She stopped him so she could read the names, and found that the writing wasn't complete names. *Ger, Badajoz,* she read. *Don, Talavera.* With a chill, she knew that he'd recorded the battles where they had died.

Then one drawing said only, *Hilyard.*

"He didn't die?"

"The bloody flux in a muddy village. We didn't even know the name. We lost more men to disease than to battle."

She took the folder and flicked through it quickly, seeing name and location on every one. "You only drew dead men?"

"They were alive at the time." Before she could ask, he said, "I generally gave the pictures to the sitters. These are men who died before I had a chance. I've wondered if the relatives would like them. They're not very good."

"Good enough," she said, staring at one near the end. *Dare, Waterloo.*

There were a great many Waterloo ones, but this sketch had leaped out at her because she recognized the long face and merry smile. "He looks ready for a great adventure," she said, touching the paper. "I think his mother would like this. They don't have a recent likeness."

"You knew him?"

"He's a distant cousin." She traced his smile. "He looks so happy."

He picked up the paper and studied it. "Drove us crazy. We all knew it was going to be hell, but Dare saw it as an adventure. He was Con's friend. Part of a bunch of Harrow men who call themselves the Company of Rogues. He was one of the enthusiastic volunteers that we scoffed at, but you couldn't scoff at Dare. At least he knew he didn't know."

All the pictures disturbed her, but Dare's in particular.

He and Van were of an age. Van could so easily be dead. Was that why he was showing them to her? "Why did you want me to see these? They don't change anything."

"Don't they?" He flipped through the pages and pulled another one out, one not obviously different from the others except in being a little more clumsy. A picture of a sinewy, grizzled man who looked cynical but kind.

"Sergeant Fletcher. He taught me how to survive. When you were marrying Celestin, the scrubby school-boy was drawing his first picture of a walking corpse."

The clock on his mantel tinkled the hour.

He gave her the picture. "Don't think that I'm a child, Maria, not knowing what I want and need. You are my heart's blood. Perhaps we all know when we meet that one person who is the perfect match." He took another sheet out of the folder, the very last sheet, and gave her a picture of herself. "Not drawn from life, of course."

It was just head and shoulders. Her hair was loose, as she never wore it, tendriling down the front of a simple gown. She looked serious, but not unhappy, and unlike any self she had seen in a mirror.

"You have a gift, but this isn't really me."

"It's the Maria I see." He began to tidy the papers. "I will leave tomorrow if you insist, but my feelings will not change." He tied the strings and looked up. "You do not have to protect me from myself."

She caressed his scarred cheek. "How can I not? Love does that to us."

"I'm not your child, Maria. I'm your lover." He kissed her then, proving it, and loved her in the wild-fire way.

She lay there afterward, sweaty and sticky, stroking the lean length of his powerful body.

I'm not your child, Maria. I'm your lover.

When you were marrying Celestin, the scrubby school-boy was drawing his first picture of a walking corpse.

He was a man, mature enough to be fair mate for her. He was more than her lover, though. He was the man she loved as she had never thought to love. She would marry him quickly, joyfully if she could give him at least hope of a child.

Could she be his mistress? Let him marry a suitable young woman who would bear him children?

No. Never. If he married someone else she could never corrode his marriage like that, and she didn't think he would consider it.

So . . . As he'd said, they could be happy without children of their own. The title would die, but if he didn't mind . . .

Was she being weak or strong?

Would he—and this was the crucial question—would he come to regret it?

She turned and looked at her mate, her destiny. He was sleeping, lashes long on his cheeks, looking at ease. Perhaps he had not slept much these past nights.

She had the sudden realization that her life had flowed to make this moment possible.

When she had entered society at sixteen—shy, proud, and rather awkward—Van had truly been a scrubby schoolboy. They would never have found each other. The years since had been necessary to bridge the gap of years and experiences.

Without the army, Van might not have become her match. With his wild nature, he might have become one of the callow, irresponsible young men of the *ton*.

If she'd not married Celestin, she would now be settled with some other man, not free to love. Without the pleasures and pains of that marriage, she would never have been able to deal with Van's complexities.

Fate had shaped them and finally tossed them together for this brief trial. This was her golden moment. Her only chance. She brushed silky hair from his forehead, tussling with courage and honor in her mind . . .

His lashes rose and he smiled, confused for a moment, then warm. "Marry me, Maria."

She was struck dumb again, but surrendered in a whisper. "If you're sure . . ."

His eyes shut, then opened, and she saw the gloss of

tears. "I'm sure. Maria!" He gathered her in for a hug that made her squeak. They broke apart, laughing.

"I feel wicked," she protested. "Wrong."

He grinned. "Of course you do. You are lying ravished in an unblessed bed. But marriage will fix that."

"I'm not sure our sort of ravishment is right even with a blessing."

"Oh it is, it is," he murmured, nuzzling at her breasts.

She suddenly held him there, held him close, stabbed by the thought that no child would ever suckle at her breast. And that she was binding him to her barren fate. She was a greedy, wicked woman.

"Promise me you won't regret, Van."

It was a whisper because he could not promise that, but he said, "I promise."

They lay for a moment, but then he stirred, pulled apart, and sat shamelessly naked facing her. "I've shown you the things. I still have the words."

She sat up, too, suddenly wary. "Words? What more is left to say?"

He looked down for a moment, then met her eyes. "I don't want to raise false hopes. It's still in the hands of fate. But you may not be barren."

The pain of tears swept through her. "Van, don't! We have to accept the truth."

"Then accept it. Listen." It was an officer's command and she stilled.

"I've spent time with Oncle Charles and Tante Louise, and things they said didn't entirely match Natalie being your husband's daughter. For a start, the idea only stirred about six years ago."

"That was when Natalie's parents died and she came here. The truth came out because her mother was beyond scandal. And why else would she come to live with Maurice? Van—"

"She came here because there was nowhere else" he interrupted. "The wars wreaked havoc with Celestin's family in Europe. She also came here, I believe, because it suited him." He took her hand, her ringless left hand. "I set Hawk to making inquiries, Maria. It's his forte.

Celestin was almost certainly not in the right place at the right time."

She looked at him, her brain feeling fogged. "What? Why would he lie? It doesn't make sense. It doesn't matter anyway, Van. There are four others!"

"All definitely false."

She stared at him. "They can't be."

"They are. It can't have been hard to find women unfortunately with child willing to call a man the father in return for an income."

She pulled her hand free, moved back, back against the headboard. "Such women would say anything for money, too. Did you arrange this to try to persuade me into marriage?"

She was suddenly reminded of the man she had first met, the one who'd threatened and disarmed her. He neither attacked, however, nor shrank from her. "I knew you might think that. That's why I wanted our feelings settled first. The matter of children doesn't matter that much to me, Maria. I'm sure that's undutiful of me, but you matter more than the damned title. I set Hawk to finding out the truth to remove the last barrier in your mind. That's all. Talk to the women if you want. I think you'll be convinced."

His leashed anger stung, but a trace of doubt lingered. "Why would Maurice do such a thing, construct such a painful, complex lie?"

"Because he was a self-made man who cared about appearances. He doubtless wanted to found a dynasty, and when it didn't happen, he couldn't bear to have people think it was his fault."

That rang with the clarity of absolute truth.

"So he constructed another facade!" she exclaimed. "The swine. The worm. The toad! I felt so *guilty*. So *flawed*." She launched herself toward him. "Oh, Van, please forgive me! I should never have even thought you might have made it up."

He pulled her into his lap. "Of course you should have thought it. I was desperate enough." He brushed hair off her face and looked into her eyes. "It might still not happen. There might not be children."

She smiled up into his eyes through tears. "But there might be. That's enough. And you are more important to me, too, than children of our bodies." All the same, she ran a hand down her belly. "But think, there might be a child growing now!"

He covered her hand with his. "And we'll certainly be willing to work hard at putting one there. I've always been lucky, you know." He rolled her down beneath him on the bed and reached out to take a silver box off the table.

She could hardly think for hot muscles weighting her, but she focused on it. "What now?"

He opened the box to show her a ring, and a piece of sharp stone. The ring held a fine, flashing ruby in a circle of diamonds.

"A new ring?" she said. "'I still have the other."

"My Maria needs a ring with fire in the heart." Still over her, his erection pressing between her thighs, he slid the ring onto her finger. "A new ring for a new beginning."

She looked at it. "You were very sure of me."

"I wasn't sure at all. But the only way to fight is to convince yourself that you'll sweep all before you."

"Thank God you always did." She brought the ring to her lips, tears escaping. "I'll always cherish the other one, too." She looked back at the box. "And the stone? A flint . . . ?"

He put the box aside, but kept the flint in his fingers. "When you burst into my room that day I'd already pulled the trigger—"

"Van!"

"—but the flint failed. This flint. Sheer demon's luck, but mostly luck in having a valet who loves me more than I deserve, and finding a woman willing to fight my devils with me."

He tossed it on the table. "Marry me in Hawk in the Vale, Maria, soon?"

She traced the demon on his chest, and knew they

could make it little more than a memory of darker times. "Can we share our happiness with everyone there? A grand party for all? Your friends will attend?"

"Hawk and Con? I'm sure of it."

She hoped he was right. She suspected that Major Hawkinville still disapproved, and the Earl of Wyvern seemed to be a dark mystery. If his friends failed him she would fill any void, but if she could, she'd heal the connections to them, too.

With love so strong, and happiness burning in them like a winter fire, how could they fail?

"A wedding, my lord. In four weeks. In Hawk in the Vale. A celebration to show that sometimes we poor mortals can find heaven here on earth."

Author's Note

I hope you enjoyed "The Demon's Mistress." I'm sure you guessed that there will be stories about the other two Georges—Con and Hawk.

First we have *The Dragon's Bride,* on shelves next month. As you learned here, Con Somerford has unexpectedly inherited the title of a distant branch of the family, the Demented Devonish Somerfords. Despite it being an earldom, there is nothing he wants less, but duty calls him to at least visit the fortresslike home of the Earls of Wyvern, perched high on the Devon coast. He must set his property in order. It will not be easy because he knows the place is infested with smugglers, but there is another reason he has delayed.

Eleven years ago, he visited Crag Wyvern with his father and older brother. There he met a girl of his own age, and discovered a magical friendship. There they went too far, and became lovers—and then she cruelly rejected him when she discovered he was not the heir to Wyvern.

Now he has the title. If he returns, Susan Kerslake might still be there, and despite eleven years he doesn't know if he'll want to murder her, or kiss her. And who do you think is the first person he meets at Crag Wyvern, late on a dark night, in the middle of a smuggling run?

As for Hawk, he is reluctant to return to Hawkinville Manor, but he's going to find that it holds a dearer place in his heart than he thought—and that it is threatened by a young woman who has inherited the wealth of a distant relative, Lord Deveril. Foul Lord Deveril was commonly known as Lord Devil, and thus she is known as the Devil's Heiress. Such a woman should be easy prey for the man known as The Hawk, shouldn't she? But Clarissa Greystone is not at all what he expected, and soon he is engaged in a battle with her and with her protectors, the Company of Rogues. And also, perhaps, with his own wary heart.

Be ready for *The Devil's Heiress* in August 2001.

For more details on these books, please visit http://www. poboxes.com/jobev. I welcome letters by E-mail to jobev @poboxes.com, or care of my agent. Please send them to Jo Beverley c/o Meg Ruley, The Jane Rostrosen Agency, 318 East 51st Street, New York, NY 10022. A SASE is appreciated.

About the Author

Jo Beverley is widely regarded as one of the most talented romance writers today. She is a four-time winner of the Romance Writers of America's cherished RITA Award, and one of only a handful of members of the RWA Hall of Fame. She has also received the *Romantic Times* Career Achievement Award. Born in England, she now lives with her husband and two sons in Victoria, British Columbia, just a ferry ride away from Seattle.